P9-DCL-155

Notes from the Underbelly

Risa Green

 NEW AMERICAN LIBRARY

New American Library
Published by New American Library, a division of
Penguin Group (USA) Inc., 375 Hudson Street,
New York, New York 10014, USA
Penguin Group (Canada), 10 Alcorn Avenue, Toronto,
Ontario M4V 3B2, Canada (a division of Pearson Penguin Canada Inc.)
Penguin Books Ltd., 80 Strand, London WC2R 0RL, England
Penguin Ireland, 25 St. Stephen's Green, Dublin 2,
Ireland (a division of Penguin Books Ltd.)
Penguin Group (Australia), 250 Camberwell Road, Camberwell, Victoria 3124,
Australia (a division of Pearson Australia Group Pty. Ltd.)
Penguin Books India Pvt. Ltd., 11 Community Centre, Panchsheel Park,
New Delhi - 110 017, India
Penguin Group (NZ), cnr Airborne and Rosedale Roads, Albany,
Auckland 1310, New Zealand (a division of Pearson New Zealand Ltd.)
Penguin Books (South Africa) (Pty.) Ltd., 24 Sturdee Avenue,
Rosebank, Johannesburg 2196, South Africa

Penguin Books Ltd., Registered Offices:
80 Strand, London WC2R 0RL, England

First published by New American Library,
a division of Penguin Group (USA) Inc.

First Printing, April 2005
10 9 8 7 6 5 4 3 2 1

Copyright © Risa Green, 2005
Readers Guide copyright © Penguin Group (USA) Inc., 2005
All rights reserved

NEW AMERICAN LIBRARY and logo are trademark of Penguin Group (USA) Inc.

LIBRARY OF CONGRESS CATALOGING-IN-PUBLICATION DATA

Green, Risa.
    Notes from the underbelly / Risa Green.
        p.   cm.
    ISBN 0-451-21416-1 (Trade pbk.)
    1. Motherhood—Fiction.   2. Married women—Fiction.   3. Pregnant women—Fiction.
4. Student counselors—Fiction.   5. Children of celebrities—Fiction.   I. Title.
    PS3607.R445N68   2005
    813'.6—dc22   2004017148

Set in Minion
Designed by Ginger Legato

Printed in the United States of America

Without limiting the rights under copyright reserved above, no part of this publication may be reproduced,
stored in or introduced into a retrieval system, or transmitted, in any form, or by any means (electronic, me-
chanical, photocopying, recording, or otherwise), without the prior written permission of both the copyright owner and the above publisher of this book.

PUBLISHER'S NOTE
This is a work of fiction. Names, characters, places, and incidents either are the product of the author's imagination or are used fictitiously, and any resemblance to actual persons, living or dead, business establish-
ments, events, or locales is entirely coincidental.

The scanning, uploading, and distribution of this book via the Internet or via any other means without the
permission of the publisher is illegal and punishable by law. Please purchase only authorized electronic edi-
tions, and do not participate in or encourage electronic piracy of copyrighted materials. Your support of the
author's rights is appreciated.

FOR HARPER

my sun,

my moon,

my stars

Acknowledgments

I owe a huge amount of thanks to the following people (listed in the order in which they appeared in my life) for making this book a reality.

My fabulous husband, Michael Green, who selflessly indulged my constant complaining about the fact that I worked three jobs (counselor, mother, writer), who read and reread the same stories so often that neither of us could tell if they were funny anymore, and who, despite much evidence to the contrary, insists that Andrew Stone is a total figment of my imagination. Dolly, I love you to death. My delicious daughter, Harper, who literally inspired me from within. Harper, my love, you were worth every second of being pregnant and then some. Kate Phillips, my fairy godfriend who read the first draft and made things happen with a wave of her magic wand, and Modi Wiczyk (a fairy godfriend in his own right) who started the ball rolling at Endeavor and who, most importantly, taught me that I Am the Talent. Jack Kappler, for validating my writing, for being a really nice guy, and, of course, for finding me Barbara. The one and only Barbara J. Zitwer, my amazing, funny, brutally honest agent who saw something in the first draft and who encouraged me to keep going and to rewrite the whole thing from scratch, even when I said that I didn't want to. I don't know what I would do without you—you have been such a source of strength and such a cheerleader for me. Thank you for everything. Everyone at New American Library, but especially my wonderful editor, Anne Bohner, who just got me from day one and who included me in every step of publication. Thank you, thank you, thank you. And finally, to the classes of 2000, 2001, 2002, 2003 and 2004 of Milken Community High School, for being all around fabulous kids, for making work fun, and for providing me with a wealth of teenager-related material.

1.

No More Classes, No More Books, My Husband's Giving Me Dirty Looks

I always feel the same way on the last day of school. I imagine that it must be similar to the way that ex-cons feel when they step out of jail for the first time—the sensation that their hearts might explode with the promise of total freedom, combined with the disbelief that they won't actually be there again tomorrow. Of course, there is also the giddy sense of anticipation—three entire months of midweek shopping excursions and empty ten A.M. Tae Bo classes—that I experience that ex-cons probably don't, but whatever. The point is, whether it was in my past life as a student or in my current reincarnation as Mrs. Stone, director of college counseling, I have always loved the last day of school.

Last days just don't exist in other jobs. For example, when I was practicing law (an endeavor that ended almost as quickly as it began, given my utter, utter distaste for hundred-hour workweeks and the tedium of drafting such exciting documents as mortgage loan warehouse agreements), there was no such thing as a last day (at least, not until I quit). Each twenty-four-hour period ran into the next, sometimes without my going home in between, and the piles on my desk grew higher and higher until my office looked like a maze of paper stacks. Vacations made no difference. I always found it kind of hard to relax, knowing that each day spent lounging by a pool meant a future Friday or Saturday night spent playing catch-up with the new pile that, inevitably, formed during my five measly days off. No, in the real world, there is no such thing as a last day. Which is why I am, happily, no longer in the real world. I am in education. Even better, I am in elite private education, which translates into decent pay, short hours, long vacations, an absence of pesky, state-mandated requirements, and, of course, come each June, a last day.

On this particular last day of school, I shut the door to my office behind me, and I step out into yet another perfect Los Angeles summer afternoon. With the sun shining down and three entire months of freedom ahead of me, I feel like skipping to my car, but, of course, I don't, both because I am wearing three-inch wedge heels and because I am not someone who skips. Plus, I spy a group of students who are still hanging around in the school parking lot. As I get closer, I can overhear them making plans for the final days before they go off for the summer—to CIT in the Berkshires or to "study" in Europe on a program that their parents think will look good for college but that they, and I, and colleges, all know is just an excuse to spend eight weeks hooking up with other résumé-padding kids from various U.S. suburbs. And, of course, to get drunk without the hassle of having to get a fake ID.

If this were not the last day of school, I would probably wave and say hello to them, but my summer has officially started and I have about zero interest in talking to these delinquents during the very first few minutes of my vacation. So instead, I discreetly avoid them and head straight to my car, pretending that I haven't seen them despite the fact that they are standing no more than twenty feet from where I am parked. But I am busted.

"Hey, Mrs. Stone." It is Mark, one of my counselees. "Nice car. Are you gonna put the top down?"

One of the advantages of having formerly been a lawyer who was worked practically to death at a huge LA law firm is that I made way more money than I possibly had the free time to the spend. As a result, I socked away enough cash to allow me to continue to consume as if I were still a lawyer, despite the fact that my salary is about a third of what it used to be. In any event, the car to which Mark is referring is a two-seater Mercedes convertible that I love to death and that makes me feel like Christie Brinkley in *National Lampoon's Vacation*—although I rarely drive alongside middle-aged men in green station wagons and seductively lick my lips at them. Normally a teacher would have to worry about driving such a flashy car to a high school, but at Bel Air Prep it is no problem. At Bel Air Prep, half of the kids got the more expensive version of my car for their sixteenth birthdays, and the parking lot is lined with them.

I squint at Mark as I ponder his question. I hardly ever put the top down, mainly because I have never quite mastered the whole convertible, long-hair-blowing-in-the-wind thing. I look fabulous in parking lots and at red lights, but the second that I get up over three miles per hour, my hair blows straight into my face and gets enmeshed in my lip gloss. I've tried varying levels of window and I installed a windscreen behind my seat, but I always end up bearing a scary resemblance to Cousin It, if he were ever to get behind the wheel of a luxury roadster. I once even tried to do the Jackie O. thing and wrap a scarf around my head, but I looked utterly ridiculous and pulled it off before I even got out of the garage, as my next-door neighbor was standing outside and I was too embarrassed to wave at her with a big old scarf tied under my chin.

Today, however, I am feeling reckless. *Lip gloss be damned,* I think. *It's summer, I'm free, and I am definitely going topless.*

I look Mark straight in the eye.

"As a matter of fact, I am. And if you'll excuse me, I'm off to vacate for a few months, so I really have to run."

With that, I hop in the car, push the button that automatically lowers the top into the trunk, and leave Mark and his cohorts eating my dust. Hasta la vista, *babies,* I think.

Like any true Los Angelino, I immediately pick up my cell phone and start dialing. Time to check in with the old ball and chain. After two rings, he picks up.

"This is Andrew Stone."

"I'm *done,*" I announce. "How jealous are you?"

"Very jealous. Congratulations. Are you meeting us at agility?" Unfortunately, this is not a reference to a funky yoga class or a New Age-y sex workshop. No, he is referring to the doggie agility class that he takes with Zoey, our three-year-old Wheaten Terrier. In case you're not a die-hard Animal Planet fan, agility is a competition in which dogs run as fast as they can through an obstacle course comprised of tunnels, weave poles, a seesaw, jumps, and various other death-defying equipment. Not that they do it alone—the dog's "handler" (aka Andrew) is crucial, because

4 · Risa Green

the handler runs next to the dog and tells him what to do and where to go next. Andrew says he does it just for fun, but this is total bullshit, as Andrew never does anything just for fun. He considers it a real sport and he takes it Very Seriously. As in, he went out and bought some PVC and made his own weave poles that he set up in our living room and that he makes Zoey practice with three nights a week. I think he's secretly hoping that the teacher will tap him to become a professional handler.

I unglue the hair from my lips.

"Yeah, I'm going. I'm on my way there right now." I used to go to agility with them every week, but then the class switched to Saturday mornings, which is when I go hiking with my friend Stacey, and hiking won. Tonight's class is a makeup, though, so I'm going to support Zoey. I think it's good for her self-confidence to have a cheering audience every once in a while.

"Oh, good," he says. "Okay, so let me finish up here and I'll see you in a little bit. I love you."

"I love you, too," I say. " 'Bye." I hang up and gather my blowing hair, then attempt to hold it in a ponytail and steer with my elbow while I dial my friend Julie.

"Hello?"

"Hey, Jul, it's me. Are we still on for dinner?" Julie is one of my closest friends, a fact that, even after seven years, continues to shock me on a daily basis. We could not possibly have more opposite personalities. I lean toward misanthropy and sarcasm, while Julie is the nicest, sweetest, most positive, well-meaning person on the planet. Every stupid saying about making lemonade and half-empty cups was definitely written by someone just like Julie. Of course, it doesn't hurt that she leads a totally charmed life and has never had a bad thing happen to her, ever. Normally, I hate people like Julie and make fun of them endlessly behind their backs, so I really have no good explanation as to why I tolerate her sunniness and enthusiasm. The only thing that I can think of is that it's my body's way of telling me that I need it, kind of like how anemics sometimes crave red meat.

Anyway, Julie and I were supposed to have had dinner plans for the last three Fridays in a row (with Andrew and her husband, Jon, but since they usually sit across from each other and talk about business, they don't count), but Julie canceled on me every time. One week she didn't feel well, one week she was really tired, one week she had to have dinner with her parents. If I didn't know that she psychologically wasn't capable of it, I would have thought that she was blowing me off.

"Hey, Lara. I'm so sorry about before. We're definitely on for tonight."

"Oh, really, what happened? Did your better plans fall through or something?"

"I know you don't really think that. What time do you want to go?"

"I don't know. We're taking Zoey to agility at five, and then we just have to drop her off at home and feed her dinner. I swear, sometimes I feel like I'm a soccer mom for my dog. Is seven okay?"

"Perfect. I'll see you then."

I arrive at the park and drive all the way to the back of the parking lot, from where I can see that the other dog handlers are still setting up the agility course. I hate setting up the course. I helped out during the first few classes that I went to because I felt guilty just sitting there while everyone else schlepped tunnels and hurdles around the field, but then I figured out that if I just showed up ten minutes late, I wouldn't have to deal with it. As I wait for them to finish, I open up the mirror in my visor and spend a few minutes trying to get my fingers through the knots that have formed in my hair. When I see the last piece of equipment go up, I grab a blanket out of my trunk and stroll across the grass.

Andrew and Zoey are nowhere to be found, so I spread out the blanket away from everyone else and plop myself down. I have absolutely no interest in conversing with the agility crazies. As far as I know, Andrew is the only male handler in the entire "sport" of agility. The rest of them are a bunch of middle-aged, overweight lesbians who are totally obsessed with their dogs and are clearly using them to replace the children that they never had. They all have bumper stickers on their cars that say things like *Sheltie on board* or *My dog is an honor student at West LA Obedience School*, and they all buy their clothes from some catalog that specializes in dog logos and breed-specific accessories. One time one woman came to class practically in tears because she had lost one of her favorite German shepherd earrings. I mean, come *on*. I love Zoey and everything, but I'm not about to make her a staple of my wardrobe.

But before I have time to figure out how best to avoid making eye contact with anyone, I hear Andrew calling my name.

"Lara! Lara!" I look up and see Zoey, who is headed, full throttle, toward where I am sitting. She's barking like a maniac, and Andrew is running behind her, gripping her leash and trying in vain to keep her from ripping his arm off.

"Zoey, easy, Zoey. Zoey, heel! Heel, Zoey!" To this day, I have no idea why he even pretends that Zoey understands what it means to heel. Or that she would do it even if she did understand it. She's a terrier, for God's sake. Terriers don't do obedience. Andrew is panting and out of breath by the time he reaches me.

"I swear, I'm going to put a muffle on this dog one day."

I cock my head sideways. "Do you mean a muzzle?"

He looks at me and thinks for a second. I have clearly thrown him for a loop. "Is that what it's called?" he asks, and I nod my head yes. "Really?"

I roll my eyes at him. Andrew has only read something like two books in his entire life, and as a result he can barely speak English. He's a really smart guy, but he sounds much dumber than he is because he's always messing up his idioms and getting words wrong. I stand up and grab the leash from him.

"Andrew, leave the poor dog alone. She just wants to say hi to her mommy." At this, Zoey jumps up and pounces on me, and in return I kneel down and smother her head with kisses. As per our usual hello routine, Zoey is licking my face and my mouth so intensely that we are practically making out. "Hi, bunny, hi, sweetie, did you miss your mommy today? Mommy missed you so much. Oh, I love this girl, I love you, yes, I do." Our love fest continues for about ten minutes, during which time Zoey's tail is wagging so fast that I think she might achieve liftoff. I swear, if I could harness the energy in that tail, I could easily power a small city.

Just then the teacher of the class, an enormous woman named Jean who has trained her dog using voice commands because she is too heavy to run alongside him, calls for the class to begin.

"Okay, everyone. Take a look at the course and then line up. We're going to be working primarily on jumps today, so make sure you have lots of water ready for your dogs." At this, Andrew gets so excited that I think that he might run off and hurdle one of the jumps himself.

"Yessss!" he says, pumping his right arm. "Jumps are Zoey's best skill," he whispers to me. "This is *great*." I nod at him indulgently, and then I sit back down on my blanket while he goes to get in line.

The first pair to go is a little black Pekingese named DJ whose flowing hair is so long that she looks like she floats over the ground, and her handler, a large, pasty woman named BJ who looks as if she might shatter the earth with every step. BJ is wearing a polo shirt with a Pekingese where the horse or alligator would belong on a normal person's polo shirt, khaki walking shorts, and white socks embroidered with little black Pekingeses (Pekingesi?) on them. DJ takes off, and while BJ huffs and puffs alongside her, she gracefully sails over the first two jumps, then flounders when she has to turn around to find the next one. At this, Andrew leans over to whisper his commentary.

"That's just bad handling. DJ could be so good, but BJ always confuses her. She always does back crosses when she should be doing front crosses." I fake-smile at him and nod so he will think that I care.

During the next three dogs, I completely lose focus and begin to daydream about the pale pink skirt with the white eyelet trim that I saw in the window at Barneys, which is for sure going to be the first purchase of my summer vacation. As I begin to imagine how great it will look with the new white Gucci clutch that I just bought myself for our four-year wedding anniversary, I am rudely interrupted by Andrew, who is yelling at me to watch.

I look over and see that it is their turn to run the course. Andrew has positioned himself about thirty feet in front of Zoey, who is sitting behind the first jump, hunched over with her front paws out like a swimmer poised for a race. Their eyes are locked, and Zoey is anxiously awaiting his signal. When Andrew is ready, he waves his right arm.

"Okay, Zoey, over!" he yells. My little Wheatie princess takes off like she's been shot out of a cannon, and, I have to say, she rocks. She hits every jump, turns right when Andrew motions right, turns left when Andrew motions left, bounces through the weave poles like a Ping-Pong ball, and then sits down in front of Andrew and waits, breathlessly, for her peanut butter–flavored treat. I am bursting with pride and clapping like she has just hit the winning run for her Little League team.

When Zoey dispenses with her reward, the two of them come hurtling toward me. I begin to roll around on the ground with Zoey, and Andrew is like a little kid begging for compliments.

"Did you see that? How good was she? How good of a handler am I?"

"You're good, honey. You're both incredible. You two should be on *Amazing Animals,* really." I am well aware of the fact that, in his mind, this is by far the highest compliment that I could possibly pay him.

"Do you really think so?"

"I do," I say, and he beams at me. Looking at him, I can't help but wish that I were that easy to please. It would certainly make things simpler for both of us.

When class is over, we drop off our agility star at home and head straight to the restaurant. Julie and Jon aren't there yet, and since it's a beautiful night, Andrew and I decide to wait for them outside. A few minutes later, Jon pulls up in front of the restaurant and Julie steps out of the car. As much as I love Julie, I can't stand the way she dresses. She's always appropriate and put together, but in an Ann Taylor–meets–Laura Bush kind of way. The girl just has no edge whatsoever. You know what I mean— pearls, jeans with waists that actually sit on the waist, lots and lots of twinsets, Ballet Slippers on her nails. And the hair. The hair is always the same. Perfect, shoulder length, a shiny, natural chestnut, perpetually blown out. She always looks like she's running off to have tea, or to a PTA meeting in Greenwich.

Anyway, as Julie walks over to where we are standing, I immediately give her the once-over (as all girls do, no matter how good of friends we are with the once-overee, so don't even try to pretend that you don't do it). As I look her up and down, I can't help but notice that she looks kind of fat. Her shirt is way too tight on her stomach, and she just seems . . . thick. But otherwise, everything else is the same. So of course, I do what any good friend would do. I give her a kiss hello, tell her that she looks amazing, and ask if she's lost weight. She looks at me like I am crazy.

"No! Are you kidding?" I see her glance at Jon and he smiles back at her. "Actually, we have something to tell you." She pauses, dramatically, for effect. "I'm pregnant. We're having a baby!"

She's pregnant! My first thought is, *Ohhh, well, that explains the fat.*

My second thought is, *Oh, crap, now all she's ever going to talk about is babies.* I give a mock scream and hug her.

"Oh, my God! Congratulations! I am sooooo excited for you! How far along?"

"Four months today. I've been dying to tell you for so long, but I wanted to tell you in person, and I haven't seen you in the last month at all."

Four months! I think. I readjust my critical eye and look at her stomach again. I know plenty of people who have children, but aside from a second cousin whom I haven't seen in ten years, I've never known anyone while they were actually pregnant. But four months sounds pretty far along to me, and she doesn't look pregnant at all. She just looks like her shirt is a size too small. I wonder if this is normal or if this is just typical Julie good fortune, but I don't want to ask.

I look over at Andrew, who is grinning from ear to ear and hugging Jon and Julie like they're moving away to Czechoslovakia. I can see the wheels turning in that little head of his, and I hope he's not getting any stupid ideas. You see, having a baby is kind of a sore spot for us right now, as in, he wants to and I don't. Or, the way I see it, he thinks he wants to, and I know that I don't. Seriously, what does he know about having kids? Given that he doesn't actually know anyone under fifty who has a child, he's obviously getting all of his information from television and movies, which, as I remind him whenever this comes up, is *fiction.* I mean, yeah, it looks like a blast when some movie star and a couple of five-year-olds are dancing around a bedroom and singing Supremes songs into a hairbrush, but that's not exactly *real.*

I, on the other hand, work with kids every day. Spoiled, bratty, nobody's-ever-said-no-to-them, real-life kids, and I see exactly what happens to their parents. These people—who I'm sure were totally cool, normal, people at some point in their lives, and who *had* lives at some point in their lives—have been completely reduced to cartoon versions of themselves. Either they're so petrified of being disliked by their kids that they turn into whimpering, sniveling doormats who can't ever bear to see their precious angels fail and take it upon themselves to fight every last teacher, administrator, and college official to make sure that they don't, or they're so totally clueless and uninvolved that half the time they're shocked to remember that they even have kids, especially when those kids do things like set fire to a hotel bathroom at prom, or organize a crime syndicate involving stolen final exams. I mean, really, why the hell would I want to go and do that to myself? And I know that we're talking about teenagers here, and that I would have to get through babyhood and toddlerhood and elementary school and the preteen years before I even got to that point, but all of that sounds like a lot of work, and I'm already a pretty busy girl, you know?

Plus, with regard to the more immediate future, it helps to know that I don't even like babies. They're loud, they're messy, they can't do anything for themselves, and most of them are really ugly. Oh, be quiet, they are, too. And I know what people say about how, when it's yours, everything is different, but I'm not so sure. I just can't picture myself with a baby. Not right now, anyway.

I'm sure I'll change, though. I keep telling Andrew that I'll do it eventually, I just need some more time to enjoy my life before I hand it over to someone else, that's all. My theory is that, when the time is right, my nurturing side will kick in and I will suddenly find myself sobbing at diaper commercials, and then I'll know that I'm ready. It just hasn't happened yet. But it will. I think. Maybe.

Andrew, however, doesn't want to hear any of it. He's been up my butt about this ever since I turned thirty last month, and he just won't let it go. Of course, one of the reasons I think that Andrew wants a kid so badly is so he'll have someone to play with. I mean, he's practically a kid himself. Not chronologically or anything, but definitely at heart. Consider the following: (1) He doesn't like the taste of alcohol (except for wine coolers, but I have informed him that under no circumstances is he allowed to ask for one anywhere, ever), so when we go out to dinner with our friends and everybody orders a glass of wine, Andrew orders a hot chocolate. (2) He is a member of about nineteen different "men's" softball leagues, and he names his bats (Black Thunder, the Stonewaller, and Morty) and sometimes sleeps with them before a big game. (3) His favorite store in the entire world is called the Soda Pop Shop. Seriously. The manager is this crazy black lady with a big Afro who knows all kinds of trivia about soda, and Andrew spends hours chatting her up about the history of ginger ale or the healing properties of root beer. He always comes home from there all excited about some new soda that he can't wait to try, and he buys cases of them at a time, as if one bottle of Kick-apoo Joy Juice or Blueberry Cream couldn't possibly be enough. Do I need to go on? I have no idea how the two of us ended up together, but somehow, it works.

Except for when it comes to this baby thing. He has this whole fantasy going about how he'll take the kid to see all of the cheesy Hollywood movies that I refuse to go to with him, and how they'll have soda-tasting parties together, and how he'll finally have somebody to go to the arcade with on Sundays who will play that stupid Japanese dancing game with him, and he wants all of this to happen *now*.

Ugh, there is no telling what this Julie–Jon news is going to do to him. Suddenly I am finding myself very, very nervous.

Our table is ready, and as we sit down to eat, I realize that I am going to have to feign some degree of interest in Julie's pregnancy. I know slightly less than nothing about having or taking care of a baby, and I really am not in the mood to learn right now. But since Julie is my friend and this is a big deal to her, I guess I can pretend to be nice. I quickly come up with a strategy: Whenever she gets going on an unbearable baby tangent, I will just tune her out and eavesdrop on Andrew and Jon. *Good*, I think. *I have a plan.*

I pull my napkin out of my glass and place it on my lap.

"So," I ask, "how are you feeling? Is it really bad?" Julie practically jumps out of her seat, she is so excited to talk about this.

"No, I feel great. I was supertired in the very beginning, but I didn't have any morning sickness at all." Of course she didn't. "But when I was at the doctor's last week, I met this woman in the waiting room, and she's been sick the entire nine months. She has to carry around a little cup with her to spit in because she can't even stand the taste of her own saliva." This is quite possibly the most disgusting thing that I have ever heard, and I make a face indicating such.

"Are you craving weird foods?"

"Not really. I've been eating more bread than I normally do, but that's about it." *Right*. As Julie begins to review every last carbohydrate that she's consumed in the last four months, I let my ear wander over to the other side of the table, where Andrew is playing the man version of my game with Julie.

"So how much do you think a baby costs?" Oh, that is so Andrew. Get right down to the money. I see Jon looking a little puzzled, probably because he's loaded and the cost of a baby never even crossed his mind.

"I don't know," Jon says. "I mean, there are clothes, and private school, and stuff." Andrew seems perturbed by this, and I know exactly why. He simply can't fathom the idea of not having an exact accounting of expenses, as well as a complete cost-benefit analysis. When we do have kids, I won't be surprised if he draws up a business plan for them.

"I don't understand," Andrew says. "Didn't you do a spreadsheet or anything first?" I knew it. It's scary how well I can read his mind. Although I didn't figure on the spreadsheet part. Andrew has this weird obsession with spreadsheets—he creates them for everything. He built one when we got married, when we remodeled our house—he even made one when he was having trouble with his golf swing and he couldn't figure out what was wrong. It's not his fault, really. He's just a total control freak. He truly believes that all of life's problems can be solved by breaking them down into little columns in Excel.

Jon gives him a look and tells him that no, he didn't create a spreadsheet for their unborn child, and I can see that Andrew is disappointed. No doubt he was hoping to get a copy of it.

I've lost interest in the guys, so I turn back to Julie.

". . . and then today I had an omelette for breakfast. It's funny, because my sister couldn't even go near eggs when she was pregnant, but I haven't had that with any foods at all. I think that I must be having a girl. Everyone says that you don't get as sick with girls."

I sense that I am expected to marvel at her luck, which I do with great fake enthusiasm. I also sense that she is waiting for me to excitedly ask her more questions. Let's see . . . unfortunately, I have a limited arsenal of pregnancy-related knowledge, and it is running out fast. Suddenly the pink Barneys skirt flashes before my eyes. I really just need to go buy it first thing tomorrow morning. But then I have a stroke of genius. *Oh!* I think. *I can ask her about clothes. Perfect.*

"Have you bought any maternity clothes yet?" Based on the tightness of her shirt, I already know the answer to this question, but since Julie doesn't work and therefore spends the majority of her time figuring out how to spend Jon's money, I also know that I can count on it as a good conversation starter.

"No," she says, looking somewhat crestfallen. "I tried some stuff on a few weeks ago, but everything was still way too big. I think I'm probably ready now, though." She looks down at her stomach. "I just can't wait until I'm really showing and everyone knows that I'm pregnant." At this I cock an eyebrow.

"Really?" I ask, sounding skeptical. I can't comprehend why anyone would want to be really showing. I think that pregnant women who are really showing look like bowling balls with heads.

"Are you kidding?" she asks. "Everyone is so nice to pregnant women, and you get so much attention. My sisters all had the best time." Sounds horrid, all that niceness. Time to check in on Andrew and Jon again.

". . . term life insurance, I think. Although I heard about some variable life insurance plan that lets you put in money tax-deferred up to twenty-five thousand. . . ."

Ugh. Being a guy must be so horrendously boring. I'm still not exactly sure how the news is impacting Andrew. I can't decide if he's just asking these questions out of curiosity, or if he is actually starting to make plans. I'm so hoping it's the former.

Back to Julie. Correction. Back to Julie, my friend who is *pregnant.* I look at her, and this time I am totally sincere.

"I really can't believe you're having a baby. I just cannot believe it."

"I know," she says. "Isn't it crazy? I'm going to be somebody's *mom.*"
Yes, I think. *It is crazy. Because that means that I'm going to be the very good friend of somebody's mom. I'm going to be Aunt Lara. Ick. I hate the way that sounds.*

2.

Jack Sprat Could be Such a Brat; His Wife Could Be So Mean

Andrew is curiously silent on the drive home from dinner, and I am careful not to say anything that might steer the conversation toward our own baby prospects. But it seems that I needn't have worried, because, as we pull into the driveway, he still has not said anything more about it other than to note how happy he is for them. I'm reluctant to believe my good fortune, but by the time we get into bed, I am beginning to think that I'm off the hook. I, by the way, am exhausted—it's now almost ten o'clock—and it is aeons past my bedtime. Andrew, however, is wide-awake, and he's scrolling through the shows that we TiVoed during the year and saved for the summer rerun season. Because God forbid we should have nothing new to watch. We might actually have to do something with our lives. Andrew finishes his audit and turns to me.

"Do you want to watch a *Law and Order?*" he asks.

"I think I just want to go to bed. I'm wiped."

"Okay, well, do you care if I read?"

"You're *reading?*"

"Yes," he says, in a fake, I'm-so-offended tone. "I'm reading." He picks up a huge hardback book with a picture of a white-haired man on the cover. "Jack Welch. It was on sale at Costco. I thought it looked interesting." I make a mental note to myself to start a betting pool with our friends over how far he'll get before Jack Welch ends up on the floor, right next to the book about everyday engineering that he thought looked interesting about three years ago and still hasn't opened.

"Go ahead," I say. "Read away. I'm going to sleep." I kiss him on the cheek and roll over. "Good night," I tell him. "Don't stay up too late." I give him ten minutes, tops.

Two minutes later, I hear him close the book and put it down on his nightstand. Like I said . . .

He turns off the light and I feel a tap on my shoulder. He's probably going to ask me if I'd mind it if he puts the television back on. I pretend to be asleep, but Andrew knows full well that I am a semi-insomniac and that it takes a good hour before I am out. So he taps me again. In the cute baby voice that he reserves for occasions when he wants something that he knows I will say no to, he starts to whisper.

"Dolly?" *Oh, no.* The cute voice and a pet name? I try not to sound annoyed.

"Yes?" I say, not moving from my sleep position. There is a long pause, and I finally roll over to look at him. He is smiling at me. Playfully. I sigh. "Honey, if this is an attempt to have sex, I'm really sorry, but I don't feel like it tonight. Starting tomorrow we can do it every day, I promise." Andrew ignores this and keeps smiling at me until I am no longer able to hide my annoyance. "What?" I yell.

"Let's have a baby," he says, still using the cute voice. I knew it. Damn that Julie for getting knocked up. I sit up and roll my eyes in a here-we-go-again kind of way.

"Come on, Andrew, you know how I feel about this topic."

He drops the cute voice and starts to whine. "Yes, but I don't understand *why* you feel that way. You just turned thirty years old. Don't you want to get started?"

"Andrew, it's not a contest. Just because Julie and Jon are having a baby doesn't mean that we have to also. We should do it because we're ready, and I'm not ready."

"I just don't understand why. We have a house, we've traveled, we make enough money. I mean, what are you *waiting* for?"

Now I start to whine. "I've told you this a million times. I'm waiting to be ready, and I'm just not ready right now."

He rolls his eyes at me. "Well, how do you know that you're not ready? Do you seriously think that one day a big ready light is going to go on over your head?"

I glare at him. I can't possibly say out loud what I am thinking. I know that I'm not ready because every time that I even think about having a baby, I keep going back to the fact that I still need to lose five pounds, and that I'm not ready to give up vodka martinis for nine months. Not to mention the pink skirt. There would be no point in buying it if I can only wear it for a few weeks, and I really, really want it. So how can I be a mother? Mothers don't think this way. Mothers are supposed to be *un-selfish*.

But, as I said, I can't tell him all of this. So I dodge the question.

"Andrew, do you remember how I was when we got Zoey?" I look over at her—she's lying upside down in her round, leopard-print doggie bed, all four legs sticking straight up in the air. Upon hearing her name, she opens her eyes and perks up her ears, so I lower my voice to a whisper. Zoey definitely understands English, and I don't want her to hear what I have to say next. "Do you remember? I had postpartum depression with a *puppy*. I cried every single day and I told you every night that I hated her puppy guts and that I wanted to give her back. Imagine how I'll be with a baby."

This is not an exaggeration, by the way. I really did hate Zoey when we got her. It wasn't entirely my fault, though. Andrew never should have given her to me as a surprise birthday present. I had made it very clear that I wanted a hot-pink, 100-percent cashmere pashmina. I felt so cheated when he gave me a puppy instead. I mean, pets are not birthday presents. They're presents for *everyone*. If you're going to surprise some-one with a dog, fine, but don't do it for a birthday. It's a complete waste of a perfectly good gift opportunity. And to top it off, she was a stubborn, destructive pain in my ass. She chewed four pairs of my shoes, she ate a blue ballpoint pen that leaked all over the couch, she peed everywhere, and I had to spend ten minutes chasing her around the house every time she saw me pick up her leash. Plus, we couldn't go on vacation the whole summer because we had nobody to watch her and she was still too young for a kennel. Of course, I came around and now I love her to death, but I'm a dog person. I'm not so sure that things would have ended so hap-pily for us if I had started off hating the entire species.

Andrew looks at me like he was anticipating this. I hate it that our mind reading works both ways.

"Lara," he says. "Zoey is a dog. I know you love her, but you didn't give birth to her." I start to interrupt him, but he puts his palm up in the air to stop me. "Honey, just listen. I believe you that you're not ready. I do. But I also think that being pregnant will change you. There is a reason that it takes nine months—it gives you a chance to get used to the idea. I don't think anybody is ever really ready to have kids. It's just the kind of thing where you hold your nose and jump in. And then you'll be ready because you'll have to be."

Hmm, I think. *I wonder where he got that from. There's no way that he came up with it on his own.* He smiles at me lovingly and brushes a wisp of hair away from my face. *Sorry, honey,* I think. *I'm not going to let you win that easily. If I'm going down, I'm going down swinging.*

"Well," I finally say, crossing my arms. "If you're so smart, why don't you be the mother?" I know, I know. Definitely not my best work, but it was the only thing I could think of. I give him a big pout, and Andrew lets out a sigh.

"Look, all I'm asking is that you think about it, okay? Just think about it."

"Fine," I tell him. "Are we finished now? Can I go to sleep?"

Another sigh. "Yes, you can go to sleep." I roll over and he kisses me on top of the head. "I love you, okay?"

"I love you, too," I say, and wonder, for about the eight millionth time since we met, why in the hell he puts up with me.

I am dressed in a gorilla suit, and I am walking down the street in Pennsylvania, where I grew up, pushing an old-fashioned metal baby carriage. The sky is ominously dark, and the wind is blowing my hair wildly, which is kind of weird because the gorilla suit covers my head. Suddenly a huge black bird swoops down and lands inside of the carriage. It looks like a cross between a crow and a pterodactyl. I try to shoo it away, but it won't go. I desperately look inside to make sure that the baby is okay, but the baby is not okay. The baby is actually a giant, adult-size man-child, who is naked except for a hot-pink cloth diaper that is pinned with a pink rhinestone brooch in the shape of a snake. He's wearing a braided Rapunzel wig that is tied at the ends with pink bows, and when I see his face, I cringe in horror. His skin is wrinkled with old burns, and his nose is huge and hooked and raw. Suddenly I realize that it is Freddy Krueger from *A Nightmare on Elm Street*. I start to scream . . . and then I am awake.

I sit up and try to catch my breath. What the hell was that? I mean, it doesn't take a rocket scientist to figure out the subtext, but what was with the gorilla suit and Freddy the tranny baby?

I look at the clock. Three twenty-six. Suddenly I am furious. I am supposed to be on *vacation*. I am supposed to be sleeping like a rock because I have no worries and no stress. I am supposed to be relaxed.

I am not off to a good start.

I get up and go into the kitchen to get a glass of water, and then sit down at the table. Maybe Andrew's right, I think. Maybe I will never feel ready. I'll just keep making excuses for why it's not the right time, and the next thing you know, I'll be forty-four years old with a closetful of dog T-shirts and dried-up ovaries. Okay, fine. He wants me to think about it? I'll think about it.

True to my scary, type-A personality, I feel an overwhelming urge to make a list. I grab a pad of paper that some random real estate agent left on my doorstep *(Moving? Call Sherri Levine! Everything I touch turns to SOLD!)*, and I make two columns.

BABY CONS   BABY PROS
_____   _____

Here we go. Cons first because I am a negative person and that is how I naturally think. I write down the first thing that pops into my head.

>   *Will get fat.*

I really am so vain. But that's a topic for a different list. Right now, I need a pro. Ah. I know.

>   *Still young,*
>   *easier to lose weight after.*

This, by the way, is a medical fact. I have read in several different fashion magazines that a woman's metabolism doesn't start to slow down until after thirty. That means that, if I got pregnant right now, I would still be thirty once the baby was born. Hmm. Very interesting. I pick up the pencil again.

No sleep, no spontaneity.

The pro is an easy one.

*Have insomnia,
am never spontaneous.*

I'm getting into the groove now. The next one comes almost immediately.

Maternity clothes.

While I try to think of something that could possibly be a pro with regard to maternity clothes, I look back over my list and realize that my pros are not really pros at all. They're actually just counterarguments to the cons. *Come on, Lar,* I tell myself. *Think of something positive.* I try to think.

Still thinking.

Got it.

Baby clothes, esp. girls.

I picture the tiny plaid shift dress with the tiny plaid shoes that I saw in Burberry last week, and I smile. They are pretty cute. Although probably not that cute when covered with spit-up and diarrhea.

I'm starting to get a headache. It feels like there's a giant hammer that is banging on my temple from the inside out. I put the pencil down and start to rub the spot where it hurts, and I suddenly realize that it's not a hammer that's banging in my head but the con that I've been trying to ignore since I started this exercise. Maybe if I write it down it will be satisfied and stop banging on my brain. I pick up the pencil and take a deep breath, then write:

I am not cut out for motherhood.

There. I said it. Well, not actually *said* it, but it's close enough. What is it they all say in AA? Admitting that you have a problem is the first step? Fine. I've admitted my problem. I have no idea what the second step is, but seeing it there on paper is not nearly as scary as I thought it would be. Actually, I'm finding it oddly comforting.

I stare at my list for a few minutes, letting it absorb into my brain. It looks lopsided without the last pro. I pick up the pencil again.

?????

I'm not going to force it. I think I've made quite enough progress for one night.

3.

Shoo, Boss, Don't Bother Me

Andrew is shaking my shoulder. I open my eyes and see him hovering over my side of the bed with the phone in his hand.

"Lara," he's semiwhispering. "Lara." I look at the clock. It is eight thirty. What kind of a person calls someone at eight thirty on a Saturday morning? And why is Andrew waking me up to talk to such a person? I roll over and kick him away with the heel of my foot.

"I'm *sleeping*. Tell whoever it is that I'll call them back." I close my eyes and try to get back into the dream that I am having about the hot Tae Bo teacher at my gym before I lose it. But Andrew apparently has ESP and knows that I am dreaming of another man, which can be the only possible explanation for why he is persisting in his attempt to rouse me.

"Lara," he says, shaking my shoulder. Forget it. The dream is gone. I open my eyes again, hoping that they convey every last ounce of the irritation that I am feeling toward him right now. If they do, he doesn't seem to notice. Andrew covers the mouthpiece of the phone and whispers. "It's *Linda*."

I am yelling at him at the top of my lungs. "Who the hell is Linda and what the fuck does she want on a Saturday at eight thirty in the morning?" Andrew closes his eyes. When he reopens them, he hands me the phone.

"Linda. Your boss."

Shit. There is no way that she didn't hear that. Then I remember that it is not only a Saturday morning but also summer, and I hope that she did hear it. I take the phone from Andrew, clear my throat, and put on a fake sweet voice.

"Hi, Linda. What's going on?"

"Lara, hi. I'm so sorry to bother you at home during your vacation, but there's been an emergency." *Oh, no.* Someone must have died. That's the only thing that I can think of. I hope it wasn't one of the kids in a stupid drunk-driving accident. I lower my voice.

"Is everyone okay?" At this, Linda begins to stutter.

"Oh, no, I mean, yes, everyone is fine. It's not *that* kind of an emergency." I start to get the feeling that it is not any kind of an emergency. I start to get the feeling that Linda is going to ask me to do something for her. I say nothing, hoping that my silence is long enough to express the full extent of my irritation. I think that, for eight thirty on a Saturday morning on what is supposed to be the first day of my summer vacation, there has already been entirely too much going on in the irritation department. Linda takes a deep breath and starts talking.

"Victoria Gardner is one of your students, right?" She is. Victoria is a junior with crappy grades. She has purple hair, four visible piercings, and no friends. Her nickname is Tick, and I'm not sure I want to know why.

"Sort of," I say. "I mean, I really only met her once. She blew off every single meeting with me the whole year. When I called home, the only person who would talk to me was the mother's personal assistant, and she had no idea what was going on." I distinctly remember this, mostly because I spent a good hour with my colleagues discussing the hilarity of a woman who doesn't work having a personal assistant. Linda sighs again.

"Yes, well, do you know who she is?" I have lived in this city long enough to know that this phrase is code for, *Do you know why she's important?* I was not aware that Tick was important, although I am not surprised, given her attitude. And, of course, the personal assistant.

"No," I answer. "Who is she?" I can't wait to hear this one. In the Los Angeles private-school world, you never know. It's not like New York, where all of the rich kids' parents are corporate big shots or real estate moguls. In LA, she could be anything from the illegitimate child of a porn star to the heiress of a discount fashion empire. As long as you have money, nobody discriminates.

"Her father is Stefan Gardner, the director." *Oh, really?* I think. He's huge. I'm impressed, but I pretend not to be. I don't want to get sucked into anything by being starstruck.

"Okay," I say, clearly intending this to mean, *So what?* If Linda doesn't cut to the chase soon, I'm going back to bed.

"Well, her mother called me last night, *at home.* Apparently Victoria got her SAT scores back yesterday, and they were not satisfactory."

"What does that mean, exactly?" I ask. And why should I care? I'm not an SAT tutor. If she wants a list of referrals, I'm happy to tell her where to look in my Rolodex.

"She got a ten-ten." For our school, that's pretty bad, but it's not unheard-of. And again, I'm not sure what I'm supposed to do about it. But Linda continues. "Anyway, her mother thinks that she bombed it on purpose, because her PSAT scores from last year were in the twelve hundreds." She pauses, and I can tell that she's about to get to the point, and that it's not looking good for me. "Her mother would like for you to meet with Victoria a few times this summer. To get her on track for college."

I am stunned. Stunned both that the mother asked this of Linda, and that Linda is actually asking this of me. *No way,* I think. *No way.*

"But, Linda, school is over. Does this woman understand that I'm on vacation? It's not my fault that her kid is a mess and that she didn't get the information when she should have. I must have left her mom ten messages this year, and she never even called me back. And now, *now* she decides that I'm important?" I am so furious that I'm actually shaking. "I'm sorry, Linda, but no. I'm not going to indulge that kind of behavior. Just because her father is in entertainment doesn't mean that they don't have to play by the rules." Zoey jumps up onto the bed and sits down on my leg. I can tell that she's trying to figure out if I'm mad at her. I rub her ears and smile at her while Linda talks.

"Lara, you're meeting with her. It's not a choice. Her father is not just in entertainment. He happens to be the school's biggest donor, and if I want to make my budget next year and be able to pay the teachers' salaries, I need him to be happy." Oh, so now the salaries of the poor teachers are in my hands. That's nice. Nothing like a little guilt first thing in the morning.

Satisfied that she's not in trouble, Zoey lies down and rolls over onto her back.

"This is ridiculous," I yell. "What if I have plans? What if I'm going away for the whole summer?"

I can tell by Linda's tone of voice that she is growing tired of me. "You told me three days ago that you were looking forward to just staying home and doing nothing until August."

God. Why do I have to be so boring?

"Honestly, Lara, it's just a few meetings, it's not that big a deal. And they're willing to underwrite a stipend to your salary, so you'll be compensated. Now, I told her that you would call her this afternoon to set something up."

"Fine," I say, spitting the word out. "But you owe me." Linda hangs up and I slam down the phone, and Zoey cranes her neck to the side to see what all of the commotion is about.

"Some vacation this is turning out to be," I say, and she licks my hand in sympathy.

An hour and a half later, I'm still fuming. I'm supposed to be meeting my friend Stacey at ten o'clock to go hiking, as we do every Saturday morning, but I got so wrapped up in my post-Linda lividness that I didn't even leave the house until ten, and now I'm going to be fifteen minutes late. I hate being late for anything, so I am racing down Sunset Boulevard, trying to eat a piece of string cheese and drive at the same time. But Sunset starts to get really curvy in the Palisades, and I can't pull off strings of cheese with just one hand. So I eat the thing in three big bites, even though it's completely disgusting that way. By the time I get to Temescal Park, I am already sweating from the effort.

Stacey is waiting for me in the parking lot, and I am, as usual, immediately annoyed by how skinny she is, considering that she subsists exclusively on chili cheese fries, porterhouse steaks, and beef gorditas from Taco Bell, not to mention the fact that the only time she exercises is on Saturdays, with me. Meanwhile, I haven't had a carb in almost two years (okay, whatever, I had three bowls of cereal and a blueberry waffle for dinner last week, but I had my period so it doesn't count), and I work out like a fiend, but I couldn't get one leg into a pair of Stacey's pants, and I'm a size four.

Anyway, she's standing in the middle of the parking lot, and she's got a pink bandanna wrapped Aunt Jemima style around her head, and she's wearing a tight, Day-Glo orange Hello Kitty T-shirt and bright purple workout pants. Anyone else would look ridiculous in this color scheme, but somehow it works on her. As I get out of the car, she frowns and looks at her watch.

"You're late. What's wrong?"

I jut out my lower jaw. "Sorry. I was *working*."

Stacey scoffs at this.

"No way, babe. You don't get to use that one. That excuse is reserved exclusively for people with real jobs." I knew that she would have some smart-ass remark like that. Stacey and I met in law school, and she has spent the last six years in indentured servitude at a fancy boutique entertainment firm in Century City. She thinks that because she martyred herself and stuck it out at a firm, nobody else is entitled to work-related complaints. She, on the other hand, complains constantly about how miserable she is in her job, but she would never quit, for several obvious reasons. (1) she has no life outside of work and no interest in cultivating one; (2) she thrives under pressure and wouldn't last three minutes alone with herself in a room without a crisis to deal with; and (3) though she would never admit it, she totally gets off on working with celebrity clients and feeling vicariously important through them.

Aside from making fun of people, Stacey never talks about anything but work, she has no free time, and she uses her job as an excuse to get out of anything that she doesn't want to do, which is just about everything. It's no wonder that I'm her only friend—nobody else would put up with her crap for more than five seconds. Personally, I think that the long-term exposure to fluorescent office lighting is causing some kind of a personality cancer in her. I mean, if you think that I'm bitchy, Stacey makes me look like one of the Bobbsey Twins.

"Don't worry," I tell her. "I won't complain to you."

"Good. Because I got home from the office at three thirty in the morning, and I have to go back in after lunch." She starts walking. "Come on, let's go. If we don't hurry up we'll get stuck behind the Persian men." She's right. There's this very strange phenomenon that occurs every weekend in the Santa Monica Mountains that involves old Persian men who get up at the crack of dawn to go hiking in groups of twenty. I swear, the average age must be somewhere around seventy-five, and they wear dress pants and button-down shirts and carry walking sticks like they're climbing Mount Everest. The worst part is, if you have the misfortune of getting stuck behind them, you are doomed to taking no more than four steps per minute and listening to them yell at each other in Farsi for an hour and a half. Needless to say, we book it to the trail.

Stacey and I have been doing this hike every Saturday for the last four years, and while I still find it difficult, it's no longer the huge challenge that it was when we first started out. Stacey, however, wheezes like Darth Vader the whole way up to the top and has to take water breaks every ten minutes. Of course, this might be due to the fact that our hike is quite possibly the only two hours each week when she breathes uncirculated air, but as a result, the responsibility for keeping us entertained during the uphill portion of the climb sits squarely on my shoulders each week.

But not today. As we start trudging up the trail, I am silent. I can't stop thinking about my conversation with Linda, and there isn't anything else that I want to talk about right now. I'm confident that if I keep this up long enough, she'll give in out of sheer boredom. After about three minutes, she caves.

"You are so fucking passive-aggressive," she says. "Just tell me."

I smile at her and begin to recount the whole story. When I get to the part about who Tick is, she interrupts.

"Her dad is Stefan Gardner? I just worked on his contract for a three-picture deal that he's got with Sony. The wife is such a bitch. She gets a coproducer credit on all of his movies—not that she does anything for it—and she demanded that the studio lease him his own private jet to use on each film. When they said no, she threw a fit and threatened to take his all of his projects to Dreamworks. What a piece of work. I've heard that Stefan is a nice guy, but she definitely wears the pants in that family."

I want to tell her that she probably should not be sharing this information with me, as it is technically privileged, but I know that she knows this, and besides, I am very interested.

"Well, that's just great," I say. "Because I have to work with her kid all summer and try to get her to care about her SAT scores. And if I don't, the teachers apparently won't get paid next year. So I'm just thrilled to know that her mother is demanding and impossible to please. I wonder if maybe that's why her kid is such a fuckup." As soon as I yell out the work *fuck,* the entire Persian constituency of AARP descends upon us on their way down the trail. Per the unwritten rule that all hikers must smile and heartily greet each other, each one of them shouts good morning to us in broken English. Stacey and I both hate this rule, but I at least fake-smile and nod at them. Stacey just scowls. When they have all passed us, we resume our conversation.

"Anyway," I say, "I love my job, but I don't love it that much. Can you believe that they're making me work during summer vacation? I'm *tired* of kids after nine months with them. I *need* twelve weeks off."

I think that I hear her snort at me, but it's hard to tell with all of the panting. She starts talking, pausing to exhale twice after every third word.

"First of all, you are such a little brat. Nobody *needs* twelve weeks off. Ninety-nine percent of the working world gets two weeks' vacation every year and survives just fine. And if it makes you feel better, I haven't had a vacation in almost three years. And the last time I *did* take a vacation, they called me in Hawaii two days after I got there and told me that I had to come back right away. The studio was refusing to pay José Eber a thousand dollars a day to blow out the hair of one of my clients, when we had specifically negotiated for that in her contract."

What can I possibly say to this? No, it doesn't make me feel better, and if anyone's job is fake, it is definitely hers. But I don't feel like getting into an argument over it, because, as I already told you, it would be pointless.

Suddenly a random thought flashes into my mind. *Huh,* I think. *I just thought of a better pro for my maternity-clothes con. Maternity* leave. *That's about twelve weeks. It would be like getting two summer vacations in one year. Interesting. I'll need to write that down on my list when I get home.* Thinking of my list reminds me that Julie is having a baby. I turn around to look at Stacey, whose face is now the exact color of her bandanna.

"Oh, I forgot to tell you," I say. "Julie's pregnant." This is sure to change the subject. Stacey can't stand Julie. They were both bridesmaids in my wedding, and for my bachelorette party the three of us spent a long weekend in Vegas and stayed in the same hotel room. For Stacey, the constant flow of cheeriness was like Chinese water torture. By the third night, I seriously thought that she was going to suffocate Julie with a pillow in her sleep. Or at the very least, pull a Jan Brady and cut off all of her gorgeous, shiny hair.

"Oh, how perfect," Stacey wheezes. "At least now she'll have something to do with herself all day." In addition to being outraged by Julie's über-happiness, Stacey is also deeply offended by the fact that Julie has never worked a day in her life.

"You are so mean," I say. "Not everyone defines themselves through a job, you know." We have reached the boulder that is halfway to the top, and we stop for a minute so that Stacey can catch her breath.

"Oh, whatever," she says, taking a long swig of water. "I really think that you're schizophrenic or something. It just makes absolutely no sense how one person's two closest friends could be me and her. It's like being best friends with Gandhi and Hitler."

I laugh. "Yeah, and I think we know which one of you is Hitler." I start walking and put on my lecturing professor voice. "Each of you fulfills different needs in my life." This time I definitely hear a snort.

"I didn't realize that you had such a strong need to vomit. So does Miss America know whether it's a boy or a girl?"

"She doesn't know yet, but she thinks it's a girl."

"Of course she does," Stacey says. "Just what the world needs. Yet another woman who will contribute absolutely nothing to society. I just don't understand this obsessive need of everyone to procreate. There are plenty of kids. It's not like the world is running out of them anytime soon. In fact, I think it would be a great idea if they took one entire continent and put it aside for people who don't want children. God, that's genius, isn't it?"

In case you couldn't tell, Stacey hates kids. Hates them. Once, when we were in law school, Stacey and I were out to dinner, and a kid in the booth behind us was pretending that his imaginary friend wanted to play with us. He couldn't have been more than five or six years old. Anyway, after about ten minutes, Stacey finally looked at the kid and said, *Oh, is this your friend, sitting right here next to me?* The kid smiled and said yes, and then Stacey pointed her finger like she was making a gun, and pretended to shoot the imaginary friend. *Well, now he's dead,* she told him. The poor kid was so hysterical that his mother had to take him out of the restaurant. I was mortified.

"Yes, you're a regular Isaac Newton. Anyway, as soon as Andrew heard the news, he started in on me again."

"Oh, God," she says. "He has got to give it a rest. What did you tell him?"

"I told him that I'm not ready, and he wanted to know what I'm waiting for. I think he really means it this time. I don't know how much longer I can stall him."

"Look, Lara, do not do this if you don't want to. You will resent him forever if he pushes you into this."

I know she's right. I have considered this. But I really don't know how much longer it will be before he starts to resent me for making him wait. But Stacey wouldn't understand this. The concept of marital compromise is not one that would make sense to her.

"I know" is all that I say. "I know."

Zoey is so happy to see me walk in the door that she is running around in little circles and making these adorable, soft grunty noises. I pet her for a good ten minutes, and then I take off my dirty shoes and socks and head upstairs. There is a distinct dirt line of demarcation on each of my ankles where the tops of my socks ended. Andrew is off playing golf for the day—a game the appeal of which I will never understand—and I have nothing on my agenda except for a shower, a manicure and a pedicure, and, of course, a call to Cheryl Gardner.

I decide to get the call to Cheryl over with so that it isn't hanging over me for the rest of the day. Plus, if I am really upset afterward, I will still have time to shop away my sorrow before all of the stores close. I open the fridge and take out a container of green grapes, and then I find the scrap of paper on which I wrote down her number. As I dial, I walk into the den and sit down on the couch. Zoey is right behind me, and she sits down by my feet, waiting expectantly for me to send a grape or two in her direction.

There's an answer on the third ring.

"Hello, Gardner residence." It's got to be the personal assistant. I can't believe that they have this woman working on Saturdays, too. No wonder they thought nothing of asking me to work during my summer vacation.

"Hi," I say, my voice ten octaves higher than normal. *No,* I think. *I am not going to be polite.* I lower my voice back to normal. "Could I please speak with Mrs. Gardner?"

"May I ask who is calling?" the assistant says.

"This is Lara Stone, Victoria's college counselor."

"Oh, just a minute, Mrs. Gardner has been waiting for your call." She says this in a tone that suggests that I am somehow at fault for keeping this woman waiting. *Great.* I brace myself for the impending hostilities, and then drop a grape on the floor and watch as Zoey rolls it around in her mouth. There is nothing funnier to me than watching a dog try to eat a grape. I hear activity on the other end of the phone, and then a young, bubbly voice is exploding in my ear.

"Hi, Lara! Thanks so much for calling me back today. I'm so sorry if we're ruining your vacation. Linda didn't think you'd mind, but I want you to tell me if this is too big an imposition." I am completely caught off guard by this. I was so not expecting disarming and nice, and now I have no choice but to drop the chip from my shoulder. I hate myself for what I am about to say.

"No, no, it's not a big deal. I wasn't really doing anything anyway. I mean, how many *Wonder Woman* marathons can you really watch on TNT in one summer?"

She laughs. "I love that show! I used to have Wonder Woman Underoos when I was a kid." So did I. How old is this woman? "God, it would be so great to have that truth-lasso thing she had. I could use it on Tick to find out why she hates me so much."

I don't know if I'm supposed to laugh at this or not, but I find it interesting that she calls Victoria by her nickname.

"Yeah," I say. "Do you want to tell me what happened?"

"I have no idea. She got a twelve-fifty on her PSATs last year without even trying, and then this year she had a private tutor for four months, and she gets a ten-ten. I know she did it on purpose, but she won't admit it. She won't even talk to me. We hired a private college counselor and got nowhere, so I'm hoping that maybe you can get through to her. Linda said that the kids love you."

Oh, no, I think. *Not again.* I love these parents who can't deal with their own kids, so they want me to do their parenting for them. I can't even tell you how many times a year some mom will call me up and ask me not to tell her kid that she called, but could I just sit him down and explain to him that he really shouldn't do his homework in front of the television? I'm always like, *Oh, yes, and should I tell him that I know he does his homework in front of the television because I have a spy camera set up in his room, or is it better to say that I'm channeling the dead person who used to live there and that that's who ratted him out?*

"Well," I say, "I don't know about that, but I'll see what I can do."

"Fabulous," she says. "So do you think you could see her on Monday? Tick's band is practicing at one, so maybe around ten?" *Noooo,* I think. Not ten. Ten is Tae Bo with the hottie.

"Um, could we do it later in the day? Maybe around three?"

"Oh," she says, sounding disappointed. "I've got someone coming to the house to do my hair at three, and then Tuesday we're going to be on set with Stefan all day. I really don't want to put this off too long. Are you sure you can't do it at ten?" Oh, I see. Nice, but only on her terms. Got it. Fine. I'll skip Tae Bo and just go on the treadmill or something in the afternoon. The sacrifices that I make.

"I guess I could switch my schedule around," I say. "Where should we meet?"

"Why don't you come here?" she says. "I'll have Lori bring in breakfast." Lori, the assistant. What a shitty job that woman has.

"Okay," I say, trying to muster some enthusiasm. "I guess I'll see you then." I hang up the phone and head straight for the shower. This definitely calls for shopping.

* * *

The pink skirt is gone. All they have left are three size tens. The saleswoman apparently thinks that it will make me feel better to tell me that they just sold the last one in my size this morning. I take it as a sign that my summer is going to totally suck, and I end up buying two shirts that I most definitely will never wear.

4.

Hickory, Dickory, Dock, I Hate My Biological Clock

The next morning, I drag Andrew with me to breakfast. I say drag because, short of an occasional piece of dry toast or an English muffin with peanut butter and jelly, Andrew doesn't actually eat breakfast. And it's not because he doesn't get hungry in the morning. It's because he doesn't feel that pancakes and waffles and French toast are worth the calories. He says that they're dessert foods posing as breakfast foods, and that if he's going to eat dessert, he would rather have a chocolate brownie sundae or a glazed doughnut. And, of course, to make him even more impossible, eggs make him gag. Really. I didn't believe him either, but then I hard-boiled some eggs one time while he was at the gym, and when he walked in the door he *freaked out*. He was home for something like three-eighteenths of a second before he smelled it, and then he ran through the house with his hand over his mouth, flinging open all of the windows, alternately retching and screaming at me. He threatened to divorce me for three straight hours. I was like, *Okay, honey, on what grounds? Irreconcilable breakfast differences?*

Anyway, Andrew is currently sitting across the table from me and trying to avoid making eye contact with my veggie-and-goat-cheese omelette. The plan was that he would eat the toast that came with my meal, since I pretend not to eat carbs, but I forgot to ask the waiter to bring the toast on a separate plate, so now Andrew is eating nothing. Because the toast might have touched egg. I know. Believe me, I know.

The two of us are already off to a bad start this morning. In addition to the fact that I am torturing him by ovum, we fought during the entire car ride to the restaurant. Granted, it might have been partly my fault. I have a tendency to get a little nasty when I'm hungry, and since I woke up this morning with a gnawing, empty pit in my stomach, it didn't take long before I snapped at him. However, in my defense, he was being really annoying. Do you know those people who sing along to the radio and always get the lyrics wrong? That's Andrew. It drives me fucking crazy. And, to add insult to injury, he does this ridiculous thing that he calls bomping. It's kind of like humming, but he just says *bomp, bomp, bomp* to the tune. After a while, he starts to sound like the sound track to a bad seventies porno.

Anyway, as I said, I was *starving* and in no mood, and about halfway to the restaurant "Jack and Diane" comes on the radio, which, as you know, happens to be an amazing song that quite possibly defined our entire generation, or at least it did for those of us who grew up in hick towns. Honestly, one would think that anyone who came of age in the eighties would for sure know the words to "Jack and Diane," right? Wrong. He bomped his way through the entire musical introduction, and then, right when the lyrics started, he turned his head to look at me and pretended to sing into a microphone.

"Itty bitty, 'bout Jack and Di-ay-an."

Itty bitty. Itty fucking bitty about Jack and Diane. What does he even think that that means? And so I lost it on him.

Of course, after I yelled at him he got mad at me for yelling at him, and he made me apologize sixteen times. Which I did, albeit in a nasty tone and without a hint of remorse. But now that I have some food in my stomach and I am no longer a vicious, hungry monster, I'm actually feeling bad for lashing out at him. So I soften my voice and attempt to smooth things over.

"I'm sorry, okay? Please don't be mad at me." He sticks out his lower lip to illustrate that I have hurt his feelings.

"What are you sorry for?" he asks. We've been through this routine a million times. My part is to tell him that I'm sorry for being mean.

"I'm sorry for being mean." He nods solemnly.

"You were really mean."

"I know I was, and I said that I'm sorry."

"Say it one more time," he demands. I sigh.

"I'm very sorry, okay?" He nods again.

"Apology accepted."

Just then a little boy runs past our table with his arms spread open like wings, and he knocks into my chair, which causes me to spill my water all over my lap. His parents are on the other side of the restaurant, completely ignoring him. But before I have a chance to get in a dig about how fun it must be to have kids, Andrew clears his throat.

"So I've been doing some research."

I take another bite of my eggs. "Research on what?" I ask.

He sits up straight in his chair and pushes his shoulders back. "On pregnancy."

I swallow loudly and raise my eyebrows. "Really. What kind of research?"

"I was looking at statistics on getting pregnant after the age of thirty. It's not as easy as you think. On Oprah's Web site there was a whole thing about these women who waited to have kids until they were in their mid-thirties or early forties, and then they couldn't get pregnant at all because it was too late." So that's where he got his little speech from the other night. I'm not sure whether I should be more concerned about the fact that he's doing research on pregnancy or that he's conducting his research on Oprah's Web site.

"Okay," I say, "but I'm not in my mid-thirties." He nods. "I know, but it could take years to get pregnant, and then if we have to do in vitro it can take even longer, and by then you could be thirty-five or even older, and that's when you're most at risk for birth defects and Down syndrome." The kid runs by our table again. As he approaches my chair I give him a nasty glare and he goes scurrying back to his mom. This time I seize my opportunity.

"Did you see that?" I say. "I'm the mean lady who gives dirty looks to kids in restaurants. Don't you understand? Kids annoy me. I find them annoying. How can I be a mother?"

"Our kids won't be like that," he says. "We won't let them be." I turn around to look at the kid, who is now standing in the booth and squeezing ketchup into piles on top of the table. "Remember how we were with Zoey?" Andrew says. "We disciplined her and we didn't let her rule the house, and now she's a sweet, well-behaved dog. It'll be the same thing with our kids."

Maybe he's right. Maybe it's not the kids who annoy me, but their parents. I mean, it's not the kid's fault if nobody ever tells him no. If nobody ever told me no, I'd probably do stupid stuff just to see what happens, too.

"I don't know," I say. "It just doesn't appeal to me on any level. First of all, the whole idea of being pregnant completely turns me off. I don't want to be a fat cow for nine months, and what if I get morning sickness? Julie told me about some woman who had to spit in a cup or something. Plus, I don't even want to think about going through labor. And breast feeding? Breast feeding is the grossest thing in the entire world. Nobody should be sucking on my boobs except for *you,* and when you do, there shouldn't be food coming out of them. It's disgusting." Andrew's face has changed and he looks angry. *Uh-oh.* I hope I haven't gone too far. He lowers his voice, and I instantly know that I have.

"Lara," he says. "I am sick of listening to your lame excuses. You've been putting me off for over a year, and I let you have your time. But now it's my turn. I want to have a baby, and I don't want to wait anymore. I'm thirty-one years old, and as it is, I'll be almost fifty by the time our first kid graduates from high school." He pauses for a moment, and when he starts talking again his voice breaks. "My dad was fifty when he died. I'm not willing to wait much longer."

I am stunned, and I can feel the tears welling up in my eyes. So that's what this is all about. His father. I should have realized it before. Now it's all starting to make sense. I'm trying really hard not to cry, both because I have upset him and because I know that I'm not going to win this one.

"So what are you saying?" I ask him.

He stares at me, and I can see that there are tears in his eyes, too. "I'm saying that, if you care about our marriage, you might want to reassess your priorities."

I inhale sharply, like I've just been sucker punched in the gut.

Okay, then. I guess my ready light just got turned on for me.

Ten hours later I'm sitting on the floor of my bathroom, naked, whispering into the phone.

"Hi, it's me," I say.

"Why are you whispering?" Julie asks.

"Because I don't want Andrew to know that I'm on the phone."

"Why?"

I take a deep breath and debate for the fiftieth time whether I should tell her. I should. I don't have anyone else to ask. But what if she tells people? Julie has such a big mouth. She won't. If I tell her not to, she won't. I should tell her.

"Lara, what's wrong? Are you okay?"

"Yes, I'm fine. I have to ask you a question, but you have to swear to me that you will not tell anyone. Not even Jon." As I say this, I know for sure that she is going to tell Jon. *Shit.*

"I swear, I swear. What?"

I take another deep breath. "Let's just say that, theoretically, Andrew and I had sex without a condom or anything else. How would I know if I was pregnant?"

"Oh, my God!" she screams. "Are you guys trying? This is *so amazing!* How fun would it be to be pregnant together?"

Oh, no. What have I done here? I just now come up with the idea of telling her that the condom broke by accident, which would have been a perfect cover. *Shit, shit, shit.*

"No, I mean, we're not really *trying.* I'm not charting my temperature or anything like that. We just decided to stop using protection and see what happens."

I don't tell her that I have already seen what happens. What happens is that sex sucks. I couldn't enjoy myself at all because I was such a nervous wreck. The whole time I kept thinking that this was it—we could be making a baby and my life would never be the same again. And I kept thinking about how I couldn't change my mind if I did get pregnant. It's not like you can have an abortion when you're married and thirty and your husband is pressuring you to have kids. And then, once I got past that, I became totally neurotic. I kept thinking about how I would never sleep once she started to drive, about the inevitable fights over tattoos and dating college guys, and about the stress of trying to get a kid into private school in LA. In ten minutes, I thought about every single thing that a parent must worry about over the course of a child's entire lifetime. Then Andrew came, and I swear I could hear the sperm arguing over which one was going to impregnate me. Honestly, if that's how it's going to be every time, there is no possible way that I will ever have an orgasm again.

"Anyway," I say, "I just want to know if you felt different right away or not."

"Okay," she says, sounding serious. "First of all, you can't just start trying like that with no preparation. Have you been taking prenatals, or at least folic acid?"

I have no idea what she's talking about, and my heart starts to pound. Great, I'm already messing up at motherhood.

"No, am I supposed to be? I thought prenatals are for once you're already pregnant."

She takes a deep breath.

"Look, it's not a big deal. Plenty of people get pregnant all the time by accident without it and they have perfectly healthy babies."

I can tell that there is a *but* to this sentence, and she's not sure whether to say it. If it's that bad, I need to know.

"But?" I say.

She hesitates, then begins to talk very fast. "But taking folic acid reduces the risk of brain defects when the baby first starts to form."

Oh, my God. Oh, my God. I am *so* not cut out for this.

Sensing my despair, Julie starts to backpedal. "Lara, you're probably not even pregnant. It never happens on the first try like that. Just first thing tomorrow go out and buy some prenatal vitamins at the drugstore and start taking them twice a day. You'll be fine."

She's right. She's got to be right. There's no way that one day makes a difference.

"Oooh!" Julie exclaims. "Do you eat eggs? Eggs have a ton of folic acid in them."

"Yes!" I shout, then lower my voice. "I had eggs this morning for breakfast."

"Perfect. See, you have nothing to worry about." I exhale. Thank God I didn't let Andrew talk me into getting oatmeal.

"Okay, so, did you feel any different right away?" I ask her.

"I did. I knew the next day. My boobs hurt, and I was really emotional, and . . . I don't know, I just knew it. But my sisters didn't feel anything at all. They didn't know until they took the pregnancy test. Everyone's different."

Wow, that's a big help. "All right. Thanks. Just don't say anything to Jon, please? I made Andrew swear not to tell anyone, so he would kill me if he knew that I told you."

"I promise. Just, before you go, can I tell you a couple of things to watch out for?"

Oh, no. How else am I endangering the life of my potential unborn child? "What?"

"Just in case you are pregnant, there's a lot of stuff that you shouldn't have." She starts to tick off a list of the verboten. "No coffee—actually, nothing with caffeine in it—no alcohol, of course, no unpasteurized cheeses, like Brie or soft mozzarella, nothing with aspartame, no sushi, nothing with raw eggs in it, like Caesar salad . . . umm, what else? Don't eat a lot of tuna or swordfish—they have a ton of mercury—and don't take any medicines, even over-the-counter ones. . . . I guess that's it. I'm sure your doctor will give you a list when you go to see him."

I am beginning to wish that I had never called Julie. Talk about a buzz kill. "Great," I say. "Well, thanks for ruining my life." For a moment it actually sounds like she is saying, "Tsk, tsk," and I am trying to remember what it is about her that I like.

"It's really a great thing, Lar. I promise you that if you are pregnant, you're going to love it. It's all worth it."

Speak for yourself, babe. "I'm sure that you think it is," I say. "But I've gotta go. I'm afraid Andrew's going to think that I'm in here with a coat hanger. I'll talk to you later."

I open the bathroom door and walk back out into the bedroom. Andrew is lying in bed, half-asleep, with his I-just-got-laid smile plastered on his face.

"Are you okay?" he says.

"I'm fine." I crawl into bed next to him and put my head on his chest.

"Do you think we made a baby tonight?" he asks. Oh, God, I hope not. I just need a little more time to adjust to this.

"I have no idea," I say. "Ever since I went off the pill my cycle's been completely irregular." Yeah, how convenient for him that I'm not on the pill anymore. When my doctor found out that I was turning thirty and had been on the pill for almost fifteen years, he suggested that I take a break from it for a little while, just to make sure that my ovaries actually work, in case we wanted to have a baby anytime soon. I never should have listened to him. I could have bought myself at least three more months.

"Mm-hm," he mumbles. He's in that relaxed, half-comatose place where guys go after sex, and I realize that I could probably get him to agree to anything right now. I am contemplating whether I should ask him to upgrade my engagement ring to a three-carat princess cut, but he starts talking again. "Can I ask you a question?" he says.

"Yeah, what?"

"Are you going to be a total bitch when you're pregnant?"

I snort. Any other woman would probably be offended by this remark, but I know what he's getting at. I mean, if I'm a vicious monster normally when I'm hungry, what will I be like when I'm fat and uncomfortable and eating for two? I hug him and give him a kiss on the cheek. "You can bet your ass I will be."

"That's what I thought," he says, closing his eyes. "Okay. Good night."

"Good night," I say. And, I think, *God help us.*

5.

There Was an Old Woman Who Lived in Jimmy Choos

The next morning, promptly at ten A.M., I pull up to the gate at Beverly Park. A guard comes over with a clipboard and I tell him that I have an appointment with the Gardners. The gate swings open and, as I drive through the neighborhood, I am shocked by the enormity of the houses. I shouldn't even call them houses. They're definitely estates. Gigantic, monstrous estates. I cannot even imagine Tick Gardner living in one of these places. With her Kelly Osbourne hairdo and combat boots, she must feel so completely out of her element. I pull into the circular driveway, and before I have a chance to get out of my car, one of the huge, double front doors swings open.

"Mrs. Stone?" It is Lori, the assistant. I recognize her voice. She's about twenty-two, brunette, and really pretty. She's wearing a beige velour Juicy sweat suit, and I immediately suspect that she's sleeping with the dad.

"Hi, you must be Lori." I reach out to shake her hand.

"It's nice to meet you. Mrs. Gardner will be down in just a minute. She wants to talk to you before you meet with Tick."

I follow her into the house, which is apparently the final destination for every last piece of marble on earth. Just as Lori is directing me to have a seat on one of the six green Italian leather couches in the living room, I hear expensive heels clicking somewhere in the distance. I look behind me and see a petite, gorgeous blond woman coming down the double spiral staircase. She's wearing my pink skirt, and I know instantly that she is the person who beat me to it yesterday morning. Any positive feelings I might have been having toward her completely vanish.

She walks the fifteen miles across the living room and, as she approaches me, opens her arms and leans in to give me a hug.

"Lara, I'm so glad you're here! Thank you so much for doing this." I am shocked by how young she is. There's no way she's more than thirty-seven, and if she is I want the name of her plastic surgeon.

"Hi, Mrs. Gardner, it's so nice to finally meet you in person," I say.

"Please, call me Cheryl. I always feel weird when people my age call me Mrs. Gardner."

Uh, sorry, I think. *People your age?* Oh, my God, do I look thirty-seven? That's it. I'm making an appointment to get Botoxed the second that I get home.

"Why don't we go into the dining room? Lori's brought in an amazing brunch."

I follow her through the house, trying to calculate how much they must have spent on it. I figure at least ten million for the property, probably another three to five on decorating. If there is such a thing as a next life, I hope that whoever I come back as is smart enough to know to go to film school.

As we enter the dining room, I see that there's a buffet spread out on the table that consists almost entirely of things that I am not allowed to eat. There's a wheel of Brie, a bowl of Caesar salad, a wooden tray lined with some kind of sashimi, another bowl of Chinese chicken salad, and a giant bed of lettuce, atop which is sitting a huge ball of tuna. Oh, and a big pot of coffee and a pitcher of mimosas made with Veuve.

"I hope you don't mind," Cheryl says. "I'm on Atkins, so I told Lori not to bring in any carby foods. I can't even pass by a bagel place, let alone have them in my house." I am tempted to just make a giant plate of everything and down about four mimosas, but I can hear Julie's voice in my head telling me about birth defects and learning disorders and deadly bacterial infections, so I spoon some Chinese chicken salad onto a plate and try to spread it around so that it doesn't look so empty. Lori eyes me suspiciously.

"Can I get you something else?" she asks.

"No, no," I say. "I'm fine. I was really hungry when I woke up this morning, so I had some eggs before I came." This, actually, is not a lie. I was so paranoid about the whole folic acid thing that I made myself a six-egg omelette for breakfast. Ooh, that reminds me, I need to remember to pay attention to my boobs to see if they hurt. "I'll just have some water, if you don't mind." Lori and Cheryl exchange a look, and Lori shrugs and disappears into the kitchen. We both sit down at the table, and I cut to the chase.

"So, what did you want to talk to me about?" She cuts off a huge chunk of Brie and pours herself a mimosa. Lori reappears with a bottle of water, sets it down in front of me, and then vanishes again.

"Yes," she says, sipping her drink. "Here's the situation, Lara. It's very important to me and to Tick's father that Tick goes to a reputable college. You know, somewhere with a good name. Tick wants to be in New York next year, so we were thinking maybe Columbia, or even Princeton, since it's not too far from the city. Now, I know she'll need to get her SAT scores up, but assuming that she does, I'm just curious as to what you think her chances are." When she says Princeton I almost spit out my water. I can't think of a person less suited for Princeton than Tick Gardner. Even if we suspended reality for a moment and supposed that hell had frozen over and she could get in, she would hate it there. But it's a moot point, because she won't get in. Not a chance. But then I remember that I'm sitting in a $10 million house, and I wonder if they're planning to donate a building. It would have to be a pretty big damn building, though.

"Um," I say, trying to be tactful. "Princeton and Columbia are pretty big reaches, even if she does get her SATs up. At those schools, SAT scores in the thirteen and fourteen hundreds are considered average." I pause, giving her a chance to jump in at any time. She doesn't. "Do you have any connections there, or were you, um, maybe thinking about making a donation? Because that might help her."

She gives me a steely glance. "I was hoping that we wouldn't have to throw money at this. I'd like to see Tick get in on her own, and not feel like we bought her way in."

Interesting. The trophy wife has morals. Or else she's just cheap. In any event, I try to backpedal. "Oh, I didn't mean that you should. I totally agree with you. It's just that, you know, you picked two of the hardest schools to get into, and even though Tick's smart, her grades just aren't at the level of the typical—"

She interrupts me. "In ninth and tenth grade she had all As and Bs. It's only this past year that her grades went down. And that C minus in Chemistry wasn't her fault. She had a horrible teacher who hated her."

I love how, with private-school parents, it's always the teacher's fault when a kid gets a bad grade. I think it's time for my don't-shoot-the-messenger routine.

"Look, Cheryl, if it were up to me, every kid would get into their first-choice school. But it's not up to me. All I can do is tell you what it takes to get in, and to get into Princeton or Columbia, not only does she need to have straight As, but she needs to have them in honors and Advanced Placement courses, and even then she still has only about a one in five chance of getting accepted. I'm not telling you that she shouldn't apply; I'm just telling you that, realistically, her chances aren't great and you might want to consider some schools that aren't in the Ivy League."

Cheryl looks like I've just informed her that Neiman Marcus is closing its doors forever. I mean, the woman seems positively *crushed*. I usually hate this part of my job, but I have to admit that it is perversely satisfying to know that I am most likely one of very few people in the world who has ever told this woman that she can't have something she wants. She shakes her head, and her lower lip is quivering. Oh, God. Is she really going to start crying on me?

"Stefan is not going to be happy about this," she whimpers. "I don't know how I'm going to tell him."

I say nothing. If she thinks that I'm going to tell him, she can find herself another college counselor to have over for brunch. I clear my throat and try to take another approach: "Have you even asked Tick what she wants? Because, to be honest, I really can't see her being interested in either one of those schools. You know, if you want her to be more motivated, it might help if she actually wanted to go to the college that she's trying to get into." It is immediately clear to me that Cheryl has never considered this before. The glow from the lightbulb that just went on in her head is almost blinding. She beams.

"You know, you are absolutely right. I can just tell Stefan that Tick doesn't want those schools, and he'll never even need to know that she can't get in."

Right, I think. Because obviously Tick's college search is all about Stefan. And she wonders why her kid hates her.

"See," she says, "this is why I needed you to come over. Maybe we should find her so that you two can get started." She takes her napkin off of her lap and stands up, and I feel a twinge when I see my skirt again.

I realize that I have to pee, so I ask her where the bathroom is and she points me down a long, marbled hallway. The bathroom is about the size of a hotel suite. It's all black marble and it looks like they locked somebody in there with a monogram machine for two weeks. Everything says *CGS* in superfancy script. The towels, the soaps, the top of the toilet seat, the trash can, even the center stone of the floor is inlaid with tiles that spell out their initials. I wonder if they think that their guests will forget whose house it is for the five minutes that they are alone in the bathroom. Like, mid-pee someone is going to think, *Wait, where am I again? Oh! That's right, I'm at Cheryl and Stefan Gardner's! Thank goodness they have that monogram on the floor.*

As I sit down to pee, I take the opportunity to squeeze each of my boobs to see if they feel tender. I'm not one of those women who gets sore boobs from my period, so I'm not exactly sure what I'm feeling for, but they don't seem any different. I am shocked to find that I feel a twinge of disappointment about this. *Hmm,* I think. *Is it possible that I want to be pregnant? And if so, how can that be?* I begin to suspect Andrew of playing happy-motherhood brainwashing tapes to me in my sleep.

I wash my hands and, turning sideways to look in the mirror, I lift up my shirt. My stomach is perfectly flat. It's really amazing how much less bloated I am when I don't eat carbs. I take a deep breath, and then exhale and push it out as far as I can. I suck it in again, fast. Nope. Definitely do not want to be pregnant.

When I emerge from the bathroom, Cheryl is at the other end of the hallway waiting for me, and she motions for me to follow her up the stairs. As I ascend the staircase, I start to hear some kind of horrendous punk-rock music that grows exponentially louder with each step that I take. By the time we get outside of Tick's room, Cheryl practically has to scream for me to hear her.

How can she listen to that noise? It reminds me of the time that I went to a Def Leppard tribute band concert and the lead singer was tripping on acid and yelling into the mike about how he was the real Lizard King. Hey, I was in high school and it was the eighties, okay? My point is, the music she's listening to is god-awful. And she must be doing permanent damage to her ears.

I suddenly realize that my inner voice is starting to sound just like my mother, and I am momentarily panic-stricken. I wonder if I can pin-point the exact moment between my twentieth birthday and now that I turned into Bea Arthur in *The Golden Girls*.

Cheryl is banging on Tick's door, and it takes a good minute or two before Tick realizes that someone is banging on her door. The so-called music stops.

"What?" she yells from behind the door. Her tone of voice is nasty and I instantly recognize it. It is the same tone of voice that I use with Andrew when he interrupts me while I'm reading or talking on the phone. Or when I'm annoyed with him for not knowing the words to songs. Okay. I really need to try to be nicer to him. If he ever talked to me like that, I would definitely cry. Cheryl, however, is unfazed.

"Tick," she says sweetly, "can you open the door, please? There's some-one here to see you." Cheryl looks at me and smiles apologetically. I am horrified as I realize that she didn't tell Tick that I was coming. The bitch has completely set me up.

The door swings open and Tick is standing in front of us, furious. Her hair, which is now dyed a dark, dark black, is messy and stringy-looking. She's wearing jeans with a thin black silver-studded belt and a vintage KISS T-shirt, and she's barefoot. I never noticed before, but she has a re-ally good body. I have a feeling that that's about the only thing she inher-ited from her mother.

I don't want to make eye contact with her, so I look past her into her bedroom. I have to say, it is just about the funniest thing that I have ever seen. Cheryl clearly picked the décor, and it's frilly and girly and horrible. We're talking pink and white and lace. But what's funnier is the way that Tick has subverted it into a kind of Dada-esque punk masterpiece. Hon-estly, Duchamp could not have done a better job. Scattered over the light pink berber carpet are several white Flokati rugs, the tips of which have been dyed black and dark purple. The canopy atop the white four-poster bed has been removed and replaced with a huge black cloth banner that says *Black Flag* in white graffiti letters. Running across the top of each pink-washed wall is a border of hand-stenciled tulips, each of which has been meticulously turned into a skull and crossbones. In one corner of the room is a professional drum set, and in the other corner is the pièce de résistance: an enormous distressed white antique pedestal mirror, the glass of which is covered by a life-size cutout of a skinny, sickly-looking guy who looks like he's about to OD on heroin at any second. The whole thing looks like a virgin who's been defiled by Gene Simmons himself. It's genius.

Tick puts her hands on her hips and, upon seeing me, gives her mother a look of death.

"What is she doing here?" she says, flicking her head in my direction. I'm going to kill Linda for this.

"Tick, I asked Mrs. Stone to come over to talk to you about college, since you didn't go to any of your meetings with her this year."

I smile awkwardly at Tick, and I feel like an idiot. She ignores me.

"There's nothing to talk about. I'm not going to college."

Cheryl looks at me like she's embarrassed, which she should be, and then turns back to Tick. This time her voice is firm. "Tick, do not start with me this morning. You're going to talk to her or I'm not letting your band into this house to practice. End of discussion." Tick looks like she's going to shoot fire out of her eyes, and Cheryl nods at me to go in. As soon as I cross the threshold, Cheryl makes a quick exit, leaving me stranded with a hostile teenager who has several studded items in her possession that could potentially inflict serious bodily harm. *Great.*

I am so uncomfortable that I don't know what to do. I stand there while she picks some stuff up off of the floor, and neither of us says anything. Finally, after about a minute, she breaks the silence.

"She's such a bitch," she mutters. It is unclear whether she is talking to me or to herself. *All right,* I think. *How am I going to handle this?* My usual strategy for dealing with upset teenage girls is to start off by just agreeing with whatever they say. I never try to offer solutions because I hate it when Andrew does that to me, and I always end up getting mad at him. Seriously, it's been the subject of so many fights between us, I could write it as a Mad Lib. Here, I'll show you:

Me:	*(crying or trying not to)* I hate *(fill in person, job, or just life in general)*. It will never get better. My life is so miserable.
Andrew:	Well, why don't you *(fill in some kind of stupid advice that usually involves talking to the person responsible for my misery)*. That way you are in control of the situation and it will be better.
Me:	Ugh! That is so annoying. I don't want to do anything about it; I just want you to agree with me that my life is *(fill in appropriate negative adjective)*.
Andrew:	Fine, your life is *(use same negative adjective from above)*. Are you happy now?
Me:	Yes.

In this case, however, I don't think that I can agree with Tick that her mom's a bitch. Of course, I do agree with her, but that is probably not an opinion that I should voice out loud. I decide to try the play-it-straight angle.

"Look," I say to her. "I know I'm the last person you want to be talking to right now. And to be honest with you, this is not exactly how I had planned to spend my first day of summer vacation. But we're here, so we might as well use the time productively."

Based on the fact that she is still picking things up with her back to me, I think it's safe to assume that she is unmoved by my speech. I wish I had a better knowledge base of underground punk bands. I'm tempted to tell her that I used to love the Violent Femmes, but I am afraid that this will cause her to roll her eyes at me. I have never felt so out of touch in my life. I resolve to start TiVoing shows on MTV immediately.

"You know," I say to her back, "your room is awesome. Your mom must have been furious when she saw it." She turns around to face me with a wicked smile. *Aha.* I've struck a chord.

"You have no idea," she says. "She was so pissed off. She has this big vein in her forehead that sticks out when she gets mad, and I thought it was going to pop. My dad thought it was cool, though, so I didn't get in trouble." She turns around and goes back to the pile on the floor.

After a lengthy pause, I push on. "I would think you'd be dying to get away from her after you graduate." She hesitates for a second before answering me. I can tell that she's deciding whether to engage in this discussion or to tell me to fuck off. If she tells me to fuck off I'm leaving and I'm not coming back. Linda can fire me if she wants to.

"I am," she says. *Damn.* I was kind of hoping for a "fuck off" so that I'd be able to get out of this gracefully. "I'm getting an apartment in New York the minute I turn eighteen."

Ah, yes. Tick wants to be in New York, so we were thinking Princeton or Columbia. Nice of her to leave out the fact that Tick was thinking *School of Rock.*

There must be a boyfriend. I'll bet he's a couple of years older, not in college, and unemployed. Probably wants to be a musician and has her convinced that if they move to New York together, they can get discovered there and live happily ever after. On Stefan Gardner's dime, of course. Why do girls have to be so stupid and predictable? I, however, will feign adult stupidity for the purpose of moving this conversation forward.

"By yourself?" I ask innocently.

"No," she says. "With my boyfriend. He's in my band."

Bingo. I am so good. This is just like how, ten minutes into a movie, I always ruin it for Andrew by leaning over and telling him exactly how it's going to end. I really should have gone to film school. I could have a big house and a screwed-up kid just like her. Ooh, speaking of having kids, time for a boob check. I cross my arms in front of my chest and subtly push. Still nothing.

Okay, back to Tick. Here's what I'm going to do: I'll indulge her stupid, teenage line of thinking, then try to plant a seed. I am so manipulative, it almost scares me. But then it occurs to me that I must not be that good, because I have been completely outmanipulated by Cheryl. She has managed to get me to do exactly what she is too chicken to do herself. Purely out of spite, I have a sudden urge to tell Tick that running off to New York with her gold-digging boyfriend sounds like a fantastic idea, and that I think she should drop out of high school and just get on with it now. But I don't.

"Oh, wow," I say instead. "So are you going to try to get signed by a record label?"

"Yeah. I know it sounds stupid, but Marcus—my boyfriend—he's also the band manager, and he knows a lot of people in the city. There are already some executives who are interested, but they want to meet me first before they do anything."

I picture the scene in *Fame* when Irene Cara meets with the "photographer" who tells her to take off her shirt so that he can get a better idea of how she'll look on camera. I try really hard to sound sincere. "It's not stupid at all. I'm sure you're really good." Then I pretend to hesitate, like there's something that I'm not saying.

"What?" she says. "If you're going to tell me that it's really hard to make it and that I should have something to fall back on, I've already heard it from my mom, thanks."

"No," I say, "that's not what I was going to say at all. Look, I don't care if you go to college or not. My job is to help people who want to go, not to try to convince people who don't." At least, it was until this morning. "I was going to say that you should be careful that the record company doesn't take advantage of you, that's all. You know, you always hear about these famous musicians who have no money because the record labels screw them over." She doesn't say anything, but I can tell she's interested, so I keep going. "My friend is an entertainment lawyer, and she does a lot of contracts for the labels. It's crazy how they exploit the talent. They get them when they're first starting out, and the bands are so happy to get signed that they'll agree to anything. But then they have a hit, and all of a sudden they're famous and they're stuck in these ridiculous contracts, and by the time they pay their managers and their agents they have nothing left." I wave my hand as if it's nothing to worry about. "But, I mean, I'm sure your boyfriend already knows how the music business works, since he's the manager and everything."

She stares at me for a second, like she's deciding whether I'm lying or not. "Yeah," she says. "He's been in, like, four different bands, and a lot of his friends are signed and stuff."

I stand up. "Okay, well, I guess I should go, then. It doesn't seem like you really need me." I walk over to the door, and she goes back to the pile on the floor as if I have already left. I put my hand on the doorknob, but before I open it, I cast my line.

"Hey, you know, if you ever want to talk to my friend, I'm sure she wouldn't mind. It can't hurt to get a few strategic pointers from the enemy, right?" Her head starts to whip around, but then she catches herself and turns it back to the floor. Wouldn't want to appear too eager, I suppose. *Whatever,* I think. She took the bait.

"Yeah, thanks," she mumbles. "I'll talk to Marcus about it."

I open the door and step out into the hallway, and I practically collide with Cheryl. I feel like I'm in an episode of *Three's Company,* where Chrissy's been listening through the door with a glass to her ear again. Except that Chrissy is wearing Jimmy Choos and my pink skirt instead of knee-high athletic socks and terry-cloth short shorts. She waves at me to follow her down the stairs, which I do.

When we reach the bottom, she turns to me. "Well," she says, "that was quick. Did you discuss any good colleges for her?"

I give her my best steely stare. "We didn't discuss colleges at all," I say.

"Well, then, what did you discuss? I didn't ask you here to hang out with my daughter for half an hour."

Oh, that's it. That is so it. "No, Cheryl, you asked me here to be the bad guy for you. I don't appreciate being blindsided. If I had known that Tick wasn't interested in college, I might have been a little bit more prepared. But since I didn't know, you're just going to have to let me do this my way." I start walking toward the door, and Cheryl's lip begins to quiver again. I wonder if she was an aspiring actress before she met Stefan. I hope she saved the casting couch, because that thing was good to her.

"I know, I know," she-fake cries. "I'm sorry. I just couldn't tell Linda that I needed you to convince her to go to college. You have to understand, Stefan is very prominent in the community, and if people find out that Tick is rebelling, everyone will be talking about it. It could even end up in the tabloids."

First of all, it's not that hard to figure out that Tick is rebelling. I mean, the combat boots and the piercings are pretty much a dead giveaway. And second of all, I get the sense that she expects me to feel sorry for her, which I don't. Not one bit. I raise my eyebrows and say nothing, and she gets the hint. She looks at me sheepishly.

"So what do we do next?" she asks.

I sigh. "Nothing. Do nothing. Don't mention college; don't mention me. Just leave her alone. She'll call me, I promise." She makes a skeptical face, which annoys me. I feel the need to firmly repeat myself. "Leave her alone, and she will call me."

"Are you sure?" she says.

No, lady, I'm not sure. I'm just telling you this because I think it will be fun for me to have to explain to my boss why I lied to our biggest donor.

"I'm sure," I say, as I walk out the front door.

Well, almost sure, anyway.

6.

Hey, Diddle Diddle, There's Something in My Middle

omorrow is finally the day. PT day. It's about friggin' time it got here, too, because I've been driving myself crazy for the last three weeks. Oh, I'm sorry, you're confused? Here, let me backtrack a bit. You see, after that first night that I Andrew and I had unprotected sex (and got my period a few days later), I started doing some thinking, and basically I came to the conclusion that if I was going to be pushed into having a baby, I might as well just get it over with now. I mean, really, what is the point of randomly trying to get pregnant? You know that you *could* be pregnant, so you have to eat and (not) drink responsibly, but the chances of your actually *being* pregnant are slim to none. So actually, every month of randomly trying is like another month of pregnancy, except without the getting-fat part. Personally, I'd rather just get fat and be done with it. Plus, when I did the math, I also realized that if I didn't get pregnant by August, I would mess up my whole school year. There's just no way that I can be on maternity leave in the fall. It's my busiest time. And—get this—if I got pregnant now, in July, I would have the baby in March, which would mean that I would get to take three months' maternity leave and then have another three months of summer vacation. Six entire months off! Need I say more?

Anyway, once I came to all of these realizations, I decided to get down to business. It felt a lot like the college application process, actually. You know, you do your research, you try to figure out all of the best angles to use, and then you send in your applications and hope for the best. See, look at this:

- Research: I spent almost an entire week on the Internet reading about ovulation and how to track it, and when the best time to have sex is, and I started examining my vaginal discharge like it was some kind of ancient Dead Sea Scroll that holds the answer to life after death. Of course, I still have no idea how one is supposed to tell the difference between regular discharge, which is colorless and thin, and ovulation discharge, which is allegedly colorless and thin and stretchy, like egg whites. I actually broke open a few eggs just to get an idea of what I was looking for, but I never noticed any extra stretchiness when I actually checked the stuff, so then I went out and bought about fifteen ovulation kits, on the theory that those might be more reliable.
- Angles: The deeper the better. Missionary position and doggie style, to be exact.
- Sending in the applications: Just in case the ovulation kits weren't accurate, I decided that Andrew and I would simply have sex every day for three weeks, so that there would be no possible way for me to miss my thirty-six-hour window of peak fertility.

I swear, it was like we were honeymooning again. Every day Andrew would come home from work and I'd be waiting for him in the bedroom, ready to rip his clothes off. And once I figured out how to put the whole we-might-be-making-a-baby idea out of my head, the sex was fantastic. I haven't had sexual energy like that since I was in college. The only difference was afterward: Instead of collapsing on top of each other into a sweaty heap, I'd lie in bed with my legs straight up in the air for ten minutes, and Andrew would walk around the bedroom, beating on his chest like he was a caveman who, per his evolutionary duty, had just done a bang-up job of spreading his seed. And just in case you were wondering, yes, I did find myself asking what the hell has happened to us on several different occasions.

But anyway, now that you're all caught up, I was saying that tomorrow is finally the day that I get to take the damn pregnancy test and see if all of my hard work has paid off. I'd better be knocked up, by the way. Six months' vacation is entirely too good a thing to let slip through my fingers.

Six-oh-three A.M. I lift the covers off of me and silently slip out of bed. I haven't told Andrew about today. I want to surprise him if it's positive. It's really weird—obviously I'm not a sappy person, but I keep having this cheesy fantasy about how I'm going to tell him that I'm pregnant. I imagine myself sneaking into his office while he's out to lunch or in a meeting, and leaving some kind of baby paraphernalia on his desk. When he comes back, he'll settle into his chair and, just as he's about to start typing on the computer, he'll spot the rattle/tiny shoe/baby outfit. A bit puzzled at first, he'll pick it up, and then I'll emerge from behind the door with tears in my eyes, nodding my head, and as it registers with him his eyes will start to well up, too, and we'll walk toward each other until we meet in an embrace. Then we'll both walk out of his office and he'll yell, *I'm going to be a dad!* and all of the secretaries will applaud while we make out.

Of course, this fantasy is inherently flawed for several reasons: (1) I'm me; (2) Andrew works by himself and doesn't even have a secretary, let alone a whole roomful of them; and (3) even if I did do something like that, he would definitely think that I was playing a joke on him and would just end up getting mad at me. I am, however, willing to bet every last pair of shoes that I own that that is *exactly* how Julie told Jon.

Still naked, I open the cabinet under my side of the bathroom sink and fish out the pregnancy test that I bought during my ovulation-induced shopping spree. I rip off the wrapper and take a moment to read the directions, which instruct me to pee on the stick and then wait one minute. If there's a line in each window, I'm pregnant. If there's only one line, no dice. I take a deep breath and sit down on the toilet, holding the stick underneath me. I start to pee, and, of course, it gets all over my hand. Somebody really needs to make a roach clip for these things. When I'm finished, I wash off my hand, place the pee stick on a piece of toilet paper on the floor, and stare at it. Immediately a thick, bright purple line forms in the control window, but the other window remains blank. *It said to give it a minute,* I tell myself. *Don't look until it's been a minute.*

This is a very long minute. I look back down at the stick. The other window still looks blank—but wait . . . what is that? I pick it up and hold it two inches from my face. There's the faintest purple line in the other window—it's so faint I think that I'm seeing things, but, oh, my God, it's definitely a line. My heart stops, and I take a brief moment to wonder if this is really something that I want to be happening right now. I'm not at all sure that it is. I can feel my blood vessels constricting from the panic. What the hell was I thinking? Why do I always have to be so damn anal about everything? Why couldn't we just have tried for a few months? Oh, my God. *What have I done?*

Screw the surprise. I have to tell Andrew. Now.

Still holding the test stick, I fling open the bathroom door, run into the bedroom, and jump onto the bed, where Andrew is soundly sleeping. I violently shake him and thrust the peed-on pregnancy test in front of his face.

"Do you see two lines there? Because I see two lines there. Holy shit, Andrew, I'm really pregnant!" Amazingly, even in the midst of my terror, even with all of my doubts and second thoughts, I am still expecting some kind of a romantic moment to ensue. I envision him crying, or picking me up and swinging me around, or, better yet, professing his profound gratitude for the self-sacrifice that I am making in order to help him fulfill his unresolved feelings about his father's death. But Andrew still has not opened his eyes. I shake him again.

"Andrew, did you hear me? I'm *pregnant*. We're having a *baby*." He opens his eyes and gives me a groggy look.

"Does this mean that we're not having sex tonight?"

Okay, wait just a minute. Did he just say what I think he just said? He did. I heard it. I punch him on the arm, hard.

"Are you kidding me? I tell you that I'm pregnant and you want to know if we're having sex tonight? You're lucky if I'll let you sleep in this *bed* tonight, Andrew." I get up from the bed and go to my closet to get some sweats. I have no desire to be naked in front of him right now. In fact, I have no desire to look at him right now. Zoey follows me into the closet and I slam the door shut behind her. I hear Andrew get up from the bed.

"Dolly?" he says. "Dolly?" He knocks on the closet door. Oh, yeah, he knows he's in trouble. I blatantly ignore him and sit down on the floor to pet Zoey. She rolls over and gives me her belly. Loudly, I start talking to her.

"Zoey, guess what? Mommy's pregnant! You're going to have a little brother or sister! What's that? You're so excited and you can't wait? Oh, I know, bunny, I love you so much, too. I love you more than anyone else in the whole entire world. Way more than I love your daddy."

"Lara," Andrew whines from the other side of the door. "I'm sorry. I didn't mean it. Of course I'm excited. I'm so excited. It's just . . . you woke me up out of a dead sleep; I didn't know what I was saying."

Okay. For the record, I will admit that waking up to a pee-soaked stick being shoved in your face at six-oh-seven A.M. is not exactly the most pleasant way to greet the morning, but that is still not an excuse. And neither is the fact that I woke him up out of a dead sleep. I firmly believe that anything one says when in a coma, on drugs, or coming out of a deep sleep absolutely represents one's true feelings, unfiltered by the conscience. I start to cry.

"You are mean, and you don't love me or our baby." I realize that I am feeling unusually emotional right now, as I typically cry about as often as the Barneys semiannual sale. I wonder if this has something to do with the hormones. It must.

"No, honey," he says. "I do. I love you, I swear. Please let me in. Please? I don't want to start off our family this way. I'm sorry. Please." I can tell he's really upset. Good. He should be. I reach up and open the door, and Andrew laughs when he sees me sitting on the floor, still naked, with Zoey's head resting on my leg.

"Would it be inappropriate for me to tell you that you're the hottest pregnant woman I've ever seen?"

I pretend to mull this over. "Yes," I say. "It would. I'm now the mother of your unborn child. I'm not allowed to be hot."

He sits down on the floor next to me and gives me a hug. "I love you," he says. He leans his head down and kisses me on the stomach. "And I love you, too," he says to it.

Well. Not quite the stuff of fantasies, but I guess it'll have to do.

Okay, I know that you're not supposed to tell anyone that you're pregnant until you've passed the three-month mark. I looked it up online, and apparently the rationale for this rule is that, should you miscarry during that time, no one will need to know and you will thus be spared the pain of having to talk about it over and over again with everyone you blabbed to in the first place. And yet, while I appreciate the logic, there is simply no possible way that I can keep this to myself any longer. It's been only four days, and I'm about ready to die. I have to tell someone. I'm willing to take my chances.

So, after I get out of the shower, I pick up the phone and call Julie.

"Hi, it's me. What are you doing for lunch today?"

"Actually, I was supposed to meet my sister, but she just canceled on me five minutes ago. Maya was walking around barefoot on their deck and she got about fifty splinters in her feet, so she has to take her to the pediatrician."

"Great. I mean, not great, that sucks for Maya, but great that you're free. Do you want to meet somewhere at noon?"

"Sure. I have to go to Beverly Hills to get some gifts for people beforehand, so can we meet at the Ranch?"

Ugh. I hate the Ranch. The food is good, but it's like a breeding ground for rich LA women who don't work and pass their entire lives on Beverly Drive, shopping and getting their hair done. Like Julie.

"Yeah, that's fine. I'll see you later."

At two minutes to twelve, I pull up to the valet and get out of my car. Julie is sitting at an outside table for two, but she's pulled up an extra chair for all of her shopping bags.

"Hi," I say, leaning down to give her an air kiss. "I didn't realize you were bringing your friends."

"Very funny. Unfortunately, none of it is even for me. Sometimes I feel like I spend my entire life buying presents for people." I am tempted to tell her that, actually, she does spend her entire life buying presents for people, but I bite my tongue. "Both of my sisters' kids have birthdays in July, I have a bridal shower and a baby shower in August, I have to send a thank-you gift to Jon's sister for letting us stay at their place in New York, and I needed a hostess gift for Jon's boss's wife because she's having us over for a dinner party next week. It's ridiculous." A hostess gift. Who buys hostess gifts? Should *I* be buying people hostess gifts? Have I been operating as a rude, unthankful guest for my entire adult life? I hate Julie. She always manages to make me feel socially inadequate.

I realize that I haven't noticed her stomach yet. I peer over the table to check her out.

"Wow," I say. "Look at you. You look pregnant." Julie grins from ear to ear.

"I know. Can you believe how big I am already? I definitely think it's a boy now. Everyone is telling me that I'm carrying like a boy." I shudder at the thought of Julie with a boy. The only men in her life are Jon and her dad, neither of whom are particularly teeming with Y chromosomes. Her dad spends every waking moment playing golf at his country club, and Jon's favorite thing in the whole world is the Perle de Caviar facial at the Four Seasons spa. Trucks and dirt bikes and *Star Wars* action figures would be totally lost on them.

"Well," I say, "shouldn't you be able to find out soon?" Julie stops smiling and pouts at me.

"Didn't I tell you? We're not finding out. Jon wants it to be a surprise. He says that he's always imagined that moment when the doctor pulls the baby out and yells, '*It's a Boy!*' He doesn't want to miss out on it."

I am trying so hard not to laugh. It must be killing her that she can't go out and start decorating the nursery yet. "You do realize that that's absurd," I say. "Who in this day and age doesn't find out the sex of their child?"

"Lots of people don't," she says defensively. "Some people like doing things the old-fashioned way."

I snort at her. "Well, we're definitely finding out. I want to know the second they can tell." Oops. That was not what I wanted to say.

Julie raises her eyebrows and gives me a sideways glance. "Is there something I should know?" she asks.

I take a deep breath. "Actually, yes. That's why I wanted to have lunch today. I'm pregnant."

Julie jumps up from her seat and the table hits her smack in the center of her big belly. I hope she didn't just decapitate little Jon Junior, but she seems unfazed. She runs over to my chair and gives me a huge hug. She really is big. I wonder if it's bad that I'm feeling a little repulsed by it.

"Oh, my God! Oh, my God!" she screams. "I am so happy for you! Oh, my God!" She is literally jumping up and down, and every patio diner and sidewalk passerby is staring at us. I am mortified.

"Shhh! Julie, please. Nobody knows yet. I'm only telling you because I need to be able to talk about this with someone, and you're the only friend I have who's ever been pregnant."

"Okay," she whispers, taking her seat again. "I'm sorry. I'm just so excited for you. This is so exciting. We'll be like Drew Barrymore and Brittany Murphy in *Riding in Cars with Boys*. Didn't you love that scene when they stood next to each other with their bellies touching? It was *so* adorable." I give her a look that informs her that I do not watch movies with names like *Riding in Cars with Boys,* and that we won't be touching bellies anytime soon. She sticks her tongue out at me. "You are no fun. When are you due?"

"I don't know. I only found out four days ago, and my doctor won't see me for another two weeks. March something, I guess."

"Well, let's see, it's the end of July now. . . ." She starts counting on her fingers. "July, August, September, October, November, December, January, February, March, April. Probably around the beginning of April, I think."

"No," I say. "It can't be April. You just counted ten months. I figured it out and it should be March."

Julie gives me a pity smile. "Oh, Lar, it's not nine months. It's forty weeks. It's ten months. They start counting from the first day of your last period, though, so the good news is that you're already finished with your first month." No. That can't be right. If it's ten months, why don't they just say that it's ten months? There was a movie called *Nine Months*. Why didn't they call it *Ten Months* if it's really ten months? Why perpetuate a rumor like that? I feel like I'm going to cry. This is terrible. So now I'm only going to have five months off? It's not even worth it.

"They should tell people that," I say. "They should tell them *before* they get pregnant."

Julie gives me one of her cheerleader smiles. "Oh, come on, it's not that bad. Think about it this way: It's only thirty-six and a half more weeks!"

I want to shoot her. I want to find a gun and shoot her down right here in front of all of the other Stepford wives, as a warning to anyone who ever tries to be cheery with me again.

But Julie doesn't seem to notice my hostility, or else she's just ignoring it. "I am *so* glad you told me about this. I mean, aside from just being honored that you told me before anyone else, there is so much that you need to do. First of all, you have to call right away to get into Susan Greenspan's class. If you heard that you can wait until you're three months, you can't anymore. I know a lot of people who didn't get in. Here, I have the number in my Palm; let me get it for you." She starts digging in her giant Louis Vuitton bag.

"Who is Susan Greenspan?" I ask. "What are you talking about?" She stops digging and looks at me as if I just asked her who Britney Spears was.

"You haven't heard about Susan's class? *The* Mommy and Me class? Seriously?"

I feel embarrassed for being so obviously not in-the-know. I shake my head.

"Susan Greenspan is, like, the Mommy and Me guru. *Everyone* takes her class. It's supposed to be amazing. People swear by her. But it's, like, impossible to get in. It fills up like that," she says, snapping her fingers. "But this early on, you should be fine. Just call first thing Monday morning. The last thing you want is to be worrying about getting off of a waiting list when you've got a newborn." She finds her Palm and writes the number for me on a napkin. I still can't get past the fact that she has just used the terms *waiting list* and *Mommy and Me* in the same sentence.

"Okay," I say, taking the napkin from her. "So what else am I horribly uninformed about?" Julie is loving this. It is very rare that she knows more than I do about anything, which is one of the reasons why I keep her around.

"Do you know about Your Baby?" she asks, knowing full well that I don't. I give her a look indicating that I know that she knows full well that I don't. "Right. It's a Web site. Your Baby dot com. It's free, and if you sign up with them they'll send you an e-mail every week telling you what's happening with the baby. Like, for me, this week my e-mail said that the baby has eyebrows now and the teeth are starting to form above the gum line. Isn't that cool?" That *is* kind of cool. It appeals to me on a checklist type of level, as in: Eyebrows, check. Teeth, check. Development of amygdala, hypothalamus and cerebral cortex, check.

"Okay," I say. "What else?" She thinks for a few seconds.

"Oh! Have you ever seen *Real Births?*" I give her another look. "No," she says somberly. "You work during the day, so you probably haven't." But then she quickly perks up again. "But you're on vacation, so you can watch it now. You *have* to watch it. I'm totally addicted to it. I watch it, like, four times a day." Ah. So that's what she does all day long. I knew there had to be something.

"What is it?" I say. "It sounds cheesy."

She puts her hands up in protest. "Nooo, it's so good. They profile real people who are pregnant and they film them doing some kind of prebaby event, and then they show them actually having the baby. I love it. It'll make you so excited." I doubt this, but I guess it can't hurt to check it out. If nothing else, I'm sure it will provide me with hours of amusement.

"Well," I say to her. "You have been a wealth of information. I don't know what I would do without you."

"The pleasure is all mine, darling," she says in a bad Zsa Zsa Gabor accent. "And when you're ready, I'll let you know about everything else you need to do."

"You mean there's more?"

"Oh," she says, "you have no idea."

For once, I'm pretty sure that she's right.

7.

Merrily, Merrily, Merrily, Merrily, Working on My Scheme

I. Am. So. Tired. I've never experienced tired like this before. Andrew is convinced that I have chronic fatigue syndrome. I'm only two weeks into this pregnancy thing, and I feel like I've been carrying an elephant around on my back for ten years. Thank God I'm not working right now. I don't know how I would be able to do it. Yesterday I spent the entire day in bed, and I think I slept for, like, twenty hours. I only got up to pee. I even made Andrew come home from work in the middle of the day to bring me lunch so that I wouldn't have to get up and make something. And when he complained about it (which I knew he would), I informed him that it takes a lot of energy to make a baby from scratch, and that he'd better get used to waiting on me hand and foot. Oh, yeah, I'm already milking this thing for all it's worth.

Of course, he was furious when I then somehow found the strength to get up at eight o'clock this morning to go hiking. Truthfully, I can't think of anything that I would like to be doing less right now, but I had to see Stacey. Tick Gardner e-mailed me yesterday and she took the bait. Thank God. I was starting to get nervous that my plan had failed, and that I would have to come up with some kind of a scam to get another meeting with her. I mean, I am coming up with a scam to get another meeting with her, but at least now I don't need another scam to get her to go along with my original scam. Oh, whatever. You know what I mean. Now all I have to do is convince Stacey to get in on the grift, and I'll be all set.

Well, convince Stacey and somehow manage to make it up this

mountain without collapsing. Did I mention how tired I am? I stop walking to take a swig of my water, and Stacey passes me.

"Wait," I shout to her. "I need to rest for a second." She turns around and gives me an impatient look.

"What is wrong with you today? This is the third time you've stopped."

"Nothing. I just didn't sleep that well last night. I'm really tired." I can't bring myself to tell her about the baby yet. It's going to put her into a complete tailspin. Anyway, I'm not lying. Come on, everybody, all together now: I *am* really tired.

But before Stacey has a chance to make some snippy comment about how exhausting my summer vacation must be, we are confronted by a beaming Persian octogenarian.

"Good mohrning! Go Dodge hairs!" Stacey and I look at each other and I realize that she's wearing a Dodgers cap.

"Your hat," I whisper. "He thinks you're a Dodger fan."

With enough enthusiasm to sink a ship, Stacey limply raises her fist. "Yeah, go blue."

Our new friend emphatically raises his fist back to her. "Go blooh!" he yells, and continues down the trail. "Go blooh!"

We both laugh and start walking again. *Okay,* I think. *Here's my opening.*

"So, do you remember how I told you that I had to meet with Stefan Gardner's kid?"

"Oh, right," she says. "How did it go? Did she hate you?"

"Pretty much. It turns out she wants to be a rock star. She thinks she's going to move to New York and get discovered. With her boyfriend, the band manager."

"Typical. So why did they call you?"

You must tread carefully here, Lara-san. "Apparently, it's my job to change to her mind. Not that I recall ever seeing that duty listed in my job description, mind you. You were right about the mom, by the way. She's totally nuts. All she cares about is Stefan's image, and how it will look for him if his daughter doesn't go to a good school. I had to talk her down from Princeton and Columbia."

Stacey hoots at this. "I told you she's a hard-ass. And the irony is,

Stefan probably never even heard of Princeton and Columbia. He could probably care less where she goes."

I stop again to take a drink. Did they make this mountain bigger since last week? "You're probably right," I say. "Anyway, I think that the whole band thing is an act. I think she's just trying to piss off her mom. If I can make her see that going to college would actually allow her to get away permanently, I think she'd be into it." We start walking again. Only a few more minutes to the top.

"So how are you going to make her see that?"

Wait for it . . . wait for it. . . . "Um, I was kind of thinking that maybe you could help me." I brace myself as Stacey stops dead in her tracks.

"Excuse me?" she yells. I hold up both of my hands like I'm stopping traffic.

"Wait. Before you start freaking out, just listen to me."

She's already shaking her head no. "I'm not going to freak out, because I'm not going to engage you in this discussion. If I wanted to help people, I would have become a public defender. But I didn't. I became a corporate entertainment lawyer. By definition, I do not help people."

"And that is exactly why I need you." Ooh, I have an idea. "Look, forget I said the word *help*. I didn't mean it. Let's think of her as a new client. She's in a band. She wants to get signed by a label. You represent labels, so you can give her some practical corporate entertainment advice."

She's shaking her head again. "And how am I supposed to bill for this?" I swear, I have no idea how Stacey has lived in a desert climate for this long without melting.

"I don't know," I say. "Doesn't your firm do any kind of pro bono work?"

She looks at me like I am an idiot. "Hello? Did we not *just* have this conversation? Don't help people, remember?"

I roll my eyes at her. "Call it client development if you want to. I'm sure that you can think of something." She glares at me while she mulls it over.

"What is it exactly that we would be talking about?"

Yesss. I got her. "You just have to explain to her how the labels screw the talent, and then convince her that the musicians who always get the best deals are the ones who know something about the business and don't rely on their managers to make all of the decisions for them. I'll take care of the rest."

She looks at me skeptically. "That is total bullshit. All musicians rely on their managers to make decisions for them. That's why they have managers."

Oh, I love this. All of a sudden Miss Corporate Entertainment Lawyer is worried about telling the truth. "I don't care. The goal is not to get her a good record deal. The goal is to get her to think that college is a good idea."

Stacey shakes her head again. "No. I'm sorry. I'm not going to lie to her. I'll talk to her, but only if I can say to her what I would say to any other client in her position."

Oh, God. Of all the times for Stacey to get a conscience. I'm not sure if letting her loose on Tick unsupervised is such a good idea, but I'm too out of breath to argue.

We round the final bend of the uphill part of the trail, and walk the rest of the way to the top in silence. I almost fall down when we get to the clearing. I bend over and put both of my hands on my knees while I try to catch my breath.

"Okay," I say, panting. "How about this: The three of us meet for lunch. You can say anything you want, but I get to be there to do damage control." She bites her lip. "Please," I say to her. "I really need this."

"Fine," she says. "Call my secretary on Monday and set something up." I nod my head. "But I'm not sugarcoating this for you. Got it?"

"I've got it," I say.

Why do I get the feeling that this is the worst idea I've ever had?

For someone who is supposedly swamped with work, Stacey sure has a lot of free time available for lunch. No wonder she works until three o'clock in the morning. I'd work until three o'clock in the morning, too, if I took two-hour lunches every day. As I dial Tick's cell phone, I make a mental note to remember this the next time she says that my job is easy.

"Hello?"

"Hi, Tick? It's Mrs. Stone."

"Oh, hi." Silence. No *How are you?* Nothing. Kids are so rude these days.

"Listen, I spoke to my friend and she can meet us for lunch any day this week. When would be a good day for you?" There is a long pause. "Tick, are you there?"

"Yeah. Um, I was thinking, I don't really know if I need to meet with her. I think Marcus has it under control."

No, she is not. Uh-uh. No way am I letting her out of this. I put on my huffy voice. "You know, Tick, I went to a lot of trouble to get this meeting set up for you. If you thought that Marcus had it under control then you shouldn't have asked me to do it in the first place."

She lets out an annoyed sigh. "I'm sorry if I *inconvenienced* you, but I just don't really have time right now. . . ."

Oh, please. Does she really think that she is any match for me? I've got fifteen years of bitchiness on her. And I'm pregnant. "Tick, I'm sure if I called your mother she would find a way to clear your schedule." *Take that, you novice.*

Tick laughs. "Go ahead, call her. Do you really think she wants me meeting with someone who can help me get a record deal?"

Okay, fine. Touché. I hear male laughter in the background and I realize that she must be with Marcus. If she thinks she's going to show off for him at my expense, she can think again.

"No," I say in the most patronizing tone I can muster. "I'm sure she doesn't, but I think I'll get her attention if I tell her that I won't be your college counselor next year because you were so rude to me." I feel like we're Alexis and Krystle Carrington. If we were face-to-face, one of us definitely would have slapped the other by now. Through the phone I hear the male voice tell her to just hang up. But she doesn't.

"First of all, I don't care, because I'm not going to college, and second of all, you can't do that. You can't refuse to be my counselor." She sounds like she's going to cry at any second.

What the hell is going on here? I soften my voice. "Okay, do you want to tell me what's going on? Because if you really weren't going to college, then I don't think you would be so upset about not having a college counselor next year."

Silence. *Oh, shit.* I know what's going on. I know exactly what is going on.

"Tick, just say yes or no. Can you not talk about this in front of Marcus?"

"Yeah."

I knew it. This whole not-going-to-college thing was his genius idea.

"Is he going to be with you all day today?"

"Yeah."

"How about tomorrow?"

"No."

"Okay. Do you want to meet me for coffee tomorrow so that we can talk about this? I can meet you at ten at the Starbucks in Century City mall. Is that good?"

"Yeah."

"All right. I'll see you then."

"Yeah, whatever." Click.

It's ten-oh-nine. If she's not here by ten fifteen, I'm leaving. I sit down with my decaf chai latte and pick up one of those free city magazines that they always have stacks of in coffee shops. I flip through it and I immediately feel old. All of the articles are about bands and movies and clubs I've never even heard of.

Just then Tick walks up to my table. She's in her combat boots, which squeak every time she takes a step, and she is carrying a black messenger bag that is bursting at the seams with stuff and that is easily enormous enough to house a Hobbit or two. Honestly, the thing must weigh at least forty pounds. She drops the bag on the floor and plops herself down in the chair across from me. I look at my watch: ten thirteen.

"Sorry," she says.

In the interest of not sounding downright elderly, I decide to spare her my lecture about how being late is a sign of disrespect. "It's fine," I say. "I'm glad you came." I fold up the paper and put it on the table next to me. "So, do you want to tell me what's going on?" For a second, I think she might bolt, but then she seems to surrender.

"It's really complicated," she says with a sigh. Well, of course it is. Teen drama is always really complicated.

"I think I can handle it," I tell her, trying to contain my growing impatience. Does she not understand that there are many better things that I could be doing right now? Like taking a nap, or reading three months ahead in *What to Expect When You're Expecting*.

"Fine," she says. She picks up the paper wrapper of a straw and starts twisting it while she talks. "Marcus and I have been together for, like, eight months. He's totally cool, and . . . I don't know, he just, like, totally gets me. I mean, he's older, so he's over all of that stupid high school boy crap, and since we're in the band together and everything, it makes it really intense."

Oh, no. I concentrate really hard on sending her an ESP message to not tell me about her sex life, because I really do not want to know.

"So anyway, things with us are really going well, and the band is *really* starting to get good."

Hah! It worked. I *knew* I had a sixth sense.

"I mean, Marcus booked us at the Whiskey in September, and he thinks he's going to be able to get us into the Knitting Factory, which is so cool. . . ."

Jeez, kid, cut to the chase already. "Okay," I say, cutting her off. "So what is the problem?"

She nods her head. "*Okay*, the thing is, he's worried that if I go to college next year, everything is going to get ruined. He thinks that I'll, like, find some other guy if we're apart, so I told him to just come with me, you know? But then he was like, 'Yeah, so I'm just supposed to follow you around and wait for you to get done with your classes and to come back from fraternity parties.'" She snorts. "Like *I'd* really go to fraternity parties. So then I told him that I'd go to school here in LA, which is, like, the hugest sacrifice for me, because he knows how bad I want to get away from my mom, but he was like, 'No, you won't have time to practice and do shows, and if you live on campus I'll still never see you.' So then he was like, 'Well, what if we just move to New York together?', and then I can get away from my parents and we can be together and really work on the band And since he knows people there, he thinks we can get into a bunch of really good clubs, and he's, like, positive that we'll get signed." She takes a deep breath and then stares at me for a reaction.

My reaction is that this guy is a possessive, controlling asshole and that she must break up with him immediately. But I'll work up to that. I don't want to come on too strong.

"But that's not what you want?" I ask.

She sighs again. "I mean, it is, kind of. On the one hand, it would be fun to be in New York with him, completely on our own, you know? But then I think about going to college, and it could be really cool, and, like, what if the band doesn't get signed? Then what do I do?"

Well, I think, *your dad's a bazillionaire; I'm sure you could figure something out before you'd have to resort to the streets.*

"You're right," I say. I'm about to tell her that it's always good to have something to fall back on, but I catch myself. I remember her comment from last time about how she's already heard it from her mom. "Have you said any of this to Marcus?" I ask.

Another sigh. "Whenever I bring it up to him he gets really mad, and we've almost broken up, like, five times over it." I am starting to feel suspiciously like the Well-meaning Guidance Counselor in an *ABC After School Special*. I am trying to think of a sensitive, tactful way to tell her to dump this loser, but my thoughts are interrupted by the person sitting at the table behind us.

"I'm sorry, but that's the most ridiculous thing I've ever heard." I don't even need to turn around. I know that voice. It's Stacey. She stands up and walks over to us, and Tick is giving her looks like she's the band geek who dared to sit at the cool kids' table at lunch.

"Tick," I say, "this is my friend Stacey. The one I was telling you about. I swear, I did not tell her to come here." I turn to glare at Stacey. "What are you doing here, and who told you that you could eavesdrop on our conversation?" She throws a haughty stare in my direction and then gives me the finger. Nice.

"I work in the building next door, genius, and I come here *every* day at ten thirty. I saw you talking to a kid with black hair and a dog collar, so I figured it must be her, and since you wanted me to meet with her anyway I sat down."

Well, I think, *aren't you just Little Miss Encyclopedia Brown?*

Stacey reaches across the table to shake Tick's hand. "Nice to meet you," she says, then gestures toward the empty chair at our table. "May I?"

Tick looks at me and I nod. There's a Starbucks on every damn corner in the entire city of Los Angeles, and I have to pick the one next door to Stacey's office. This has disaster written all over it.

Stacey sits down and immediately takes over.

"Anyway," she says, "as a neutral observer, I see three separate issues here. One is your relationship with Marcus, who sounds like a real prick, by the way."

Oh, lovely. I begin mentally drafting my resignation letter and trying to think of grounds on which to sue Stacey for this. I wonder if tortious interference of contract would work. I glance at Tick for a reaction, but she doesn't seem to be fazed by the prick comment. Maybe I'm underestimating her. I'll let Stacey continue and see what happens from there.

"Two," she says, "is what is going to happen to your band, and three is whether you're going to go to college. They don't necessarily have to be mutually exclusive."

I look at Tick again because I'm not sure if she knows what mutually exclusive means.

"What do you mean?" she says.

"I mean, you can go to college and still be in the band, but the band doesn't have to have Marcus in it if he can't handle your being in college. First of all, just from a business standpoint, there are all kinds of conflicts going on. For one thing, you should never date your manager, because if you break up he can turn everyone else against you. And second, the band manager should never be a member of the band, because no one will want to give him honest feedback about whether it sucks. I mean, this is just Music Industry 101 kind of stuff." I realize that Stacey has been doing her job for so long that she actually speaks in bullet points. But her bullet points do have a point.

"So what should I do?" Tick asks.

I can't believe this. She's actually listening to Stacey. Stacey glances at me and I make a face as if to say, *Go ahead.*

"If it were me, I would tell Marcus that if he really cares about the band, he should step down as manager and hire an outside person to do it. And then I would tell him that if he really cares about you, he should want what's best for you, and if that means college, then he needs to deal with it." Tick looks positively petrified by this suggestion.

"But what if he gets mad at me?" she says. Stacey laughs at her.

"Listen, honey, it's not show friends; it's show business. If you can't handle your boyfriend getting mad at you, then maybe you're not cut out for the entertainment world."

Oh, God. Who does she think she is, Samuel Goldwyn? I take this as my cue to jump back into the conversation.

"Wait a second," I say. "Let's forget about Marcus for right now. Stacey's right: Lots of people go to college and play in bands. It sounds to me like you're the one with all of the talent and Marcus knows it, or else he wouldn't be so upset about your leaving. Right?" She looks embarrassed and shrugs her shoulders. Stacey and I exchange glances, and I can tell that she knows exactly where I'm going with this.

"What does he play?" Stacey asks. Tick cocks her head.

"Lead guitar. And sometimes backup vocals, but his voice isn't really that good."

"Okay," Stacey says. "So you've got a guitarist with a mediocre singing voice, and he's pinning all of his hopes on you. You're the one with all of the leverage, so call his bluff. Tell him that you're going to college with or without him. And if he says no, then dump him and replace him. You'll definitely find a new boyfriend in college, and I'm sure that if you go somewhere with a half-decent music department, you'll be able to find somebody who can sing and play guitar. Just don't let it be your new boyfriend."

Stacey pauses and takes a sip of her gigantic chocolate mocha latte with whipped cream. That thing must be two thousand calories, and she has one every single day. I just don't understand how she stays so skinny.

"You see," she says, "this is what people mean when they say that you should learn from your mistakes." Tick is hanging on her every word, like Stacey is some kind of a guru. A skinny, workaholic guru who hasn't had a real relationship or seen the inside of her apartment in six years, but hey. If Tick is buying it, Stacey can keep dealing it.

"Where did you go to college?" Tick asks.

Stacey smiles and nods her head. "NYU, baby, the best college in the world."

Oh, no. Oh, no. I forgot that Stacey went to NYU. NYU is almost as hard to get into as Columbia now. Every kid who ever watched *Felicity* wants to go there. *Shit.* Tick looks at me.

"Do they have a good music department?"

I try to hedge. "Yeah, I mean, it's okay—"

Stacey cuts me off. "Okay? It's NYU. It's the cultural mecca of the entire collegiate universe. All of their performance departments are amazing."

I rub my temples. "Yes, it's very good. It's just that it's not that easy to get in—"

Again, she cuts me off. "What are you talking about? I was the biggest fuck-up in high school—" I shoot her a look to remind her that there are children present, and she rolls her eyes at me. "Lara, I'm sure she's heard the word *fuck* before." Tick laughs at this, and I realize that I have just become the bad guy again. "Anyway, I was the biggest screwup in high school and I got in. I had something like a ten-fifty on my SATs. As long as you write a good essay you're fine."

I want to kill her. I love how everyone in the world thinks that they're qualified to be a college counselor.

"Stacey, that was twelve years ago. Things have changed. People do not get into NYU with a ten-fifty anymore. You need to be at least in the thirteen hundreds, you need good grades, you need AP courses, you need calculus. It's not the same school that you applied to."

Stacey is shaking her head and making faces at me. "No way. Why is it so hard?"

I really don't feel like explaining to her that when we went to college, the population of teenagers was at an all-time low, and now, with all of the baby boomers' kids going to college and all of the baby boomers willing to spend their money to send their kids to college, applications are up about 40 percent at every school, so the demand is far outweighing the supply. Not to mention the fact that the SAT was recentered in 1994, so a twelve hundred from 1989 would be equivalent to a thirteen hundred today, which means that colleges have raised the bar for scores since then. Of course, this information would not only put them both to sleep, but it would make me sound way more boring than I already am. So instead, I give her the easy answer.

"Because" I say, "it just is." Wow. I'm already starting to sound like a parent.

Tick gives Stacey a knowing smile and then turns to me. "Well, that's where I want to go." Yes, I gathered that. I purse my lips and give Stacey a look. "It's perfect," Tick says. "If Marcus wants to be in New York so bad, he can come with me, and if not, then I can still get away from my mom and be in the city."

"Okay," I say, throwing up my hands. "If that's what you want, that's fine, but you're going to have to really work hard. You'll need to pull up your SAT scores, and you're going to have to do amazing in the first semester of senior year. I'm talking straight As. I can't stress to you enough how important that is, especially since your grades went down so much last year."

She is totally ignoring me. "Yeah, fine. I can do it." She turns to look at Stacey. "Thank you *so much*. You, like, totally helped me get some clarity with this. I'm going to talk to him right now."

Stacey smiles at her. "Remember, don't cave. If he really wants to be with you, he'll do what you want, and if he doesn't, then fuck him. Here." Stacey pulls out a business card from her wallet. "Here's my card. Call me and let me know how it goes."

Oh, please. I want to throw up, and it's not from morning sickness. Tick beams at her and grabs the card out of her hand.

"Thanks!" she says, picking up her bag. "I definitely will." Her combat boots squeak as she gets up from the table and heads out the door, giving us a little wave. Once she's gone, Stacey turns to me.

"That was fun. You really do have the easiest job in the world."

"Oh, whatever. You got lucky. She just as easily could have hated you."

"Never. I have a way with teenagers. They think I'm cool because I curse and make a lot of money and work in entertainment. Trust me."

"Yes, but if you worked at their school you wouldn't be able to curse and you wouldn't make a lot of money and you wouldn't be in entertainment, so therefore they wouldn't think that you're so cool."

She ponders this for a moment. "Yeah, well, good thing you have me to be your cool friend, then, huh?" She is so annoying sometimes.

"Yes, Stacey, it's a very good thing. But your being cool doesn't help me get her into NYU. This is going to take some serious working it on my part. You have no idea."

"She's Stefan Gardner's daughter. I'm sure they would love to have her."

"It's NYU," I say. "Celebrity kids are a dime a dozen there. If he's not donating, they don't care who she is. You see, this is why my job is hard, Miss Two-hour Lunch Break."

She ignores this. "Yeah, well, since you're so good at it, I'm sure you'll think of something."

I close my eyes and shake my head. *Shit.* I'd better.

8.

The Contents of My Stomach Go Round and Round, Round and Round, Round and Round

I can't believe that this is the last weekend of my summer vacation. Aside from conceiving a child, I've accomplished absolutely nothing over the last two and a half months. I barely went to the gym because I was always too tired, I couldn't see the point in doing any shopping, and the only books I read were about pregnancy. A total waste of a summer. And, to make matters worse, tomorrow afternoon I get to spend my last Sunday of vacation at the first birthday party of Julie's niece. Julie seems to think that it will be good for me to have some exposure to babies, so she's made me and Andrew promise to go. Apparently some friend of her sister's will be there with a six-week-old or something.

I don't know. Maybe she's right. It probably wouldn't hurt for me to at least see what a real live baby looks like before I actually have one for myself.

Right now, however, I am famished. I had my first appointment with my obstetrician this week—the baby's fine, I'm due April eleventh, yadda, yadda, yadda—but the really important thing he told me is that pregnant women only need an extra three hundred calories a day to sustain a fetus. Three hundred calories! That's like two glasses of orange juice, or an extra bowl of cereal. It's *nothing*. I mean, my fetus must have some kind of a hyperthyroid disorder, because I well exceeded those three hundred calories two hours ago and I still feel like I haven't eaten for four days.

I'm not going to have another snack, though. My doctor said that a normal amount of weight gain is between twenty-five and thirty-five pounds, and I fully intend to be on the low end of that spectrum. I'll just suck it up and hold out until dinner.

Of course, it's Andrew's fault that I have to wait. It's already six thirty and he's still not home from golf. I swear, whoever came up with the idea of daylight saving time was definitely a golfer. All of that stuff about the farmers who needed more daytime hours to plow the fields is total bullshit. It was definitely some Scottish guy who thought it would be a genius way to squeeze in another nine holes. At this rate, I'll be lucky if I'm eating by eight.

I sit down on the couch and turn on the television, and Zoey plops down next to me. Hopefully I'll find something absorbing enough to take my mind off of the gnawing pit in my stomach. As I scroll through the channels, I come across an old *Facts of Life* rerun. Perfect. I used to love this show when I was a kid.

Two minutes into an argument between Mrs. Garrett and Jo, I start to wonder what it was about this show that left me with such fond memories. I mean, it is horrifically bad. The perky naïveté of Tootie and Natalie is borderline unwatchable. Even Zoey got up and walked away. But there's nothing else on, so I get up and go back into the kitchen. I open the refrigerator to see if any new, zero-calorie-yet-intensely-satisfying snacks have magically appeared since the last time I opened it, and Zoey comes running over, looking for a handout. I probably should feed her dinner. There's no reason why both of us should starve to death.

I scoop some kibble into her bowl, and then get her chicken out of the fridge. Yes, I feed her chicken. It's not a big deal. I buy precooked, prepackaged grilled chicken strips, and then I just tear up a few pieces and sprinkle it over her kibble. They sell it in the refrigerated aisle, right next to those processed meat-and-cheese snacks they call Lunchables. Lunchables seem to be marketed to busy moms as an easy and nutritious meal to stick in a lunch box, but I have to tell you, I may not be a mom yet, but I would sooner put a rattlesnake in my kid's lunch box than one of those Lunchable things.

I open up the chicken package, and I am suddenly overwhelmed by the smell of it, which is weird because I've been feeding Zoey this chicken every single night for the last two years, and this is the first time that I've ever noticed that it even has a smell. And it's not a bad smell—it doesn't seem rancid or anything like that—it just smells . . . I don't know . . . chicken-y. Really, really chicken-y.

I think I'm going to puke.

I run to the bathroom and start heaving over the toilet bowl. Well, at least now I don't have to worry about those extra calories that I ate today. When I'm finished with my hurling, I sit down on my knees, shut the lid, close my eyes, and rest my head on top of the toilet seat. I find it impossible to believe that millions of women go through this every year, yet there has never been mass rioting over how unfair it is. I, for one, am totally ready to take to the streets.

When I open my eyes again, Zoey is sitting by my side, staring up at me intently. Poor thing, she's probably wondering what happened to her dinner. I reach down to pet her on the head.

"Oh, Zo, Mommy doesn't feel so good," I moan. She locks eyes with me and cocks her head to the side. Out of nowhere, I hear a scruffy voice.

"It's the chicken," the voice says.

I shift my eyes from side to side, trying to figure out where it is coming from. I sit up and look at Zoey—hard.

"Did you just say something to me?"

She straightens her head and opens her mouth. "The chicken. It's nasty."

Oh, my God. Is the ability to communicate with animals a secret side effect of being pregnant? *Hah!* I *knew* Zoey could understand English.

"It is, nasty, huh? I'm sorry, bunny. I'll never give it to you again. Only the good stuff from now on, I promise." She closes her mouth and it looks like she's actually smiling at me. Then she stands up and walks out of the bathroom.

That's it? My dog speaks to me and all she wants to say is that she doesn't like the chicken?

"Wait!" I yell after her. "Zoey, come back!" There are so many things that I want to ask her—does she wish we had another dog or would it just make her jealous? Does she like the pink rhinestone collar that I just got her or does she think it's too much? Why does she always whimper whenever the kid who lives in the house behind us goes swimming? But it's too late. She ran out through the doggie door and is already barking at the two pugs who live next door. I wonder if she's telling them about what just happened. I wonder if they believe her.

Bright and early the next morning, Andrew and I put on our Sunday best and head out to Julie's sister's house. By the way, who the hell plans a birthday party for ten A.M. on a Sunday morning? Really, people, just because you have kids who wake up at the butt crack of dawn does not mean that everyone else should have to suffer right along with you. Have a little common courtesy, for God's sake. And to make things worse, the party is in the Valley, which might as well be the middle of the Arabian Desert. It's already a thousand degrees outside in the city, so I'm sure it'll be at least a thousand degrees hotter there.

FYI, I'm pretty cranky this morning. I've been so nauseous since I barfed last night, and I have a zit on my chin that could body double for a baked potato. And to top it all off, Andrew started in on me five minutes before we left because he doesn't like the gift that I bought, even though it is a perfectly acceptable gift for a one-year-old. It's a toy that looks like a cookie jar and that plays classical music when you stick different-shaped pieces into it. Getting it was no small feat, mind you. I had a mini-meltdown in the toy store because I couldn't figure out where the toys for one-year-olds were, and, of course, being pregnant, such a dilemma is cause for tears. But once I recovered and got someone to help me, it seemed like the most educational and least annoying toy available. But Andrew thinks it's boring. As if any gifts for one-year-olds are not. As if one-year-olds are not.

As we pull into Julie's sister's driveway, I check the dashboard to see what the outside temperature is, and, as predicted, it is already one hundred and one degrees at nine fifty-six in the morning. Fabulous. But before I can get out of the car, Andrew leans over and puts his hand on my stomach.

"I'm excited about this," he says. "It'll be fun to be around so many babies."

I promptly remove his hand. "Yeah, well, don't try pulling any of that stuff in public yet. Nobody knows except for Julie, and I don't want an inquisition today. Just try to contain yourself."

"Sorry," he says in a fake-insulted voice.

We both get out of the car, and I can already hear the Barney theme song blaring from the backyard. Against all better judgment, we head toward the music. Andrew and I walk around the side of the house and open the gate that leads directly into the yard, and we are presented with Julie, her sister, and their mom, frantically running around and trying to tie balloons to anything that doesn't move. Despite the fact that Julie is five months more pregnant than I am, she orders me to go inside and sit on the couch, but she makes Andrew stay to help. *Sucker.*

We must be the first to arrive, because nobody else is in the house. I plop myself down directly under an air-conditioning vent and gently dab at my chin in an effort to remove the sweat that has pooled there without disturbing the intricate layers of moisturizer, white concealer, powder, skin-colored concealer, and more powder that I applied this morning with the hope that my zit might pass for a large, flesh-colored cyst instead of the red, flaming volcano that it is.

Within minutes, however, the doorbell begins to ring, and lots of little loud people accompanied by big tired-looking people come pouring in. As I scan the crowd, I am pleasantly surprised to find that both the moms and the dads are present; however, it becomes immediately clear to me that this is because it would be physically impossible for one adult to carry both a child and enough gear and supplies to outfit a small commando operation in Nicaragua.

Very interesting. I actually already did know that babies require a lot of stuff, but the carrying-the-stuff job could turn out to be an excellent ploy to force Andrew into spending Saturday afternoons with me instead of playing golf.

I smile. Maybe this baby thing won't be so bad after all.

And then I see the asses.

A little background info: During my first year of law school, I put on a ton of weight and ballooned up to a size eight, and it's taken me years to finally get it off and keep it off. Up until then, I was always able to eat whatever I wanted to, but after I turned twenty-one it was a different story. My metabolism suddenly morphed into the Merchant of Venice. It was like, *Now that you're finally legal and don't have to worry about getting arrested every time you set foot in a bar, you're gonna pay for every drunken binge that you have from now on with a pound of flesh. Literally.* And believe me, there were a lot of drunken binges that year. Twenty-seven of them, to be exact. Hence my obsession with the gym and with not eating carbs. It's not only because I'm superneurotic. It's also because it is a constant struggle for me to stay under one hundred and thirty pounds, and because at any moment every fat cell in my body could easily triple in size if I have just one too many pieces of bread with dinner. So of course, this whole pregnancy thing is totally freaking me out. I am absolutely petrified that I will never get skinny again once I have this baby.

I just have no idea how my body is going to respond to pregnancy—or how hard it's going to be to lose the weight afterward—but if the butts on the mothers in this room are any indication, I am totally screwed. Honestly, every single one of them is larger and fatter and more cellulite-ridden than the next, and I suddenly begin to think that I've been brought to this party for a reason. Like the Ghost of Asses Future is trying to show me what's in store.

I think I might need to cry. I've got to find Andrew.

I get up from the couch and make my way to the backyard, but as I step through the sliding glass doors, I am stopped dead in my tracks by an immensely swollen, incredibly sweaty, impossibly large pregnant woman. She's about a foot shorter than I am and she's easily packing an extra two hundred pounds on her. She's also wearing a horrible yellow maternity dress with a flower pattern on it that reminds me of my parents' kitchen circa 1975. Fabulous. If this is not a sign from God that I'm going spend the rest of my life as a moose, I don't know what is.

"Do you know where I can find some water?" she asks me.

"Um," I say, trying to avoid making eye contact. "I think I saw a cooler inside."

"Thanks," she says. She smiles at me awkwardly, as if she is embarrassed. "It's really hot."

"I know," I say, pretending not to notice that she's sweating like a man. "It's miserable out there."

There is a part of me that really wants to get a good look at her, but she is so gross that I just can't do it. I'm tempted to put my hands over my eyes and peek at her through my fingers, but before I even have a chance to consider just how rude that would be, she disappears inside. Okay, now I'm definitely going to cry.

I desperately scan the yard for Andrew, but all that I can see are scream-ing babies and lots of women who look like they could really use a pitcher of vodka. I start walking in step to the refrain that is running through my head. *What have I done. What have I done. What have I done. What have I done.* The tears are dangerously close as I finally spot An-drew in the corner of the yard, sitting under an umbrella. He's watching some poor soul dressed in a Teletubby outfit dance around on the grass, surrounded by a circle of women sitting on the ground. The women all have their babies on their laps, and they're singing the Teletubby song and trying to get the babies to clap their hands. In response to this, half of the babies are screaming their heads off, and the other half are sticking blades of grass in their mouths. On the periphery of the circle are the dads, video cameras glued to their faces, zooming back and forth from the Teletubby to their screaming and/or grass-eating progeny. Although this scene is troubling to me for several reasons, I am most baffled by the videotaping. It is simply beyond me why anyone would ever want to see this again.

I pull Andrew aside and tell him that we need to have a conference.

"What's wrong?" he asks.

The tears start as soon as I start to talk. "What's wrong? What's wrong? What's *not* wrong? Every single baby here is a monster. And have you happened to notice the butts on their mothers? Their kids are all *a year old.* How have they not lost the weight after a whole year? Am I being unrealistic? Do you think that I'll ever be able to lose the weight? And that pregnant woman? Did you see her? She's huge. Is that normal? How can a seven-pound baby make you that fat? I don't think I can do this. And her outfit?" I angrily point my finger at him. "If that's what mater-nity clothes look like, we are going to have a *serious problem,* because the hell if I'm going to walk around in some tent pretending it's a dress." I am really sobbing now. "How could you do this to me?" I yell. "This is all your fault. I'm going to be a horribly dressed, miserable fat cow and it's *all your fault!*"

Andrew stares at me, and I can tell that he's wondering where the pod people have stashed his wife. He begins to speak in a calm, slow voice.

"First of all, there is no way that any of these women were as thin as you before they got pregnant. And even if they were, they probably never worked out, and I'll bet that they ate as much as they wanted to the whole time. But you're eating healthy, and you're watching your calories, and you're exercising, and after you have the baby you'll go on a diet and you'll work out and you'll be fine."

I suppose that he is making sense. I have been going hiking, and I have been trying to stick to that three-hundred-extra-calories-a-day rule. I'm just going to have to be vigilant about it from now on. I'm starting to feel somewhat sorry for accusing him of ruining my life. In what I hope comes across as a show of remorse, I stick out my lower lip and sniffle.

"But what about the clothes?" I whimper. He looks relieved to see that the old me is back again, and he smiles.

"There is no way that all maternity clothes look like that. Madonna was pregnant, Sarah Jessica Parker was pregnant, plenty of famous people have been pregnant and looked great the whole time. But listen, if you can't find any clothes that you like, then we'll just go have some made for you, okay?"

In case you were wondering why I married Andrew, this is why. Any other man would have thrown me out of a window ten minutes ago, but Andrew actually indulges my tantrums. I think that he secretly enjoys them. I sniffle at him again.

"Do you promise?"

"I promise."

"Okay," I say, wiping the tears from my eyes. "I feel a little better now, thank you. I'm going to go find Julie."

"Good. I'm going to stay here and watch the Teletubby some more. A few of us are betting on how long it'll be before he collapses from heat exhaustion."

I give him a kiss on the cheek and head back toward the house. When I find Julie in the kitchen, she practically accosts me.

"*There* you are," she says. "I've been looking all over for you. The baby is here." You would think that Elvis just showed up, she is so excited. She takes me by the arm and steers me into the den toward a woman who is sitting by herself on the couch and guarding a portable car seat.

"Lara, this is my sister's friend whom I told you about, the one who just had a *baby*." She puts entirely too much emphasis on the word *baby*, as if I am new to the English language and have no idea what it means.

Julie points to the car seat and, upon peering inside, I see that there is, indeed, a sleeping baby in there.

While Julie fusses over him, I give the friend the once-over and quickly determine that she is Not Like Me. By this I mean that she is not wearing a stitch of makeup, she has a short, hi-I'm-a-new-mom haircut, she desperately needs a manicure, and she is wearing a baggy gray T-shirt with purple elastic-waistband pants and Birkenstocks.

Ooh, better make that a manicure *and* a pedicure.

I'm sure Julie told me her name, but I already forgot what it is, and Julie just left to go take some pictures of the birthday girl. *Oh, well.* I sit down on the couch next to her and silently thank God that people can't yet tell that I'm pregnant. I would hate to have to talk shop with this granola bar. I just want to try holding her kid for a minute or two and get out.

"Wow," I say, looking at the car seat. "Congratulations. Julie said he's six weeks old; that's great."

"Thanks," she says. "It is great." There is an awkward silence, and then she reaches over and pokes me in the stomach. "So, I hear you've got one in the oven!"

I resolve to kill Julie once and for all, assuming that I don't kill myself first. But before I can even put on a fake smile and try to respond, the baby begins to squirm and make googly noises. It seems that the god of excruciating pregnancy small talk has decided to spare me this morning.

I lean down and peer into the car seat at Not Like Me's baby, but the second that he sees me he begins to scream like someone is sticking needles in his eyes. I wonder if my zit scared him. I glance at Not Like Me.

"It's me, isn't it?" I say. "Are babies like dogs or something? You know, the way that they can smell fear?"

Not Like Me laughs. "No, of course not. He's just hungry; that's all."

"Oh," I say. She picks the baby up and lays him down across her lap, and I ask her if she needs me to get anything for her.

"No, thanks," she says. "I'm fine. I've got everything that I need right here."

She starts fiddling with her shirt, and I notice that it has two pockets running down the front of it that I hadn't seen before. To my total horror, Not Like Me reaches inside the left pocket and whips out the biggest, brownest nipple that I have ever seen on any human or animal. Without a hint of embarrassment, she sticks the baby in front of it, and before I can say, "Moo," the nipple disappears into his face. She looks up at me and smiles.

"So, are you planning on breast feeding?"

I am dying to inform her that there is no fucking way that I'm planning on breast feeding if it means that I'm going to grow udders where my tits used to be. But I force myself to look at her eyes and, in my politest voice with my politest fake smile, I respond. "You know, I'm not sure."

Then, before she can rope me into any further discussion on the topic, I give her another fake smile and lie that I need to go get some food. "Eating for two, you know," I say, patting my stomach. She nods and knowingly smiles right back at me.

I think it's about time to kill Julie.

I make a beeline for the kitchen, but I am once again foiled by the enormous pregnant lady, who this time is asking me for directions to the bathroom. I wonder what vibe I could possibly be giving off that is causing her to think that I am hospitable. This time I make the mistake of looking right at her, and I want to throw up. She's sweating so badly that her dress is plastered to her stomach, and her belly button is protruding out like a little erection. Between her and Not Like Me, it is a hands-down tie as to who is more revolting. I mumble something about not living here and continue toward Julie, whom I grab so hard that I practically rip her arm out of its socket.

"What's the matter?" she asks, sounding alarmed. She probably thinks that I dropped the baby on his head, or accidentally pushed down on his soft spot.

I begin to yell at her in a loud whisper. "What are you trying to do to me? You make me come to this party, and then you leave me alone with some stranger who sticks her naked, gross boobs in my face, *and* you told her that I'm pregnant? I told you not to tell *anyone.*" I stare at her expectantly, waiting for an apology, but she rolls her eyes at me like I am the stupidest person in the world.

"She doesn't count. You don't know her, and she doesn't know anyone who you know, so I am one hundred percent allowed to tell her."

Oh, really, I think. *I wasn't aware of that loophole in the pregnancy secret-keeping statute book.*

"It doesn't matter," I say. "She's disgusting. I can't believe you thought that I would want to talk to her. And what's with that pregnant chick? Why didn't you warn me about her?"

"I know," Julie says, getting a serious look on her face. "And she's still not due for four more weeks. Thank God neither of us will be that big until the winter."

Uh, speak for yourself, sweetie, I think. I don't know what Julie's been eating, but I am certainly not going to ever look like *that.*

"Anyway," Julie says, "come on. You don't have to talk to her anymore; I just want you to try holding the baby. It'll be good for you."

"No way," I tell her. "I am not going back in there. I've been traumatized enough for one morning."

"Fine," Julie says. "Then go sit in the living room and I'll see if she'll let me bring the baby to you for a little while."

"Whatever," I say. As long as I don't have to look at those boobs again, I'll do anything she wants.

Julie and I go our separate ways and I take a seat in the living room, where about a dozen people whom I have never seen before have taken refuge from the heat. They're all talking about which nursery schools they're applying to, and the more I listen, the more anxious they are making me.

". . . I joined Beth Shalom two years before I got pregnant, because they only admit temple members to the nursery school, and they check to see if you join just to get in. My friend joined when her son was only four months and they still wouldn't take her."

"I know—at Children's Village, they tell you to apply when you're still pregnant. They only have four spots a year because there are always so many siblings who get priority, and . . ."

"I heard that at the Fourteenth Street School, they ask you flat-out in your interview how much you'll be able to donate, and they expect at least ten grand on top of tuition. But, you know, I think it's worth it, because they're the biggest feeder into all of the good elementary schools. . . ."

Is this real? They're talking about *nursery* school. The hypercompetitive side of me kicks in and I start to panic about the fact that I haven't done anything about this yet. And then I remember that I never even called what's-her-name for that Mommy and Me class that Julie told me about. *Shit.* I have to do that tomorrow.

Suddenly my anxiety attack is interrupted by a tapping on my shoulder. I turn around to see Julie, who is holding Not Like Me's baby out to me as if he were a sacrificial offering. Everyone stops talking to gush, and then it gets silent as they wait for me to take him.

"Wow," I say. "Is that how you're supposed to hold a baby? It seems like it would be a little uncomfortable to have to hold your arms straight out like that all of the time."

Julie gives me a giant pity smile for the benefit of the crowd. "No, Lara, this is not how you hold a baby. This is how you give a baby to someone else to hold. You're going to have one, so you might as well learn what to do with one."

At this, all of the nursery school neurotics open their mouths and let out gasps of surprise, after which I am inundated with questions regarding my due date and advice about prenatal vitamins. Apparently the secret-keeping loophole applies to crowds, as well. I give Julie a look of death and she smiles back at me. I really had no idea that she could be so bitchy. I'm not sure if I like it.

Reluctantly, I reach out to take the baby, and Julie starts yelling instructions at me like a drill sergeant.

"Watch his head! Keep him at an angle! Don't scratch him with your nails!"

"Julie, stop it," I snarl. "You're making me nervous." The baby is squirming and his head is flopping all over the place, but I finally get him properly positioned.

There. I did it. Mission accomplished. That wasn't so bad. I look up at my audience, victorious. I'm about ready to call it a day, but everyone is still watching me, and it seems that they are waiting for me to do something else. I wonder if there is an actual protocol for holding a stranger's baby in front of an audience. I look down at the baby, who now has spit-up trickling down the side of his mouth. Maybe I'm supposed to talk to him.

"Hi," I say, in a voice about five octaves higher than normal. He's a really ugly baby. "You're so cute." He stares back at me just like everyone else in the room.

After about thirty seconds more of me smiling at him and him doing absolutely nothing back, I have completely lost interest. I want the baby off my lap, now. I need a drink, I need to pee, I need to find Andrew; I need to do lots of things that I can't do with an ugly, drooling baby on my lap. But of course, I can't say that I want the baby off my lap, what with all of these people judging me. I don't want them to go home and talk about what a horrible mother I'm going to be, since I can't even sit with a baby on my lap for more than thirty seconds. It's bad enough that they already think that I'm negligent for not having gotten on a wait list for nursery schools yet. And I don't know why I even care what these people are going to say about me when they get home, but I just do.

I smile at everyone to show that I am thoroughly enjoying this experience, and then I kind of bounce my arms a little bit, hoping for some sort of a reaction from the baby.

Still nothing.

I begin to wonder if all babies are this boring, or if there is just something wrong with this one.

But then it dawns on me that maybe he isn't boring at all, but that maybe there is something really wrong with *me*. I mean, Julie turns into a puddle whenever she even thinks about babies, and here I am with a real live baby on my lap and I can't muster up even the remotest of positive feelings toward him. *Damn it.* I knew I wasn't cut out for this. I knew it. Is it possible for someone to just be missing the maternal gene entirely? I can feel the tears welling up in my eyes.

I think I'm going to cry. Again.

I whisper to Julie that I think I'm feeling some morning sickness coming on, and I practically throw the baby back at her. I pretend to head for the bathroom, and as I pass the den I see Andrew in the corner, talking with some dads and shoveling cookies into his mouth. My voice breaking, I inform him that I need to leave *right now*.

By the time we get to the car, I am in full-fledged tears. Again.

"Now what's the matter?" Andrew asks.

"You were wrong," I sob. "I'm not ready for this. I'm going to be the worst mother ever."

Andrew looks at me, not quite sure how to manage this one. "Why do you think that?" he asks.

"Because I don't have any maternal instincts at all." Sob. "I sat with a newborn baby on my lap for two minutes—two minutes—and all I could think about was how soon I could get him off of my lap. I'm pregnant and I'm supposed to love babies, and I didn't even care about him." Pause, then sob. "No, actually, I hated him. I'm pregnant, and I hate babies. There is something fundamentally wrong with that." Double sob. "And I think I'm too selfish. I don't want to wear some ugly shirt with slits in it. I want to wear *my* clothes. I like my clothes. I don't want to have to cut my hair short, and I don't want to have disgusting boobs." I realize that he didn't meet Not Like Me and thus has no idea what I'm talking about, but I keep going anyway. "They were disgusting. And if you saw them you wouldn't want me to have them, either."

Andrew sighs loudly, and I can tell that he's getting tired of humoring me.

"Honey, when it's your own baby you will love it."

I shake my head. "No. I don't think that I will." Sob that is much louder and more dramatic than I intend for it to be. "Some people are just meant to be mothers, and I am clearly not one of them." Andrew says nothing in response to this and proceeds to concentrate on backing out of the driveway without hitting the iron gate.

Despite the sobbing, I don't think that he fully grasps how upset I am right now. So I sniffle dramatically and dab at my eyes.

"I wish I weren't pregnant," I say.

"You don't really mean that."

"I do. Yes, I do. I wish I weren't pregnant, and I wish I weren't having a baby." Very loud sob that does nothing but inspire disgust in him.

"Well," he says. "Then you really are selfish."

Okay, that's fine. I deserved that. We drive home in silence, and I continue to sniffle and pout and dab at my eyes, just so he doesn't forget that I'm in the car.

By the way, so you don't think that I'm a total bitch, I know that I'm wrong. I know that I should be thankful that I was able to get pregnant so quickly, or even at all, and that millions of people would kill for what I have. I know this. And if you're one of those millions, I'm sorry—I really am. But I just hate the way that this pregnancy is making me feel. I mean, I barely recognize myself anymore. I'm so damn weepy and inse-cure, and—here's what it is, really—I just feel so out of control. And I guess I'm just not used to feeling that way. I make lists and I organize things and I count calories and I have routines in place for every aspect of my life for the express purpose of feeling *in* control, and now, because of this *baby*, all of the list making and organizing and calorie counting and routines—all of my usual methods of operation—they don't work any-more, and I don't know how to deal with it except to just get angry and resentful and to lash out at my husband.

And so here's what I've decided. I am not going to take it anymore. I am going to fight this thing to the death. Get ready for the WWF Smack-Down of the Century, people. We've got the Mother of All Anal Reten-tion in one corner and Mother Nature in the other, and we'll see who comes out on top.

I hereby declare my independence, and I, Lara Stone, hold these truths to be self-evident:

I am not going to look like that pregnant woman at the party.

I am not going to wear hideous-looking kitchen dresses.

I will be back in a size four by the time my maternity leave is over.

I am not going to get gross boobs.

I am not going to burst into tears more than once every week—no, better to not be unrealistic—I am not going to burst into tears more than once every four days.

I will prevail.

9.

Hi-ho, Hi-ho,
It's Back to Work I Go

I f the last day of school is my favorite day of the year, the first day is by far the most abhorrent. To me, there is nothing worse than knowing that I have not even one day behind me, but just a long, tireless span of nine months ahead. Kind of like being pregnant, now that I think about it.

Of course, when I got in this morning, it was as if my vacation had never even happened. Within three minutes, I had a horde of anxious seniors in my office, all dying to tell me that they've completely changed their minds about where they want to apply and can I please give them some suggestions for schools that meet their new, ridiculous criteria. It's like they think that they can order up a college the way that they order up a cappuccino: *yes, I'll take a medium-size student body in a big city, but hold the math and science requirements and give me the racial diversity on the side, thanks.*

Ah yes, another exciting school year.

When I finally get a minute to myself, I pick up the phone and simultaneously log on to the internet. I rationalize that the first day of school is a fake work day, during which no actual productivity is expected, so I might as well take care of some personal stuff while I have the chance. I dial the number that Julie gave me for that Susan woman, and while I wait for her to pick up, I type in the Web address for Yourbaby.com.

A cheery voice answers the phone.

"Mommy and Me, this is Susan."

"Um, hi," I say. "I'd like to sign up for your class. I'm due April eleventh." The Your Baby Web site pops up on the screen and I click on "Become a Member."

"Oh, well, congratulations! Let me see, April, April . . ."

I am prompted to enter my name and address and to make up a password, and then to put in my due date or my date of conception. I type in *April 11* in the due-date field and wait for the screen to change. "Ah, here we go. Why, don't you have good timing! I only have one spot left in my April birthday class and it now belongs to you. What's your name?"

"Lara Stone," I say. A new screen comes up, welcoming me to Your Baby and providing me with a list of the wonderful benefits of membership. At the bottom, it asks if I would like to receive weekly e-mails about the progress of my baby's growth. This must be what Julie was talking about. I click on "Yes."

"Okay, Lara Stone. The class will start in the middle of June, and it's a twelve-week session. Each session is three hundred and fifty dollars, and you can sign up for new sessions until your baby is eighteen months." I do some quick calculating in my head and realize that she's running quite a racket with this Mommy and Me thing. "I'll contact you a few weeks before the class starts with the exact date and time, so until then, just enjoy being pregnant!"

Yeah, right. Not likely. I log off of the Web site.

"All right," I say. "That sounds great, thanks."

"Thank *you*," she sings. "Good-bye!"

I decide that this woman is entirely too happy for me, but I'll stay on the list for now. I can always drop out as it gets closer. I'll have to see how cranky I am in June.

Just as I am hanging up, there's a knock at my door, and I see Tick peering through the wide horizontal glass pane that is standard on all office doors at the school. I wave at her to come in.

"Hi," I say. "How was the rest of your summer?" She sits down on one of the three chairs in front my desk and drops the enormous bag on one of the other ones. I notice that her hair now has four blue streaks running through it, and that she has a decapitated Barbie head hanging from one of her combat boots.

"It pretty much sucked," she says.

"Did you talk to Marcus?" I ask.

She rolls her eyes back in her head, as if hearing his name makes her want to forgo consciousness altogether.

"Yeah. We broke up. He was such a dick about it, too. He didn't even care that I want to go to college; all he cares about is himself. Do you know what he said to me?" I shake my head no. I can only imagine. "He said that I'm an idiot because my dad would have paid for us to live fat in New York, and I'm throwing it away to go waste four years of my life learning about nothing. I was like, Excuse me, pay for *us* to live? Did he think that my dad was, like, going to give him an allowance or something?"

I resist the urge to tell her that yes, that's exactly what he thought, and I shake my head in disgust. "You're better off without him," I say. "What's going on with the band?"

"Oh, of course everyone blamed me. Marcus convinced all of them to stay with him and find a new lead singer. Your friend was, like, so right about not dating the manager." She lets out a long sigh. "I just want this year to be over so that I can go to college and get the hell out of here."

Oh, thank God. At least she still wants to go to college.

"Okay," I say. I'm kind of afraid to ask if she's still interested in NYU. "Have you thought about where you want to go?" She looks at me and curls the left side of her top lip, like Billy Idol used to do.

"Yeah," she says. "NYU, remember?" Her tone suggests that there is another word to that sentence that she has left off. Like *moron,* or *idiot,* or *doofus,* or whatever word kids use today to describe people who are infinitely dumber than they are.

"Yes," I say, "I remember. But where else? You can't only apply to NYU." She does that lip-curl thing again. I bet she doesn't even know who Billy Idol is.

"Why not?" she asks. "I don't want to go anywhere else. I want to go to NYU."

I think I'm going to try to be more like Stacey. Maybe I'll get through to her if I'm rude.

"Yes, well, I want to go to Hawaii and drink piña coladas on the beach for the rest of my life, but I don't think that's going to happen."

She gives me a smart-ass smile. "It could. My dad owns a hotel in Hawaii. I'll see if he can arrange it for you."

You see, that right there is what is wrong with the entertainment industry. People should not own entire hotels in Hawaii. And if they do, they shouldn't tell their children about it. I take a deep breath.

"Okay, just humor me for a moment. I'm not saying that you won't get into NYU. I'm just saying that you have to consider the possibility that you might not. Look, it's my job to plan for the worst-case scenario, and right now the worst-case scenario is that you apply only to NYU, you don't get in, and then you're stuck living at home next year and going to community college. Is that what you want?"

She shakes her head. "No. I'd rather die first." Frankly, so would I, if I had her mother.

"Exactly. See, when you think about it that way, going somewhere else doesn't sound so bad, does it?"

She shakes her head again. "So where else is there?" she asks.

Okay. Now we're getting somewhere. I go right into college-counselor mode. "Well, that depends on what you want. You have to figure out what your criteria are, and then try to find a college that fits them." I swivel around in my chair and pull a huge college reference book off of my bookshelf. Tick waves her hands at me.

"All I care about is being in New York and playing in a band. Nothing else really matters to me."

I flip the book open to the New York section and start turning the pages. "Okay, well, there's Fordham, but that's a Catholic school—do you care?"

She makes a face. "No. Nothing religious. I don't believe in organized religion." She makes a peace sign with her fingers and affects a deep, hippie voice. "Music is my religion, man."

I laugh. I'm beginning to suspect that she's much smarter than she lets on. Maybe she did trash her SATs on purpose. I pull out a pad of paper.

"Okay," I say, writing while I talk. "So it has to be in New York, it has to have a music scene, and it can't be religious." I continue to look through the book. "There's Eugene Lang, at the New School. That's really artsy, and it's a small school, so you'd have—"

She cuts me off. "How small?" she says, looking at me skeptically.

I consult the book. "About five hundred students. It's pretty small."

She is vigorously shaking her head. "No way. Too small. I don't want to be somewhere that's all gossipy and incestuous. It needs to have at least a few thousand people."

I give her a look. "I thought that all you care about is being in New York and playing in a band."

"Fine. You're right. I guess I didn't really think about it."

"Okay," I say, shutting the book. "I think you need to do some thinking about it before we can continue this conversation." I pull another, smaller book from my shelf and hand it to her. "Why don't you take this book and see if there are any schools that appeal to you? When you have a better idea of what you want, come back and we can start putting together a list, okay?"

She nods and, after a few minutes spent rearranging the contents of the bag, she manages to find a spot inside for the book. Has she never heard of a locker? She glances at the clock and stands up.

"I've gotta go to math. I'll see you later." She opens my door and starts to leave, but then she stops in the doorway and turns around. "Thanks," she says.

"You're very welcome."

She half smiles at me and walks out, her combat boots squeaking through the office. I am sure it is the pregnancy hormones, but I am so touched by this that for a brief moment I feel like I'm going to cry.

When I come back from lunch, I have four phone messages and an e-mail from Yourbaby.com. I assume that it's probably just a confirmation of my log-in and password, but when I click on it I see that it is my first weekly update, decorated in the background with cartoon baby faces and yellow ducks. I don't know why I listen to Julie. I should have known that this was just another one of her attempts to convert me.

YOUR BABY NOW: Nine Weeks

Hello, Lara!
You might not be growing yet, but your baby sure is! He still weighs almost nothing, but he's already starting to look like a real person! He even has eyes! As for you, you may have been feeling like you're on an emotional elevator lately, but rest assured that mood swings are something that almost all pregnant women experience.

Yeah, I think. *So I've noticed.* I scroll down to see what else it says.

Today's Hot Topic: Do you find yourself having to urinate all the time? See how other pregnant women deal with their "urge to go" on the Your Baby bulletin board!

How come nobody can write about baby stuff without using bad puns and exclamation points? And who has time to spend chatting with strangers about how often they have to pee? Delete. If Mommy and Me turns out to be anything like this, I think I'll pass.

I pick up the phone and dial into my voice mail. The first three messages are from parents of my students who want to know the following: (1) If we have a live-in housekeeper, can we count her as a dependent on our financial aid forms? (2) We're planning a trip back east to go visit colleges, and I'm wondering if you know whether Syracuse, New York, is north or south of Boston? and (3) If I (white) and my husband (also white) were both born in South Africa, but my son was born here, can he check the African American box on his applications?

Do you see what I deal with? Now do you understand why I need three months off every year?

The fourth message is from Linda, and she sounds pissed.

"Lara, it's Linda. Please call me as soon as you receive this." Click.

Well, welcome back to you, too, I think. I dial Linda's extension and she picks up on the first ring. She knows it's me because the school phone system has an internal caller ID.

"Hi, Lara," she says, but her tone is not friendly.

"Hi. What's up?" I say, trying to sound casual.

"I received a call first thing this morning from Cheryl Gardner. She says that you met with Victoria one time this summer for twenty minutes, that you didn't even speak about college with her, and that she never heard from you again. I thought I made it clear to you how important it is that we accommodate these people."

Oh, man. I can't believe that Tick sold me out like that. I'll bet Cheryl has no idea about Marcus or the band or NYU or anything.

"Actually, Linda, that's not true. I did meet with Tick again this summer, and we were in touch by e-mail, and then I met with her again today just before lunch. Tick must not have told Cheryl about it."

Linda lets out a loud, annoyed sigh. "Of course she didn't tell Cheryl about it. Teenagers don't tell their parents anything." She shifts to an I'm-the-boss tone. "I want you to call Cheryl right now and fill her in on everything that has happened. And from now on, do me a favor and keep her in the loop. I don't want to get any more phone calls like that from her."

I'm guessing that now would not be a good time to tell her that I'm pregnant.

"I'll call her right now," I say. "Sorry, I didn't realize that she would be so angry."

"No," Linda says, "clearly you didn't."

I can't believe that Cheryl went over my head like that. Why didn't she just call me over the summer if she was so worried about it? It's not like she ever had any misgivings about bothering me at home before.

I pull out my phone list of students and their families and dial Cheryl's house. I want to get this straightened out right away so that Cheryl can get on with begging my forgiveness.

"Gardner residence."

"Hi, Lori. This is Lara Stone. Is Cheryl around?"

"Yes, Lara, she's right here. She's anxious to speak with you." Lori hands off the phone and Cheryl gets on.

"Hi, Lara," she says curtly. "I'm assuming that you spoke with Linda."

Oh, lady. Do not mess with me. You are about to get so hosed. "Yes," I say, "I spoke with Linda. But frankly, I wish you had just called me first, because I did meet with Tick again. Twice." *That's right, you snotty little tattletale. I am good; you are evil.*

"Well, how I was I supposed to know that, Lara? If you had told me I wouldn't have had to go to Linda in the first place."

Oh, that is *so* not the point. But I can't argue with her. It's not worth the phone call that I'll get from Linda. I take a deep breath and swallow my pride in one big gulp. Let me assure you that it tastes really, really bad going down.

"You're right," I say. "I should have called you after I met with her. But we've had some really productive meetings and she's very interested in NYU."

"NYU," she says, with a scoff. "That's not a very prestigious school, is it?" She must be kidding. I convinced her kid to go to college instead of moving to New York and playing in a band with her skank boyfriend, and now she's taking issue with the choice of school?

"Actually," I say, "NYU has become extremely selective over the last five years. It's much more highly regarded than it used to be."

"But it's not ranked in the top ten," she says matter-of-factly. "It's not even in the top twenty-five." I wonder if she has actually memorized the *U.S. News & World Report* annual college rankings list. I am tempted to quiz her: *Quick—which school is thirty-seventh in student-to-faculty ratio?* But I am too afraid that she might actually know the answer.

"No, it's not," I say, "but we already discussed that Tick's chances for a top school are not that realistic, and to be honest, I don't even know if she can get into NYU."

"I don't see how that's even possible," she says. "You know, you're always so negative, Lara. Tick is a very smart girl, and I think that maybe you're leading her toward lesser schools on purpose." Okay, I've had it with her. Who does she think she is, calling me negative?

"First of all, I have not led Tick anywhere. NYU was completely her idea. And second, I am not negative; I am cautious. There is a difference. But really, Cheryl, this isn't about me. This is about Tick, and with Marcus gone and the band breaking up, she's having a pretty hard time right now. The fact that she's interested in college at all is a huge step, and I think it would help her to feel that you're being supportive of her choices."

Cheryl says nothing, and I can't tell if it's because she's mad or because she actually thinks that I have a point.

"Do you have children, Lara?" She's mad. She definitely did not know about Marcus and the band breaking up.

"No, I don't." But I do have a fetus with eyes.

"Well, until you do, you might want to leave the parenting advice to those of us who know what we're talking about."

Those of *us*? Is she kidding? I must have missed the memo naming Cheryl the arbiter of good parenting. I suppose that I should be flattered, though. She's obviously feeling threatened by me.

"Fine," I say. "The next time I meet with Tick, I'll let you know what happens."

"Please do."

Okay, I think, hanging up the phone. *That went well.*

This day cannot possibly end soon enough. I'm exhausted, I'm still really upset by my conversation with Cheryl, and I just want it to be over. Do you remember the clocks from high school? You know, the round kind, with black numbers big enough for a legally blind person to see, and that red, hypnotic second hand that, if you weren't careful, could suck you into watching it sweep around over and over again, until you started to anticipate exactly when, ever so slightly, the minute hand would begin to quiver, and then, finally, as the thin red line aligned with the twelve, spastically jump to the next number with a loud, clicking noise, marking the passing of yet another excruciating minute spent listening to some horrendous teacher drone on and on about something that you would never remember once the test was over? That's the kind of clock that I am staring at right now, willing it to magically skip ahead twenty-seven minutes so that it will be three thirty and I will be free to go home and take a nap.

I'm supposed to be meeting with Mark—you might remember him: He's the kid who commented about my car on the last day of school last year. He stopped by this morning and asked if he could come in at three o'clock to go over his college list. He's only three—well, now four—minutes late, but I'm praying that he forgot, because I'm really hungry and I want to go down to the vending machine in the teacher's lounge to get some peanut-butter crackers. If my assistant, Rachel, were here, I would just tell her to tell Mark that I'll be right back, but she had to go to some computer training thing, so if I leave the office I'll have to lock the door, and you know that if I do that, Mark will show up the second I leave and think that I blew him off.

I'll give him five more minutes.

Tomorrow I am going to have to bring some snacks to keep in my desk.

Four minutes and fifty-two seconds later, Mark comes running in the door, just as I'm standing up to go. *Damn.* I'm really getting hungry.

"Sorry, sorry, sorry," he says as he breezes in. "I got stuck talking to Mr. Frye after History and he wouldn't shut up."

"It's fine," I say, sitting back down. "What do you have for me?"

He takes a seat and starts rifling through his backpack, which is crammed with crumpled papers.

"Mark," I say, "it's only the first day of school. How are you already so unorganized?" He finds the paper he's looking for and tries to smooth it out on the side of my desk.

"I don't know," he says. "It just happens. My friends have decided that if I were a superhero, I would be Disheveled Man. I would have the ability to make things messy just by looking at them."

I laugh. I actually like Mark a lot, despite the fact that he is the president of the Business and Investment Club and one of about six kids in the entire school who identifies with the Republican party. He's like an Alex P. Keaton for the new millennium. We've developed a little banter where we make fun of each other's politics—I call him a fascist and he calls me a tree hugger—and every now and then we'll debate the previous night's *West Wing* episode. He's a little bit obsessed with money, and he's definitely kind of nerdy, but he's pretty smart and he works obscenely hard in school, and he's got his act together more than most kids. I actually think that he's going to have some great college prospects for next year.

He hands me his list and I look it over. George Washington, Georgetown, Columbia, Penn, Emory, Washington University, Northwestern, Berkeley. I look up at him.

"Berkeley?" I say, raising my eyebrows. "Talk about tree huggers. I don't know if that's quite the place for you, Mark."

He nods at me.

"I know," he says. "My dad is making me apply. It's his alma mater." He rolls his eyes. "Don't worry, I'll never go there. I'm just doing it to get him off my back."

I give him a concessionary nod. "Okay, that's fair, I guess. So what's the problem?"

"There's no problem. I just wanted to run them by you to see if you think I have enough backups. I don't know, do you think they're all reaches for me?"

"I mean, I don't think they're *all* reaches for you, but it might not be a bad idea to—" Suddenly, midsentence, the muscles in my throat and my abdomen begin to convulse, my mouth involuntarily opens, and the next thing I know, I am producing a series of retches, the force and volume of which I heretofore would not have believed was possible. There's nothing actually coming out, mind you; I'm just retching.

I hold up a finger to Mark and, still retching, run out of my office to the nearest teacher's bathroom, which, thank God, is private and can be locked from the inside.

I quickly bolt the door behind me and continue with my dry heaving. In the back of my brain, some instinct that I never knew I had is telling me that the only way to stop this is by getting something to eat. So I leave the bathroom and, still retching, though much more quietly now, I book it down to the teachers' lounge, where, upon seeing that it is empty, I again give thanks, and then stick my dollar into the vending machine and frantically push C16 for the peanut-butter crackers, which I fish out from the receptacle, unwrap, and inhale in three large bites.

Miraculously, the retching stops. I am sweating, and my abs feel sore, like I just did twenty minutes of stomach crunches. And not the fake ones where I only lift my head off the ground, but the real kind, where I actually get my shoulders up, too.

I sit down at the table and dab at my forehead with one of those brown industrial paper towels that are ubiquitous in school bathrooms, cafeterias, and science labs, and then I suddenly remember that Mark is sitting in my office, no doubt wondering what the hell happened to his freak of a college counselor.

I run back up the stairs. Sweating even more profusely than before, I sprint to my office, but as I get within eyesight of my window I slow to a leisurely stroll. I open the door and walk back in as if nothing has happened, trying to pretend that everything is A-okay and that a sudden burst of violent, convulsive gagging accompanied by disgusting, earsplitting, strangulation-like noises is a normal, everyday occurrence that requires neither explanation nor comment.

"So," I say to Mark, sitting back down in my chair. "As I was saying, you might want to pick one or two more schools that aren't as selective as the rest of these, just to be safe." Mark looks at me for a second, trying to decide what to make of this, but given that he is just as embarrassed to have witnessed this display as I am to have displayed it, he gratefully follows my lead.

"Yeah, that's what I thought you would say." Mark is not, however, very good at hiding the fact that he's desperate to escape, as he has picked up his bag and started slowly backing away from me, as if he just learned that I am in possession of a highly contagious and fatal Ebola-like virus and am threatening to throw it on him if he makes one wrong move. "Okay," he says, still walking backward. "So I'll do some more research and see if I can find a few more schools to add to my list. Can I e-mail it to you?" Oh, yeah. He's afraid.

"Yes," I say. "That's fine. I'll let you know what I think when I see what you've added."

By this point he's backed himself all the way through the doorway and is ready to run. "Okay. Thanks. I'll see you later."

"'Bye!" I say, trying to sound cheery. I look up at the clock. Three thirty on the dot. I turn off my computer, grab my purse, and lock the door behind me.

As I walk to the parking lot, I recall how, at the faculty meeting this morning, the vice principal gave us a little pep talk to get the year off to a good start. He told us that there is an old superstition among educators—something like, "If the first day goes well, the year will be swell. If instead it is bad, a poor year will be had." When he said it this morning, I thought it was supercorny and I rolled my eyes for the benefit of the sarcastic, gay math teacher who was sitting next to me. But after the day that I've had, I'm thinking that maybe there might just be something to it.

10.

Pop! Goes My Ego

It's starting. I noticed it for the first time about a week ago. I was fine in the morning—totally normal—but by the time I got home from work, I had to unbutton my pants, and by the time I was ready to go to bed, there was an actual bulge in my stomach. It wasn't a big, round bulge or anything that you would imagine a pregnant stomach to look like. It was just a little pookie that I couldn't suck in, no matter how hard I tried. And believe me, I almost collapsed a lung I tried so hard. When I woke up the next morning it was, miraculously, gone, but at the end of the day there it was again, making me look as if I alone had consumed the pasta inventory of the entire Italian countryside. It went on like that for the whole week—gone in the morning, back at night—but then this morning, right smack in the middle of my fourteenth week, the very beginning of my second trimester, the bulge was still there when I woke up. It seems that I am (audible gasp) Starting to Show.

It's incredibly depressing, by the way, this pregnant-but-not-really-showing-so-therefore-just-looking-tubby phenomenon. It makes me want to wear a blazing neon sign around my neck that says, *Not Fat, Just Pregnant,* or even one of those *Baby on Board* T-shirts that I always thought were so stupid back in the eighties but that now make complete and total sense to me, although, come to think of it, I still would never actually wear one, no matter how unfairly porky I appeared. And I don't even know why I care if random strangers or vague acquaintances or people at work (I know, I know, I just haven't gotten around to telling

Linda yet, but I'm for sure telling her on Monday) think that I'm fat, because all of our real friends and family already know that I'm pregnant (except for Stacey—she's been going back and forth to Mexico City every few days, handling some problems on a movie that one of her clients is filming down there, so I haven't seen or talked to her in almost a month), but there's just something about the idea of people whispering about me behind my back—*Ooh, that Lara, she used to be so thin, but now she's really starting to let herself go again. I wonder if her husband is looking at younger, thinner women yet?*—that is very upsetting to me.

But I digress. The point is, I am showing, albeit not in an obvious way, but enough that, when I tried to put on my favorite pair of jeans this morning, it took me a full five minutes and more than a reasonable amount of grunting and pulling and lying down on the bed and deeply inhaling to get them closed. And then, after all of that effort, I realized that there was no possible way that even one oxygen cell could possibly squeeze past the waistband and reach the lower half of my body, and so I had to take them off after only twenty minutes because I got scared that I might permanently lose feeling in my legs.

And then I tried on all of the other pairs of jeans that I own, including the one pair of superfat jeans that I kept from my law school days just to remind myself of how bad things could get if I'm not careful, and the same exact thing happened.

So I am now wearing sweatpants, and I have absolutely nothing casual to wear out to dinner and the movies tonight with Julie and Jon, which means that I must go shopping for some maternity clothes immediately, because there is no way that I am going to be one of those women who runs around in my husband's sweatpants for nine months.

I have been standing on Beverly Drive, outside the door of Pea in the Pod, for a good ten minutes already. Despite the fact that the pregnant mannequins in the window appear to be wearing perfectly acceptable outfits, I have been able to muster only about 70 percent of the courage required for me to actually enter the store. The other 30 percent is still stuck on the image of that hideous, 1970s kitchen-looking dress that the pregnant beast from the first birthday party was wearing, and no matter how much I try to reason with it—*Look, just look at the pregnant man-nequin; it's* fine—it simply will not come around.

But as I conspicuously turn my head in both directions, trying to appear as if I am waiting for someone and not as if I am casing the joint, I spot one of my students coming out of the Ron Herman store across the street, loaded down with shopping bags. Any lasting reservations that I am having about this undertaking are quickly tossed to the wind, and I duck into Pea in the Pod for cover. I simply cannot risk being seen looking fat and standing outside of a maternity store by anyone associated with my school until I have told Linda the news myself. I know Linda. If she finds out about this from anyone but me, she will always wonder what else I am keeping from her.

So that's that. I'm in. I do a quick lap around the store, just to get a sense of what it is that I am dealing with, and I am totally shocked by how normal—stylish, actually—the majority of the clothes are. There are boot-cut pants, cashmere sweaters, denim skirts, all knockoffs of what regular stores are selling this season, but bigger, and with elastic waistbands. And when I start looking at the labels, I almost fall down when I see names that I recognize. Chaiken makes maternity pants? Anna Sui! Seven jeans! I have died and gone to heaven. This is so much better than I ever imagined. It's almost like real shopping.

I look up to find a salesperson to help me with the sizes, and my eye is caught immediately by the woman who has been hovering at arm's length, like a sort of military plane, ever since I walked in the door. She looks about twenty-two, cute, dressed in a trendy outfit, very thin. Not what I was expecting *at all*. For some reason I imagined that all of the salespeople in the store would be pregnant, and that they would just keep hiring a new crop every nine months or so. Not that I think that Pea in the Pod should be actively trying to violate the equal opportunity laws; it's just that I don't get why anyone who is not pregnant would want to work here. I mean, isn't the employee discount the whole point of working in a retail clothing store?

The unpregnant sales associate with the mysterious motives is now practically on top of me.

"Do you need any help with sizes?" she asks.

"Yes," I say. "I have no idea how this works. This is my first time."

She—Sherry is her name—explains that if I was a size four before I got pregnant, then I would wear a small in maternity clothes. Small. I love that word. I decide that I like her and that I will accept her advice and not snarl at her every time she offers to help me. Together, we determine that I am not yet ready for any maternity shirts, so we go through all of the jeans and choose five pairs for me to try on. Sherry, who has quickly become my new best friend, cautions that some of them will for sure be too big and that I will have to grow into them.

I nod to show that I understand this caveat and disappear into the dressing room.

I try on the first pair—a really cute pair of Bella Dahls that Sherry says just came in and have been flying off the shelves—but, as she warned, they are enormous. They pull up over the belly and I have to roll them down about six times to keep them from falling off. I tell Sherry that I think I'll wait to buy these until they fit me, but she grimaces.

"They're our most popular jeans. I don't even know if we'll have them in a few months. We had to wait almost eight weeks to get the last shipment, and we had a waiting list for those."

Ooh, she's good. Preying on my fears like that. Fine. I'll take them now.

The next three pairs are also way too big, but not nearly cute enough to buy for insurance against possible future wait lists. I'm starting to get a little nervous, because I need a pair of jeans that I can wear now—tonight—but when I try on the last pair, the dark blue Sevens with the low under-the-belly elastic waistband, I emerge from the dressing room smiling.

"Oh!" says Sherry. "Those look awesome! They make you look *so* thin!"

Although I do agree that they look pretty good, I don't quite trust that Sherry is being 100 percent honest with me. In fact, I am fairly certain that her comment is actually a tactic pulled straight from the Pea in the Pod employee training manual.

Be sure to always tell the customer that the most expensive items make her look so *thin. This will not only boost the confidence of your customer, but will also increase sales for you, and may even lead to repeat business.*

Of course, I have neither read nor seen the Pea in the Pod employee training manual, if such a thing even exists, but if it does, then I imagine that this is the kind of thing that it would say, and if it doesn't, then hey, corporate Pea in the Pod people, you might want to take some notes here.

While I am checking myself out in the mirror and Sherry is gushing about how she can't believe how amazing my legs are—

Also, always make a point of complimenting at least one of the customer's body parts, aside from, of course, her abdomen.

—the woman in the dressing room next to me comes out wearing the same exact pair of jeans. Sherry immediately stops talking, and my neighbor and I look each other squarely in the eyes. I clench my fists and squint at her, like the men in old Western movies do just before they are about to have a showdown.

As an aside, let me just pause here for a moment to tell you that Julie warned me about this this morning, when I called to ask her where one goes to buy maternity wear. Apparently, shopping for maternity clothes has become a competitive sport, falling somewhere between hot-dog eating and Ultimate Frisbee throwing on the scale of sport-worthiness. And there are rules. Rule number one is that all shoppers must size each other up in order to determine whether they look better or worse than their opponents.

My adversary, let's call her Shorty, is about five-two, probably on the heavy side to begin with, and is carrying in such a way that she looks like she's got a spare tire to a Hummer hanging around her waist. I check her out and, I'm sorry to say, the Sevens just don't look very good on her. Not to be conceited or anything, but so far, I think it's safe to say that I am in the lead.

Shorty glances at me sideways.

"Well, how far along are you?" she asks in an accusatory tone. Rules number two and three: Upon face-off, take any and all steps necessary to determine exactly how pregnant your opponent is, and then be sure to make yourself sound as far along as possible in order to justify why you are as big as you are. (Note: After you deliver, the inverse of this rule goes into effect. Always round *down* your baby's age in order to justify why you are still as big as you are.)

"Not quite fifteen weeks," I answer expertly, as if I have been playing this game my entire life.

"Oh," Shorty says in a well-that-explains-it kind of tone. "I'll be nineteen weeks on Friday."

Nice try, honey, I think, *but I am not about to fall for a fake-out.* Today is only Saturday, which means that she just turned eighteen weeks yesterday, which means that she is not even three and a half weeks ahead of me and, therefore, has lost fair and square. The rules clearly state that if you are not at least a full month farther along than your opponent and your opponent looks equal to or better than you, then the game is over, end of story.

I turn my attention back to the image of me kicking Shorty's ass in the mirror, and proceed to let her know that I know that we both know that I have won by turning around and pulling at the fabric that, even in a size small, is still hanging loosely around my butt.

But it seems that I have underestimated Shorty's skills, because she tries to toss one in below the belt.

"You know," she says, "I wouldn't buy those jeans in that size. They might fit you now, but you're going to gain weight, and there's no way they'll fit you like that in another few weeks. You haven't even popped yet."

I look to Sherry, whose job description apparently includes referee duty, and she calls a flag on the play.

"Actually, if they fit you now, you'll probably be able to wear them until almost the very end. They don't look tight on your legs at all, and if you haven't gained weight in your legs by now you probably won't."

Always try to sound as authoritative as possible in all matters having to do with pregnancy and weight gain, even if you have no idea what you are talking about. To guarantee your sale, assure the customer that her weight gain is well below that of others you have seen, or, in the alternative, that she will not continue to gain any further weight.

I shoot Shorty a now-nobody-likes-a-sore-loser look and claim my victory.

"I'll take two pairs," I say to Sherry, and just about float out of the store.

When I arrive home, Zoey is sitting on the chair in the foyer, awaiting my return. When I say that she's sitting, I don't mean that she's lying down, curled up in a ball, as most dogs would be. I mean that she's actually sitting up like a person, her back resting against the chair, as if she were just hanging out and reading the paper. Sometimes I really wonder what goes on in this house when we're not home. I would not be at all surprised to learn that she has a regular poker game going with the Pugs next door.

I place my shopping bags on the floor and go over to give her some love, but as I approach her, she nods in the direction of my purchases.

"Whatcha got there?" she says in that same scruffy voice.

Oh, good. I was starting to wonder if I'd imagined it the last time. I smirk at her. "My new, very stylish maternity jeans."

She jumps down off of the chair and walks over to inspect them. "Hmm," she says, sounding unimpressed. "Daddy's going to be mad."

I scoff. "Daddy is not going to be mad. Daddy just pretends to get mad. Don't worry, I know how to deal with Daddy."

By "deal with Daddy," I am referring to the little game that Andrew and I play, where I spend more money on clothes than he wants me to and he gets angry with me. It goes like this: I buy a ton of new stuff, and the first thing he wants to know is how much it all cost. I tell him, and he then gives me a whole song and dance about how I'm going to put us in the poorhouse, at which point I offer to give him a fashion show and concede that, if he doesn't like anything when he sees it on me, I'll take it all back. Of course, we both know that he will like everything on me when I'm dancing around in it half-naked, and that he will like it all even more after we've had sex, so he never makes me return any of it, I always promise not to do it again, and a month later we go through the whole process once more.

Zoey shrugs at me, if you can even call it a shrug. She really lifts her head more than her shoulders, since she's standing on all fours, but I get the intent.

"We'll see," she says. "By the way, you're looking a little fat. You should lay off the carbs." *Uch.* Like I need this from my *dog?*

"For your information, I'm not fat; I'm pregnant. And I liked you much better when you couldn't talk. I had no idea that you were such a bitch."

She does that openmouthed smile thing, and her tongue hangs out over the side of her lower lip. "Yeah, well, no shit, Sherlock. Where do think the expression comes from?" Oh, how clever. A bitch and a smart-ass. But just then she hears someone walking by outside, and she takes off through her doggie door, barking at the top of her lungs.

By the time Andrew finally gets home from golf, I have tried on each pair of jeans with every single set of shoes that I own, and am dying for an audience. The second he walks in the door, I drag him upstairs with me to our bedroom.

"I got the *best* maternity jeans today," I say, leading him by the hand. "Go sit down; I want to show you." Knowing better than to argue with me, he turns on the television and takes his place on the chaise at the foot of our bed. I disappear into my closet and put on the first pair of jeans to kick off the fashion show. Then I twist my hair up into a sexy, messy ponytail and put on a fresh coat of lip gloss. Ready.

I strut out of my closet—picture it—I'm topless, wearing the Sevens with the elastic waistband sitting just below my bulge, and my black, stiletto-heeled Gucci ankle boots, and I am so excited about them and how they make me look *so* thin that I am practically high. When I reach Andrew at the end of the catwalk, I spin around so that he can admire me from all angles.

"What do you think?" I ask. "Aren't these great? They're Sevens."

"Yeah," he says. "They're okay. What's with the sweatband at the top?"

"It's not a sweatband. It's an elastic waistband. Instead of a zipper and a button, so that my stomach can get bigger?"

"Ah," he says, nodding his head.

Normally, by this point in the fashion show he has already thrown me to the floor and is tearing off whatever clothing I have just modeled for him. But he's not the least bit aroused by me right now. In fact, he's not even looking at me anymore, as he has semiengrossed himself in a show about the construction of the Golden Gate Bridge that he has found on the Discovery channel.

I'm starting to get the sense that my usual tactics are not going to work here. This damn bulge is like kryptonite—it's thwarting my powers over him, and there is nothing I can do about it. *Well,* I think, *Superman would fight on anyway, and so will I.*

I grab the clicker and turn off the television.

"I'm not finished yet," I say.

"Oh," he says. "There's more?" I shoot him a look and then go back into my closet. I put on the Bella Dahls, leaving them unrolled and pulled all the way up, so that he can see how they work. But when I do my spin at the end of the catwalk, he is horrified.

"They come all the way up to your boobs," he says.

"They're supposed to," I say, as I start rolling them down. "Eventually my belly will fill them out, but for now I'll just have to roll them down, like this."

"But if you roll them down it'll make a big lumpy thing under your shirt."

For the record, any positive body-image feelings that I was having have completely vanished. I pout.

"Well, I don't know what you want me to do. I need jeans; none of mine fit me anymore."

He closes his eyes—closes his eyes!—and squinches up his face like he's just seen something too icky to even describe. "I want you to take them back. I'm just not ready to see you like this. The Seven ones are okay, but these are really awful. I'm sorry." With that, he turns the television back on.

Wow, I think. *Strike one for the pregnant chick.* I wish Shorty would walk out of my closet so that he could see what a good deal he's got. Instead, Zoey strolls into the room and jumps up onto the bed, settling herself into the mass of decorative throw pillows.

"Fine," I say. "I'll take them back." He looks at me again, one eye still on the TV.

"How much did they cost, anyway?" Without moving her head, Zoey shifts her eyes in my direction. I ignore her.

"For these and two pairs of the Sevens it was around six." Andrew hits the pause button on the TiVo remote.

"Hundred?" he yells. "You spent six hundred dollars on three pairs of maternity jeans? I didn't think you'd spend six hundred dollars on clothes for the whole pregnancy!" I look at him like he has lost his mind. Is he kidding me? This is a man whose mother would drop two grand on a Chanel purse in the eighties without even pausing to think. He knows exactly how much things cost; he just doesn't like to believe that I will actually buy them.

"Andrew," I say, in an annoyed, how-dare-you-you-bastard voice. "Please do not start with me. Maternity clothes are expensive, and whether you like them or not, I need to have clothes. I need stuff to wear to work and I need stuff to wear to go out and I need some casual stuff for the weekends. But don't worry. Now that I know how attractive you find me in them, I won't spend a penny more than I have to."

I am in tears. Again. But Andrew turned back to the television and tuned me out somewhere around "stuff to wear to work," so he doesn't even notice. I go back into my closet and Zoey jumps off the bed and follows me.

"Shut up," I say to her, pointing my index finger. "I don't want to hear it." She dog-shrugs again and walks out, probably to go lie down next to Andrew for a belly rub. Traitor.

Sobbing, I take off the jeans and put them back in the bag, all the while hearing about the miracle of engineering that is the Golden Gate Bridge in the background.

When we get to the restaurant, Julie and Jon are already seated at the table, waiting for us. We are late because I couldn't find a shirt long enough to hide the elastic waistband on my new jeans, and I went through yet another round of tears while flinging every top that I own onto the bed while Andrew and Zoey hid in the kitchen.

"Ooh!" Julie exclaims, upon seeing me. "Cute jeans. They look great on you." At this, I smirk at Andrew. I have not spoken one word to him since my failed attempt at seduction four hours ago, and I fully intend to continue giving him the silent treatment throughout the evening, interjected only by sarcastic looks and you-are-so-mean-I-hate-you glances.

Julie's stomach, by the way, is huge. Huge huge. The rest of her looks amazing—her arms and legs appear to be downright skinny—but I can't tell if it's because everything else just looks small in comparison to the atomic missile that she is carrying in her midsection, or if all of the fat has actually accumulated only in that one spot. She's not due for another five weeks, but she is positive that she's going to be early.

"Are you nervous?" I ask. I am nervous. Just looking at her makes me nervous.

"Not really," she says. "We did Lamaze, and I was in the delivery room for all of my sisters' babies, so I think I know what to expect. And I've been watching *Real Births* every day." She lowers her voice to a whisper. "Actually, I haven't told anyone because I don't want to jinx it, but I applied to be on the show."

"You *what*?" I say. Now, I haven't actually seen the show for myself—I never got around to watching it, and I keep forgetting to TiVo it—but just based on Julie's description of it, I am fairly certain that this is the most ridiculous thing that I have ever heard.

"I applied. I think it would be really cool to have my pregnancy and the birth of my first child on a professional, edited television show. It would be like having my own documentary." She sees that the look of horror has not left my face, and she attempts to convince me. "Come on, how cool would it be to watch it with the baby twenty years from now?" Not cool. Way uncool. If my mom wanted to watch a cheesy video about my birth with me when I was twenty, I would have been mortified.

"But Jul, it will be on *television*. People will see you grunting and pushing—oh, my God, do they show crotch shots?—I mean, won't you be embarrassed?"

She rolls her eyes at me. "Please, it's daytime television. They don't show anybody naked. They just show you from the neck up, and I'll have drugs, so it's not like I'll be screaming or anything. It'll be fine. It'll be *fun*."

I am thinking that, if this actually happens, I don't know if I can be friends with her anymore. How can I be friends with someone who does something like this? It's just as bad as—no, it might even be worse than—being best friends with a girl who goes on *The Bachelor*, and having to watch her humiliate herself on national television by "falling in love" with a guy she's known for only twenty minutes, and then, if she makes it to the end, having to actually be there when he comes home to meet her family, and to have to sit at her parents' dining room table and ask him absurd questions about how he views her in comparison to the other three girls, and whether he would consider picking up the great life that he must have in order to even have been chosen as the Bachelor, and moving it to Idaho, or Nebraska, or wherever it is that those twenty-three-year-old girls come from who want to get married, are dying to get married, *must* get married to this man, and can already picture themselves, at twenty-three, as Mrs. the Bachelor, as the Mother of the Bachelor's Children. Yeah, I'm pretty sure that this is worse.

"Do they tape your friends?" I ask.

This is a perfectly legitimate question. I need to know if I will be expected to play any part in this nonsense so that I can conveniently be out of town when it happens. Julie shakes her head at me.

"No. I mean, maybe. It depends on what we decide to use as our pre-baby event. If I have them come to a party, then yeah, I guess you might be on tape. But I don't think I would want to do that. I think I'd rather do something private, just me and Jon. Don't you think that that would be better?"

"I think it all sounds crazy, but that's just me." I realize that I have hurt her feelings, and we both peruse the menu in silence.

I have no idea what to order for dinner. I really don't want pasta again, but nothing else appeals to me anymore. Ever since the chicken incident I have been repulsed by all forms of poultry. And fish. And virtually all red meat except for really well-done hamburgers with lots and lots of ketchup. Oh, and mangoes. Mangoes make me gag. Something about the texture, I think. Okay, I guess it's going to be pasta again.

I shut my menu and look back up at Julie.

I should just let it go. I should use this natural break in the conversation to move on and change the subject. I should tell Julie all about what happened with Shorty today, or about what an insensitive jerk my husband is, or about my now-permanent bulge. But I can't. I just can't.

"I just find the whole idea of childbirth to be disgusting," I say. "I don't know why you would want the whole world to see you looking so . . . I don't know . . . so *primitive.*"

Julie looks at me like I just told her that I will be having the grilled, boneless filet of baby for dinner.

"I *love* that it's primitive," she says, sounding deeply offended. "I think it's beautiful. You know, when you take away the money and the clothes and the jewelry and the hair coloring and everything else, we're just the same as cavewomen, and childbirth is the only thing that reminds us of that anymore. I wish that I were strong enough to do it without drugs. I admire those women who have natural childbirth. It's so real. I mean, think about it: Women have been having babies the same way for thousands of years. It's amazing. It's a miracle."

Yeah, yeah. Miracle, schmiracle.

"Well, I don't buy it," I say. "For thousands of years doctors did amputations without anything but a shot of brandy and some wood to bite down on, but I don't see people lining up for that procedure. Plus, you can't tell me that if someone had offered a cavewoman a warm bed and an epidural that she wouldn't have taken it in a heartbeat. I mean, come on, you have to admit that having a baby is a little bit gross."

I realize that Andrew and Jon have stopped talking, and that the restaurant has all of a sudden gotten very quiet just as I am yelling this deeply held conviction at the top of my lungs. People at nearby tables are staring at me, obviously wondering why this mean, chubby woman would berate an innocent pregnant lady about childbirth like that. Andrew places his forearms on the edge of the table and buries his face in them.

"But," I say loudly, for all to hear, "that's just my opinion. Obviously you can do whatever you want."

I think that I may be wearing Julie down. She usually just gives me a pity smile when I say obnoxious things to her—*Oh, you poor, misguided girl, you don't really think that*—but this time she looks like she's actually kind of mad. Oh—no, forget it. There's the pity smile.

"You know, Lara," she says. "They say that happy mommies make happy babies. You would be so much better off if you just surrendered to this and accepted it for what it is. The more you fight it, the angrier and more stressed out you're going to be, and I really believe that babies can pick up on that from inside the womb."

Oh, puh-lease. Like that est shit is going to work on me.

"Well," I say, "since I will never surrender, I guess I'm just going to have one grumpy-assed baby, aren't I?"

Andrew picks his head up to shake it at me, and I give him a look that says, *Do not even attempt to pass judgment on me right now or you* will *be sorry.* He turns his gaze up toward the ceiling, as if to ask God why he must be put through these trials over and over and over again.

But you know, maybe Julie's right. Maybe I am predisposing my child to a lifetime of orneriness. Like, the apples don't fall far from the tree and all of that jazz. To be fair, though, you can't help what kind of a tree you are. I mean, Julie is a Golden Delicious tree; that's obvious. And Jon's a little blander, maybe a Macintosh. Andrew is probably a Granny Smith— good, but a little tart for some people's tastes—and I, of course, I am a crabapple tree. No question about that one. I wonder what you get when you cross-pollinate a Granny Smith with a crabapple? God, I'm going to have tart little crabapples lying around at my feet, aren't I?

Okay, I'm making a midyear resolution. From now on, for the sake of my unborn child and my own future sanity, I'm going to make an effort to be nice. Or at least nic*er*. It can't be that hard.

11.

It's Not Easy
Being Mean

Okay, so the nice thing is harder than I thought. I actually did pretty well for most of the day yesterday. Of course, Andrew played golf all day and I sat home by myself and read a book, but still, I noticed a marked improvement in my thoughts. Even this morning I was doing great. Andrew was still sleeping when I left, so I woke him up by gently brushing his hair and giving him little baby kisses—I'm sure he thinks it was a dream—and I got in the car and I even waved to my neighbor across the street who was outside putting something in her mailbox.

But then the line to get onto the freeway was three miles long, and it took me almost twenty five minutes to even get in view of the on-ramp, and when there were only two cars ahead of me and I was finally about to start moving again, some guy in an SUV came up out of nowhere on my left and edged his way in front of me—which really is so rude, because why should he not have to wait his turn like everyone else?—and so, for the rest of the time that we were in line, I laid on my horn and gave him the finger until I caught myself and remembered that nice people don't do things like that; a nice person would have waved him into the line instead of yelling, *No way, no way, asshole,* and almost getting hit trying to keep him out. So then when I finally got on the freeway, I decided to try to redeem myself and to make amends—you know, to let bygones be bygones—so I pulled up next to the guy and waved and smiled, but he thought that I was still harassing him, so then he gave me the finger, and then I rolled down my window and started screaming at him about how nice it must be to be better than everyone else and to not have to ever wait in line, except that I think I may have punctuated my speech with a few obscenities that probably should not be repeated.

But except for that minor relapse, I did well all morning—I said hello to everyone and I smiled and I was really on a roll—until about ten o'clock, when one of my kids came in with an absolutely atrocious essay that contained every single faux pas that I have, at least a million times, warned them against making. And after I read it, I was so annoyed that I snapped at him and asked him if he thinks that I just say things because I'm kidding or if he just thinks that I have no idea what I am talking about when it comes to college admissions. But then I remembered that I am nice now, so I apologized and sat him down and calmly went over it with him again, and even though I caught him staring out the window six different times, I didn't say anything or even clap my hands in front of his face to get his attention, which I think was really nice, all things considered.

And then, after he left, I even sat down and took a minute to try to analyze why this made me so angry—because nice people don't just fly off the handle for no reason; there must be an underlying cause—and I came to the conclusion that I wasn't angry with him at all, but that he just happened to represent everything that I am really starting to hate about my job, which is, namely, the fact that it *never* changes.

Yeah, every year the kids are different, you know, genetically, but with a few exceptions, they're all more or less the same. Year after year, they all have the same extracurricular activities—camp counselor! Honors Society tutor! Prom Committee Cochair! Year after year, they all want to go to the same colleges—Penn! GW! Michigan! Emory! And, year after year, they all end up writing the same boring, predictable college essays.

What book, fiction or nonfiction, has been the most meaningful to you? Why, that standard junior year curriculum classic, *The Catcher in the Rye*, of course! (Or, for the shallower, more materialistic crowd, *The Great Gatsby*.)

Who has been the most inspirational person in your life? Why, my grandfather, who else? He came here from *[poor, foreign country]* with nothing but twenty dollars in his pocket and now he's a successful *[doctor, business owner, antique rug dealer, television producer]* whom everyone looks up to and admires!

How are you making a difference in the world? Why, I spend three hours every six months serving nasty food to scary shoeless people because my school makes me fulfill a stupid community service requirement, but thank God that they do, because now I have something to write about for this essay!

Every now and then I'll get an AP English kid who comes up with something new, but nine times out of ten it's the same old story. Even their crises are the same—*I mailed my application to Arizona State five weeks ago and they still don't have it! I retook my SATs and I went down thirty points! I want to go away to college but my parents are making me stay in state because it's cheaper!*

Yes, nothing changes all that much in the world of private school college counseling, where kids grow like weeds among the Los Angeles sprawl, never experiencing any setbacks except for an occasional rain shower and multiple divorces.

The irony of it, of course, is that the predictability of my job is exactly what appealed to me about it in the first place. Having been a lawyer, where every day could potentially turn into an all-nighter and unforeseen contingencies lurked around every corner, I loved the idea that it was so easy and consistent. But lately it's been getting to me. I don't know if it's because my personal life is so out of whack now or what, but I'm starting to wonder if I might not be wasting my own Ivy League education on all of this unoriginality.

Plus, I'm finding it very difficult to get my work done this year. I just can't seem to concentrate on anything but me and how the goings-on in my uterus are affecting me. I spend hours of potentially productive work time scouring the Your Baby site for relevant pregnancy information. Seriously, I have spent entire mornings plugging different height and weight combinations into the Your Baby pregnancy weight gain calculator (e.g., if I am five feet, seven inches [which I am in shoes], and weighed 126.4 before I got pregnant [which I did for about five minutes back in June, after two weeks of being really, really, really good about not eating carbs], then I should gain approximately thirty pounds, which I suppose is okay but is still more than I wanted to gain. But if, however, I am five feet, six-and-a-quarter inches, and weighed 129.8 before I got pregnant [which I am not saying is true, but is just a random combination that I was testing], then I will gain approximately thirty-four pounds, which is totally unacceptable and almost sent me into cardiac arrest), and entire afternoons reading article after article about things like how to ease nausea, what sleeping positions are best for your back, and what questions to ask your obstetrician at your monthly checkups.

And then, of course, I keep thinking that if I'm like this now, when I'm only pregnant, what I am I going to be like once the baby is born and I have an actual child to obsess about? How will I ever get anything done?

I don't want to quit, though. Not that I even could, mind you. Andrew started another new business back in January (his third since graduating from college), and we need my income, at least until things are more stable with his company. It's something about the startup phase, and reinvesting profits to generate more cash flow—I don't know; I try to pay attention, but I always lose interest when he starts walking me through his spreadsheet projections, so I never quite get the full story—but it doesn't matter, because I don't want to quit. Despite my semiregular fantasies about becoming a housewife and living a life of Julie-like leisure, I really can't imagine my life without work, even if it is boring work. Plus, if I had nothing to do all day, I'd probably develop an addiction to painkillers, or get involved in a platonic yet dangerously flirtatious online affair with some stranger whom I'd meet in a *New York Times* Sunday crossword puzzle chat room, or God knows what else.

But at the same time—okay, and this is where it gets a little scary, because while the sentiments that I am about to share are completely out of character for me, they are there, deeply and firmly rooted and *there*—I don't want to work full-time and have someone else raise my kid while I'm at the office all day, because we've all seen the made-for-TV movies about what happens to children like that. You know how it goes. It starts off kind of funny, but a little bit pathetic—like, the kid got tired of eating TV dinners every night, so she taught herself how to cook gourmet meals by the age of eight (as illustrated by a montage of images showing her in various places—her bedroom, on the school bus, in the bathroom— always with her nose buried behind *The Joy of Cooking*—and then sitting at a kid-sized table, sharing her delicious four-course meals with her dolls, who are propped up in the other chairs with plastic china place settings in front of them).

When there's a PTA bake sale at school, she covers for her mom by making a three-layer rum cake all by herself (chosen because she thinks that the rum makes it sophisticated and adultlike and nothing that anyone would ever suspect was made by a child), because she knows that there is no way that Mommy will ever have the time or the memory required to bake something from scratch, and she would rather die a slow death than show up with a box of Entenmann's chocolate-covered doughnuts like she did last year.

But then, by the time she turns fourteen, it's not really funny anymore, because now she's hanging out with older guys and doing hits of E at her house after school just because she can, yet all the while fully functioning and still maintaining her A average so as not to alert any of her teachers, or—yeah, right—her parents. And then, finally, one day in the middle of senior year, just when the oblivious, self-absorbed, career-ladder-climbing mother is starting to think that she's home free, that she's somehow made it through adolescence without dropping any of the balls that she's been keeping in the air for the last eighteen years, the Spanish-speaking cleaning woman (who loves this child like she is her *own*) is the only one who even realizes that Jenny (it's always Jenny) didn't come home after school, and Mom sheepishly tells the police that Jenny was supposed to be at soccer practice or play rehearsal or whatever extracurricular activity Jenny was lying to her about being involved in, but when she called the soccer coach or the drama teacher she learned that, no, Jenny hasn't shown up for months, we thought you knew, and so now she is missing.

And only then does the mother give Jenny her undivided attention, posting flyers on telephone poles and spending the wee hours of the morning cruising the parts of the city where you have to drive with your doors locked, until finally, by some one-in-a-million, totally chance encounter with a young homeless boy outside of a 7-Eleven that she just happened to run into to get some coffee, she finds her, living in a cardboard box, strung out on drugs, begging people for change or for their leftover pizza crusts, with the unspoken but very obvious implication that she has been prostituting herself.

And so the mother cradles her in her arms and takes her home, and vows through her tears to quit her job and never leave Jenny's side again, because obviously the only possible reason why this could ever have happened is because she chose her career over her child, and we, the predominantly female, eighteen-to-thirty-four-year-old audience, are left shaking our heads about what an enormous mistake that turned out to be.

So you see, it seems to me that the only solution is to work part-time once the baby is born. I think that it's a perfect compromise. It'll make things here less boring, and I'll still get to spend quality time with the baby. And I'll be able to go to the gym. I mean, really, if I work five days, when am I supposed to go to the gym? How could I ever justify my horribleness if I spent eight hours away from my baby and then went and worked out for another hour and a half right afterward?

I'm thinking that three days a week would be good, but I'd be willing to take four if that's all I can get. Of course, I'll still have to have some kind of a babysitter on the days that I'm home, so that I'll be able to get work done if I need to, but I'm pretty sure that part-time is the only way to go.

And that, my friends, is exactly what I am going to propose to Linda this afternoon, although without the part about going to the gym and with much more emphasis on the part about spending quality time with the baby.

The phone rings.

"College Counseling, this is Lara Stone," I say.

"Hi, Lara, it's Cheryl Gardner." *Cheryl. My, my, my.* I've sent her two or three e-mails to let her know what's been going on with Tick lately (*Hi, Cheryl—Tick registered for her SATs this week. Hi, Cheryl—Tick decided that she's going to apply to NYU, USC, Trinity, and U. Conn. Hi, Cheryl—Tick decided on an essay topic today for NYU*), but this is the first time that I've actually spoken to her since our falling-out back on the first day of school.

"Hi, Cheryl," I say cautiously. *Nice. Remember to be nice.*

"Listen, Lara," she says. "I have to come over to school this morning for a Parents Association Meeting, so I was wondering if I could come meet with you first for a few minutes. I just want to touch base with you about where things are, and ask a few questions, if you don't mind."

"Sure!" I say. "I'm open all morning." I am the queen of niceness. I am Miss Congeniality.

"Great. I'm on my way to Coffee Bean now, and then I'll be over."

When she arrives, at ten twenty, she is all Marc Jacobs and Stella McCartney, with silver glam aviator sunglasses perched atop her freshly colored blond hair, a magnificent, deep-purple Birkin bag swinging from her arm, and two large coffees in her hands. *Shit.* I can't drink coffee.

She hands one of the cups to me and puts the other one on her side of my desk, and I stand up to greet her.

"Thanks for the coffee; that was so sweet of you, but I . . ."

She looks me up and down and then puts her hand over mouth, Betty Boop–like. "Oh, my God, you're pregnant, aren't you?"

Oh, no. Is it that obvious? Does everyone at school know and is just pretending not to? Does Linda know? "Um, no, I mean, do I look pregn—"

She puts her hands up to indicate that I can stop stammering. "What are you, fourteen, fifteen weeks?" I nod, stunned by her accuracy. She sits down on one of the chairs in front of my desk, and crosses her arms as if she is extraordinarily satisfied with herself. "I used to do the billing for an ob/gyn before I met Stefan. I can usually call it to the day. It's a gift."

Huh. So she has held a job. And one that requires actual thinking. Who knew?

"It's very impressive," I say. "But nobody around here knows yet, so if you wouldn't mind . . ."

She smiles and pretends to zipper her lips shut. "Don't worry; I won't tell a soul." She takes my coffee and removes it from its place in front of me. "I guess you can't have this, then."

"No," I say, "I guess not." I give her a wistful smile as she dumps it in the trash, and I open my file drawer and pull Tick's file from it. But Cheryl, apparently, is not quite over my pregnancy revelation.

"I *love* babies," she says. "It's the best time in your life, when your kids are young. . . . God, I haven't been around a baby in years. It's just so great. You have this little, perfect, helpless thing that needs you and loves you and only wants to be with you." She stops for a moment and sighs, then shakes her head sorrowfully. "It goes by so fast. One day it's 'Mommy, Mommy, Mommy,' and then before you know it, they're slamming the bedroom door in your face and telling you to leave them the fuck alone."

I don't quite know what to say to this—I'm thinking that *Well, maybe if you made your kid feel like you gave a shit about her she wouldn't be quite so hostile* isn't really appropriate, so I decide to go with self-deprecating humor.

"Yeah, well, at least you got a good thirteen or fourteen years out of her. I'm pretty sure my baby will be saying, 'Mommy, I hate you' by the time we leave the hospital."

"No, no," she says, "you'll make a great mom. The kids here adore you. Tick just loves you." She pauses and shifts in her seat uncomfortably. "I'm sorry about what happened the last time we spoke. I just . . . She shuts me out of everything, and it's so hard because I've always had the best relationship with my mother—I still do—and I always thought I'd have that with my own daughter. . . ." She sighs again and then waves away whatever she was thinking. "Anyway, I didn't mean to take it out on you. It's just difficult to see her open up to other people."

Apology accepted, I think. It's about six weeks late, but I'll take it.

"Don't worry about it," I say. "You're not the only one. I see this with so many families, but as soon as the kids move out and go to college, all of a sudden they love their parents again. It'll pass."

"Well," she says, "we'll see." She has definitely opened up to me more than she intended to. I should change the subject before she changes her attitude.

"So," I say, opening up Tick's file. "What did you want to meet about?"

Cheryl proceeds to inform me that she did some asking around, and that she learned that the children of many prominent entertainment people have attended, or currently do attend, NYU, and that, despite its unfavorable spot in the rankings, it must, therefore, not be such a bad school after all.

Upon making this determination, she then arranged for Tick and Stefan to have a long talk about college (which I already know, because Tick came into my office, frantic, the day before said long talk was scheduled to take place), and that, after giving him several good reasons why she wants to go to NYU (which reasons I myself devised in preparation for said long talk) and showing him a list of prestigious and successful NYU graduates who were not prestigious and/or successful before entering NYU (which list I provided, to further bolster her case), Stefan agreed to let her go there, should she be admitted (which I also already know, because Tick came in the day after her talk with him, elated, and profusely thanked me for my help, without which she never could have convinced him).

And then Cheryl proceeds to inform me that the Gardner family is willing to make a donation in order to seal the deal (which I did not know and, in fact, am quite shocked to learn). So much for Tick doing this herself, and not feeling like she bought her way in.

"Well," I say, taking in this new piece of information. "That could change everything."

Cheryl smiles, already very well aware of the fact that tossing around large sums of money usually does effect change. "Yes," she says. "So what I want to know is how we go about this."

By *this*, I assume she means trading cash for a spot in next year's freshman class. I flip through my Rolodex and pull out the business card of the guy at NYU who reads the applications from Los Angeles. His name is Ed Jellette, and he's a good friend of mine. In fact, the only good thing about Tick's choosing NYU is the fact that I actually know someone there with pull.

"There should be a development office or an office of gift planning or something like that, but I don't have a contact there. If you call this guy"— I tap Ed's card—"he can put you in touch with the right person. Just tell him that I referred you to him and that you're interested in making a gift." I hand her the card and she snatches it from me.

"Great," she says. She looks at the clock and tells me that she has to run to her meeting, and blows a kiss at me. "Thanks, Lara, you're a doll." As she is walking out the door, she turns to me again and eyeballs my stomach. "You know, you really should tell Linda soon. She's going to figure it out for herself if you wait much longer."

Right, I think. *Thanks.*

The door to Linda's office is half-open, and she is sitting behind her desk with her back to me, furiously typing on the computer. I lightly, timidly knock on the door, and she spins around in her seat, glancing first at me and then at the clock. I was exactly on time for our appointment, but I waited outside her office for three minutes before knocking so as not to appear overanxious. She waves me inside.

"Come in, come in. Have a seat." I sit down in one of the chairs across from her desk, and she gives me a perplexed look. "You look different. Have you lost weight?" God, I must really be fat.

It just occurs to me that Linda does not have children. Actually, I don't know if she does or not, but if she does, she never talks about them. I think she's been divorced for something like twenty years. I look around at the pictures in her office, but they're all of her and the same three girlfriends standing in front of various landmarks around the world. Yes, definitely no children. Which is kind of weird for someone who's in charge of running a high school. You know, I think that if Linda and I were the same age, we could have been really good friends. She would *love* Stacey.

"No," I say, laughing nervously. "I didn't lose weight. Actually, that's kind of why I'm here. I'm pregnant." The blood drains from her face.

"Please do not tell me that you're leaving."

Ooh. Fear. That's a good sign.

"No, no. I'm not leaving. And I'm due in April, so I won't even be missing that much of the school year. I planned it very well." Linda exhales and smiles.

"Oh, thank God. Well, in that case, congratulations! What wonderful news!"

This is just about the fakest congratulations that I have ever received. She might as well have said, *Great job on ruining your life,* or *Good luck with the little shit.*

"Thanks," I say. I smile at her, and cross and uncross my legs. "So I was hoping that maybe we could talk about some kind of an arrangement for next year."

She raises her eyebrows at me. "An arrangement? What kind of an arrangement?"

I unfold a piece of paper that I have been concealing in my hand. I have typed up a proposal for her of exactly what I want, and I hand it to her across the desk. She takes it and reads it over for a few minutes. When she's finished, she looks up at me, her eyebrows still raised.

"So you're asking for three days a week next year? Is that right?"

"No," I say. "Not really. I'm asking if I can *come in* three days a week, but I'll work from home the other two days, and I'll still do everything that I normally do. I won't need anyone to cover for me the other two days or anything like that."

Linda looks back at my proposal and begins to shake her head. "I don't know, Lara. I don't know how it would look if our director of college counseling only worked part-time. It might send the message that we're not serious about our college placements. I'm not sure the board of trustees would go for it."

No, no, no. This is not going as planned. She's supposed to tell me that she can't live without me and that of course I can work part-time if that's what it will take to keep me happy.

"But the colleges won't have to know that I'm not there, and I'll take phone calls at home—I can transfer my phone so that it rings right in my house—it'll be just like I'm at school. You know that I can handle this. I can do this job with my eyes closed. I wouldn't be asking if I didn't think that I could make it work." She still looks unconvinced. I think I'm going to have to pull out the big guns. I'm going to have to remind her that we have a debt to settle.

"Linda, I have always gone above and beyond the call of duty for you. I have always done whatever you needed me to do, whenever you needed it. All I'm asking for in return is that you let me spend a little extra time with my baby."

Linda pushes out her cheek with her tongue. She knows exactly what I'm talking about.

"And where are things with Victoria Gardner?" she asks.

What? That's it? She's just going to change the subject without even giving me an answer? "Can we talk about that later? I'd like to resolve this—"

"No. This will help us resolve it. What's happening with her?"

I have no idea what she's getting at here, and I must look as bewildered as I sound. "I guess she's fine. I meet with her every week or so, and she wants to go to NYU next year."

"Do you think she can get in?"

I still don't see the relevance in this and I am getting really annoyed. I sigh, loudly. "Not on her own, no, but I have a strong contact in the admissions office, and it looks like her parents are willing to donate, so she's probably got a good shot."

Linda looks pleased by this. "Okay. Here's the deal. You get Victoria into NYU, and I'll let you have your three days a week. Her father sits on the board, and if she gets in, I'll make sure he knows that you're to thank for it. If he's happy, I can guarantee you that they'll agree to whatever you want. But if she gets rejected, I don't see how I can ask him to do you any favors next year. Do you see what I mean?"

Oh, no. This is so not okay. This is wrong. This is unethical. This is definitely not nice. I'm not supposed to have any self-interest in whether a student gets into a college or not. That would give me an incentive to lie, or to push for her more than my other students, or to call in serious favors with Ed. . . .

"It's a deal." I stand up and shake her hand, and Linda flashes me a coy smile. Okay, so I'm not nice. Deal with it. Did you really think that I could stick to that act for much longer anyway? It's not that bad, though. I mean, her parents are donating, for God's sake. She'll get in with or without me. And besides, I'm doing this for the good of my baby. There's got to be something inherently nice about that, right? Right?

12.

Sticks and Stones
May Break My Bones,
But Baby Names
Will Kill Me

As part of my never-surrender, fight-to-the-death plan for pregnancy, I've been working out like a fiend for the last two weeks. Now that I'm into my second trimester and I have my energy back, I figure that I might as well channel it into a good cause. I've been taking step classes on Mondays and Wednesdays after work (modified to avoid jumping, but still an excellent cardio and overall leg workout), and I just got back from the tone and sculpt class that I've been taking on Saturday mornings while Stacey has been out of town. I'm convinced that if I keep lifting weights, I won't get those pregnant-woman sausage arms. And, contrary to a certain stupid pregnancy book that says that you should just embrace your fatness and stop exercising because it's not worth the risk to the baby, my doctor says it's fine. In fact, as long as I skip the sit-ups at the end and keep an eye on my heart rate, he thinks it's downright great.

My doctor is very LA, by the way. Mid-fifties, very hip, drives a Carerra (I know because I always see it in the spot that says *Reserved for Dr. Lowenstein* in the office parking lot), lots of thick, black, JFK Jr.–type hair. He's got a few celebrity clients (mostly B- and C-list actors from sitcoms that aired on Friday nights in the eighties and early nineties), and he's a got a wall of their signed headshots proudly displayed in his office (*To Dr. Lowenstein, Thanks for the TLC! Love, Erin Moran*). I'd lay odds that he's writing a screenplay.

I throw my keys down on the kitchen counter and hit play on the answering machine. God, my triceps are still on fire from that class. The first message is from Andrew.

"Hi, Dolly, it's me. My tee time got changed and I didn't get off until eleven, so I probably won't be home until six. Don't be mad, okay? Love you." Did I mention that I hate golf? Next.

"This is the reservation center. Congratulations! You've been selected to win a free Hawaiian cruise! To accept your prize, please—" Delete. That national Do Not Call list is such a load of crap. I feel like the telemarketers just use it to get even more phone numbers. Next.

"Hi, it's Stacey. The movie finally wrapped, so I'm back. Real Mexicans have nothing on Taco Bell, by the way. Can we hike tomorrow? I'll see you at eight thirty unless I hear from you." Oh, we are definitely on. I could use one more cardio day, and it'll be really good for my butt. Nice.

As I hit the delete button, I suddenly remember that Stacey hasn't seen me in six weeks and has no idea that I'm pregnant. I have to warn her. I can't just show up to our hike with a person in my stomach unannounced—it'll completely freak her out.

I pick up the phone and dial her office. It's Saturday, but she's definitely there.

"This is Stacey."

"Hi! Welcome back."

"Oh, shit, don't tell me you can't go tomorrow. I really need to go. I haven't seen daylight in weeks."

"No, I'm going, I'm going. I can't wait. I just need to talk to you first." She hesitates. "What's wrong? Did I do something?"

"You didn't do anything. There's just something I have to tell you, and it can't wait until tomorrow." Oh, she's going to think I'm such a sellout. Maybe if I put on a really cheery voice she won't yell at me. "I'm pregnant!" I yell with as much cheer as I can muster.

"What? You're what? I can't believe you. You are so soft. How could you let yourself get manipulated like that?"

"I'll take that as a congratulations. Thank you."

"Whatever. You know it's true. How the hell are you going to be a mother? Aren't mothers supposed to be nice?"

"I can be nice. You've just never seen it because you bring out the worst in me. In fact, I've been making an effort to be nicer. Lots of people think I'm nice."

She snorts. "Yeah? Name one." I have to think about this for a minute. Andrew, no. My mom, no. Linda, no. Various former boyfriends and sorority sisters to whom I no longer speak, no. Zoey! Zoey must think that I'm nice. Oh, but she's not a person. Not really, anyway. Julie. I'll have to go with Julie.

"Julie thinks that I'm nice."

Stacey scoffs at this. "No, she doesn't. Julie thinks that you have the *potential* to be nice, so she's taken you on as a charity case, to try to reform you."

Huh. I've always wondered why Julie was friends with me, but that is not a reason that I had thought of. It makes sense, though. Puts the pity smile in a whole new light.

"Look, it doesn't matter. It's done, I'm having a baby, and I can't undo it now, so you might as well be happy for me."

"Fine. I'm thrilled for you, okay? Just do me a favor—don't ever talk to me about poopy diapers or how cute it is when the kid spits up. I can't deal with that new-parent crap."

"I swear to God, sometimes I think you're hiding a penis under those pantsuits. Don't worry; I'll never talk to you about baby stuff—I promise."

"Good." She pauses. "So you can still go hiking when you're pregnant?"

"According to my doctor, I can hike until the very end. I'll see you tomorrow."

"Oh, my God, you're huge."

After spending six weeks out of the country, this is the first thing that she has to say to me. I should introduce her to my dog. I'm sure they'd get along famously.

"I am not huge. I'm still wearing most of my regular clothes."

She carefully inspects me from head to toe. "Well, you're huge for you. And your arms look fat."

I knew it. My arms are always the first place that I gain weight. I'm going to have to step up the weight lifting to two days a week. "Can we go?" I ask.

We start toward the trail in silence. I have so many pregnancy-related things that I want to complain about, but I'm not going to give her the satisfaction of thinking that I've changed and that I can only talk about babies now.

"So," I finally say. "How was the movie?"

She rolls her eyes. "It was a disaster. The lead actors hated each other, and they were complaining the whole time about how this one got a bigger trailer, and that one got to have special food prepared. It was awful. And the crew was mostly Mexican, and half of them didn't speak English, so the director was constantly having to explain things to them. Don't ask. It was horrible."

"Mm. Sorry, that sucks." Another long silence. Then Stacey pipes up again.

"So when do you find out?"

I have no idea what she's talking about. "Find out what?"

"If it's a boy or a girl. You are finding out, right?"

Oh, I know what she's doing. She feels bad about yesterday, so she's pretending to be interested. This is exactly what I did to Julie when she told me about her baby, remember? It's a nice gesture, but I don't need her to do me any favors.

"Look, you don't have to act like you care about this. I know how you feel about it, so we can just talk about other things. It's fine."

"I don't care about it, and I fully intend to talk about other things. But since you're having it, I'd like to at least know what it's going to be. So when do you find out?"

Fine. If she wants to make herself feel better, I'll be the bigger person and let her. "In three weeks. November twenty-second."

"Do you have a preference?"

Of course I have a preference. I really, really, really want a boy, if for no other reason than because girls scare me. Think about it—it's a much safer bet that I won't completely screw up a boy. I figure that I'm significantly less likely to be blamed for eating disorders or bad relationships or general insecurities twenty years from now, and, despite the double standard from which it stems, there will simply be much less worrying involved with a boy, and that is always a plus for me.

Andrew, by the way, is praying for a boy. Not because he's afraid of girls, the way I am, but because he's just dying for someone to play sports with. He played baseball in college, and he can hardly contain his excitement about going to Dodgers games and buying little baby baseballs, and fulfilling his own failed dreams by training the kid for the majors while he's still in utero. You think I'm kidding. I told Andrew about something I read on the Your Baby Web site—about how the father is supposed to speak to the baby so that it gets used to his voice from inside the womb—and now he spends forty-five minutes every night outlining the rules of baseball to my belly button.

The only kink in his grand master plan is genetics. He's absolutely petrified that the kid will take after my side of the family. You see, as far as coordination goes, my family members are somewhere between not and not at all. For example, my father doesn't like to sweat, which means that he will exert himself only enough to get out of the heat and into an air-conditioned room. It takes my mother about twenty minutes just to get from a sitting to a standing position, and my brother is a tall, lanky guy who majored in art history and whose childhood dream was to become a museum curator. He played sports as a kid, but he played more because it was something that everyone else did than because he really enjoyed them or because he was very good at them, which he wasn't. He was always much better at drawing, and that makes Andrew very, very nervous.

Last week Andrew actually tested him. My brother moved to LA a few years ago, and we usually see him about once a month for dinner, but last week Andrew called him up out of the blue and invited him to an afternoon game of tennis. This was, by the way, inherently unfair from the start. My brother hasn't played tennis since he stopped going to summer camp when he was fourteen years old, and Andrew plays in a weekly game that usually ends with someone furiously breaking a racket. Anyway, three hours and seven sets later, Andrew won forty-two games in a row and was completely freaking out. He called me from the car in a panic.

"I have serious concerns about the athletic ability of our child," he said. "Your brother has no hand–eye coordination whatsoever and he is really slow. Plus, he is lazy and totally uncompetitive. He didn't even care that I was beating him."

This, by the way, for Andrew, is much more important than the actual athletic prowess that my brother may or may not possess. Whether one gives his best is how Andrew determines whether that person is a true athlete. I know this because of Zoey. A few months after they started their agility class, Andrew got cocky and signed them up for a competition. They got up at six o'clock in the morning on a Sunday and drove for two hours to a town called Filmore, where they then waited five more hours for their turn to have a single two-minute run on the agility course. But when their names were finally called, Zoey choked. Instead of running the course, she ran off the field and hid under someone's lawn chair, and they got disqualified. The entire two-hour drive home, Andrew was furious. I will never forget the phone call I got after it was over.

"I am so disappointed in her," he moaned.

"Honey," I told him, "she's just a dog."

But he could not be dissuaded from believing that Zoey is, at heart, a quitter with no drive to succeed. He was devastated by the fact that she didn't take pride in her performance, and after the tennis match, that's exactly how he felt about my brother.

"Honestly, Andrew," I said to him. "Did you just play with him so that you could assess his athleticism?"

"Yeah. Did you really think that I thought your brother would be a challenging opponent? I just wanted to see how bad it really was, and it's bad. We'd better hope that our son gets my athletic gene or we are in serious trouble."

It was then that I realized that we can't win. No matter what gender our child is, one of us is bound to turn him or her into a basket case eventually. But hell, let it be a boy so that at least Andrew can take the blame when Junior needs therapy because he wasn't named Little League MVP when he was eight. Fine with me.

I don't want to jinx anything by saying it out loud, though, so I just give Stacey the old party line. "I don't really care, as long as it's healthy."

She rolls her eyes at me. "I knew you'd say that. It's so annoying."

I roll my eyes back at her.

"Well, do you at least have names?" she asks.

Ah, the dreaded question. I really don't want to talk about it now. Not with her. Especially not with her. If I talk about it, I will definitely cry. I must change the subject.

"Let's talk about nonbaby things, okay? Tick is applying to NYU early decision, and her dad is even going to make a donation. You were such a big help, you have no idea." It's too late, though. She can sniff out fresh blood like a buzzard.

"That's great, but why did you dodge my question about the names? Don't tell me you're going to be one of those people who keeps it a secret until the baby is born. I will never speak to you again if you do that."

It's clear that I am not going to be able to get out of this. I haven't been a lawyer for five years, and my negotiating skills are no match for hers. Fine. *Fine.*

"Fine." I take a deep breath. "I have names, but I can't use them." *Don't cry, Lara. Do not cry.*

"Why not?"

I exhale loudly. "Because my names do not work."

Stacey cocks her head to one side. "Why, what are your names?" she asks.

"If you must know, they are Brook and Jade."

"Those are both girl names."

"B-R-O-O-K for a boy, Jade for a girl." I had a really good guy friend from high school named Brook whom I adored, and it's been my boy name since I was sixteen years old. Jade came later. In college, I think. I know it's popular now, but I've always loved it.

Stacey looks confused, as I knew she would.

"I don't understand. I mean, Brook sounds a little gay for a boy, but what's the problem?"

Oh, here we go. "Stone," I say. "Our last name is Stone. See the problem?"

"Brook Stone, Jade Stone." Stacey starts cracking up. "Oh, my God, no way. That is so fucking hilarious. What are the odds?"

Yeah, yeah, tell me about it. It breaks down like this: Brook Stone is simply a ridiculous name. There are no two ways about it. He'll go through his entire life with people asking him if he's got any personal massagers or travel alarm clocks handy. And Jade Stone? A total stripper name. You might as well buy her a pole for her sixteenth birthday.

Believe me, I have spent countless nights lying in bed, desperately trying to rationalize how I can get away with it. I've heard the urban legend about the people with the last name Pig who named their kids Ima and Ura. I went to high school with a guy who, born in the seventies, was named Tony Orlando, and it was always my greatest wish that he would date a girl named Dawn. But surely I cannot be one of those people who would do something like that to my children. I just don't think that I have the heart to go through with it.

Stacey, by the way, is stopped in the middle of the trail, bent over in hysterics. I cross my arms and shift my weight to one leg.

"If you fall down and roll off the side of this mountain, I am leaving you there to die."

She tries to catch her breath and wipes the tears from her eyes. "I know, I know, I'm sorry; it's just so funny." I ignore her and start walking again, but she runs to catch up to me. "Okay, I'm done. Sorry. Come on, let's try to think of some names." I am deliberately walking as fast as I can in order to stay ahead of her.

"I don't want to think of names. I'll figure it out myself." She is scrambling behind me, completely out of breath.

"Come on, I'm sorry. Ooh, listen, I thought of a good one. What about . . . what about Lime? Lime Stone? What do you think?" She breaks up again and I do my best to ignore her. "Just kidding, just kidding, wait, seriously, I have one, for real. If it's a boy, you could name him Fred." She hoots at herself. "And his middle name . . . his middle name could be"— she can't even get control of herself long enough to form the words—"it could be Flint."

"Ha, ha," I say, "you're a riot. Can we walk now?"

She is gasping for air and she shakes her head. "Oh, no, I've got it— oh, this is the best one, I promise. What about"—she is laughing so hard now that she is holding her stomach and snorting like a pig—"Rosetta! Rosetta Stone, get it?"

Yeah, I get it. Hilarious. She's her very own one-woman comedy troupe.

But it doesn't matter. None of it matters. The truth is that I couldn't have used my names anyway, even if they did work. Because of Jewish tradition, we have to name our baby after Andrew's father, whose name was Philip. Unlike most people, who name their children after themselves or living relatives or soap opera stars, Jews have to name their children after dead people. But in order to spare the next generation from having to run around with names like Saul, Sadie, Irving, and Phyllis, most people cheat. Most people name the baby something that nowhere even resembles the name of the deceased, and then the dead person's first name becomes the baby's middle name. Or, more often, the baby gets a middle name that starts with the same initial as the dead person's first name. Like, for example, if we were naming my baby after my grandmother, whose name was Ida, we clearly would not be naming our baby Ida. Instead, we would give her a cool first name and then make her middle name something with an I, like Ilene or Ilona. Since nobody cares about middle names, it doesn't matter if I don't love it, and I still get to name my baby whatever I want and say that my child is named after my grandmother.

But Andrew doesn't want me to cheat at all. We're, like, the least religious Jews this side of Israel, but when it comes to naming our baby, all of a sudden he's an Orthodox rebbe (well, he's not making me name the baby Philip if it's a boy—that would be grounds for divorce—but still). He's insisting that the baby's name has to start with a P and that the middle name has to start with a J, because his dad's middle name was Joel. The only concession that he's willing to make (but that he would strongly prefer that I not accept) is that if it's a girl, I can switch the order and use the J for her first name and the P for her middle name. So, yes, I suppose that I actually could have used Jade—how ironic, now let's move on.

Frankly, I think it's an outrage. I mean, choosing a name for your child is a huge decision. Probably one of the biggest decisions that you make as a parent, am I wrong? No, of course I'm not wrong. Your name is something that affects you every single day of your life. It speaks volumes about who you are, and, more important, about who your parents are. Let's be honest—people will judge me based on the names that I choose for my children, and having restrictions placed upon me like this is completely unfair and stifling to my creative process.

Of course, I've tried to explain all of this to Andrew, but he's holding firm. A P and a J. That's the deal. I wonder if I could put an asterisk next to the name, the way they did for Roger Maris's home run record. Like, on her driver's license it could say, for example, *Paula Julia* Stone.*

> ** Please note that Ms. Stone's mother was forced to begin Ms. Stone's names with the letters P and J, respectively, and therefore, the names Paula and Julia in no way represent Ms. Stone's mother's actual taste, personality, or sense of originality, but instead represent only the best that she could come up with under the circumstances.*

Yeah, that probably wouldn't work. Well, I'm just not going to worry about it until I know if it's a boy or a girl. There's no point in getting myself all worked up over male and female names when I'm only going to need one or the other. I'll just put it out of my head until I know for sure.

There. It's gone.

13.

She'll Be Poopin' on the Table When She Comes

So, I told everyone at school that I'm expecting. Linda announced it at the faculty meeting last week, and then I told my kids this morning at a workshop that I held on how to write a college résumé. But the kids didn't even care. All they wanted to know was whether I would be here next year in case they decide to transfer. Although Mark did come up to me afterward to ask if that's what was wrong with me that day. He looked greatly relieved to know what it was. But other than that, not a single question. They're way too busy with their own little dramas to worry about mine.

Unlike the teachers. As soon as they heard the news, I got accosted. All of a sudden, every random history or English teacher who had ever had a baby was my best friend. *When are you due? Is it a boy or a girl? Who's your doctor? How much weight have you gained?* That last one was shocking to me. I was like, *Look, people, just because I once ran in a three-legged relay race with you at faculty orientation does not mean that you are privy to highly personal information about my* weight, *okay?* For the record (and feel free to use it if you are ever in this situation), I tell people that I have gained "enough," just because I know that it is vague and unsatisfying and bitchy enough to convey my annoyance but not so bitchy as to alienate anyone permanently.

But, oh, the stuff that they say right in front of me! You would not even believe it. For example, yesterday I was in the teachers' lunchroom, totally minding my own business, when a group of foreign-language teachers came in. I guess my presence inspired them to wax nostalgic about their own pregnancies, because they started telling me the dumbest, most boring stories about fetal hiccups and acid reflux, and then the topic turned to how much weight they had gained. At first, they were only talking about themselves:

I was an absolute cow. I gained ninety pounds with my first one and I never was able to lose it all.

Oh, that's nothing. I was so bloated I couldn't wear any of my shoes for six months. I had to wear Birkenstocks the whole time because they were the only things that fit my feet.

Please. My butt got so big it was hard to tell whether I was carrying the baby in front or in my behind.

But then they all turned to look my way. The ringleader—I think she teaches French—looked right at me and said, *Lara, your butt hasn't gotten very big yet, has it?* And then she asked me to turn around so that she could see. Turn around so that she can assess the size of my butt! Of course, I declined, and said something about how I hadn't really noticed a difference, but no, that wasn't good enough for her; she had to find *something* about me to pick apart, so she kind of squinted at me and then said, *Well, your face is starting to fill out. You can really tell that you're pregnant by your face.* I was like, *Did she just tell me that my face is fat?* Because how rude is *that?* So, of course, now, on top of worrying about my fat arms, I also have to obsess over whether I have chipmunk cheeks and a double chin. I swear, some people have no concept of boundaries. They should take a lesson from the kids and learn a thing or two about being ambivalent and uninterested.

And speaking of ambivalent kids, Tick's hair is blond. Platinum blond. If it weren't for the squeaky combat boots and the ginormous bag, I wouldn't have even recognized her when she came into my office just now. It actually looks really good, though. She's got kind of a punk Marilyn Monroe thing going on, and it's much more flattering than that horrible black, Goth do that she had before.

"I like it," I say. "It's a good look for you."

She smiles at me. "Thanks. I hope you like the essay as much as you like the hair." She reaches across my desk and hands me two typed pages.

It's about time she got this to me. The early decision deadline for NYU is November fifteenth—just three days from now—and I've been bugging her for a rough draft for weeks. I really wasn't sure if she'd get everything together in time, but it looks like she actually did it. That is, assuming that the essay isn't completely horrible and that we don't have to spend the next three days rewriting it from scratch. I just don't know what to expect from her. I feel like it could go either way—she's either going to completely surprise me or utterly disappoint me. But at least her topic is good. None of that *Great Gatsby* or *Oh, I so admire my grandfather* crap. The question was: *Tell us about a person, place, or event that has particular meaning for you, and why.* As soon as I saw it, I knew immediately what she had to write about, and when I told her my idea she flipped. I just hope she didn't screw it up. I can't tell you how many times I've helped a kid come up with an amazing topic to write about, only to have them completely fuck it up in the execution.

I put the pages down on top of my desk and pull out a red pen. Tick bites her lower lip.

"Go easy on me," she says.

"Shh," I tell her. "Let me read it."

New York University Essay
Victoria Gardner

I will never forget the day that we moved into our new house. I was fourteen at the time, although my parents had been building and decorating it since I was twelve. My mom obsessed day and night about what color the curtains should be, and what kind of stone should go on the kitchen counters, but I didn't care about anything except for my bedroom. In our old house, my room was like a time capsule from 1986. It still had all of my baby furniture in it, and the walls were papered with barnyard animals. I couldn't wait to get into my new room, and I dreamed about how I would decorate it all by myself, how I would fill it with things that I love, until it was 100-percent, unmistakably mine.

When we pulled into the driveway that day, I was trembling with excitement. I burst out of the car and into the house, and ran up the stairs to the room that would be my refuge, my oasis, my shelter from the storm. I flung open the door, and, to my surprise, the room was already decorated. The floor was covered with thick pink carpeting, and the walls were stenciled with a border of pastel tulips. The white four-poster bed was smothered in a ruffly pink comforter, and topped with an eyelet-lace canopy. In the corner of the room was an antique wicker rocking chair covered in the same fabric as the comforter, and there were large framed sketches of girls holding bouquets of flowers on two of the walls.

I remember thinking that there must be some kind of a mistake. This couldn't be my room. Where were the dark purple walls and the vintage posters of early punk bands like the Ramones and the Sex Pistols? Where is the plastic lime-green retro chair, the oversize black beanbag and the Frank Lloyd Wright–style area rug that I had spent hours fantasizing about? Maybe they thought that this room was supposed to be a guest room, and my room was somewhere else. Maybe the decorator had mixed up her customers and had brought that stuff to the wrong house. There wasn't anything wrong with it—the furniture was nice, and the room was pretty—it just wasn't *me*. But when I ran downstairs to find my mom, I learned that there was no mistake. That was my room, and at that moment I realized that my mom knew nothing about me at all.

I pleaded with her to send everything back and to let me decorate it the way I wanted to, but she wouldn't hear of it. I knew right then and there that if I was going to make my room my own, I would have to find creative ways to do it. Over the next few months I scoured flea markets and record stores, I rummaged through countless garage sales, and I acquired a collection of tiny paintbrushes. Once I had everything that I needed, I went to work. The lace canopy came down and I put up a huge banner for the band Black Flag that I got for five dollars at a record store clearance sale. The pink carpet got covered with three white rugs that I found at the Salvation Army, which I partially dyed dark purple. I spent an entire weekend transforming every last pastel tulip into black skulls and crossbones, and I reupholstered the rocking chair with vintage rock T-shirts that I sewed together myself. Finally, the girls with the flowers got shoved under the bed, and I papered my walls with pictures of things that I love, like my band, my friends, and other musicians who inspire me.

When I was finally finished, I stood back and took it all in with pride. My mother was furious when she saw what I did, but at least now she knows who I am. Looking back, I'm actually glad that I didn't get to decorate it myself from the start. Because now my room not only reflects who I am and what I like, but it also rejects the notion of who I am supposed to be, and who my mom, and others, want me to be. By starting with something completely antithetical to my personality, my room is not just what I am, but also what I am not. There is no place in the world that is more meaningful to me than my bedroom.

When I finish reading it I have tears in my eyes. I look up and Tick is staring at me, waiting for a reaction.

"You think it still needs work, don't you?" she asks.

"No," I say, shaking my head. "It's perfect. Really and truly. It's one of the best college essays I've ever read. It's original, it's creative, it answers the question, it tells me something about you—it's amazing. You did an amazing job."

"Really? You think it's good?"

Actually, I think it is so good that I am stunned. In a million years I would not have believed that she could produce an essay like this. This is a kid who got straight Cs in English last year.

"It's great," I tell her. "Your writing is fantastic. I had no idea."

She blushes. "Well, you know, I read a lot, and I used to write all of the lyrics for the band. I guess I kind of have an ear for that stuff." She lets out a sigh of relief. "I'm so glad you like it. I was really nervous about showing it to you."

"Tick," I say. "Can I ask you a question?"

She nods her head. "Sure."

"Did you screw up your SATs on purpose last year?" She shifts her eyes away from mine and I know that the answer is yes. "Why?" I say. "Why did you do that?"

"I don't know," she says. "It was Marcus's idea. I knew the answers, but I promised him that I would get them wrong. I was really mad at my mom, and I wanted to do something that would piss her off. I just wasn't really thinking about college, you know?"

I nod my understanding. "So do you think that you did better this time?" I ask her. "Because they need to be much higher for you to even have a chance. I mean, your essay is great, but a great essay won't get you into college if your grades and test scores aren't up to par." She took her SATs again last weekend. If she can crack thirteen hundred, and with this essay to back it up, I think that I can convince them to overlook just about everything from last year. And it helps that she's applying early decision. The standards for early are a little bit easier, and we'll know by December fifteenth if she's getting in or not. Which, I will admit, serves my needs, too, because then I can get on with making my plans for next year.

"Oh, definitely," she says. "I know I did better."

"Good," I say. "Let me know when you get the scores, and in the meantime I think your application is ready to go. By the way, how are your grades so far this quarter?"

"They're pretty good, I guess. Mostly Bs, but I think I might be getting a C in Trig. It's really hard."

Oh, no. Cs are bad. Cs do not help my cause. I shake my head. "You can't have a C, Tick. I told you that your grades this quarter are crucial. If NYU sees that you're not doing well senior year, they'll think that you're slacking off. Especially after your grades last year. You need to be able to show them that last year was a fluke and not a trend. So get your grades up, okay? No Cs." I hope I don't sound desperate.

"Okay, okay," she says. "I'll try to do better."

I can't believe that my fate is in the hands of a volatile seventeen-year-old who is bad at math. How did I get myself into this position?

She stands up and hoists her two-hundred-pound bag onto her shoulder, and then she stares at me for a minute.

"Is there something else?" I ask.

She nods in the direction of my stomach. "Do you think it's a boy or a girl?"

Oh, right. I forgot that she knows I'm pregnant now. "I don't know," I say. "I think it's a boy, but that might just be because I want it to be a boy." I don't know why I am being so honest with her. I haven't said that to anyone. Not even to Andrew.

"Oh, really?" she says, sounding surprised. "I see you with a girl."

I shake my head. "No, girls scare me. Look at you and your mom. I'm afraid of having a relationship like that."

She makes a noise that sounds like it is partly a laugh and partly a sigh. "You'd be good with a daughter. If my mom was like you, our relationship wouldn't be the way that it is."

Hmm. Maybe she's not so ambivalent. I'm certainly learning a lot about the real Victoria Gardner today, aren't I? Actually, I'm really starting to like her. She's got a wicked sense of humor that I love, and she's not nearly as judgmental as I'd first imagined. Exactly the opposite, actually. She's much more accepting than most of the snotty kids in her grade. I think she's actually embarrassed by who her dad is and how rich they are, so she gravitates toward the artsy, not-into-material-things crowd. I mean, she could be driving a BMW like the other kids—she could be driving a Rolls if she wanted to, probably—but she drives a 1978 VW bug. Really, I've never met a less pretentious teenager from LA. She's definitely shaping up to be one of my favorite students this year.

But I can't let on that I feel that way. If she thinks that I like her, she'll just try to take advantage of me. I learned that lesson my first year in this job, when I befriended all of the kids and I gave them my home number, and then I got phone calls at all hours of the night about breakups with boyfriends and problems with parents. One time a kid even called me to pick him up from a party because he was high and he was afraid to tell his dad. So after that, I decided to play it superstrict and no-nonsense, and I always maintain an aura of cool distance from them. It's hard sometimes, but they respect me more. It makes them feel like they've really accomplished something if I compliment their work or crack a smile.

"Yeah, well," I say, "the grass is always greener. Who knows? If your mom were like me, your relationship might even be worse." Tick smiles and pushes a strand of her platinum hair out of her eyes. She can see right through me; I know it.

"Yeah, probably. But I have a feeling it's a girl, so you'd better get used to the idea." She shifts her bag to her other shoulder and turns to leave. "See you later."

"Good-bye." I say. "And get that C up."

She rolls her eyes at me and walks out.

When I get home from work, there is a breathless message from Jon on my answering machine.

"Hi, it's Jon. Julie wanted me to call you; she went into labor around four o'clock this morning and she just had the baby about twenty minutes ago. It's a girl! Her name is Lily Michelle, seven pounds, nine ounces. Ten days early, can you believe that? We're in room 3204 if you want to come over. Okay, we'll call you later. 'Bye."

Oh, my God. Julie just had a baby. Julie is a *mother*. Julie just went through *labor*. I picture Julie, her perfect hair all disheveled, white as a sheet, wearing one of those ugly green hospital gowns and sitting on one of those doughnut pillows, cursing at Jon for doing this to her. Oh, this is too good to miss. I've got to get over there right away.

Twenty minutes later I am wandering the halls of the Cedars-Sinai maternity wing, trying to find room 3204. 3226, 3230, 3234—I think I'm on the wrong side. I double back toward the elevator and head down the hallway that is parallel to where I was before. But I don't even need to look at the room numbers this time, because I can already see the crowd from halfway down the hallway. Julie and Jon's entire family is there—we're talking, like, fifty people—and there's a camera crew.

There are monster cables and light reflectors running up and down the hallway, and as I approach I see that one of the camera guys is filming Julie's mom, who is rambling on about how this is grandchild number seven for her, and that seven is her lucky number because every time she's played roulette in Vegas she always wins on seven black, although the black part doesn't really fit in this case, but still, seven is what counts. I can't believe this. I can't believe that they actually got on *Real Births*.

I've got to get out of here.

I try to turn around and leave without being noticed, but Julie's younger sister grabs me by the arm. She is wearing a full face of makeup and her hair looks like it was set with hot rollers by Dolly Parton's stylist on *Steel Magnolias*.

"Lara! Jon said you were on your way. Can you believe they got picked to be on the show? Isn't this exciting?" If I recall correctly, this sister is an "actress" whose claim to fame is a Playtex tampon commercial that aired three years ago. I wonder if she thinks she's going to get discovered on her sister's *Real Births* episode. That would explain the hair, maybe.

"Yeah," I say. "I had no idea. Julie told me that she applied, but I didn't know they actually were doing it."

"I know!" she squeals. "They just found out a few days ago. The couple who was supposed to do it changed their minds at the last minute, so they called Julie and said they would use her if they could start right away. They just filmed their prebaby event *yesterday*. Thank God she didn't go into labor before or they wouldn't have had enough material for the show."

Yeah, thank God. Before I have a chance to ask what the prebaby event was, Jon spots me and comes over. He has a pink bubblegum cigar dangling from his mouth.

"Hey," he says, kissing me on the cheek. "Isn't this cool? I'm a dad *and* I'm on TV."

"Yeah," I say. "Congratulations. How's Julie doing?"

"She's fine now. You can go in and see her if you want. The baby's still in the nursery."

I make my way past the throng, trying not to trip on the wires taped to the floor, and I push open the door to Julie's room. She looks nothing like what I imagined. Her hair is perfect, she's wearing cute, flowery pajamas, she looks flushed and healthy, and there isn't a doughnut pillow in sight. There is, however, a strange woman with a television camera sitting in the corner of the room. *Shit.* If I had known that there would be cameras, I would have at least put on some lip gloss.

I give her a kiss hello and sit down on the edge of the bed.

"Hi, Mom," I say to her. "So, Lily Michelle, that's pretty."

"Thanks," she says, smiling. Her eyes look a little glassy, like she hasn't quite come off of the drugs yet. "We named her after my Grampy Max."

I remember Julie's Grampy Max. He moved in with Julie's mom and dad after Julie's grandmother passed away, and he died in his sleep about a year ago. I think he was something like ninety-two. All I really remember about him is that he refused to wear his false teeth, so Julie's mom used to have cases of baby food delivered to her house every week.

And, by the way, do you see what I mean about how people cheat on the name thing? This is not just me being difficult. Even Julie and Jon did it.

"Okay," I say. "Enough with the pleasantries. I want to hear all about it. Was it awful?"

Julie glances at the camerawoman and flashes a big smile. "No, it really wasn't that bad. They put me on an epidural right away, and after that it's kind of a blur. Jon said I pushed for forty-five minutes, but I don't remember feeling like it was that long, and then that was it. Oh, and they gave me some oxygen at one point, because I started to hyperventilate when her head was coming out. But I didn't need an episiotomy, and my doctor was massaging me the whole time, so I didn't tear. It really wasn't a big deal." She glances at the camerawoman again and gestures for me to lean in closer. She lowers her voice to a whisper. "The worst part was that I pooped on the table. Right in front of Jon and the camera crew and everybody. It was kind of embarrassing."

Kind of embarrassing? I think that I would die if I did that in front of Andrew, let alone in front of total strangers. Andrew and I have serious bathroom issues. We would never use the bathroom in front of each other. We don't even *discuss* using the bathroom in front of each other.

It all started when we were in college. I used to sleep at his place every night, and every morning I would make up any excuse that I could think of to get out of there so that I could go home and poop in private. Andrew for sure thought that I had some kind of an OCD thing about getting the mail. And he was just as bad. He used to sneak out to the pizza place on the corner at three o'clock in the morning in the dead of winter, under the pretense of needing a Coke.

By the time we actually moved in together, things had reached a whole new level of denial, and after two weeks of us both enduring horrible, cramping stomachaches, Andrew finally decided that he couldn't take it anymore. He went out and bought some potty-training book called *Everyone Poops,* and presented it to me as a moving-in-together present. He inscribed it and everything. I was horrified, but that, at least, paved the way for the creation of the Stone-Levitt Bathroom Contract, which I drew up during my first year as an associate at my law firm and which we both signed. In blood. It reads as follows:

WHEREAS Andrew Stone and Lara Levitt (hereafter collectively referred to as "the Couple") hereby both acknowledge that they are equally uptight with regard to all things involving poop and pooping; and

WHEREAS the Couple desires to enter into this contract for the sole purpose of setting forth procedures in the event that a member of the Couple must take a poop (hereafter referred to as a "Poop Event");

THEREFORE, the Couple hereby agree to the provisions set forth below:

(1) Immediately upon the request of the pooping party, the nonpooping party must retreat to a location that is not within earshot of the bathroom in question (such location having been approved by the pooping party prior to the Poop Event); and

(2) The pooping party shall not be required to actually state to the nonpooping party that a Poop Event is about to occur. Simply instructing the nonpooping party to leave the immediate vicinity shall serve as notice that a Poop Event is imminent; and

(3) Once the Poop Event has concluded, the nonpooping party shall not enter the bathroom in which the Poop Event has occurred, unless and until the nonpooping party has been given clearance by the pooping party. Should the pooping party tell the nonpooping party that (s)he may enter the bathroom "never," then the nonpooping party must forgo all rights to said bathroom until the earlier of: (a) the following morning, or (b) the time at which clearance is given, pursuant to this section (3).

By signing below, the members of the Couple do hereby agree to be bound by all of the terms and conditions set forth herein, pursuant to the laws of the State of California.

Lara Levitt
Lara Levitt, Couple member

Andrew Stone
Andrew Stone, Couple member

Needless to say, pooping on the table in front of Andrew is a deal breaker for me. Now that's a self-evident truth that I can add to my Declaration of Independence. I will not poop on a table in front of my husband. No way.

I look at Julie, who is red with embarrassment.

"You pooped on the table?" I yell. *Oops.* I didn't mean for that to come out so loud. I lower my voice. "Did Jon say anything?" I ask.

"No, he pretended like he didn't even notice, but I know that he did. My doctor said that it happens all the time, though. I'm sure he'll forget all about it."

I don't want to tell her that I disagree. Seeing your wife with her knees up by her ears, trying to squeeze something the size of a watermelon out of her crotch is one thing, but seeing your wife with her knees up by her ears, trying to squeeze out a watermelon and instead squeezing out a big poop is something entirely different, and not something that one is likely to forget anytime soon, if ever.

"Yeah," I say, unconvincingly. "I'm sure he'll forget." There is an awkward pause, so I change the subject. "I see that the *Real Births* thing worked out for you."

At this, Julie gives the camerawoman a little wave. "I know! I'm so excited. It's going to air really soon, too. They're going to come over next week to do the follow-up visit, and then it only takes a week or two to edit, so Maggie—she's the producer; I think she left already—she said that it should be on by the end of January. Come on, admit that it's kind of cool."

I will never admit this, but since the woman did just have a baby an hour ago, I will try to be agreeable. "I think it's great for you. I'm glad that you're happy." There. See, I *can* be nice. "So what was your prebaby event?" I ask.

Upon my mentioning this, Julie's whole face lights up. "Oh, I'll show you. It was amazing. You really should do it." She reaches over to the table next to her bed and hands me a large white envelope. "Go ahead, open it."

I open the envelope and pull out a dozen or so pictures, varying in size from four-by-six wallets to eight-by-ten portraits. Some are of Julie by herself; some are of her with Jon. All feature Julie's enormous pregnant belly, with the rest of her strategically draped in a sheer, gauzy robe thing. I begin to sort through them.

First is the black-and-white profile shot: Julie, seminaked in the gauze thing, staring off pensively at the horizon, and standing with her back arched, the belly fully exposed, looking somewhat like the figurehead of an old sailing ship.

Then there's the full-frontal shot: Julie, still seminaked, lying down on her side with her hands resting on top of the belly, looking down at it and smiling a Virgin Mary smile.

There are also two of her with Jon: The first one is the same profile shot as before, but with Jon kneeling down on the floor in front of her, his head resting on the belly, while both of them stare off pensively at the horizon. And then there's the clear favorite: Julie sitting on a chair, with Jon sitting on the floor in front of her, his back to the camera, and the belly at his eye level. He's finger painting on the belly—I swear that I am not making this up—and you can kind of make out that he's writing *Daddy loves you,* while Julie gazes down at him, one hand lovingly resting on his shoulder.

As I flip through them, I try to keep a straight face in order to conceal the fact that I think they're icky and weird. When I've seen them all, I look up at her.

"These are"—I pause as I search for the right word—"very unique."

Julie beams. "Aren't they? The photographer was so amazing. She's also worked as a director, so she really knew how to make us understand what she wanted. It was an incredible experience. I'll give you her number when I get home."

Yeah, okay. Just what I want, a permanent record of the ugliest period of my life. Please. I've already imposed a no-photos rule at all holidays and/or parties, and, in the event that any pictures are inadvertently snapped, I fully intend to rip them to shreds, just as I did during my sophomore year of high school, when I thought it would be a cool idea to get a perm.

Our conversation is interrupted by a quick knock on the door, and then a nurse comes in pushing little Lily Michelle in a glass-enclosed metal hospital cart. She parks the cart next to the bed and I peer inside. This kid could not have been more aptly named. She looks exactly like Julie's Grampy Max—all shriveled and wrinkly and bald, with no teeth. It occurs to me that maybe the reason why Jews name babies after dead people is because babies look like old men right before they die. Maybe, thousands of years ago, before there was any understanding of genetics, people thought that babies were actually dead people reincarnated, so they just gave them the same name so as not to cause any confusion. Oh, come on, it's possible.

Anyway, trailing the nurse is Lily's entourage (mainly Jon, Julie's mom and dad, and Jon's mom and dad), followed by the paparazzi (mainly Julie's sisters, Jon's sisters, and Jon's grandparents), who are snapping pictures right and left and have three different video cameras poised to capture every second of Lily Michelle's life from here on out. Sensing that a Big Moment is about to occur, the camerawoman in the corner stands up and turns on a huge, blinding light, and everyone crowds around me and Julie on the bed. I realize that, as the only non–family member in the room, I probably don't deserve such a good seat. Do you know how, at weddings of friends, you would never presume to be so important as to sit in the front row? It's kind of like that. I stand up and, ducking to avoid blocking the camera, I make my way to the back of the room, where I can watch the Big Moment from an appropriate, not-a-close-relative distance.

As everyone holds their breath, the nurse lifts the baby out of the cart and gently hands her to Julie, who gathers her up in her arms as flashbulbs pop all over the place. The baby seems to look right at her, and then, as if she is satisfied that this is where she belongs, she closes her eyes and rests her tiny head against Julie's chest.

It's pretty damn heartwarming. Jon is crying, Julie is crying, their parents are crying, the sisters are crying, even the camerawoman is getting teary. Jon goes over and first kisses Julie, then Lily, on the tops of their heads, and now even I'm getting choked up. I'm also getting the sense that the Big Moment has suddenly become a Huge Private Moment at which I clearly do not belong, so I open the door and quietly slip out of the room, unnoticed.

The hallway outside is bustling with nurses and visitors and pages over the intercom system, and all of the noise quickly brings me back to my senses. *God*, I think. *I can't believe that that schmaltz made me cry.*

You know, maybe there's hope for me yet.

14.

C is for Cranky; That's How I Like to Be

O kay, I need to vent for a few minutes about how much I hate people. All of them. I mean, can you please explain to me why it is that every random stranger in the universe feels the need to strike up a conversation with me just because I'm pregnant? Why? I would never go up to a total stranger who's minding her own business in line at the grocery store, or dropping her car off with a valet, or waiting for a table at a restaurant, and just out of the blue start talking to her for no reason whatsoever.

Of course, it wouldn't even be so bad if they were just saying hello or asking me if I needed help carrying anything, but that's not what they do. It's just one insipid comment after the next. Everywhere I go, it's, *Oh, look, you're pregnant!* Or, *Now, now, somebody's having a baby soon!* What am I supposed to say to this? *Wow, your powers of observation are outstanding!* Or maybe, *Huh, thanks for telling me; I thought it might just have been something that I ate.*

And then there's this dialogue, which I have about seventy-five times a day:

Random Stranger:	So, when are you due?
Me:	April eleventh.
Random Stranger:	Oh, really?! My brother/father/sister/ boyfriend/ great-aunt's best friend's birthday is April ninth!
Me (fake-smiling):	Oh, wow.

I just don't understand this line of questioning. Why should I give a rat's ass when some total stranger's relative was born? And what kind of a response are they looking for, anyway? *Oh, great, give me your card, and if it's born on the ninth, I'll call you to let you know. Maybe my baby and your brother/father/sister/boyfriend/great-aunt's best friend can have a double birthday party together!* Please.

And, really, what is with people feeling entitled to analyze my body out loud, in public? *Boy, you're really showing! Your stomach is huge! Have your legs gotten bigger since last week?* Or the one that really pisses me off: *You look so great for a pregnant woman.* Yeah, you think it's a compliment, but it's not. What it really means is, *Considering that you are supposed to be getting fat, you don't look nearly as bad as you could. However, if you were not pregnant and you looked like this, then actually you would look like shit.* Compliment, my ass.

Oh, and let's not forget about the ones who tell me how "cute" I look. I mean, come *on.* I am not cute. First of all, I'm too tall to be cute, and second, I am way too obnoxious. But apparently, the rule is that any pregnant woman who was relatively thin before she got pregnant and hasn't turned into a total cow is deemed to be "cute" by all who see her. And I know what you're thinking. You're thinking that having random people tell me that I'm cute is better than having random people tell me that I look like a beached whale, and I'll give you that, I will. But what I don't understand is (a) why a woman who looks as if she is about to topple over at any minute is thought of in the same way as puppy dogs and infants, and (b) why a random stranger needs to tell me anything.

Hey—don't get up—I'm not finished. I still have to complain about the smiling. I hate the fucking smiling. Every version of it bugs me. There's the oh-you're-so-cute smile, which generally comes from twenty-somethings who have never had children and think that pregnancy is fun and happy, like in the movies. Yeah, well, here's a news flash, kids: It's not.

Then there's the oh-I-know-how-miserable-you-are sympathy smile, given by smarter, more mature women who actually have been pregnant and know just how much it sucks. The please-avoid-making-eye-contact-with-me-because-your-stomach-is-making-me-uncomfortable smile is used exclusively by men who still have functioning penises, and the oh-I-feel-so-bad-for-you-you-poor-swollen-woman pity smile can generally be counted on from everyone else. I swear to God, if one more fucking person smiles at me, I'm going to knock their teeth out.

And men? Men are pigs. Every last one of them. Now that I'm really showing, it's like I've ceased to exist in their eyes. I mean, you'd think that it would be the opposite, right? Clearly, I have had sex, and I might even be easy. You'd think that a guy would figure that he'd have a pretty good shot with me, since somebody else obviously did. But no, they just ignore me. They ignore me when I'm trying to open a heavy door, they ignore me when I'm the only person in a room standing because they're hogging all the chairs, they ignore me when I struggle to carry my groceries, they even ignore me when I am attempting to lift my luggage into the overhead bin on an airplane. I swear, last week I had to go to a conference for work, and I was on the plane, obviously by myself, obviously pregnant, and obviously having difficulty lifting my rolling carry-on bag. There were men in front of me and behind me and not one of them offered to help me out. Can you believe that? And by the way, I have been on dozens of flights by myself when I was not pregnant, and I can assure you that I never had any trouble getting a guy to help me lift my luggage then. But no, God forbid a man should help a woman if he doesn't think that there's even a remote possibility of getting sex out of it. No way.

In fact, the only men who even take the slightest interest in me are guys who either just became dads or whose wives are also pregnant. And these guys are, like, at the opposite end of the spectrum from normal guys. These guys are regular Chatty Cathys. They feel that it's okay to touch my stomach (I won't even go there—let's just say that several people have almost lost limbs in such attempts) and to ask me all manner of personal questions, like whether I've gotten any stretch marks (no) or varicose veins (eww, no).

At the gym, it's like they're stalking me. For whatever reason, new dads seem to think that the mere fact of my presence means that I'm seeking their weight-loss advice. I'll be sitting on a bench, quietly doing some bicep curls, and some guy will saunter over to tell me about how his wife went into labor in the middle of doing some leg presses but she still finished out the set anyway, and if I just keep it up and don't get lazy at the end I'll lose all of the weight right away, unless, of course, I'm breast feeding, and then it might take a little bit longer. But hang in there, 'cause you're doing great.

I'm always amazed at the words of wisdom that all of these men have about pregnancy. I mean, I'm sorry, but if you don't have a vagina, I don't really want to hear from you, buddy.

Even Andrew sucks. The only time that he's not completely oblivious to the fact that I'm pregnant is when it works to his advantage. He'll sit on the couch and watch football while I haul things up the stairs, but if someone inconveniences him, all of a sudden my pregnancy is magically in the forefront of his thoughts. Let me tell you, there is no one in the world who plays the pregnancy card better than Andrew. No one. His trick is to muster up all of the indignation that he possibly can, and then act as if he's both morally outraged and deeply insulted that his wife is not being treated in a manner appropriate to her condition. He could win an Academy Award, his performances are so outstanding. If we're in line at the movies, it's, *Can't you see that my wife is* pregnant? *I don't think that she should have to stand in line when it is obviously putting a strain on her back. Can't you just let us in now?* If we're checking in for a flight, he'll tell the flight attendant, *My wife is* pregnant; *are you really going to make her sit in a middle seat where she can't stretch her legs? Couldn't you give us the bulk-head, or maybe bump us up to first class?* And if he needs to get out of something, forget it. *Tom, I'm so sorry, but I'm not going to be able to make it to dinner tonight. My wife is* pregnant *and she's not feeling that well, so I'm going to stay home and take care of her.* Yeah, right.

The ridiculous thing, though, is that people buy it. If he's dealing with a man, the mere mention of the word *pregnant* is like a Get out of Jail Free card. And if he's dealing with a woman, she'll invariably find his compassion and concern for me to be so sweet that her heart melts and she gives him whatever he wants on the spot.

Personally, I find the entire thing to be revolting and totally unfair. I mean, here I am, making a baby from scratch and suffering through the back pain and the swelling and the aching feet, but I never cash in my chips because I'm always afraid of sounding like a whiny complainer. Meanwhile, my husband is out there getting all of the sympathy and Man of the Year awards because he has no problem exploiting me. Honestly, it's no wonder that men rule the world.

Zoey stands up and stretches her back.

"Now are you finished?" says the scruffy voice. I stop pacing and sit down on the couch, kicking off my shoes.

"Yes," I say. "I am. Thank you for listening; I feel much better now."

She rolls her eyes at me. "Whatever," she says. She stands up and goes into the kitchen, and I hear the ca-cling of the doggie door as she pushes herself through to the backyard.

Andrew is singing.

"You thought you'd found a friend. To take you out of this place. Bomp, bomp, bomp, bomp, lend a hand. Bomp, bomp, bomp, bomp, bomp, bomp, bomp. 'Cause it's a beautiful daaay. Shy calls your feelin' it's a beautiful day-ay-ay, don't let it—"

"It's not 'shy calls your feeling,' Andrew," I say, interrupting him. "It's 'sky falls, you feel like.'" But he ignores me and continues to butcher Bono.

"Bomp, bomp, bomp, imagination, bomp, bomp, bomp." He's banging on the steering wheel and bobbing his head up and down, and I have to laugh. I don't think that he could do anything to annoy me right now, because right now we are on the way to my five-month checkup, which means that we are on the way to finding out whether the alien inside of me has a penis or not.

A commercial comes on, mercifully putting an end to the bomping.

"I think we could have the bris at our house," Andrew says. "I'm thinking maybe fifty people, a few deli platters, some chocolate rugalah, snip, snip, snip, and we're done. Don't you think?"

"Yeah," I say. "Fine with me." He is so sure that it's a boy. I'm carrying really high in front, and according to several thousand random strangers, this is a definite sign of boyness. I, however, not being a believer in old wives' tales related to me by virtual unknowns, would prefer to actually see the penis before I start painting the nursery blue and pondering male P and J names.

I really can't wait to get this name thing settled. I'm so sick of people asking me if I have a name yet. After the episode with Stacey, I learned my lesson and stopped telling people about my name dilemma. Now I just say that we haven't gotten a chance to buy any baby-name books yet, and that we'll start thinking about it as soon as we're not so busy. And speaking of books, Stacey did manage to make up for her despicable behavior. As a good luck/apology present, she sent me this book called *Anticipating the Schoolyard Taunts: What to Consider Before You Name Your Baby*. I don't know where she found it, but it's fabulous. Take, for example, Andrew. *Andrew: Nice try, but it's only a matter of time until some teacher calls him Andy in front of his whole class, and then he'll be forever known as Andy the Pansy by all those who knew him before he went to college and made a fresh start.* Genius, right?

I've decided to bring it along today for reference.

Andrew and I check in at the reception desk and take a seat in the waiting room, where we share a copy of *Ladies' Home Journal* from last March. About ten minutes into an article called "How to Stop Being a People Pleaser," the nurse calls my name *(Lara: What, was your mother hoping for a boy named Larry?)*, and Andrew and I head back to the nurses' station, where I have to pee in a cup and get my monthly weigh-in. As of my last checkup, I had gained only six pounds, and Dr. Lowenstein said that I was right on track. He said that after the first twelve weeks, I should start to gain about a half a pound to a pound per week. But I don't know what I weigh now. I've stopped using my scale at home every day because it's too depressing.

I do the pee thing first (I figure it buys me at least a few ounces), and then I remove my shoes, socks, sweater, belt, rings, and earrings before stepping on the scale. Allie, the nurse *(Allie: Is this a name? Because the last time I checked it was a dark place where unsavory characters tend to commit murder)* slides the weight around, trying to balance it.

"Okay," she says, checking my chart. "That's seven and a quarter pounds."

I smile. "I only gained a pound and a quarter since last month? Are you sure?" Wow. I mean, I know I've been working out, but I thought I'd be at least two pounds heavier by now. Maybe I should take it easy on the cardio.

Allie shakes her head and frowns.

"No, sweetie, you gained *another* seven and a quarter pounds. So now you're at"—she consults the chart again—"fourteen and a quarter pounds."

I almost fall off of the scale. That can't be possible. I've been so good. "That cannot be right," I whine. "Are you sure?"

She's already walking away, on to the next patient. She turns her head and calls back to me over her shoulder. "I'm sure. Wait for Dr. Lowenstein in room three."

As instructed, I enter room three, where Andrew is already sitting in a chair in the corner, reading a four-month-old issue of *People*.

"How did it go?" he asks nonchalantly.

I shake my head, distraught. "I don't want to talk about it." Seven and a quarter pounds. That scale has got to be wrong. I never should have had a sandwich and fruit for lunch today. From now on I am only eating protein before my doctor appointments.

I hoist myself onto the examining table and pull my shirt up over my stomach in anticipation of Dr. Lowenstein. Ten minutes later he breezes in, holding my chart in his hand.

"Hi, how are you guys?" he says, and comes over to give me a kiss hello. I've never had a doctor kiss me hello before, but he always does it. I think it's part of his LA shtick.

"We're good," I say. "We're just dying to know if we should be buying dolls or trucks."

"Well, you'll know soon enough," he says. He looks down at my chart and then looks back up at me with his eyebrows raised. "Seven and a quarter pounds?"

At this, Andrew looks up at me, too, and I wag my finger at him. "I take serious issue with your scale. I've been so good. I'm exercising four days a week, and I'm not eating a lot more at all." I turn to Andrew for backup. "Haven't I been good?"

Andrew nods in agreement. "She's been pretty good. The only extra food that she really eats is cereal. Total, right, honey?"

I nod back at him. "Two bowls of Total every day. I eat it instead of vitamins, because they make me nauseous." Dr. Lowenstein nods his head at me, like he's heard this a million times before. "It can't all be me, anyway. I mean, the baby is growing; that must account for a few pounds, right?"

Dr. Lowenstein chuckles. "The baby is the size of a computer mouse. It weighs about ten ounces." He closes my chart and places it on the counter behind him. "Look, some women just gain more. You can't control your genes. As long as you're eating healthy and exercising, you're fine."

Great. Leave it to me to have the gain-too-much-weight-during-pregnancy gene. If I end up gaining fifty pounds I will never speak to my mother again.

I lie back on the table and Dr. Lowenstein pulls out a measuring tape and stretches it across my stomach.

"Are you feeling a lot of movement?" he asks.

Oh, yeah, the movement. I don't think I told you about that. I started feeling it about three weeks ago. It kind of feels the way your stomach does when it rumbles from hunger, but without the hunger and the rumbling noise. At first I wasn't sure if it was the baby or not, but then it kept happening, so I asked Julie and she said yes, that's definitely the baby kicking. It mostly happens at night, just as I'm falling asleep. Because it's not bad enough that I won't sleep once it's born; my kid has to start waking me up five months early.

"Yeah," I say. "It's definitely swimming around in there."

"Good." He snaps his tape measure closed and offers me his hand to help me sit up. "Okay, everything looks great. Let's get you down to see Dr. Weiss. I hope you remembered your videotape."

Dr. Weiss is the special ultrasound doctor whose office is two floors below Dr. Lowenstein's. If you bring him a videotape, he'll record the ultrasound for you to keep. I would much rather watch that with my kid in twenty years than a documentary that shows me pooping on the delivery table. Oh, that reminds me.

"Um, Dr. Lowenstein, can I ask you a question?"

He turns around and sits back down on his stool. "Shoot."

"How does someone get to have a C-section?"

I'm sorry, but I need to know. After Julie had her baby I watched, like, ten *Real Births* episodes in a row, and they made me so anxious that I almost couldn't breathe. I mean, watching women in labor when you're pregnant can only be compared to witnessing your own death before it happens. And it doesn't help that 90 percent of the lunatics on the show opt for natural childbirth. I don't know what Julie finds so admirable about them. They do it squatting, or in bathtubs, or at home in their beds, and they all end up screaming their heads off and pleading with God to make it stop. It's *awful*. And I don't care what Julie says; even the ones who have drugs are miserable. She either doesn't remember or she flat-out lied to me.

The C-section episodes, though—those were amazing. They were civil and ladylike—just a little slice and five minutes later there's a baby. I mean, how easy is that? Believe me, I have tried to visualize myself doing it the regular way, you know, to make it seem more real, but I can't do it. I just can't see me, with my French-manicured toes and my blond highlights, lying in a bed with my knees up by my ears, pushing like I've been constipated for a month. Or, God forbid, pooping. No, no. A C-section is definitely the way to go.

Dr. Lowenstein raises his eyebrows at me again and picks up my chart. "How does someone *get* to?" he asks. I nod my head. "Well, obviously, one could need an emergency C-section if there's a problem with labor—"

I start shaking my head before he can finish his sentence. "No, I mean the scheduled kind, before labor." The corners of his mouth turn up in a little half smile, like he's trying not to laugh. I have a feeling that he has other patients with French-manicured toes and blond highlights.

"Well, normally a C-section is scheduled if a woman had one with an earlier child. But for first-time mothers, we might decide to have a surgical birth if we think the baby is too big, or, of course, if the baby is breach, but we won't know either of those things until a week or two before you're due."

"That's it?" I ask.

He ponders this for a moment. "Well, I suppose that we also might decide to do it ahead of time if the mother has some kind of a preexisting condition that would be worsened through childbirth."

At this, my ears perk up. "Like what?" I ask.

He looks at me suspiciously. "Like anything."

"Like severe anxiety and absolutely no desire whatsoever to go through labor or childbirth, not to mention an abnormally irrational fear of tearing and needing stitches down there?"

This time he laughs. "All right, maybe not *anything*."

Damn. Foiled again.

"Listen," he says. "You're only halfway through your pregnancy. Most women experience fear about childbirth. It's totally normal. You should do some reading about it, maybe take a childbirth preparedness class, and then we'll see how you feel. Okay?"

"Okay," I say begrudgingly. "But we can revisit this if things don't change for me, right?"

"Right," he says, patting me on the back. "Now go find out what it is that you're having already."

When we get downstairs to Dr. Weiss's office, we are greeted by his nurse, who is what I can only describe as über-happy. Her name is Katie *(Katie: Rhymes with weighty)*, and she's just so excited for us and *Oh, my God, isn't it fun to find out the sex,* and *Gosh, you guys are going to have the prettiest baby; I sure hope it gets your husband's blue eyes.* . . . She's really a bit much. Anyway, Katie shows us to the ultrasound room and gives me a gown to put on, and then she puts our videotape into the VCR that is set up below the television screen. She informs us that Dr. Weiss will be in in a few minutes and lets out one last squeal of excitement before she departs. When she shuts the door behind her, Andrew starts in on me.

"I can't believe that you asked to have a C-section. Do you realize that it's major surgery?" I find it amazing that Andrew still attempts to reason with me after all these years. He really is so tenacious.

"Yes, I do. Do you realize what the alternative is?"

He sighs. "I know, but it seems like you were a little cavalier about it."

Hmm. Cavalier. That's a big word. I wonder where he learned that one.

"I was not cavalier. For your information, I have done extensive research on C-sections over the last several weeks."

He gives me a surprised look. "You have? When? Where?"

"On the Your Baby Web site while I was at work. I read all of the articles about C-sections, and they're fine. There's hardly any risk at all, and lots of times it's even safer for the baby because there's no chance of it getting stuck in the birth canal. The only thing I couldn't find out is whether you can see the scar in a low-rider bikini." Shoot, I should have asked Dr. Lowenstein about that one. I'm sure he would know. "Anyway, we don't even know if he'll let me do it, so just relax, okay? You don't need to get your undies all in a bundle just yet."

There is a quick knock on the door and then a tall, very skinny man comes in wearing a lab coat that says *Jack Weiss, M.D.,* over the left breast pocket. *(Jack: Jack, Jack, does a lot of smack.)*

"You must be Lara," he says, extending his hand.

"I am," I say, as I take his hand and shake it. "And this is my husband, Andrew." Andrew and Dr. Weiss shake hands, and then he sits down in front of the television screen.

"So, are we finding out the sex today?"

Andrew and I inform him that we most definitely are, and that we will not be leaving here unless and until it is known.

"Okay. Let's do this, then." He squeezes some gel onto my stomach and starts moving the ultrasound paddle around. I look on the monitor and I am presented with a big, out-of-focus, black-and-white blob. It doesn't look like a baby to me, but apparently it does to Dr. Weiss.

"There's the spine; can you see that?" he asks.

No, I can't. I try squinting, but now it just looks like a smaller, more out-of-focus, black-and-white blob.

"Does it look okay?" I ask.

"Looks perfect." He moves the paddle around some more and then stops and points to the screen. "There's the head; can you see the eyes?"

Those are *eyes?* It looks like an Edvard Munch painting.

"Is that normal?"

"Totally. The eye sockets are still on the side of the head. They'll move closer together as the baby grows." Good to know. The paddle is moving again. "There are the legs; can you see them?"

I squint again. I think I see them. But they're right next to the head. In fact, they look like they're inside of the head. My heart starts to beat wildly. Oh, my God, my baby has feet growing out of its head. I'll bet it's because I didn't take folic acid before I got pregnant. I knew that would come back to haunt me. You see, this is what happens when you take health for granted and you care only about superficial things and you complain about being pregnant and you never once stop to think that everything might not just be fine. It's karma. Bad karma. I nervously clear my throat.

"Are the feet in the right place?" I whisper.

"No," he says matter of factly, and I can feel myself going into shock.

My baby is deformed, for real. I am being punished for every bad thing I ever said about having children. I am desperate to look at Andrew but he's behind me and I can't see him. I think I'm going to be sick.

Dr. Weiss glances at me and immediately assesses the situation.

"Oh, no, no, no, anatomically they're in the right place. I'm sorry. I didn't mean to scare you. I just meant no, they're not in the right place for me to determine the gender." I exhale a huge sigh of relief. That was so not funny. He really should be more careful about how he answers questions.

"You see," says Dr. Weiss, as he points to the screen again and runs his finger along the edge of the blob. "It's curled up so that the legs are running alongside the torso. If it doesn't move, I won't be able to get a look at what's between them."

"Well, what do we do?" I say, sounding panicked. "I have to know."

Yeah, yeah, I know that I should just be thankful that it's healthy and that I should be able to put such minor things as gender into perspective after having had this brush with unspeakable parental horror, but I'm sorry, I am superficial and I can't change that, so save your breath.

Dr. Weiss takes off his glasses and wipes his forehead with his arm.

"The good news is that the baby looks perfect." I stare at him as if to say that there had better not be any bad news. He sighs. "Why don't you lie on your side for a few minutes and try to wake it up, and I'll go check on my other patient." I nod at this suggestion, and he walks out of the room.

I twist over onto my side, and Andrew comes around and sits down on the edge of the table.

"How are you going to wake it up?" he asks. I have no idea. How do you wake up a fetus? Do they have special alarm clocks for this purpose? Maybe I can startle it awake. I look down at my belly and begin to jam my palms into my abdomen. Jam.

"Wake up!" Jam.

"Wake up!" Jam, jam, jam.

"Wake up! Wake up! Wake up!"

I continue to do this for several more minutes, but when I hear the doctor approaching I stop and quickly get back into position. I have a feeling that this is not exactly what he had in mind.

"Okay," he says, sitting back down on his stool. "Let's see if that worked." He puts the ultrasound thing back on my stomach and starts looking around. This time I can very clearly make out the baby's leg, and it suddenly shoots out, like someone just did a reflex test on its knee. *Oh, my God,* I think. *I just saw my baby* move. *I just saw it's tiny, little, perfect leg actually move inside of me. It's amazing. It really is a miracle.*

Suddenly I am flooded with emotion. I have never felt anything like this before. I am overwhelmed by an urge to reach inside of myself, scoop the baby up, and never let it go. I can't explain it—it's like nothing else in the world matters, and I feel warm and tingly and nurturing and filled with love. I feel, I feel . . . motherly.

Gotcha.

Jeez, how gullible are you? I look over at Dr. Weiss.

"So can you tell what it is?" I ask him. He nods at me, concentrating intently on the monitor.

"Okay—there we go. Right . . . there. Yes. I'm pretty sure that it is . . ." I am holding my breath. Ladies and gentlemen—drumroll please—the moment we've all been waiting for . . .

"A girl!" Dr. Weiss looks up from the monitor and smiles at us. "Congratulations, you're having a little girl."

My heart is nose-diving. It's not a boy. It's a girl. I'm having a girl. I'm having a bitchy, hormonal, fashion-obsessed, catfighting, mother-hating girl. *Okay*, I think. *Let's try to look on the bright side of this. A daughter could be fun. We could do vacations at spas, weekend shopping trips to Paris; it might not be so bad.* . . . I turn around to look at Andrew and he has a huge fake smile plastered on his face.

"Are you sure?" he asks.

Dr. Weiss nods. "I'm sure. The labia were very prominent."

Andrew purses his lips together. I'm sure he's thinking that the last thing he needed to know right now is that he's having a daughter and that she has prominent labia.

But Dr. Weiss is already on the move.

"Well, you two, congratulations. You're going to have a perfectly healthy, beautiful daughter." He takes the videotape out of the machine and hands it to me. "Here you go," he says. "For your viewing pleasure." He shakes both of our hands. "I'll leave you to get dressed, and then it's a left out of here and another left to get out. Nice meeting both of you. Good luck with the baby."

We both thank him and he leaves, closing the door behind him. Neither of us says a word while I remove my gown and put my shirt back on. The tension is practically unbearable.

"I feel like you're mad at me," I say to him.

"I'm not mad," he says. "How could I be mad at you? I'm just surprised. I was sure that it was going to be a boy. Everyone said that it was going to be a boy."

"You're disappointed, though; I can tell." He hesitates, trying to decide if it is legal to express this particular kind of disappointment.

"A little, I guess. But I'll get over it. I want a girl, too. Every daddy should have a little girl. I just need some time to digest it."

I nod. "I know," I say. "Me, too. Come on. Let's get out of here."

We walk down the hallway and make our insurance copayment at the billing desk on the way out. As Andrew signs the credit card slip, Katie appears and bounces over to us.

"Well?" she says. "Boy or girl? No, wait! Let me guess." She squints at my stomach and puts out her palms like she's a cinematographer framing a shot. "Boy. Definitely a boy."

Andrew and I glance at each other. We both fake-smile at her. "No, it's a girl," we say in unison.

"Oh! A girl. Wow, you're carrying so high for a girl. I never would have guessed." She takes a moment to recover, and then rebounds with a bigger smile than ever.

"So," she sings. "Do you have a name?"

No, no, no. I am not doing this now. "No," I say tersely. "We haven't thought about it yet." She looks disappointed, and then Andrew chimes in.

"It has to start with a P or a J," he tells her. I elbow him, hard, but it's too late.

"Oooh," Katie says. "How about Penny?" Is she kidding? Do I look like someone who would name my child after a dirty, all-but-obsolete form of currency?

"No," I say. "Not really me."

But Weighty Katie is unstoppable. "Paula? Paula's a good name."

I grimace at her. "I don't really see myself having a Paula."

She looks stumped for a second, but then she lifts a finger. "I know! What about Jennifer, or Jessica?"

Oh, right. Like I hadn't thought of Jennifer or Jessica. Like Jennifer and Jessica weren't the most overused names of the 1970s and 1980s, respectively. Like the world needs another Jennifer or Jessica.

"Yeah, you know, I'm sure we'll figure something out, thanks." We push the exit door open, leaving Katie standing there in the hallway, still thinking.

"Pamela!" she yells. "How about Pamela?"

Andrew and I ignore her and the door slams closed behind us. When we get to the elevator bank, Andrew comes up behind me and gives me a big hug.

"So, I guess I'm going to have three women in my life now, huh?"

Three women? "Who?" I say. "Me, the baby, and your girlfriend?"

"No. You, the baby and Zoey." Oh, Zoey. I wonder if Zoey talks to Andrew, too. Nah. He would have tried to have gotten her on television by now. "So *have* you thought about a name yet?" he asks.

"No." I say. "But I'll be sure to let you know what it is when I do."

Andrew laughs. "I have no say in this, do I?"

I shake my head at him. "Not a fucking chance."

He smiles and wraps his arms around me. "I hope she's just like you," he whispers in my ear.

Oh, honey, I think. *Be careful what you wish for.*

15.

Little Eddie Foo Foo

"**N**ew York University, this is Ed Jellette."

"Hi, Ed! It's Lara Stone, from Bel Air Prep."

"Lara, doll, how are you? I miss you and your fabulous shoes."

For whatever reason, there are huge numbers of gay men in college admissions. I've known Ed for years, and he's just about the gayest of them all. We met at my first College Admissions Counselors of America convention—it was in DC that year—and we ended up getting totally blitzed on cosmos and dancing until four in the morning at some gay bar in Dupont Circle with two other admissions guys from Skidmore and Oberlin, I think. They all love me, the gay admissions men. I'm the closest thing to a diva that's ever happened to our profession.

"And I miss you." I say. "Are you still seeing the window dresser from Armani?"

"Oh, please. That was *so* last season. No, I've moved on to bigger and better things, if you know what I mean. And what are you up to these days? Still with the hunky hubby?" The last time Ed was in LA, I invited him over to have dinner and to watch *Buffy the Vampire Slayer* with me. Andrew came home halfway through the show, and Ed's been infatuated with him ever since.

"Yes, we're still together, so don't get your hopes up. We're having a baby, if you can believe it. A little girl."

Ed gasps. "Oh, my God, congratulations. Pregnancy is very chic right now, you know. All of the big celebs are doing it." Leave it to a gay man to come up with Pregnancy as Fashion Accessory. "Do you have a name yet?"

A big lightbulb suddenly goes on over my head. I can't believe I didn't think of this before. It's been two weeks since we found out that we're having a girl, and I haven't been able to talk names with anyone yet. Really, who do I know who could give me an honest, unbiased opinion that I could actually trust? Julie wouldn't get it, Stacey will just make fun of me, and Andrew is worthless—but Ed is the perfect baby-name focus group. I mean, come on, who could be better for the job than a pretentious, urban gay man?

"As a matter of fact," I say, "I've got it narrowed down to two names. It has to start with either a P or a J—don't ask; it's an Andrew thing—and I'm deciding between Parker and Josie. What do you think?"

Ed inhales sharply through his teeth. "Oh, honey, you can't do Josie. Everyone will make jokes about her pussy. It would be tragic. Mm-mm."

Okay, I had considered this, but I wasn't sure if I was just being hypercautious. It's so cute, though. I keep picturing a little Josie with pigtails and a high-pitched, little-girl voice. But, of course, Ed's right. It won't be so cute when she's in high school.

"Good point," I say. "So then what do you think of Parker?" This is really my front-runner, anyway. I feel that it covers all of my bases. It starts with a P, which will make Andrew happy, it doesn't rhyme with anything obscene, it's unusual but not absurd, and I've got Parker Posey to back me up. And I consulted the book and the worst thing that will happen is that kids will call her Valet Parker. I can live with that. I just need it to be validated by someone with good taste. And while Ed may be someone with many flawed qualities, his taste is not one of them.

"Parker, Parker . . ." he says, thinking it over. "I like it. It's very hip. Very Sundance Film Festival. Parker Stone. Oh, yeah. She's definitely going to be the cool girl in school. Everyone will know who Parker Stone is. But she could be a total bitch, though. You know, Parker Stone, the really pretty girl whom all the boys are dying to go out with but who only dates college guys, and then she ends up losing her true love to the dorky, ugly girl who's actually a knockout when she gets her hands on a push-up bra, some contacts, and a little red lipstick. Oh, honey, you'd better be careful with Parker Stone."

I am amazed at how just uttering her name has allowed him to plan out her entire high school social life.

"Okay, Ed, you watch way too many teen movies."

"I *know*," he says. "Guilty pleasure."

Well, I guess that settles it, then. Parker it is. Parker Jade Stone. Yes, I'm using Jade, and you can just shut up about it. I love it and I can't let it go. If she's embarrassed by it, she doesn't have to tell anyone her middle name.

"Well, Mr. Jellette, you've been a huge help. Thank you. Someday I'll be able to tell her that her name received the ultimate stamp of approval."

"Oh, come on, you'll make me cry. Now, why did you really call? I know there's a hidden agenda in here somewhere."

I laugh. "It's not a *hidden* agenda. It's just a regular agenda. I need a heads-up on one of my kids. Have you guys started making decisions yet?"

"We're still in committee, but decisions are happening every day. Who is it? I can pull the file up right now."

"Victoria Gardner. Date of birth is July twenty-first, 1986." There is a long pause as he types the information into his computer, and while he waits for it to come up he hums the theme song to *Love Boat*.

"Okay, got it. Victoria Gardner. Oh, right, I remember her. She wrote about her bedroom. Great essay." He pauses again as he looks it over. "Yeah, we haven't made a final decision yet, but I don't think it's gonna happen, Lar. Those grades last year were a little scary, and her SATs were lo-ow."

"I know, they were awful, but they're from last year. She took them again; we're still waiting for the scores."

He hums again as he looks through her file. "Is she taking them again in December? Because I have her November scores right here."

I sit straight up in my seat. Tick just told me two days ago that she hadn't gotten them yet and that when she called she was told that there was a delay. That little shit. I take back every nice thing that I ever said about her.

"You do?"

"Mm-hm. Six-twenty verbal, five-ninety math."

A twelve-ten? She got a twelve-ten? I'm going to kill her.

"I had no idea," I say, writing it down. "Okay. But isn't the development office involved? Her parents are huge donors at our school and they said that they would be contacting you to discuss a donation. I gave her mom your card specifically."

"I never spoke to anyone, and there's nothing in her file. I can call over to development to find out, but usually if they're involved they flag the file and take it out of our hands."

What the hell is going on here? Something must have happened. I need to make sure that they do not deny her until I can get this straightened out. I can't believe that I'm going to say what I am about to say.

"Look, Ed, do you know who she is?" *Ugh.* I hate myself.

Ed lowers his voice like he's about to be let in on some juicy gossip. "No. Is she someone? I love this about LA private schools."

Thank God Ed is a star fucker. It's my only hope.

"Her dad is Stefan Gardner, the director. You know, *Dreamscape, Heart of Nails,* won the Oscar two years ago?" He gasps and I just know that he's started fanning himself with his hand.

"Seriously?"

"Uh-huh." He's still fanning. I can tell.

"Oh, my God. That's huge. There must be a mistake, then. I need to talk to some people about this, and I'll get back to you."

"Good," I say. "Listen, please don't deny her until we straighten this out. Defer her to regular decision if you have to, but that girl cannot get a rejection letter on December fifteenth, okay?"

"No rejections for now, I promise."

I breathe a sigh of relief. "Thank you, Ed, you are the best."

"I try. Okay, well, listen, you take care of that little Parker for me, and I'll touch base with you as soon as I know anything. *Ciao!*"

I don't know what to do first. No—scratch that—I do. I should find Tick first, so that I can rip her head off. I can't believe she lied to me. And that she did it with such a straight face. Did she honestly think I wouldn't find out? Ugh, how manipulative. *No, I don't know what's going on; they said there's a delay with the processing or something. Don't worry; you'll be the first to know when I get them, I promise.* You see, this is exactly why I didn't want a girl. A boy wouldn't do something like this. Boys aren't that smart.

I pull up Tick's class schedule on the computer. She's in Government, and the period isn't over for another thirty-five minutes. I write down the room number so that I can go stalk her when class lets out, and then I pick up the phone. I might as well just get to the bottom of this now.

"Gardner residence."

"Hi, Lori, it's Lara Stone, from Tick's school. Is Cheryl around, by any chance?"

"Oh, hi, Lara. She's not here; she's on set with Stefan all day. Is there something I can help you with?"

Yeah. Can you please steal her checkbook and send a few million over to NYU? I'd prefer FedEx, ten A.M. delivery, thanks.

"No, I really need to speak with her. Is there any way I can reach her? It's kind of important."

Lori hesitates. "I can't give out Stefan's office number, and he doesn't allow cell phones on the set, but I guess I could page her and tell her to call you right back if it's that important."

"It is. Tell her that I'm in my office, waiting for her call. Thanks so much."

I hang up the phone and take a second to shift gears, and then I dial Andrew at work. I am very excited to tell him our baby's name.

"Andrew Stone."

"Hi," I say. I can hear him typing in the background.

"Hi, what's up?" He's still typing. I hate when he does this to me. As if nothing I have to say could possibly be important enough to warrant his full attention.

"Stop typing, please." When he finally stops, I proudly deliver my announcement. "The baby's name is going to be Parker. Parker Jade." There is a pause.

"Parker? For a girl?"

"Yes. Like Parker Posey."

"Who?"

The typing starts again. He's trying to do it quietly, so I won't notice, but he doesn't realize that pregnancy has enhanced my senses. My ears and nose are so good now that I practically have superpowers.

"Have you never seen an art house film? Parker *Posey*. She's in all of those Christopher Guest movies." He is silent. "She was the neurotic dog owner from *Best in Show*?" He'll definitely know that. He totally related to that movie.

"Oh, right. Cool. I like that. Good job, honey. Listen, I'm really busy; can I call you later?"

"Yeah, I guess."

"Great. Love you, 'bye."

The dial tone buzzes in my ear. That's it? *Cool, can I call you later?* I can't believe his indifference to the name of our first child. I hit the redial button.

"Andrew Stone."

"I just announced the name of our baby to you and all you can say is 'cool'? Do you even care that our baby has a name now?"

He lets out a please-not-now sigh. "Of course I care. I said I liked it. What do you want me to do?"

"I don't know; I just thought that you would be more excited than that."

"It's a name. It's cute. I'm glad you found something you like. Okay? Can I go now? I really have a lot to do. I love you."

"I love you too," I say, feeling dejected as I hang up.

I sigh. Men are just so different. Straight men, at least. I mean, I think that this is a really big deal. I kind of expected him to say that he was coming right over to watch while I wrote out *Parker Jade Stone* over and over and over again in various styles of handwriting. You know, I really do understand the attraction of lesbianism. It must be very fulfilling to know that your partner will always have more or less the same emotional reaction to things as you. I suppose that's one good thing about having a girl. If I ever have a second baby, Parker will be excited about its name.

The phone rings. Andrew must have realized how insensitive he's being about this. I swear, I am just inches away from having him well trained.

"College Counseling, this is Lara."

"Hi, Lara, it's Cheryl."

All right, maybe it's more like yards.

"Oh, hi, Cheryl. Thanks for calling back so quickly."

"Lori said that it was an emergency. What's wrong? Did something happen to Tick?"

That Lori is such a pain in my ass. Did I ever say the word *emergency*?

"It's not an emergency. I told her that it was important. Tick's fine.

Physically, I mean." I clear my throat. "No, I was calling about NYU. I had a conversation with Ed Jellette this morning, and he said that you never contacted him, and that the development office didn't seem to have any information about you. I just wanted to know who you spoke with so that I could get this mistake straightened out before they start making decisions."

"Oh, right." She lowers her voice. "I meant to call you, but I've just been so busy. They didn't make a mistake. Stefan and I just changed our minds about donating. We've committed to several charities this year, and we're also funding some major construction at the Museum of Modern Art, so the resources just aren't available for NYU. Maybe once we have a history with them, but there are so many places that we have connections to already, and after a certain point they expect to see a financial commitment. Anyway, Tick will be fine. She's got you in her corner; I'm sure you'll be able to work something out with them."

I can't believe this is happening. They're going to support the fucking arts over their own daughter? Who cares about modern art? It's all bullshit, anyway. What, a few stupid red squares on a white canvas? That needs to be funded?

"Cheryl, you have to understand, there's only so much I can do. Tick is well below NYU's average. And she's not doing much to help her cause. She's getting a C in math, and she lied to me about her SAT scores. She told me that she didn't get them back yet, and I found out from Ed that she got a twelve-ten. NYU's average is a thirteen-seventy."

Cheryl sighs and mutters something under her breath that I can't quite make out. "I swear," she says, "she is going to be the death of me. So what are her chances?"

"They're bad. They were getting ready to deny her this morning, and I convinced Ed to wait until I spoke with you. Honestly, at this point, with a twelve-ten and her grades, she may not even get into a school that's in the top fifty." By the way, I have no idea what schools are even in the top fifty. I never use those rankings. They're stupid and they mean absolutely nothing as to whether a school is a good match for a student. But extraordinary times call for extraordinary measures. I need to speak to her in a language that she understands, and the loud gasp she just made tells me that she understands perfectly.

"Oh, no," she says. "That won't do." She pauses and I can practically hear the wheels turning in her head. "Let me talk to Stefan and I'll get back to you. I need to see what he thinks about this."

"Okay. I think that I can get them to defer her to regular decision, so that buys us a little time, but you'll need to decide fairly soon after we come back from winter vacation."

"Got it. Thanks for being so honest, Lara. So few people are these days, you know?"

Okay, now I feel guilty. But I do want Tick to get in, and it's not just because of my deal with Linda anymore. I like her. At least, I did up until today.

"Of course," I say. "It's my job."

Cheryl thanks me again and says good-bye, but as I am hanging up I hear her yelling into the phone. "Lara, are you still there?"

"Yes," I say, quickly putting the phone back to my ear. "Still here."

"Did you find out what you're having yet?"

"Yes," I say. "It's a girl."

Cheryl hesitates for a moment. "Oh, I'm so sorry," she says. "You have no idea what you're in for."

"Well," I say. "Thanks for being so honest. So few people are these days, you know."

She laughs. "Yes, I do. I'll be in touch."

Exactly three minutes before the period ends, I take my position outside of Tick's Government class. I peer in through the window and I see her sitting in the last row, her shoulders slumped. She is reading a book under her desk. No wonder she gets Cs. I am going to have a serious talk with this kid.

From the floor above, I hear a voice calling my name. I look up and I see Mark's entire torso hanging over the railing.

"Hey, Mrs. Stone, do you have a minute?"

I glance at my watch. "I have one minute exactly. Do me a favor: Stop leaning over like that; you're making me nervous." Mark stands back up and runs down the flight of stairs to where I am standing.

"I didn't know that you get nervous," he says.

I'm telling you, I have instilled the fear of God in these kids. Well, in all but one of them, apparently.

"You're down to twenty-three seconds, my friend," I say.

"Okay, I added a few more schools to my list, like you said."

"Good. Are you going to tell me what they are?"

"*Yes,*" he says, "I was getting to that." I tap my toe at him. "I'm adding BU, Vanderbilt, and NYU. What do you think?"

"Interesting choices. You realize that they're all completely different kinds of places, right? I mean, it doesn't get more apples and oranges than Vanderbilt and NYU."

"I know. But I'm thinking that I should keep my options open until I have a chance to visit and see what kind of an environment I like first-hand."

Inside the classroom the kids are starting to stand up, and I see Tick shoving stuff into her bag.

"Sounds like a plan. Just bring me the forms before winter break so that I can get them out before I go. I'm not working during vacation, *capisce?*"

"Yes, Mr. Corleone. I'll bring them by tomorrow, I swear." He salutes me and walks off down the hall, just as Tick emerges from the classroom.

Without saying a word, I grab her by the arm and lead her a few steps away from the door, to get out of the way of the throng.

"I think we need to have a talk," I say. I can tell from the guilty look on her face that she knows exactly what we'll be talking about.

"You found out about my SAT scores?" she asks.

I nod. "Why didn't you just tell me? I thought that we had moved beyond the bullshitting with each other." By the way, I'm finding the cursing strategy that Stacey suggested to be particularly effective this year. Especially with Tick.

"I know," she says. "I'm sorry. I didn't do it to be difficult; I just knew you'd be disappointed and I didn't want to tell you."

If this were real I would be very touched, but I can't help feeling like I'm being manipulated.

"Here's the thing, Tick: I don't believe you. I'm doing everything that I can to help you, and you're thwarting my efforts at every step. I don't care if your SAT scores are low. But you have to understand that it is very embarrassing for me to have to find out about them from an admissions rep. It hurts my credibility, and you need me to have credibility if I am going to convince NYU to take you. Do you get that?"

She nods. "I'm sorry. I should have told you, okay? What can I do to make you trust me?"

I lower my voice. "What you can do is change your attitude. I know you say you want to go NYU, but it's not just going to magically happen. You have some serious damage to repair, Tick. Your grades last year sucked. Now, I can explain them if you turn things around, but I will have no argument to make if they're not significantly better this semester. Do you understand? It means that you'll have to start making a real effort. I saw you in your class just now—you were reading a book instead of paying attention. That's not going to cut it. Just because your dad is famous doesn't mean that people are going to hand you things in life."

Tick's face turns bright red. I get the feeling that she's used to people dancing around the fact that her dad is *the* Stefan Gardner. Her friends probably act totally unimpressed when they go to her house, like everyone lives in a place like that.

"You know I don't think that," she says.

"No, actually, I don't. You know, for all of your vintage clothes and flea-market furniture, you still act as spoiled as everyone else here does. It's time for you to grow up and start taking responsibility for yourself. I'm sorry if I sound harsh, but I think you need to hear this."

She is crying. I made her cry. *Oh, shit.* Maybe I was a little too hard on her.

"I am not spoiled," she says, her voice breaking. "You have no idea what it's like to live my life. Everyone thinks it's so easy to have all of this money, and to have a famous dad, but it's not. It's harder than you think." She wipes her eyes with the back of her hand. "My own mother doesn't even care about me."

"Tick, I'm sure that your life comes with its own unique set of problems, and I've never been in your shoes, so you're right: I don't know what it's like. But honestly, your mom isn't that bad. She doesn't get you, but that doesn't mean that she doesn't love you. She's just doing the best she can."

Tick rolls her eyes at me. "Oh, so you're on her side now?"

"No, we're both on *your* side. We both want you to get what you want, but we can't make it happen for you. That's all I'm trying to say."

Tick has stopped crying, and she wipes her eyes with the back of her hand. "She's got you so brainwashed. She doesn't want what's best for

180 · Risa Green

me; she wants what looks best for her. She wants to be able to go to her charity dinners and cocktail parties and brag about what school her kid goes to. Don't think for one second that she's doing anything for me."

Okay, perhaps this is a better assessment. I don't know; I just want her to get in so that I can get to the gym a few days a week next year, that's all.

"Are we done?" she asks.

"Um, no. You're going to need to take your SATs again. I talked to my friend at NYU this morning, and the feeling I got from him is that they need to be higher. And just so you know, you're probably going to get deferred to regular decision."

"What does that mean?" she asks.

"It means that you won't get in early decision, but they'll review your file again with the rest of the applicants who applied for regular, and you'll hear from them in April." I smile at her. "They'll particularly be looking at your senior-year grades and your new SAT scores."

She half smiles back, in spite of herself. "Wow, you're so subtle. I get it, okay? I'll do better. Look, I'm late for my next class. I've gotta go."

"Are we okay?" I ask.

"We're fine," she says. "Thanks for being honest, at least." It probably wouldn't help to tell her that she sounds just like her mother. I think I'll just let it go at that.

When I get back to my office, I have two e-mails, one from Ed and one from Your Baby. I click on the one from Your Baby.

YOUR BABY NOW: Twenty-two Weeks

Hello, Lara!
Your baby is finally starting to look like a real little person! He still doesn't even weigh a full pound yet, but all of his features are in place. He has eyebrows and fingernails, and even his teeth are starting to form inside the gums!

Have you noticed that you're a bit clumsier than you used to be? Be careful! As you keep gaining weight, you may find yourself losing your balance, and the pregnancy hormones are causing your joints to loosen. It might be time to put away your high heels until after the baby is born.

Today's Hot Topic: Are you having heartburn and indigestion? Join our online chat and find out how other moms-to-be deal with their pregnancy tummy troubles. Plus, special guest Dr. Janie Abrams will be available to discuss your constipation concerns!

Delete. I hate these stupid updates. Now I've got two more self-evident truths to add to my Declaration of Independence:

I will never put away my high heels.
I will not discuss constipation with strangers.

Okay, let's see what Ed has to say.

From: Ed_Jellette@nyu
To: lstone@bap
Hi, Lar—
Bad news, sweetie. The Gardners never called. Do you still want us to defer?
Let me know ASAP.
Eddie

He's Eddie now?

To: Ed_Jellette@nyu
From: lstone@bap
Hi, *Eddie*—
Just spoke to Mrs. Gardner. Seems there has been a delay, but donation is still a possibility. Please do defer. Victoria will be taking Jan. SATs and I have an explanation for those grades ... senior year is

shaping up to be much better. You are my favorite
a.o. :-) Happy holidays!
Lara

I hit the send button and let out a long sigh.

Only three more days until winter vacation. I can't wait. This year has been so crappy. The kids are driving me crazy, their parents are driving me crazy—I don't know, it just seems worse than normal. It probably has something to do with the gifts. I guess I always feel this way in December, but then all is forgiven during the last week of school when the holiday gifts start rolling in. Over the past few years I've gotten five-hundred-dollar gift certificates to Barneys, an invitation to use a ski house in Aspen any weekend that I want, front-row tickets to a Madonna concert, a gorgeous Waterford crystal decanter with a vintage bottle of liquor, a day of beauty treatments from a Beverly Hills spa—one time I even got a shopping spree at Gucci because one of my parents that year was the head of their U.S. marketing team.

But this year all I've gotten are baby presents. A pink cashmere onesie from TSE. A pair of miniature suede driving shoes from Tods. A Burberry blanket. A silver spoon from Tiffany. It's really so disappointing. I mean, hello, people, the baby isn't the one writing letters of recommendation and editing essays for your kids all day; I am. You know, thanks for thinking of me, but how about thinking of *me*? I swear, it's like I've already been completely forgotten about, and this kid hasn't even been born yet. I can't even imagine what it will be like once she's actually here.

16.

Put Your Hemorrhoid In, Put Your Hemorrhoid Out

I was so right about not trusting people with my name decision. Nobody gets it. I've told just about everyone now, and they all cock their heads and say niceties that are really insults in disguise. Here's a sampling:

Julie: Parker? That's pretty. *Translation:* But not nearly as pretty as Lily.

My mother: Parker? It doesn't sound very Jewish. *Translation:* I knew that living in Los Angeles would turn you into someone who pretends to be something that she's not.

Random teachers at school over the age of 40: Parker? That's . . . interesting. *Translation:* That's horrible and weird; why would you do that to your child?

Moronic female student who wants to major in fashion design and who is wearing enormous white plastic ski glasses while sitting in my office: Parker? God, like, what ever happened to all of the normal names, like Brittany and Kaitlyn? *Translation:* N/A.

Stacey: Really? That's nice. *Translation:* I am not paying attention to a word that you are saying and clearly have other things on my mind right now.

There is definitely something going on with her. That's the second time this morning that she has had no reaction to something that would normally send her off the deep end. The first one was the hippie granola woman who tripped over a boulder and almost killed herself because she was staring at me instead of watching where she was going.

"Sorry," she said. "I just couldn't help admiring your big, beautiful belly."

It really skeeved me out, but Stacey barely even noticed, and normally she gets furious about things like that. She almost got into a fistfight with one of the Persian men last week. Now, granted, he reprimanded me for hiking—*This not safe for baby. You might slip on rocks and have abortion*—but he was, like, eighty-seven years old, and he wouldn't have whacked her in the leg with his walking stick if she hadn't told him to mind his own fucking business. But not a peep from her about the granola lady.

I wonder if she's having problems at work again. There's some female partner who has it in for her because Stacey's younger and prettier and smarter, and the bitch is always giving Stacey a hard time.

"Is something wrong?" I ask. "Did something happen at the office with Liz?"

She seems startled by this. "What? No. Work is fine. Why?"

"Why? You've let nearly fifteen opportunities for nastiness toward others get away from you this morning. I'd say that that's grounds for concern."

"Nothing is wrong," she says. "I'm just a little tired. Last night was a late one."

This is the same excuse that I used on her when I knew that I was pregnant and didn't want to tell her about it.

"Fine. Go ahead and lie to me. Whatever makes you happy."

She ignores this and we walk in silence until we get to the big log where we always stop to rest. Stacey sits down and takes a swig from her water bottle.

"I met someone," she says nonchalantly, as if this were not the hugest thing that she has uttered in the last five years.

You see? I *knew* there was something.

"Who?" I ask. "Where? When? When did you have time to meet someone?" I can tell that she was dreading this part, and that she's going to give me nothing but facts.

"I met him on the set in Mexico. He's in-house counsel for the studio, and we ended up having dinner a bunch of times. He used to work at O'Melveny downtown. Todd Saltzman. He went to Yale law and Cornell, I think."

"Sounds great," I say. "So what's the fatal flaw?" There's always a fatal flaw with Stacey. Ever since I've known her, she's been borderline Seinfeldian in her reasons for breaking up with people. He breathes like Darth Vader, he has Dumbo ears, he always smells like garlic, he says *nucular* instead of *nuclear*—you name it and Stacey has broken up with someone because of it.

She thinks for about two minutes before she answers me. Either this guy is so great that she really can't think of anything, or the flaw is so fatal that she doesn't even want to tell me. He probably has a third nipple or eleven toes or some other freakish appendage that's too embarrassing to talk about.

"He has a two-year-old," she says.

Okay, not quite the kind of freakish appendage that I had in mind. I mean, a wife, a girlfriend—a boyfriend, even—but a child? With Stacey? This is a violation of the world's natural order. This is not okay.

"What do you mean, he has a two-year-old?" I yell. "You can't be around a toddler. You'll kill it."

"Oh, look who's talking, Mommy Dearest."

"No, there is a difference. I at least *want* children. May I remind you that you have said that the world would be a better place if we reserved one continent for those who are childless and like it that way."

"Yes, and I still think that that's an excellent idea. Look, it's not like I'm adopting the kid or anything. I'm just sleeping with his father."

The cloud of stupidity that is hanging over her is making it difficult for me to breathe.

"That's great," I yell. "But what if things get serious? What if you decide to move in together?" It occurs to me that I have yet to ask the crucial question. I put my hands on my hips and glare at her. "And what's a single guy doing with a two-year-old, anyway?"

"He just got divorced," she says, again in that nonchalant tone of voice.

Is she kidding? I can't even speak. I close my eyes and quickly move my head from side to side, like I'm trying to shake off a bad dream, and she tries to explain.

"They met in law school, they were together for eight years, they thought a baby would make things better but it just made things worse, and they separated over a year ago. They have joint custody and he gets him every other weekend and one week a month."

This is so clearly a disaster waiting to happen. And what kind of a guy leaves his wife when he has a one-year-old son?

"Look," I say. "All I'm going to say is that you need to think long and hard about this one. If you fall in love with him, you become involved in this kid's life whether you like it or not. He'll start asking you to watch him when the babysitter flakes, he'll have you changing diapers while he's on the phone, and on Sunday mornings you're going to be watching Barney videos instead of drinking your coffee and reading the *Times*. And no matter what you think, no matter how mean you are, the kid will get attached to you. He *will*. So before you go any further with this, just try to remember that it's not only about you." I know that she knows that I'm right. She's just so damn stubborn that she'll never admit it. She takes another sip of her water and stands up and starts walking again.

"I'll be fine, don't worry. I have it all under control. We have an understanding about the kid. I'm not even going to meet him. We're just having a little fun, that's all."

"Yeah, well, it's all fun and games until somebody loses an eye."

She turns around and makes a face at me. "What the hell does that mean?"

"You know what it means. Just think about it."

When we get to the bottom, a group of people who are just starting out stop and applaud for me. This has been happening more and more lately, as if I've become some kind of an inspirational figure for my fellow hikers. I find it extremely disturbing. One woman in the group actually raises her fist at me and says, *You go, girl*, which is really not something that a white, Eddie Bauer–wearing person should say. Nonetheless, I pretend to take a bow, and Stacey walks ahead to her car. I scramble to catch up with her.

"I'll see you tonight?" I ask her.

We are invited to her firm's black-tie holiday party tonight. We go every year, under the pretense of me being a potential client, even though I have no interest in entertainment and never will. But Stacey likes us to be there so that she has someone to talk to and get drunk with, although this year I suppose I won't be much help in that department. Maybe I can convince Andrew to have a few sips of an apple martini, if they'll make him one with extra sugar.

Stacey presses the button on her key that unlocks the door, and the horn honks and the lights flash for a second.

"Yeah," she says coolly, stepping inside. "See you then."

I have so much grooming to do today before this party. I found a really cute dress at this funky maternity store on Melrose—it's a long black satin number with crisscrossing straps in the back and a little keyhole cutout between the boobs—but I can't even think about putting it on until I get myself cleaned up. I'm two weeks late on my highlights, I desperately need a manicure and a pedicure, I need to buy a bigger strapless bra, and I absolutely must do something about my pubic hair situation. Yes, that's right, my pubic hair situation. You see, normally, when I am not six months pregnant, I am meticulous about getting bikini waxes, and I do the full monty every five to six weeks with a Russian woman who tries to give me the perfect peepee (her words, not mine).

But these days, I'm uncomfortable enough without the added pain of having a former KGB operative pluck stray hairs from my labia with razor-sharp tweezers, so I've just kind of stopped going to her. And since my stomach is so big that I can't even see my peepee anymore, I've been operating under a rule similar to the if-I-didn't-order-it it-doesn't-have-any-calories rule, in that I figure that if I can't see what is growing down there, then it can't be that bad. But then the other night Andrew and I were about to have sex, and he couldn't even find his way in, there was so much going on down there, which is when I realized that it really is that bad and that I have to take some action. Not that I'm motivated to get a wax, but I at least think that I should trim it or something.

So, naked from the waist down, I spread a towel down on the bathroom floor and collect my manicure scissors and the pedestal mirror that I use to put on my makeup. I sit down on the towel and try to angle the mirror so that I can see past my stomach. There. *Oooh*. That's scary. I didn't realize that I was even capable of growing a bush like this.

I start hacking away, stopping every few seconds to admire my work, but as I clear away the hair near my butt I notice something. What is that? I reangle the mirror and try to lean in closer to get a better look.

Oh, my God. Eww.

I stand up and run to the phone. *Please be in the car. Please be in the car.* He picks up on the first ring.

"Hi, honey, what's up?"

I am already in tears. "I th-th-think I h-h-h-have a h-h-h-hemor-r-rhoid."

"You have a hemorrhoid?"

"Y-y-yes."

"Are you sure that's what it is?"

"I'm pretty s-s-s-sure."

"Does it hurt?" What's with the twenty questions? Does he not understand what is going on here? I have something *growing* out of my ass.

"No," I say. "But it's really, really gross." I start sobbing again. "I n-need for you to b-b-buy me some m-m-medicine." There is a pause.

"I'm not buying you hemorrhoid medicine. It's your hemorrhoid; you buy it." I cannot believe that he just said that to me.

"You are so mean, Andrew. Please, I need you to get it."

"No way. It's too embarrassing. You're home. Just go to the drugstore and get it."

"*No,*" I insist. "You have to buy it. If you buy it, it doesn't have to be for you. You could be buying it for anyone. It could be for your girlfriend, or your wife, or your friend; you're just a guy out on an errand for somebody. But if I buy it, it is definitely for me. You can't walk into a drugstore when you're six months pregnant and just casually pick up a tube of Preparation H. Come on, how cliché is that?"

"Can we discuss this later? I'm pulling into the gym."

No, no, no. I can't lose this one. I'll have to fight dirty.

"You don't love me," I whine.

He sighs. "Good-bye."

"Mean."

"*Good-bye.*"

"'Bye." I hang up the phone, temporarily defeated. There is no way that I am buying it myself. Pregnancy is humiliating enough without the whole world knowing that I have hemorrhoids. Whatever. I'll deal with it later. That always seems to work. In the meantime, I have appointments to keep.

When I arrive back home, highlighted, manicured, pedicured, and newly brassiered, I am feeling somewhat like myself again. I go into the bedroom and Andrew is lying on the chaise at the foot of the bed, watching a college basketball game.

"Hi," I say, leaning in for a kiss.

"Hi." He nods toward the bed. "There's a present for you."

Lying on top of the pillows is a tube of Preparation H, tied with a red bow.

"Oh, honey," I say. "You are so sweet."

I go over and give him a big hug, and I feel like I want to cry. Honestly, I think that this just might be the most romantic moment of my life. I mean, come on, any guy can buy you flowers, but the one who buys you hemorrhoid cream must really, really love you.

"I love you," I whisper to him.

He smiles at me. "You should."

17.

Loo, Loo,
Puke in the Loo

There is nothing worse than having to make small talk with a bunch of lawyers when you're stone-cold sober. Especially when they're not. Of course, I wouldn't have to be subjected to this if Stacey were here, but it's already nine thirty and she hasn't even shown up yet. I wonder if she had a date with her new boyfriend before this. Yeah. She's probably having fabulous, hemorrhoid-free sex right now. Lucky bitch.

I, on the other hand, am sitting by myself at a table, where I have spent the last ten minutes pretending to desperately look for something in my purse so as to avoid having to make any more conversation with these people, although I must look extraordinarily stupid, because my purse is about the size of a matchbook, thus enabling its contents to be determined in about a tenth of a second. Andrew, of course, is nowhere to be found. He disappeared twenty minutes ago to stalk the waiter with the tray of mini pizzas after failing to convince him to just leave the whole thing with us. *Sir, my wife is six months pregnant and extremely hungry; do you think that you could just leave that here and go get another one to pass around to everyone else?* When Andrew realized that the guy didn't speak English, he even tried to pull the pregnancy card *in Spanish,* but the guy knew exactly what he was up to and just shook his finger at him and walked away.

I scan the room to look for some kind of a distraction, and out of the corner of my eye I spot a crowd gathering near the entrance to the ballroom. It must be a celebrity. A few big actors show up to this thing every year, and they get accosted the entire night. Honestly, I would hate to be famous. It must be like being pregnant all the time. All kinds of strange people coming up to you and talking to you and touching you without asking, like they're your best friends. What a miserable, miserable existence. I am curious, though, so I stand up and crane my neck so that I can see what all of the hoopla is about. In the middle of the crowd is an older, not very attractive man whom I don't recognize and his date, a pretty, skinny platinum blonde who looks like she's about seventeen. Typical.

But then I do a double take. Wait a minute. She *is* seventeen. That's Tick. What the hell is Tick doing at this party? I got her to break up with Marcus so that she could go out with a creepy geriatric guy? I must get to the bottom of this, if for no other reason than because it will give me something to do. I stride over to the throng and edge my way toward her. She is sipping from a glass of champagne, and with my index finger I authoritatively tap her on the shoulder. She is so busted.

"Tick?" She whirls around, and when she sees that it is me she beams.

"Mrs. Stone! What are you doing here?"

I eye the glass of champagne and glance suspiciously in the direction of her date. "Uh, no, I think the question is, what are *you* doing here?"

She sees where I am going with this and laughs. "No, that's my dad. My mom's out of town, so he brought me. He doesn't like to go to parties by himself."

Oh, of course. Her dad. I forgot that he's a client of the firm. Well, that makes much more sense.

"Okay, you had me worried there for a minute." I give her the once-over. "You look beautiful, by the way. Your dress is gorgeous." Her dress is a long, silver mesh-looking thing that she's wearing with a stunning pair of silver stilettos. She must have gotten all of it straight from her mother's closet.

"Thanks," she says. "My mom is really good friends with John Galliano. He made it for me."

Or not.

"Yes, well," I say, brushing the back of my hand against my forehead. "I summer with the Versaces; they make me things all the time."

She blushes. "Sorry. I didn't mean to sound obnoxious." She leans in and whispers to me, "I'm a little drunk."

Noooo. Really? "I think that that's more information than I need to know, but thank you for the insight."

Her father suddenly notices that she is talking to me, and he takes her by the arm. "Victoria, who is your friend?" He has a French accent. I didn't realize that he was actually French. I always assumed that his name was Stephen and that he changed it to Stefan to give himself a Hollywood mystique. This town really can make you so jaded.

"Daddy, this is my college counselor from school, Mrs. Stone."

He looks me up and down and smiles. "Ah, the famous Mrs. Stone. I have heard much about you. You are going to get my daughter into NYU, yes?"

No, you're *going to get your daughter into NYU by writing them a big, fat check.* "I'm certainly trying," I say. "It's very nice to meet you."

"And you. Both of you, eh?" he says, glancing at my stomach. At least he didn't touch it.

I smile and put my hand on my belly. "One and a half, really," I say, letting out what I hope is an alluring, sophisticated chuckle. I don't think I've ever been faker in my entire life.

"Yes, well, you have much to look forward to," he says, putting his arm around Tick. She has him absolutely coiled around her finger. No wonder her mother is such a bitch. She must be insanely jealous of their relationship. "And how is it that you are here this evening? Is your husband associated with this firm?"

Oh, how French and chauvinistic.

"No," I say. "One of my closest friends from law school is an attorney here, and she invites me every year. She's hoping to lure me back into the legal profession."

He raises his eyebrows as if he is impressed, and he looks down at Tick. "I see. The lady is beautiful *and* intelligent. Victoria, you should pay attention to your counselor; she can teach you some things." A gray-haired man in a tuxedo is trying to cut in front of me, and Stefan nods at him. "Ladies, please excuse me. I must attend to some gentlemen who are considerably less interesting than yourselves. It was a pleasure meeting you, Mrs. Stone." I reach out to shake his hand, but he takes it and kisses the top of it instead.

Ooh, how French and charming.

Just then there is a tap on my shoulder, and I turn around to see Stacey standing behind me.

"It's about time you got here," I say. "I've been here since eight."

"Sorry," she says with a big grin. She's wearing a light pink satin dress with an empire waist that makes her boobs look freakishly large. "I was running late."

It is then that I notice that there is a man standing behind her, and that his hand is resting on the small of her back. Okay. So she was having sex. But there's no way that that's all this is about. You don't bring a guy to your firm's biggest event the year before you're up for partner if you're not serious about him.

I give him the once-over. I have to hand it to her: He's kind of hot for a lawyer. And he's wearing a fabulous plain-front, pin-striped suit with a light pink tie that matches Stacey's dress exactly. *Hmmm.*

"Stacey," I say, "you remember Tick Gardner." Tick is practically jumping up and down, she is so excited. I have to remember to get her drunk more often. She's much more fun without the badass attitude.

"No way," she slurs. "This is *your* firm? My dad's a client here."

"I know," Stacey says. "It's nice to see you again. You look . . . very adult." I clear my throat and shoot the guy a look, and Stacey shoots one back at me. "Lara, Tick, this is my friend Todd."

Todd sticks out his hand, and Tick and I both take turns shaking it.

"I've heard a lot about you, Lara," he says.

"That seems to be a theme tonight," Tick says, giggling.

Okay. I've had enough of the kid. "Tick, would you excuse us, please?" She makes a face at me and then goes off to get in line at the bar.

"So, Todd, I understand that you and Stacey met in Mexico." He nods as he takes a sip of his drink. Did I mention that I hate the fact that I am the only sober person here?

"Yes," he says. "I wasn't even supposed to be there, but there were some problems, so the studio thought it would be a good idea for me to go down at the last minute. It was fate." He gazes at Stacey and squeezes her hand. Oh, this poor guy has no idea what he's gotten himself into. He takes another sip and then turns back to me. "Stacey tells me that you work at Bel Air Prep now. That's a pretty high-powered place, huh? It must be intense."

"Yeah, the kids are pretty stressed out, and their parents are all crazy, but it's not that bad. Nothing like being a lawyer."

"Yeah, but what's it like? Are the kids really snotty?"

Why is this always the first thing that people want to know when they ask me about my job? Nobody cares about what I actually do; they just want to know what it's like to work with really rich teenagers. Like it's any different from working with really rich adults. I don't know why, but I always get vicariously offended by this question. I mean, the kids *are* snotty, but they're my kids. I would feel like I'd betrayed them if I offered up any details.

"You know," I say, trying to sound casual. "They drive BMWs and they wear designer clothes, but most of them are good kids who work really hard. They're under a lot of pressure to succeed. Much worse than when we were in high school. You couldn't pay me to be a teenager today."

Todd looks unsatisfied by my answer, which pleases me immensely, but then he starts asking me questions about the kind of law I used to practice, and we somehow end up in a conversation about reverse triangular mergers that is making me want to slit my wrists. You know what? He's perfect for her. Between the two of them, they make up approximately an eighth of a real life. I'll bet he spends so much time at work that he never even sees his son.

"I'm sorry, Todd," I say, cutting him off midsentence. "But I've got a baby sitting on my bladder, and as much as I'd love to continue chatting, I've got to get to the bathroom before I pee all over the floor. It was great to meet you."

"No problem," he says. "My ex-wife was the same way when she was pregnant. She could barely last twenty minutes. I know the location of every last bathroom in this entire city."

"You and me both." I give him a little wave and book it for the door.

The bathroom is empty, so I take the opportunity to pull up my dress and fix my thong, which has been rubbing uncomfortably against my hemorrhoid for two hours. *Ah. Much better.* It seems, however, that I have misjudged the emptiness of the bathroom, because I suddenly hear a sniffle coming from the handicap stall in the far corner. I peer under the door and I see silver strappy stilettos.

"Tick?" I say. "Is that you?"

"Mrs. Stone?"

"Yeah. Are you okay?" There is another sniffle.

"Not really," she says. "I think I might have had too much to drink."

Oh, no.

She unlocks the door and it swings open to reveal her sitting on the floor, her silver dress pulled up around her waist, with her head next to the toilet. "I think I'm going to be sick."

"Okay," I say, "do you want me to go get your dad?"

Tick looks alarmed by this. "No! Please don't tell my dad. He'll freak out. Please. Can you just stay here with me?"

What? Can *I* stay with her? She must have me mistaken for her mother's personal assistant. I start to back away from the stall.

"You know, Tick, I'm not really good with puking. Other people's puke usually makes me gag."

She looks like she's going to cry. "Please, I really don't feel well—" She suddenly jerks her head up and flings it over the toilet bowl. Her hair falls into her face and I can hear the puke hitting the water.

Ugh. Gross. When she looks up there are big, pinkish chunks covering the front pieces of her hair. I close my eyes so I don't vomit myself. *Okay. I need to get out of here.*

"Tick, I'm really sorry. I just can't do this."

Now she's crying. "Fine. Then do you think that you could get Stacey? I just need someone to sit here. This has never happened to me before."

She wants me to get Stacey? *Stacey?* What makes her think that Stacey will sit with her? She doesn't even know Stacey. Stacey will just come in here and tell her what a pussy she is for not being able to hold her liquor like a man. Please.

"Tick, trust me, you don't want Stacey in here with you right now. She'll only make things worse."

She looks up at me again. "I don't think that things can get much worse, Mrs. Stone. Stacey will be fine."

Fine, I think. *You asked for it.* I walk over to the door and put my hand on the doorknob, and I feel the baby kick me in the ribs. It might as well have been my conscience. *Shit.*

I can't leave her here.

Okay, Lara, get it together. You're going to have a kid in a few months; you'll have to deal with puke at some point, right? Right. No—wait a minute—wrong. I always assumed that I would put Andrew in charge of that department. Oh, okay. Fine. I'll face my fears.

I take a deep breath and then I turn around and walk over to the sink. I pick up a hand towel and run it under cold water.

"Here," I say, handing it to her. "Put this on the back of your neck. It'll make you feel better."

"Thanks," she says. She leans over the toilet bowl again, and I grab her hair and pull it back from her face. I can feel the puke under my fingers, but I am trying not to think about it. When she's finished, I go back to the sink and wet some more towels so that she can wipe off her face.

"I think that's it," she says. "I feel a lot better."

"Good," I say, handing her another towel. "Now let's see what we can do about getting this out of your hair." I take a comb and a bottle of mouthwash from the basket of toiletries that the florist has set up on the counter, and I begin to comb through her hair, trying to get the pieces out.

"Ugh," she says after she swigs some of the mouthwash. "I never should have had that pasta for dinner. The pink sauce was so rich."

"Okay, look, don't press your luck here. There's only so much I can take."

"Sorry," she says, smiling.

I think I have gotten out most of the big pieces, so I take another wet washcloth and run it over the strands of her hair to wipe away any left-over residue. When I'm finished, I throw all of the towels into the wooden hamper that is set up in the corner, I wash my hands, and then I sit down on the floor of the bathroom stall. Tick is lying down next to me with her cheek resting on the marble.

"You won't tell my dad about this, right?"

"No," I say. "I won't tell him. But I hope you have a new understanding of what your limits are. You're a skinny girl, Tick; you can't drink like a football player."

"I know. I'm sorry. I swear to God, I hardly ever drink. I'm not that into it. I just thought it would be fun tonight, since this was all adults and I was so dressed up and everything."

"I know. I was a teenager once, too." I smile nostalgically at her. "My parents used to have a place at the Jersey shore, and I had huge parties every time they went away. I never got caught, either, until somebody left a bottle of Coors on the floor in the corner of the living room and I missed it. My mom found it two weeks later. God, she was so mad at me."

"Do you like your mom?" she asks.

I pause as I think about how to answer that one. "I do like her. Now. We went through a rough period when I was about twenty, but things are better. Of course, it helps that she lives three thousand miles away."

Tick absorbs this information for a second. "Do you see her a lot?"

"A few times a year. She'll probably come out a lot more after the baby's born."

"I wish I only had to see my mom a few times a year. And I wish she was going to be out of town for more than just the weekend. Two weeks of winter break with her is way too much."

It must be so sad to have your kid hate you so much that she can't even tolerate two weeks with you. How do you avoid it, though? It seems like all of my students hate their parents, except for the really nerdy ones. Is it even possible to have a cool kid who likes you, or are those two things mutually exclusive? You know, I always thought that I would want my kid to be popular, but now I'm not so sure. Maybe it's better just to have a dork.

The bathroom door opens and two women walk in, and I quickly reach up and shut the door to our stall. I put a finger up to my lips to tell Tick to be quiet. The last thing I need is for people to start talking about the pregnant lady sitting on the floor in the bathroom with the teenager who smells like vomit. We listen to them talk about some sixty-year-old partner who is hitting on everything that walks—apparently he does this every year—and then one of the women starts talking about Stefan.

"Did you see Stefan Gardner? He brought his daughter. Isn't that sweet?"

"Yeah. I think I read something in *People* about her last year. They were doing a profile on the children of Hollywood." She pauses for a minute as she puts on her lipstick. "Could you imagine being the daughter of someone so rich? What a life that kid must have. She's probably such a brat."

I am outraged by this. I look over at Tick, expecting her to jump up and defend herself, but she just rolls her eyes at me. When the women are gone, I have to say something.

"Doesn't that kind of thing make you mad?"

"I'm over it," she says. "I used to get really upset, but there's nothing I can do about it. People can think whatever they want. I don't care."

I can tell that she does care, though, so I quickly change the subject. "What are you doing for Christmas?" I ask her.

"Oh, God," she says. "I hate Christmas." She rolls over onto her back and stares up at the ceiling. "Promise me that when your baby is old enough, you'll have a fun Christmas that's all about her."

"I'm Jewish," I say. "There is no Christmas for her."

Tick looks surprised by this. "Oh, you are? Fine. Hanukkah, whatever. Just make it her holiday."

"What do you mean?" I ask. "As opposed to what?"

"As opposed to a big party with lots of famous people who make everything about them. As opposed to Gérard Depardieu playing Santa Claus and Daniel Day Lewis doing a reading of *A Christmas Carol* while your kid gets to sit upstairs and watch TV with the nanny."

It actually sounds fabulous to me, and I'm wondering if I can finagle an invite, but I guess I can see how it would suck if you were the kid. "Well, considering that the most famous person I know is you, I'm not all that worried about it. But thanks for the tip."

"Yeah," she says. "No problem." Suddenly she hoists herself up and unlocks the door. "Okay. I'm ready to go back out there. My dad probably thinks that I abandoned him."

I stand up and adjust my dress over my stomach, and I go over to the mirror to check out my hair. Tick takes one more gulp of mouthwash and spits it out, and then starts to walk toward the door.

"Wait," I say to her. There is a chunk of pasta hanging from the back of her head that I missed. I reach toward her and pull it out with my hand. "There," I say. "Good as new."

Tick bites her lip for a second, and then she leans in and gives me a long, tight hug.

"Thanks, Mrs. Stone," she whispers.

* * *

When I get back into the ballroom, I find Andrew sitting by himself at a cocktail table, with four plates of food in front of him.

"Where have you been?" he asks. "I've been looking for you for almost an hour."

Poor Andrew. Remember how I said that there's nothing worse than hanging around with a bunch of lawyers when you're sober? I lied. Actually, there's nothing worse than hanging around a bunch of lawyers when you're sober and you're not even a lawyer.

"Sorry," I say, sitting down across from him. "Tick got drunk and she was puking her brains out, so I stayed with her for a little bit in the bathroom."

"You did?" He looks at me incredulously. Andrew knows that I hate other people's puke. He had food poisoning one night last year, and I actually left the house because I couldn't even handle listening to him throw up. To be fair, though, Andrew is the loudest puker that I ever met. The noise reverberates through the entire house, like he's somehow hooked himself up to the surround sound. It's incredibly disgusting.

"I know," I say, nodding my head. "Can you believe that? I even *touched* it."

He smiles at me like I just told him that I'm getting a lifetime achievement award. "Honey, I'm so proud of you. Is she okay now?"

"Yeah, I think she's fine. I just feel bad for her. She seems so . . . I don't know . . . she seems lonely. It's like when you're a kid, everything is supposed to revolve around you. I mean, I didn't even realize that my parents had a life beyond me until I was about twelve. But I don't think she's ever had that. I think she's kind of a footnote in her parents' lives. They just pay attention to her when it's convenient for them. It's really sad."

"Oh, Dolly," he says, a big, sly grin spreading over his face. "If I didn't know better, I might think that you were softening up on me."

I gasp at him in mock horror. "How dare you utter such blasphemy," I say. "I'm not getting soft; I just had a temporary moment of weakness, that's all."

Andrew smirks at me, and from out of nowhere Stacey saunters up behind him. She looks at me and puts her finger to her lips, and then she reaches down and grabs his last egg roll.

"Hey!" Andrew says, whipping around. "Get your own food, Horowitz; I worked hard for that."

"Sorry, Drew, you snooze, you lose." She pulls up a chair and sits down at the table, and Andrew pulls his plates closer to him, constructing a fort around them with his forearms. "So," she says to me, "what did you think of Todd?"

"I think he's great," I say. "He's cute, he dresses well, he's smart. I also think that you're full of shit, and that you wouldn't have brought him here if things weren't serious between the two of you." I stare at her pointedly, waiting for a response.

She rolls her eyes. "I brought him here because I thought it would be fun to have someone to talk to besides you and the people I see every friggin' day of my life at the office. He is cute, though, huh? And he can do *amazing* things with his tongue."

At this, Andrew drops his arms and slams his palms on the table. "Did I need to know that?" he says to her. Stacey reaches over, grabs a crab cake, and pops it into her mouth. She's like lightning, that girl.

"Hey!" Andrew says again, glaring at her.

Stacey holds out her hands as if to proclaim her innocence. "It's not my fault that you're predictable," she says to him. "Ooh, I think Liz Hurley just walked in." Andrew's head spins around and Stacey swipes a cube of beef satay. She shakes her head at me and stands up. "It's just too easy." Andrew looks back at us, snarling as he realizes what just happened.

"Are you leaving?" I ask her.

"Yeah. Todd's got the kid this weekend, and the sitter can only stay until one."

Andrew looks at us blankly. "Kid? What kid?" he says. We both ignore him.

"I hope you know what you're doing," I tell her.

"I told you," she says. "It's all under control."

The day after the party is shaping up to be a bad day for me. I wish that I could say that it is bad because I'm superhungover and I have a killer headache, but we both know that the closest I came to alcohol last night was the champagne that Tick barfed up in the toilet bowl. No. It's a bad day because I'm feeling fat and gross and hemorrhoidal, and everywhere

I look there are pretty, skinny women in pretty, skinny holiday party dresses, and I just feel like a cow. And you know that the only possible way to remedy this feeling is for me to go out and shop myself into oblivion. Oh, it would be so much easier if I were one of those people who could deal with depression simply by binge eating, or going for a run, or writing in a journal, but the only thing that ever works for me is therapy by credit card.

Of course, I attribute this problem, like all others, to my mother. You see, my mother was a working mom who had neither the time nor the inclination to bake cookies or pies for me. When I would come home from school upset about some trivial matter or another, my mom wouldn't offer me baked goods as a means of comfort. No, no. I would get, *I'm sorry you're upset, honey. Let's go buy you a new pair of shoes; that'll make you feel better.* Then we'd hop in the car and run off to the mall, careful to hide our purchases from my dad upon our return.

She was right, though, I always did come home feeling better. You just can't be in a bad mood when you know that you have a cute new outfit to wear to school the next day. You can see, however, how this childhood strategy might evolve into a full-fledged adult problem, which it clearly has. Especially the part about hiding the purchases from the person who paid for them.

Anyway, when I was on Beverly Drive yesterday, buying my new strapless bra, I happened to walk by A Pea in the Pod and notice that there was a huge *End of Season Sale* sign in the window, and I haven't been able to stop thinking about it since. I've spent all morning trying to rationalize with myself about how it makes no sense to be buying new maternity clothes at this stage of the game—I'll only be able to wear them for three months—but my car somehow drove all by itself and landed me here, outside of the store, where I am presently trembling with the excitement of an addict who is about to get a fix.

I am not going to spend more than three hundred dollars.

I step inside and it is immediately apparent to me that I am in trouble. It's like they're giving the place away. Pants that were one hundred and fifty dollars the last time I was in here are now going for thirty-five bucks. Sweaters are marked down 75 percent. And, of course, the spring clothes have also just arrived, and there are some really, really cute

Chaiken capri pants that I am going to need to have in both beige and stone.

The saleswoman spots me as I begin to hang things over the side of my arm. It is my dear old friend Sherry.

"Hi!" she says, running over to me. "I was hoping you'd stop by for the sale!"

Yeah, I think. *I'll bet you were.*

"I see you found the Chaikens. We just got in so much great stuff. You look amazing, by the way. What are you now, like, eight months?"

Ooh. That hurts. That really hurts.

"No," I say, trying not to cry. "I just started my seventh."

Sherry winces, knowing full well that she might have just blown any commission that she was going to make off of me today. But she has no idea who she's dealing with. If anything, she just helped her cause.

"Look," I say, trying not to sound as hostile as I am feeling. "I'm going to be very honest with you. I'm having kind of a bad day, and I'm feeling like I want to do this by myself. It's nothing you did, and you can take credit for the sale, but I'm just not really in the mood for an audience today."

"No problem," Sherry says, all smiley and sympathetic, like she's heard this a thousand times before. "I totally get it. We all have bad days. I'll be over at the register if you need anything."

Wow. She handled that really well. It occurs to me that this scenario must be covered in the handbook. *If a customer asks to be left alone, oblige her but do not take it personally. Realize that she may have just gotten her first hemorrhoid and that she is, understandably, feeling upset.* My God. Those Pea in the Pod people are geniuses.

Left to my own devices, I begin hauling armfuls of clothes into my dressing room, telling myself that I'm not going to actually *buy* any of them, but that I just want to *try them on,* just to see to how they look. But before I can pull the curtain shut behind me, the woman in the dressing room next to mine emerges wearing my Seven jeans. And, as you know, now that I have seen her, I am required by law to check her out and to see how I look compared to her.

I look like an elephant compared to her. She's petite and skinny and she's barely even showing. My guess is she's maybe just four months.

A rookie. *Okay,* I think. *I've got a three-month handicap.* I guess that makes it a little bit easier to swallow.

The Rookie sees me eyeing her and proceeds to engage me in combat. "Do you think these are too small?" she asks.

Hmm. Forceful, yet nonthreatening. An excellent offensive move.

"No," I say. "They look great on you."

"Because they're a small and I'm worried that they won't fit me later on."

I smile at her nostalgically, remembering when I was in my first trimester. I decide to bestow some of my wisdom upon this young protégé.

"I have them," I say, "and I remember that when I bought them, the small fit me great, but I bought them in a small and a medium because I thought the same thing as you. And I'm really glad I got the medium, too, because the small ones are skintight on me now. What are you, like, four months?" She looks a little embarrassed and I hope that I haven't overshot how far along she is. I wasn't trying to play dirty, I swear.

"No," she says. "Actually, I'm six months. I don't know why, I just haven't really popped yet."

Ooh. I've been hustled. Hustled by a pro. I decide to go against my instincts and be gracious, since nobody likes a sore loser. I smile at her. "You should definitely buy them in that size, then. You look amazing."

I smile again and retreat to my dressing room in shame. Well, that settles it. The only thing to do now is to hide in here until she leaves. There is no way that I am going to walk out there and stand next to her in front of the mirror so that she can feel good about herself at my expense. Not a chance.

Huh. So this is how it feels to be in Shorty's shoes.

Thankfully, I've brought about four hundred things into the dressing room with me, so I have plenty to do to kill the time. I get undressed and look at myself in the mirror. Disgusting. I'm flat-out disgusting. I have no waist, my boobs are a web of blue veins, the space that used to exist between my inner thighs has completely disappeared, and I have a dark, hairy line running from my crotch to my belly button. I have no idea how Andrew even looks at me, let alone sleeps with me. That man deserves a medal.

I begin trying stuff on, periodically peeking under the door to see if Fast Eddie has taken off yet, but she's still there. And it seems that Sherry has latched onto her, because I can hear her out there, feeding her lines about how skinny her arms look and how she's definitely not going to gain any more weight in her legs. That two-timing wench. I am now almost in tears for real, and it is becoming clear to me that I am going to have to do what any self-respecting woman would do: I am going to have to buy everything.

Once the coast is clear, I drag it all up to the register (two trips), and when the woman asks me if anyone was helping me today, I tell her that no, nobody was. Oh, please, like I'm really going to give Sherry the commission after all of that. As she zaps each tag with the scan gun, she makes a point of commenting on how cheap everything is.

Zap. "This sweater is only sixty dollars! It used to be two hundred." Zap. "Oh, my God! This skirt is thirty-nine-ninety-nine!"

When all is said and done, the total on the cash register reads, in electronic red numbers, $1214.76. *Holy shit.* This is more than three hundred dollars. This is not good. I begin to panic as I try to come up with a plan. *Deep breaths. Deep breaths. Okay.* I can put three hundred of it on the American Express card that Andrew and I share. Three hundred I can explain. It's what to do with the other nine hundred that is causing me problems right now. I look at the clothes and then at the saleswoman.

"I think I might need to put some stuff back," I say. She nods at me, and we both start going through everything in the pile.

"What about this?" she says, holding up a hot-pink cashmere halter top.

"No," I say. "I love that. And it's so cheap."

"These?" She pulls out a pair of black pants that are slit almost to the knee on each leg.

"Oh, no," I say. "Those are my favorites. What do you think about these cords?" I ask her.

She puts her hands over her heart. "You can't put those back," she says. "For twenty-five dollars, even if you only wear them once, it's still worth it."

She's right. Of course she's right. We go through every single piece of clothing in the pile, but there's simply nothing that I can get rid of. It seems that I'm going to have to break out my secret weapon. I pull a second credit card from my wallet.

"Here," I say, shaking my head in disgust. "Put three hundred on the AmEx and put the rest of it on this one."

I can't believe that I'm doing this. I can't believe that I'm using my emergency shopping credit card. Andrew has no idea that I even possess this card. I use it only if I must have something that he would never understand—like a five-hundred-dollar pair of gold shoes, or a full-length light pink shearling coat that is ridiculous for LA but is just too gorgeous not to buy—but it's been almost two years since the last time something like that happened. But desperate times call for desperate measures. I'll have to figure out later how to siphon the money out of our savings account to pay for it.

I am going to be in so much trouble if Andrew finds out about this. So keep your mouth shut, okay? He can't find out.

18.

Twinkle, Twinkle, TV Star

'm not even a full week into my vacation yet, and I'm already starting to get bored just sitting around the house. So, knowing full well that it's a huge mistake, I decide to check my e-mail account at school, just to have something to do for a few minutes. By the way, I do this every year, and I never learn. Every year I tell my kids that I won't be working over winter break. Every year I tell them that if they are applying to colleges with January first deadlines and they want me to look over their applications, they have to bring them to me before vacation. But do they listen? No. Every year, at just about this time, I get bored and check my e-mail anyway, and I never fail to have e-mails from at least six kids, all praying that I am checking my e-mail. And then, of course, I have no choice but to respond to them, and I end up getting all aggravated and annoyed by the fact that I am working over winter break, even though I said that I wouldn't be. Damn it.

The first e-mail is from Alexis, a girl who, at my last unofficial count, owns four different Louis Vuitton bags, six Pradas, a Balenciaga, two Marc Jacobs Stella bags (one in hot pink, one in powder blue), and a Dior. And that's just since September. My assistant and I have an over/under bet going on how many different bags we'll see by graduation, and we keep careful records that are updated every time one of us has an Alexis sighting on campus. Anyway, the genius wants to know if she should answer the optional question on the University of Michigan application about how much money her parents make.

To: alexisr@bap
From: lstone@bap
Hi, Alexis,
I happened to check my e-mail and saw your question. No. Do not tell them how much money your parents make. The people reading your application make about thirty grand a year, and it will only make them hate you to know that you spend that amount on purses each season. Just leave it blank. By the way, I won't be checking e-mail again. You got very lucky this time. Have a happy New Year.
Mrs. Stone

The next one is from Mark.

To: lstone@bap
From: markc@bap
Subject: PLEASE, PLEASE, PLEASE, CHECK YOUR E-MAIL
Hi, Mrs. Stone—
I know you said you're not checking e-mail, but just in case you are, I wanted to know if you could look over my essay. The question is, "What activity has been the most meaningful to you and why?" It's due Jan. 1. If you are open to bribery, I promise to get you something really nice if you read it.
Mark

I let out a long sigh. I must have asked him fifty times if he needed help with anything before vacation, and every time he said that he was fine. I should have known better. Never trust a seventeen-year-old who tells you that everything is "fine." He's just lucky that I like him. I click on the attachment and start reading.

The activity that has been the most meaningful to me is my role as president of the Business and Investment Club for the last three years. When I joined the club as a freshman, I expected to meet other students like me, who had an appreciation for money, and to hear their ideas about how to make it grow. But when I went to my first meeting, I was disappointed to find that the club was just a bunch of guys sitting around and talking about businesses that they would want to start one day, when they were older. So the next year, as a sophomore, I decided to run for president of the club, and I won.

Once I was in charge, I made some sweeping changes. I brought in guest speakers from a variety of businesses, including investment bankers, small-business owners, and CEOs of major corporations, and I also required every member to do research on an industry sector each week, and to give their opinion about the best stock in each sector. After a few weeks we realized that the stocks that we picked were doing well, so most of the club members started their own portfolios and began to invest in them. I personally invested ten thousand dollars that I got for my bar mitzvah, and in two years I have turned it into almost fifty thousand. With the money that I made, I was even able to buy myself a BMW Five Series convertible, a car that costs much more than what my parents ever would have bought me.

Being president of the Business and Investment Club has turned me into a leader and a more responsible person, and I have made some incredible connections with the guest speakers who have come to our meetings. One investment banker even told me to call him when I was in college if I ever needed an internship. I have learned so much about business and money from this experience, and as a result, I think that I am more prepared than most high school students to enter the world of business and to study it in college.

Oh, Jesus. Where do I even start with this? He may have good grades and high SAT scores, but writing is definitely not his forte. Thank God he's applying to business programs.

To: markc@bap
From: lstone@bap
Subject: Yeah, yeah, yeah, I read it
Hi, Mark,
You got lucky, my friend. I read the essay, and
here's the thing: Because I know you, I know that
you do not mean to sound as obnoxious as you do.
But if I did not know you, I would be appalled. It
starts off strong, talking about how you changed
the club as prez, but when you get into the part
about how much money you made and the car you
bought, it gets a little scary. Try this—pretend that
you are a Republican candidate and that you are answering questions on the campaign trail; i.e., be
vague and nonspecific so as not to alienate more
moderate voters. Got it?
Mrs. Stone
P.S. Diamonds are my bribe of choice.

As I am responding to the next e-mail, trying to explain to one of my less
intelligent girls that sending an application to a P.O. box does not mean
that you have to actually mail the application in a box instead of in an
envelope, a reply from Mark appears.

To: lstone@bap
From: markc@bap
Subject: I WOULD DIE 4 U
Hey, Mrs. Stone—
I had a feeling you were lying about not checking
e-mail. Don't worry; I won't tell anyone at school
that you're not as mean as you pretend to be.
Thanks for the advice. I didn't realize that it
sounded so bad, but I see your point. Except I
think that I will write it like a Democrat: Trick the
voters by pretending to be less liberal than I really

am, and then start messing everything up once I
actually get in.
Mark
P.S. I was thinking more along the lines of a plum
ambassadorship when I become President. Start
thinking about countries you would want to live
in . . . Belize, Costa Rica, maybe Brazil?

Hah. I knew there was a reason that I liked this kid so much. I just
hope that colleges can see it, too.

After another three days of vacation, I am ready for vacation to end. I'm
afraid to go anywhere for fear that I might spend more money, and—
although I never thought the day would come that I would say something like this—there really is only so much time that I can spend lying
around the house, watching daytime television. To give you just an
inkling of how bored I am, listen to this (I'm almost too embarrassed to
even admit it): I saw an ad on the Your Baby Web site for this contrap-
tion that lets you listen to the baby's heartbeat with these special head-
phones, and that also has a thing that magnifies sound so that you can
play classical music to the baby in utero, which allegedly increases a
baby's IQ. And even though I know that products like this are specifically
created to prey on the neuroses of yuppie mothers-to-be like myself, I
ordered it anyway, because I have this nagging fear that my kid is going
to come out stupid, since the only music she ever hears in utero is the
techno crap that they play in my step class and the same Madonna CD
that's been in my car for six months because I keep forgetting to put in a
new one. And so the thing arrived this morning, and I've now spent the
last three hours lying perfectly still on my bed, listening to the same, boring, "pediatrician approved" classical CD that it came with, and moving
the little microphone thingy over every last centimeter of my stomach,
trying to find the baby's heartbeat. But I can't hear the heartbeat. The
only thing that I can hear is the sound of my stomach digesting all of the
food that I've been scarfing down, since there's nothing else to do around
here all day except eat. Talk about a waste of seventy-five bucks.
But at least I have something to do tonight. Tonight Julie is having a

screening party for her *Real Births* episode. It seems that she got an advance copy of it, and she's invited over everyone in the entire world to watch one of the most intimate and personal moments of her life on a sixty-inch television. Weird, I know, but a fabulous excuse to get out of the house for a few hours. Plus, I feel like I haven't talked to Julie in ten years. It's partly my fault, I guess. I haven't been that good about visiting her since the baby was born. I went over there once, the first week after they came home from the hospital, but there were so many people there that I didn't even get a chance to talk to her. I've tried calling a bunch of times, but I can never seem to catch her at a good moment. Either she's too busy with Lily to talk when Lily's awake during the day, or she's too tired to chat after Lily goes to bed at night. I have to say, I'm starting to feel a little bit neglected.

It's probably a good thing, though. I'm sure that if we did talk, she would just freak me out, anyway. I know Julie, and all she'll want to do is try to teach me baby things and show me baby things, and I'm just not at that place yet. I don't know what it is with me, but I can't seem to get my act together to prepare for this baby. I think that I am in total denial that the pregnancy part of this is ever going to end and that I am actually going to have to raise this thing that is growing inside of me and is for some reason hell-bent on crushing my esophagus.

And just so you know, this kind of behavior is totally out of character for me. I'm not a procrastinator, and I never do anything without engaging in extensive research first. But I swear, I have been more prepared for pop quizzes in high school algebra than I am for having a child right now, and for whatever reason, I just cannot motivate to do anything about it. And it's not like I don't have time (clearly I have time). Or that I don't know where to look. I mean, I couldn't possibly have more information at my disposal. I could spend years sifting through all of the articles on the Your Baby Web site, and Julie sent me four books about baby stuff as a congratulations-on-being-pregnant gift that have been sitting on my bookshelf collecting dust since they arrived. And three months ago, my doctor gave me a huge packet detailing all of the services that the hospital offers for expectant parents—infant care classes, infant massage classes, breast feeding classes, maternity ward tours—and I haven't signed up for one of them, even though all of the information says to enroll when you're five months along in order to guarantee a spot. If this were anything else, mind you, I would have been signed up before I even got home from his office—no, actually, I would have been signed up before I even got pregnant—but for some reason, I just can't bring myself to do a damn thing. I haven't even *bought* anything for the baby yet—that's how serious the situation has become.

I don't know; maybe tonight will be good for me. Maybe seeing Julie and the baby will make it all seem more manageable, and I'll finally be able to break free of this paralysis. Then again, maybe it will send me into a complete and total tailspin and I'll end up throwing myself down the stairs. Right now I think that it could go either way.

Julie has decorated her house like it's a friggin' Oscar party. She's got a giant, almost life-size *Hollywood* sign on the banister of the staircase, there are director's chairs everywhere, and those black, chalkboardlike things that they smack shut before every take are hanging all over the walls, not to mention the giant sheet cake that looks like a movie poster with a picture of Julie, Andrew, and Lily on it. I mean, it's really a bit much for a reality-TV show that airs on the TLC network, but who am I to judge?

I spot Julie in the corner of the living room, surrounded by people I have never seen before. I give her the once-over: She looks okay. About ten to fifteen pounds more than she normally weighs, but it's only been six weeks, so I'm trying to keep it in perspective.

I wait until the crowd around her thins out before I make my approach, but when she sees me walking toward her she hurls herself in my direction.

"Lara! I am so happy you came!" She leans in for a hug. "I cannot believe that I haven't seen you since the week we got home from the hospital. It's ridiculous!"

"I know," I say, trying not to sound too sheepish. "I'm sorry. I've been so busy with work, and the holidays, and this is the first week I've had to decompress. But you look amazing." I just realized that she's not holding the baby. "Where's Lily?" I ask.

"Oh, she's with the baby nurse."

A nurse? I put on my there-are-grave-matters-at-hand voice. "Why do you have a nurse? Is something wrong?"

"No," she says. "You never heard of a baby nurse?"

There she goes, making me feel inadequate again. I can't even imagine how many things there are in Julie's world that I've never heard of.

I don't know how she keeps on top of it all. It overwhelms me just to think about it. I shake my head at her and she gives a wave of her hand.

"It's just a nurse who specializes in babies, but they come and they live with you and they show you how to do everything, like how to clean the umbilical cord, and how to give the baby a sponge bath, and how to heat bottles, and how to—"

I am tempted to put my hands over my ears and hum. You see? This is exactly why I haven't come to visit her sooner.

"Okay, I get it," I say, cutting her off. "But can't she do all of that in two days? Why does she have to live with you?"

"Oh, that's the best part. She sleeps in Lily's room, and whenever Lily gets up in the middle of the night, she brings her to me in bed, I nurse her, and when I'm done she takes Lily and puts her back to sleep. I don't even have to move. It's like room service. And Andrew and I are completely well rested, which is great because neither one of us does well on less than six hours of sleep." Seriously, how does she find out about these things?

"That's unbelievable," I say. *I've gotta get me one of these baby-nurse people,* I think. "How long does she stay?"

Julie lowers her voice. "It depends on what you can afford. They'll stay for as long as you want, but most of them are around three-fifty a day, so it starts to really get expensive after a while."

My jaw drops and I stand there looking at her, my mouth hanging open as I do the math. "Three hundred and fifty dollars *a day?* Are you kidding me? Julie, one week is an entire shoe collection."

Julie hangs her head in shame. "I know, I know. I think you can find them cheaper, though. I didn't know this when I hired Gladys, but I've been hearing that baby nurses from the East Coast are only two hundred a day, and that people are flying them in from New York and Florida."

I look at her like she's lost her mind. That is just about the most ridiculous thing that I have ever heard. I mean, I know people who have flown in hairdressers from back east for weddings and movie premieres, and I always thought that that was a bit extreme, but a baby nurse? This town is so out of control. When I tell Andrew about this he's going to freak. He'll be making spreadsheets until he goes blind.

"And how much longer are you keeping Gladys?" I ask.

Julie shakes her head sadly. "This is it. She leaves Monday morning. I know it's so expensive, but it's really been worth every penny. Gladys is an expert in sleep training, and she just about has Lily sleeping for five-hour stretches at a time now."

Jesus. For three-fifty a day she should have Lily cooking her own meals and mixing up cocktails for everybody. Honestly, I don't even know what to say to this. What do you say to someone who just spent fifteen thousand dollars to pay a woman to get up with her baby at night? *Congratulations,* that's what you say. I am so jealous, I could die. Don't ever believe that shit about how money can't buy you happiness. This is cold, hard proof that it can.

"So," I say, "will I even get to see Lily tonight?"

Julie smiles. "Of course, of course. After the screening I'll take you in for a visit. Gladys just doesn't want her around everyone. Too many germs." She motions to me to follow her as she begins to walk toward the television. "Come on," she says. "Let's get this show on the road." Then she stops walking and leans in toward me, as if to tell me a secret. "You know, *I* haven't even watched it yet. I wanted to see it for the first time with everyone else. You know, to get the full experience."

For the record, I think that Julie is taking this a little too seriously, but far be it from me to burst her bubble. I follow her toward the front of the room and squeeze myself into a spot on the couch between Andrew and one of Julie's sisters' husbands. Julie takes her place in front of us, right next to the television, and she motions to someone in the back of the room to dim the lights. As the lights go down, "Hooray for Hollywood" starts playing in the background, and everyone in the room gets quiet. I mean, really. Is she serious?

She is. She 100 percent is.

"Hi, everyone," she yells. "Thank you so much for being here tonight to share this special event with our family." Oh—just in case you thought it couldn't get any more over-the-top, a giant spotlight begins to flash around the room and then finally settles on her. Julie clears her throat and cups her eyes with her hand.

"We feel so blessed to have so many great friends and family, and this night is extra special because so many of you were there at the hospital when all of this was being filmed. Needless to say, we're so excited about our television debut, so, without further adieu, I give you . . . *Real Births—The*

Marcus Family." There are catcalls and applause as Julie presses the play button, and then the *Real Births* theme song begins to play—a cheesy, harpsichord instrumental—and the opening segment fades in on the screen.

FADE IN:

INT. MARCUS FAMILY LIVING ROOM—DAY

JULIE and JON, an attractive couple in their early thirties, are sitting on their couch, holding hands. Julie is nine months pregnant, and has the look and sound of a Stepford wife. Jon seems suspiciously happy—the kind of blank, glazed-over happiness that can be brought about only with medication.

> JULIE
> (robotically)

I've always wanted to be a mother. I'm just a very nurturing person. It's funny; I'm the youngest of four girls, but I'm the one who always took care of my older sisters.

> JON
> (gazing at Julie)

I love kids. Parenthood is going to be amazing.

> JULIE
> (gazing back at Jon)

And I can't wait for our prebaby event tomorrow. We're having professional photographs taken of us. I think that it's such a unique opportunity to capture me and Jon right now, at this moment when our whole world is about to change.

CUT TO:

INT. PHOTOGRAPHY STUDIO—DAY

Julie, Jon, and a stereotypical-looking ARTSY WOMAN dressed in head-to-toe black consult with each other. Julie is wearing a flowing, semisheer robe that is slit open to reveal her stomach. She seems to be oblivious to the fact that she looks utterly ridiculous, if not downright repulsive.

MONTAGE OF:
Images of Julie, Jon, and Julie's enormous stomach in various poses, as flashbulbs pop in the background.

ARTSY WOMAN
(clicking the camera and turning it from side to side)

Gorgeous, fabulous. The two of you are naturals!

BLACKOUT FOR COMMERCIAL BREAK
FADE IN:
REAL BIRTHS music and screen logo
EXT. CEDARS SINAI HOSPITAL—DAY
Hospital workers and random patients go in and out of the front doors.

CUT TO:
INT. HOSPITAL ROOM—DAY
Julie is lying in a hospital bed, breathing loudly. She looks pale and very real—a stark contrast to the perfectness of the previous day. A NURSE is by her side, hooking her up to an IV. Jon is on the phone.

JON

Hi, Mom. Julie's in labor . . . yeah . . . she's already four centimeters. I think you should get over here.

JULIE
(in a deep, barklike voice, grimacing in pain)

Jon, get off the phone! You're supposed to be coaching me.

Jon goes over to Julie and takes her hand.

JON
(smiling)

Okay, honey, ready: one, two, three . . .

DISSOLVE TO:
INT. HOSPITAL ROOM—SEVERAL HOURS LATER
Julie is now in a hospital gown, and there are three NURSES and a DOC-
TOR wearing surgical masks. Jon is standing by her bedside. Julie looks
disheveled, obviously in pain.

JULIE
(nearly in tears)

Please make it stop. I can't do this anymore. Make it stop. Ow,
ow, it burns, it burns. (Screaming) Why isn't the epidural
working? Why am I feeling this? Get me more drugs!

DOCTOR
(calmly)

You're almost there, Julie, just a few more pushes. We can't
give you any more medicine because we need you to push.

JULIE
(screaming hysterically)

I can't. I can't do it. Please don't make me. I can't breathe! I
can't breathe!

DOCTOR
(urgently)

Nurse, get her some oxygen, stat!

The HEAD NURSE runs to grab an oxygen mask and places it over

Julie's face. Jon is holding her hand, smiling at her lovingly. Julie begins to calm down.

DOCTOR

Okay, Julie. Just take a few deep breaths, and then I want you to push as hard as you can. Just relax; it's almost over. Ready? One, two, three, push!

ZOOM IN:

On Julie's face, which is mangled in pain.

JULIE
(screaming a primal scream)

Ugggghhhhhhh! Ugggghhhhh! Ugggghhhhh! (To Jon) You (several long bleeps)! What the (bleep) are you always smiling about? Ugggghhhhh!!!!!!

ZOOM OUT:

To Jon, who, still smiling, but with slightly less enthusiasm, looks like he is going to pass out.

DOCTOR

Okay, I've got the head! Here it comes! It's a . . . girl!

ZOOM IN:

On Julie, who is sobbing.

BLACKOUT FOR COMMERCIAL BREAK
FADE IN:
REAL BIRTHS music and screen logo

INT. MATERNITY WARD HALLWAY
Dozens of people are lined up in the hallway, and JULIE'S MOTHER, an attractive, well-dressed woman in her late fifties, is talking to the camera.

JULIE'S MOTHER

This is my seventh grandchild, can you believe it? Lucky seven. Every time I go to Vegas I bet seven black on roulette and every time I win. I told Julie, this one's going to be special. Not because of the black part—you know—but the seven, it's lucky.

CUT TO:
INT. HOSPITAL ROOM—ABOUT AN HOUR LATER
Julie is lying in bed, chatting with a visitor, looking every bit her usual self. Her hair is now brushed, she is wearing floral pajamas, and she has on a full face of makeup. The door opens, and Julie's PREGNANT FRIEND, who looks to be not a day over twenty-seven but who could definitely use some lip gloss, enters the room. She goes over and kisses Julie on the cheek.

PREGNANT FRIEND

Hi, Mom! . . . I want to hear all about it. Was it awful?

JULIE
(smiling)

No, it really wasn't that bad. . . . It really wasn't a big deal.
Julie leans in and whispers something.

PREGNANT FRIEND
(loudly)

You pooped on the table?

CUT TO:
INT. MATERNITY WARD HALLWAY
Jon is standing in the hallway with a pink bubblegum cigar dangling from his mouth. He is talking to the camera.

JON
(still smiling)

Yeah, it was a little scary. There was a lot of blood, and, um, you know, some other stuff. But the important thing is that both of my girls are doing fine, and I'm already so in love with the baby.

BLACKOUT FOR COMMERCIAL BREAK
FADE IN:
REAL BIRTHS music and screen logo
INT. MARCUS FAMILY LIVING ROOM—A FEW WEEKS LATER
Julie and Jon, picture-perfect once more, are sitting on the couch, with LILY, the baby, wrapped in a blanket.

At the bottom of screen a graphic reads LILY MICHELLE MARCUS, 7 lbs, 6½ oz.

JULIE
(gazing at Lily)

Things are going great. Lily is a little angel, and Jon is so cute with her. I can't even remember what life was like without her.

JON
(smiling)

I'm so in love with both of them. (He kisses Julie, then Lily.)

JULIE
(gazing at Jon)

It's been the most incredible experience of our lives. I'm ready to go do it again!

FADE OUT
ROLL CREDITS

The lights go up, and the room is dead silent. I think that nobody is quite sure about the proper protocol for this situation. Do we clap? Or do we run out of the room? I, for one, am mortified. I said so many nice things to Julie in the hospital that day, and they had to focus on the poop thing? Julie must be beside herself. I'm thinking that she's probably regretting not watching it ahead of time right about now.

A few people break into a polite round of applause, and I get up to look for Julie. I don't see her anywhere, so I head toward the back of the room, where Jon's and Julie's moms are in a huddle.

"Hi," I say somberly. "Where did she go?"

Julie's mom looks at me and shakes her head. "She went to Lily's room. She said that she doesn't want to talk to anyone. But maybe you should try. She listens to you." She does?

I walk upstairs and pause in front of the door that used to be the guest bedroom. I have very fond memories of this room. In fact, I got engaged in this room. Andrew and I had gotten in a huge fight, and I stayed here for three days. I was angry with him because he hadn't proposed to me yet, and I had just found out that one of the ugliest girls I knew from college had just gotten engaged to her boyfriend, and they had started dating a full six months after we did. I threw the biggest hissy fit of my life. *Amy Waldstein! Amy Waldstein could be cast as a troll from Middle Earth. Somebody wants to marry Amy fucking Waldstein and you don't want to marry me?* Poor Andrew. He had bought the ring a week before and was just waiting to get it back from the jeweler, and he ended up having to tell me and ruin the surprise because it was the only way that he could get me to come back home. I'll bet that I'm the only woman in the world whose husband started off his marriage proposal by saying that he was about two seconds away from changing his mind.

I knock on the door to the bedroom, and a strange female voice answers. "Sorry, the baby is sleeping."

So this must be Gladys. Making up cover stories must be an added perk that she throws in as part of her fee.

"Julie, I know you're in there. It's me. Come on, open up." The door opens and Julie is standing in front of me, pouting. The room looks nothing like it did the last time I was here. It's a sea of pink and there is baby paraphernalia everywhere, including a large black woman who is sitting in a rocking chair, holding Lily.

"Come in and shut the door," Julie says to me, which I do, quickly. "Lara, this is Gladys. Gladys, Lara." I wave to Gladys and she gives me a solemn wave back.

"Are you okay?" I ask. Julie's face is bright red.

"I'm just so embarrassed. I swear to God, I really don't remember it being like that. I can't believe what I said to Jon," she says, covering her mouth in horror and shaking her head. "I wasn't lying at the end—I really don't remember it being anything but a great experience. But then again, I don't remember most of that day. I certainly don't remember telling you that thing—you know, about what happened on the table." She turns even redder now, if that's possible. "I can't even believe that I said that to you."

I nod at her. To be honest, I couldn't believe she did, either.

"Look," I say. "It wasn't that bad. It was like a movie. The whole thing was actually very cliché. You know, woman has baby, screams at her husband, then forgets all of it as soon as the baby comes." She is not saying anything, so I keep talking, which, I realize as the words are coming out, is probably a bad call. "Really, the strangest thing about it wasn't what happened, but that it happened to *you*. I mean, people just aren't used to seeing you any way but perfect, you know?"

Julie looks at me and cocks her head. "What is that supposed to mean?" she asks.

"Oh, come on, Julie. You and Jon are always so *happy*. You never fight, you never talk about anything bad in your lives, you have this great family and this great house, and you always look amazing. I think it was just shocking for everyone to see the real you." Julie does not appear to understand what I am getting at here. At all.

"For your information, I always show people the real me. I *am* happy, and Jon and I *don't* fight. We have discussions. Just because I'm not bitter and always complaining all the time doesn't mean that I'm fake."

Ouch. "No," I say. "I didn't mean it that way. I don't think you're fake. I just think that you don't usually let people see you with your guard down, that's all. Please don't make this out to be more than it is. I was trying to make you feel better." She doesn't say a word to this. "Obviously, I failed." Still nothing. "Come on, Jul, don't be mad at me. Do you want to know what I really think?"

"No, not really," she says, crossing her arms. At this, Gladys lets out a little chuckle. I ignore them both.

"I think that you're really brave. And not because you did this on national television. That part I think was just stupid." I can see that she's trying not to smile, and I know that I have her. "But seriously, I think that you're brave for even going through childbirth at all." I shake my head. "I don't think I can do it. I'm scared to death. I'm a big, fat chicken, and I begged my doctor to let me have a C-section because I'm too afraid to do it the real way." At this, Julie's mouth hangs open, and I can hear Gladys *tsk-tsk*ing from behind me.

"You did?" Julie asks.

"I did."

"Is he going to let you?"

"I don't know. He told me to do some reading and to take a class, and maybe I'll change my mind. But I don't think I will. But you . . . you were so confident going into it. I wish that I could be more like you. I wish that I could be half the woman you are."

Julie looks at me skeptically. "Okay, now you're the one who's out of character. Stop being so nice; you're scaring me."

Damn. She's right. That's the second time in two weeks that I've been—dare I even say it?—nurturing. Maybe I am getting soft. God, I hope it isn't permanent.

"Sorry," I say. "I don't know what got into me. Are we okay now?"

"I guess," she says. "But I'm still not going back down there."

"Fine with me. I don't want to talk to all of your weird friends. I'll stay here with you until everyone's gone." I smile at her. "You've got a lot of stuff to teach me, anyway." I glance around at the room, which is littered with things I have never seen before. "I mean, what the hell is all of this crap?"

"Do you really want to know?" she asks, getting excited.

"No. Not really," I say. "But I'm going to have to learn about it some-time, so it might as well be now."

She looks at me mischievously. "You're gonna be a good mom, Lara Stone."

"Let's not get carried away, Jul. It was just one nice comment."

"Yeah," she says. "But there's more where that came from. I can tell."

19.

If You're Busted and You Know It, Clap Your Hands

've been back at school for almost two full weeks now since winter vacation ended, and Tick hasn't stopped by my office once. Maybe she's embarrassed about what happened at the party. I can't believe that I care as much as I do, but it's really bothering me that I haven't seen her. I feel the way you do when you have a really good date with a guy and then he doesn't call—you know, I keep replaying the whole thing in my head, trying to figure out if I did or said something that would have offended her. Oh, this is so ridiculous. I'm going to go find her. I need to make sure she registered for her SATs again, anyway.

I pull up her schedule. She's in Statistics, and the period ends in six minutes. Perfect. I'll go wait for her outside of her classroom.

It's been unseasonably warm the last few days, by the way. Mid-nineties in January. I usually love this about LA, but right now I'm just hot and sweaty and uncomfortable, and almost all of my maternity clothes are long-sleeved, so I literally feel like I am burning in hell. I hope it doesn't last, because I can't buy any more clothes. My credit card bill came last week, and I still haven't figured out how I can write a nine-hundred-dollar check without Andrew noticing. I have to pay it soon, too, because the due date is coming up and I don't want to get hit with a late fee.

As I walk down the stairs, trying to think of things that I could pretend cost nine hundred dollars—an impulsive donation to our alma mater? Doctors' bills not covered by insurance?—I do a double take as I walk past a group of tenth-grade girls huddled around a locker. They look like little clones of each other. They're all wearing the exact same outfit— brown Ugg boots, a short, Juicy Couture miniskirt, and some variation of a tank top that shows off their both their cleavage (for those who have it) and their midriffs (some of which are more flattering than others). And all of them have their skirts pulled down so that their asses are completely showing. I swear to you, they've pulled their skirts down to about the middle of their butt cheeks, and they have pulled up the backs of their G-strings so high that they're sitting on top of their hips, where their skirts should be.

For the record, I am not normally a stickler for dress code violations. I operate under a sort of see-no-evil policy, and generally pretend not to notice when girls come into my office practically naked, or when boys come in with their pants hanging down around their knees. Let their teachers send them to the dean's office, you know? I don't really want to get into that line of business. But these girls—I'm sorry. They have crossed a line that even I cannot ignore. I'm blushing just looking at them. I look around to see if there are any other faculty members around on whom I might be able to pawn off this problem, but there's nobody. It's just me and five slutty tenth graders.

I approach the girls and clear my throat.

"Excuse me, ladies," I say. When they see me, they all immediately look guilt-ridden. "Is it your belief that you are appropriately dressed for school right now?" Don't ask me why, but whenever I have to confront kids, it always ends up coming out as if I've got them on cross-examination. It seems to work, though. The girls shift their weight uncomfortably from leg to leg, and they pull up their skirts without saying a word.

"That's much better, thank you. I'm not going to send you to your dean, but if I see it again I will let him know that we've already had this conversation."

They nod, and a few of them thank me for not ratting them out. When I am out of earshot, I put my hands on my stomach and lean forward.

"If you ever leave the house looking like that, you *will* be grounded for life," I whisper. "Got it?"

Up ahead, I spot Tick from behind, as she is walking up the stairs. Her hair is dark again, and I wrinkle my nose at it. I think she looks much better as a blonde. I run to catch up with her, and by the time I get back up the stairs I am sweating like a man.

"Tick," I say, reaching out for her arm. She doesn't turn around, so I yell her name louder. "Tick!" Her shoulders heave, and she slowly turns around.

"What?" she yells back. I expect her to apologize when she sees that it is me, but she doesn't.

"Hi," I say, sounding slightly hurt. "I haven't seen you in a while, so I wanted to check in, you know, to make sure everything's okay."

"Everything's fine," she says. "Is that it?"

Okay, now I'm really feeling like the annoying girl getting blown off by the good date guy. "No," I say, trying not to let on how disappointed I am by her lack of enthusiasm for me. "Did you register for SATs?"

"No," she says. "I don't think I want to take them again, anyway. I don't really see the point."

What? *What?* I look at her sternly. "The point is, if you want to go to NYU, your scores need to be higher, and this test is your last chance to take them. That's the point."

She makes a *whatever* face at me. "I've gotta go. I'm late."

"Tick," I say. "Did I do something to upset you? Because I thought that you and I were friends." *Yeah,* I think. *I thought we had something special.*

"No offense, Mrs. Stone, but you're my college counselor, and you're, like, thirty years old. Just because you helped me out for an hour doesn't mean that I want to hang out with you all day. And I don't even want to go to NYU anymore, so you can stop worrying about it. Anyway, don't you have, like, fifty other kids to worry about?"

I am stunned by this. I don't even know how to respond. I take a moment to compose myself.

"Yeah," I say. "You know what? I do. And they deserve my time a lot more than you do. I'll see you around, Tick."

I am shaking, I am so angry with her. Fuck Linda. I don't care if she promised me a whole year off with pay; I'm not going to kiss Tick's ass if she's going to treat me like this. I do have pride, you know. I turn around and walk away, taking the long way back up to my office. I mutter to myself the whole way.

"Ungrateful little bitch. What does she mean, she doesn't want to go to NYU anymore? How can she not want to go to NYU anymore? Isn't that what she's been working toward all year?" But then a bolt of logic flashes through my anger. *Hold on*, I think. *No way.* There is no way that she's telling me the truth. Something must have happened at home. Maybe she got back together with Marcus, or maybe she had a fight with her mom. She's got to be reacting to something. I just need to figure out what it is.

I should call Cheryl and play dumb. I might be able to get some answers out of her that way. I know. I'll ask her if she's made any decisions about donating. I do need to find out what's going on with that anyway, and it's a good excuse for a phone call. I pick up the receiver and start dialing, but before I can finish, Mark appears in my doorway. I hang up and wave him inside. Cheryl can wait.

"Hi," I say to him. "How was your break? Go to any Right to Life rallies?"

"No," he says, smiling. "But I did attend a conference on book banning. It was very enlightening. What about you? Did you spend vacation chained to a tree in the middle of the rain forest?"

"I did, actually. Except it wasn't in the rain forest. It was in my house. And it wasn't a tree, exactly. It was my bed. Which is made of pine, though, so it's sort of the same thing. Anyway, I was *thinking* of all the trees while I watched television all day." Mark laughs and sits down. "So what's up?" I ask him.

"Well, first of all, I wanted to thank you for helping me with my essay. I think it turned out much better. I changed it around a little, and instead of saying how I bought my car with the money I made, I said that I'm saving it for college. What do you think?"

I roll my eyes at him. "I don't think you had to lie about it, but it sounds better, I suppose."

"Yeah," he says. "Anyway, and I wanted to tell you, I went to visit some schools after New Year's, and I think I know where I want to go."

"Great," I say. "Where did you visit?"

"I went to Boston, Philly, and New York, and I saw about seven schools. My top three are Penn, BU, and NYU. I like the real city schools.

I didn't think I would, but compared to everywhere else, they had the most going on. Oh, and I had interviews at BU and NYU, and they went really well."

"Sounds good," I say. "Make sure you follow up with a thank-you note to your interviewers."

He looks at me with pity. "I already did. And I also sent e-mails to the admissions officers who came here in the fall to let them know that I was on campus and that they're my top choices."

Why can't they all be like Mark? I fold my hands on top of my desk. "The quintessential politician," I say. "Way to work it. And how are your grades going to be?" First-semester grades come out in three weeks. That's what I should have asked Tick about this morning. *Damn.*

"They're good," he says. "As of right now, I'm getting an A or an A-minus in everything except AP Physics, but I'm still negotiating that with my teacher. But even if he doesn't change it, I think it'll still a B. But he'll change it."

"A B in an AP class is fine," I say. "Stop bugging Dr. Lin."

Mark grins at me. "Dr. Lin doesn't care. He thinks it's funny. Anyway, I just wanted to give you the update. When do you think we'll hear, anyway?"

"Mid-March," I tell him. He groans. "It's not that much longer," I say. "You'll see—those fat envelopes will be rolling into your mailbox before you know it."

"It seems like forever," he says.

I want to tell him that he doesn't know what forever seems like until he's been seven months pregnant, but I fully realize the futility in making this statement to a seventeen-year-old boy. Instead, I kick him out. "Okay," I say, picking up the phone. "Thanks for coming by. Don't be a stranger."

"Yeah, yeah," he says. "I can take a hint. See ya."

I dial the Gardners' house and I am shocked to hear Cheryl's voice answer the phone. I didn't think that she performed such lowly tasks. Lori must be on vacation. Sigh. It's so difficult when the help is unavailable.

"Hi, um, Cheryl? It's Lara Stone."

"Oh, hi, Lara. I heard you met my husband—what a small world, huh?"

Yeah. And I cleaned up your bitchy kid's puke. Did you hear about that, too?

"Yes," I say. "It's so funny." It's not funny, I know, but really, what else am I going to say to her? "So, I was wondering, did you make any decisions about NYU? Because if you're going to make that donation, we probably should get the ball rolling. I can definitely put you in touch with the right people now."

"Oh," she says. "You know, Lara, I just don't think that it can happen this year. I told you, we're so overcommitted with our charitable donations right now. We were going to buy a ski château in Switzerland this spring, but I think we may have to put it off until next year. The construction at the art museum is just turning out to be much more than we originally anticipated."

Shit. Shit, shit, shit. Oh, whatever. I don't even care anymore. I just want to know what's going on with Tick.

"Okay," I say. "I just want to make sure that you understand that Tick most likely won't get into NYU without it." This should open up the conversation. *Oh,* she'll say, sounding surprised. *Didn't you hear? Tick doesn't want NYU anymore. She's decided to go live in a Tibetan commune for four years, just to piss me off.*

"Oh," she says, sounding surprised. Okay, here we go. "Really? Because I spoke to Linda, and she seems fairly confident that you'll be able to make it happen without our help. She seems to think that you're quite . . . what was her word? . . . oh, yes, *invested* in Tick, and that you have some very strong connections with the admissions people at NYU. Isn't that right?"

Linda, Linda, Linda. Unbelievable. I take a deep breath.

"I do want to help Tick, Cheryl, and I am friendly with the admissions officer, but I can't make miracles happen. Tick isn't cooperating with me at all, and she's making it much more difficult than it needs to be."

"Hmm," Cheryl says. "Yes, Tick does get that way sometimes. But it's usually when she thinks that someone is trying to take advantage of her. But I can't imagine why on earth she would think that about you."

Suddenly everything is crystal-clear. Tick totally knows about my deal with Linda. Linda must have told Cheryl, and Cheryl told Tick because Cheryl can't stand the idea that Tick actually likes me. So now Tick thinks that I'm just using her, and she's going to screw up any chance of getting into NYU, just to spite me. I feel like I'm going to cry.

"Yeah," I say to Cheryl. "I think I will try talking to her. Thanks."

I hang up the phone while she's still talking and I run downstairs.

Tick is sitting in her Government class, in the same position she was in the last time I came to find her here. Slumped over, hiding a book under her desk. I can see that my talk with her did a world of good. She's not paying attention anyway, so I don't feel bad about pulling her out of class. I tap on the door and the teacher looks up and waves me in.

"Hi," I say, "I'm so sorry to interrupt, but I need to see Tick Gardner right away. It's an emergency." I glance back and her and she scowls at me.

"Okay, Tick," says her teacher. He walks over to his desk and consults his notes. "Homework is chapters eleven and twelve, and the questions at the end." Tick nods as she puts her things away, and then she hauls her bag up from the floor.

When we are safely in the hallway, she puts her hand on her hip and glares at me.

"What are you doing?" she says.

"We need to talk. Privately. Let's go up to my office."

"I don't really have anything to say to you," she says.

"Well, that's great, but I have some things to say to you, so let's go." We walk upstairs in silence, and when we get to my office she sits in the chair farthest from my desk. Fine.

"So," I say. "I just spoke to your mom. And she seems to think that you're under the impression that I'm taking advantage of you."

She pushes her tongue along the inside of her cheek and looks me straight in the eye. "You are."

I sigh. "No, I'm not, Tick."

"Yes, you are. If I get into NYU, you get to work part-time next year. So that's why you helped me this summer, and that's why you set up the meeting with Stacey, and that's why you've been on my case all year. And that's probably even why you helped me at the party."

I nod at her. "You're right, Tick. If you get into NYU, I do get to work part-time next year. But I swear to you, that didn't even come about until almost November."

"Oh, sure," she says. "Of course you'd say that."

"It's true. Just think about it, okay? I didn't even find out that I was pregnant until after the first time I met with you. And I didn't even tell Linda—I mean, Dr. Miller—that I wanted to work part-time until I announced it to everyone, and that was at the very end of October. Go ahead and ask her; I don't care. Plus, you didn't even decide on NYU until after you met with Stacey, so how could I have made that deal before then? Huh?"

Tick ponders this for a moment. "Still," she says. "Even if that's true, what about all year? What about the party?"

"Fine, Tick. Do you want to know the truth? Yes. I did push you to apply early decision, and I did encourage your parents to donate, and I did keep tabs on you, mostly for selfish reasons. I will admit that." There are tears in her eyes and she stands up like she is about to leave.

"Wait," I say. "Just hear me out." She doesn't say anything, but I can see that she is hesitating. "Please?" I ask. Reluctantly, she sits back down.

"Anyway, at first I did it for me. But then I started to get to know you, and I really liked you. And I felt bad for you. You just seem so lost and out of place here, and your family . . . I don't know. I don't usually get attached to students this way. Maybe because I'm having a baby—whatever. The point is, once I got to know you, I started rooting for you. I swear to God, I want you to get into NYU whether I get something out of it or not. If Linda told me right now that the deal was off, I still would try to pull every string to get you in. And the party . . . I helped you at the party because you needed help, and I care about you." I shrug at her. "And that's the truth."

She stares at me for what seems like a very long time. "Why didn't you just tell me?"

"Because. I knew that it was wrong, and I had no way to explain it to you or anyone else. Believe me, Tick, I am not proud of this."

She gives me a sideways glance. "What will you do if I don't get in?"

I sigh. "I guess I'll keep working full-time, and I'll send the baby to day care, or get a nanny to stay with her every day. I don't really have a choice."

She nods. "You know, you're the first adult who's ever really taken an interest in me. Most of my teachers just write me off, because they think I've got it made or something, and that it doesn't matter if I do well in school or not. You know, they think that I can always just live off of my dad for the rest of my life, or that he can hook me up with a cushy job. Nobody's ever cared about what I want."

"I'm sorry."

She shrugs. "It's okay. I'm used to it by now."

"No," I say. "I mean, I'm sorry that this happened. I'm sorry that I broke your trust."

"You didn't," she says. "I believe you. You know, I just wish you had told me. If I had known that you needed my help, I would have worked harder. I want you to spend time with your baby. I want your baby to get to spend time with you." She fiddles with a pin that says *Rude Girl* in big red letters that is attached to her bag, and then she looks up at me. "Do you think I have any chance of getting in?"

"I don't know," I say. "But don't try to do it for me. Do it for yourself."

She nods. "I'll do it for both of us," she says.

After work, I decide to skip the gym and curl up in the bathtub instead with the new issue of *Allure* that came today. I wonder if I'll ever have time to take a bath once the baby is born. Or to read. God, my life is going to suck, isn't it?

I'm just stepping out of the tub and slipping on my robe when I hear the garage door open, and Andrew bounds up the stairs, whistling what I think is "Zippidee-Doo-Dah," but that seems suspect, even for him. When he walks into the bedroom, he plants a huge kiss on my stomach.

"And how are my girls this evening?" he asks.

"You're in a good mood," I say. This is perfect. I have to tell him about the nine-hundred-dollar credit card bill, so I might as well strike while the iron is hot. He already got the three-hundred-dollar American Express bill—that came and went more or less without comment—but this . . . this is going to be tough to explain.

"I guess I am," he says. "Is there a problem with that?"

"No, no. It's just nice to see you so happy. Why don't you go relax in the den, and I'll get dressed and then we can decide where to go for dinner." He agrees to this plan, and a few minutes later I am sidling up next to him on the couch, trying not to think about whether the pit in my stomach could actually crush the baby.

"All ready," I say, rubbing his shoulders and giving him a few kisses on the neck.

"Hi," he says, in his are-we-about-to-have-sex-or-am-I-just-imagining-things voice. "Did my good mood rub off on you?"

"Maybe." We kiss for a minute or two, and then I pull away and begin to caress his arm. "Honey, do you remember when I went to Pea in the Pod and spent three hundred dollars?"

"Yeah," he says, as he leans in and starts kissing me by my right ear.

"We-e-e-ll, it's possible that I might have spent a little more than that." He stops kissing me and sits straight up. I think it's safe to say that I pretty much just killed the mood.

"It's possible?" he asks.

"Mm-hm."

"How much more?"

Damn. I was hoping that he might not ask me that. I take the afghan that is thrown over the arm of the couch and put it over my head.

"How much more, Lar?"

"I don't know," the blanket says in the cutest voice imaginable.

Andrew laughs. "Come on, tell me. I promise I won't get mad."

I pause. "You promise?"

"I promise, just tell me, come on."

I can tell that he is smiling, which means that the number in his head is much lower than the number that I am about to tell him. I take my hands out from under the blanket and slowly hold up nine fingers. I hear Andrew inhale loudly, and I'm guessing that he's not smiling anymore.

"Please tell me that's not a nine. Please. Please tell me that you did not spend another nine hundred dollars on maternity clothes." The blanket nods.

"Lara, are you trying to put us in the poorhouse? You know that we can't afford for you to be spending a lot of money right now. You know I'm starting a new business, and we have three months coming up when you're not going to get paid. . . ." His voice trails off and we are both silent. He pulls the blanket off my head and stares at me. "Do you even care? You don't. You don't even care." He sighs and gets up from the couch.

Oh, yeah. I'm in big trouble. I start to whine. "I do care," I say. "But I had a hemorrhoid, and there was this other girl in the store who was only a few weeks behind me but looked a million times better, and I don't know, I just couldn't control myself."

He looks at me like I really am from Venus. "What credit card did you use?" Back on goes the blanket.

"The secret one that I have that you don't know about."

"Great. Just great." He stomps his foot. "Well," he says, trying to think of something to say. "I don't want to have anything to do with it. I'm not writing the check and I'm not putting a stamp on the envelope and I won't put it in the mailbox. This is your responsibility, and you have to take care of the bill."

I am wondering if this is going to be my whole punishment, because if it is, it's pretty lame. I mean, I know how to write checks, how to stamp envelopes, and how to use the mailbox, and I don't find any of these tasks to be particularly taxing. I am not, however, about to share this information with him.

"Okay," I say, meekly. "That's fine."

"Please, just please don't buy any more clothes, okay?"

"I promise," I say.

He storms off into our bedroom, slamming the door behind him.

Zoey, who has been lying on the floor during this whole episode, lifts her head up.

"You really handled him this time," she says, smirking at me. I pick up a pillow from the couch and throw it at her.

"You'd better watch it, Zoey," I say. "You can very easily be replaced."

"You can't replace me," she says. "I'm your gorgeous, precious bunny bear. You tell me so every day."

Oh, man, I think. *This poor dog has no idea what she's in for once this baby comes.*

She lifts her nose up in the air and struts out of the room.

"Okay," I yell, calling after her, "you'll see!" But she just keeps on walking.

20.

Snips and Snails and Giant Testicles, That's What Little Boys Are Made of

I t has been almost two months since the last time Stacey and I went hiking. Every week, it's something else. *Todd and I are going to Napa. . . . Todd's taking me to his sister's house in Lake Tahoe. . . . Todd and I had such a late night, we really want to sleep in today.* I fucking hate Todd. Stacey was much more fun when she had no life. Today's excuse is that she and Todd made plans to go to brunch at the beach. She left the message on my machine last night while Andrew and I were at the movies, knowing full well that we wouldn't be home when she called. Chicken. She knows that if she got me in person I'd shame her into canceling with him. It really is ridiculous, though. I mean, aside from the fact that I miss her, I really need the cardio right now. I'm almost up to thirty pounds already and I still have eight weeks to go. If I keep this up, I'm going to be a house.

Of course, it's not like I can't just get up and go to the gym instead, but there's something about the idea of a treadmill this morning that is preventing me from moving. So as a result, I am still lying in bed at ten o'clock, contemplating what I'm going to with the rest of my Saturday. I have to go to the cleaners and to the market. And I definitely need a manicure and a pedicure. And maybe I'll see if I can go get a pregnancy massage this afternoon. Somebody got me a gift certificate ages ago, and I think it expires next week, so I really should try to use it.

I suddenly feel some rumbling in my stomach, and jump out of bed. Oh, man, I hope this means that I have to go to the bathroom. I've been so constipated lately. Every hour I run to the toilet thinking that I have to go, and every time it's a false alarm. I just sit there, pushing and pushing and pushing for twenty minutes, a half hour, and nothing ever comes out. It's no wonder. One of my pregnancy books has this picture of what a woman's organs look like when she is not pregnant next to a picture of what those same organs look like when she is pregnant, and it's absurd what goes on in there. The unpregnant organs are all happy, floating around in their natural shape with plenty of room between them, while the pregnant organs look like they're all trying to cram themselves into a studio apartment in Manhattan. And poor Andrew—he hasn't been given clearance to even go near our bathroom in almost two weeks. Every morning the poor guy takes his towel and his toothbrush and trudges across the house to the guest room, while I sit, futilely trying to poop.

But maybe this time will be the time that something actually happens. I take the *New York Times* crossword puzzle that I haven't quite finished from last Sunday into the bathroom with me, and about ten minutes later I hear the phone ring. I look at my watch. Ten eighteen. Shoot. It's got to be Andrew. I told him to call me when he was on his way home from agility with Zoey, to let me know if he was able to get a tee time late enough for us to have breakfast together. If he did, I've got to hurry up and get dressed, because he'll be home any minute. It's on the third ring already. Two more and the machine picks up. *Shoot.*

I stand up and run out of the bathroom with my sweats down around my knees, and I dive for the phone just as the machine clicks on.

"Hi, Lara and Andrew aren't here right now. . . ."

"Hello?" I say, talking over my own voice. "Hello?"

"Lar? Is that you?" It's Stacey. What is she doing? She's supposed to be at the beach.

"Hold on," I yell. I semirun into the kitchen, trying not to kill myself what with the pants around the knees, and turn off the machine. Then, phone in hand, I run back to the bathroom and sit back down on the toilet. "Hi," I say. "I thought you were at brunch."

"I need you to come over," she says.

"You need me to what? Where?"

"I need you to come over. To Todd's. It's an emergency." This is bizarre. What kind of an emergency could she possibly be having at Todd's that would require my intervention?

"Where's Todd? Are you okay?" I ask.

"He's not here. Listen, please don't ask questions; just come over and I'll explain when you get here."

Oh, yeah, right. "No," I say. "Tell me what's going on. You can't just blow me off and then call me up and order me to come over to your boyfriend's house with no explanation. I already made plans for this morning, and unlike some people, I don't cancel them at the drop of a hat." Of course, as you know, I have no concrete plans whatsoever, but my guilt trip works far better if she is kept out of the loop on this particular issue. I hear her take a deep breath.

"Fine. Todd got called to New York last night for work—there's some problem on a shoot there and they needed him right away. He had to leave first thing this morning, and he left me here alone with his kid because he didn't have anyone else to watch him. His ex is out of town."

Oh, that is so funny. I am trying so hard not to laugh.

"I told you this would happen," I say. Oh, how I love I-told-you-sos. Especially when they're directed at Stacey. "But I don't know why you're calling me. I don't know anything about kids."

"What do mean?" she yells. "You're having a baby in two months. You work with kids every day!"

"Yeah," I say, "but they're teenagers. It's a completely different genre." There is an exasperated silence on the other end of the phone. "Why don't you just put on some videos or something? I hear that television is the ultimate babysitter."

"I did," she says.

"Okay, so then what's the problem?" I think that I feel something happening in my intestinal track, and I'm trying to talk without giving away the fact that I am sitting on the toilet, because I would be totally grossed out if I knew that someone was pooping while they talked to me on the phone.

"It's the potty."

What? Did she just tell me that I'm on the potty? I thought I was being really quiet.

"Excuse me?" I say.

"The potty. Todd and his ex have been trying to potty train him, and the kid can't go. He says that he has to poop, and then he just sits there and nothing comes out. And then as soon as he gets off, he shits all over the floor. It's happened twice this morning already."

I can't help it: I bust out laughing as I try to imagine Stacey cleaning up a floor full of poop.

"It's not funny," she says.

"Oh, yes, it is. I'm sorry, but it really is. Does he always do this, or is it just with you?"

"He always does it. Todd said they talked to the doctor and it happens to lots of kids. They get all embarrassed and stressed out about doing it, so they tighten up their muscles, but as soon as they get off the potty and the pressure's off, they relax and everything comes out. It's a nightmare."

Oh, poor kid. I totally understand. My pooping issues go way deeper than just not being able to go in front of Andrew. I would hands down rather die of toxemia than poop in a public restroom, believe me.

And speaking of pooping, I'm getting nowhere with my own. I stand up and flush the toilet.

"Okay," I say. "Tell me where he lives. I think I have an idea."

When I arrive at Todd's house, I am greeted at the door by a disheveled, unbrushed, unwashed version of Stacey.

"You look like a hausfrau," I tell her.

"Fuck you," she says, jabbing me in the stomach. "We'll see how you look in three months."

"So where is he?" I ask.

"With the sitter." She flips her thumb in the direction of the den, and I peer around the corner. All I can see is a pair of feet sticking out past the edge of the couch. On the wall opposite the feet is a plasma screen, on which a little cartoon man in a hard hat, a jumpsuit, and a tool belt is running around fixing things.

"What the hell is he watching?"

She rolls her eyes. "*Bob the Builder,* it's called. It's like a *Home Improvement* for little kids, but with talking trucks instead of Pam Anderson. This is, like, the eighth time he's watching it."

I walk into the den and stand next to the couch, but he's in some kind of a television-induced trance and he's completely oblivious to my presence. He has wild, curly brown hair and he's wearing a dark-green velour Puma sweatsuit. He looks exactly like Todd. I feel a pang in my chest and I sigh. I really wish I were having a boy. I'd take *Bob the Builder* any day over PMS and catfights.

When the video finally ends, I sit down on the couch next to him. Here's my strategy: I'm going to talk to him the same way that I talk to my kids at school. No baby talk, no loud voices, just straightforward, cut-the-bullshit-because-I'm-not-screwing-around talk. This is my strategy, and I am going with it because I have absolutely no idea how else to talk to him.

I am about to say hi when I realize that Stacey has heretofore referred to him only as "the kid," and I therefore have no idea what his actual name is. Not a problem. I can work around this.

"Hey," I say as he glances at me. "I'm Lara. I'm a friend of Stacey's. What's your name?"

He looks at me and then sits up on his knees. "More Bob."

"Your name is Bob?" I ask.

"No," he says. He picks up the remote control and tries to push it into my hand. "More Bob." Oh. He wants more *Bob the Builder*.

"Actually," I say, "I think Bob is over. Why don't we talk for a little bit? I hear you're having a hard time pooping." I lower my voice to a gossipy whisper. "Between you and me, I've been having the same problem lately."

He stares at me and his lower lip begins to quiver. In a split second he is on the floor, facedown, with his hands covering the back of his head. He looks like a kid from one of those 1950s instructional movies about what to do in an air raid. Except that he's screaming.

"Nooooooo! More Bob! More Bob! Mo-o-o-o-o-re Bo-o-o-o-o-b!"

"Uh, Stace?" I yell. She is in the kitchen, taking this opportunity to scarf down a few bowls of Cap'n Crunch, her morning sugar jolt of choice. "I think he wants more Bob."

She comes stomping back into the den, still chewing. "Aiden, stop it. I told you, that was the last time that you could watch Bob. Why don't you go show Lara your Bob toys instead?"

As if the screaming fit had never happened, he is back on his feet, grinning from ear to ear. "Mohn," he says. "Aiden's boom." I look at Stacey.

"He wants you to go to his bedroom," she says. I am amazed by this. I had no idea that Stacey spoke two languages. She's obviously been spending more time with him than she's let on. Weekends in Napa, my ass. Weekends with nappies is more like it. I'll bet she's been babysitting every single Saturday morning since she met Todd. I told her that would happen.

I get up and follow Aiden into his room, where I am confronted with about fifteen variations of Bob the Builder and his various accessories, each of which Aiden picks up and hands to me, one by one.

"Thanks," I say, over and over and over again. When I'm sitting in a pile of Bob toys up to my waist, I decide to try to change the subject. "Hey, Aiden. I brought a really cool book with me. Do you want to see it?"

"Da," he says, nodding his head. I reach into my purse and pull out the copy of *Everyone Poops* that Andrew gave to me when we moved in together.

"It's called *Everyone Poops*," I tell him, flipping through the pages. "See? It's all about poop."

Aiden looks from me to the book and back to me again, and then back to the book. Then he looks at me as if to say that he can't believe I'm serious about this. "Poopoo?" he asks.

"Sure," I say. "We can call it poopoo if that's what you prefer. Do you want me to read it to you?" He nods at me shyly, and then he walks over to me, turns around, and does a free fall into my lap. *Ow.*

"All right," I say. "Here we go." I pick up the book and turn to the first page. Aiden starts grabbing at it, and he almost rips the page in half.

"Careful," I yell, and he pulls his arm back, startled. "This book has sentimental value. It's very special to me, so don't touch, got it?" He nods at me solemnly. "Okay. Let's see." I open it to the first page again and start reading. " 'Elephants make big poops, mice make tiny poops.' "

"Oooh," Aiden says, pointing to the picture of the big elephant turd, but being careful not to touch the page. "Poopoo."

"That's right," I tell him. "The elephant made a big poopoo." So much for talking to him like he's a teenager. I turn the page and the two of us proceed to examine camel poop, whale poop, and an assortment of poops

from various other mammals, birds, and reptiles. Aiden is totally fasci-
nated. He's got a good eye, too. He's very careful to discriminate between
brown, black, and white poops, not to mention ovals versus circles.
When we get to the part about people pooping, though, he clams up for
the rest of the book.

" 'Every living thing eats, so every living thing poops,' " I read. "That's
it. The end. What did you think?"

Aiden turns his head around and looks up at me. "Moooore?"

"That's it," I say, closing the book. "It's over. You see, the moral of the
story is that everybody poops. It's not something to be embarrassed
about. I mean, I know that that's easier said than done. I'm embarrassed about pooping, too, so I understand, but that's because I have
deep-seated issues about femininity and sexuality, and I also think that
on some level it's about the fact that I've rejected my father, who used to
pass gas and be gross in public all the time, which was positively humiliating for me. But you're only two. It's too early for you to have neuroses
like that." I suddenly realize that Stacey is in the doorway, and that she
has heard my entire monologue.

"Ahem," she says. "I never realized that you were so repressed." I can
feel my face getting hot, and I know for sure that I am the exact shade of
red that Stacey usually turns when we hike.

"Whatever," I say. "You asked me for my help, so don't knock it."

"Poopoo," says Aiden.

"That's right," I tell him. "We're talking about poopoo. Do you have
something to add?"

"Aiden poopoo potty," he says, staring at me and pointing to the bathroom that adjoins his room.

"Oh, my God," Stacey yells, frantically, pouncing on him and grabbing his hand. "Do you have to make a poop?"

Jeez, I think. *No wonder the kid is so uptight about it.* She's acting like
it's life or death. Aiden nods his head, but he's still staring at me.

"Come on, Aiden," Stacey says, trying to get him to move. "Hurry.
Let's go to the potty. Come on!" She reaches out to pick him up, but he
squirms away from her and starts to cry.

"Stacey, chill. You're freaking him out."

"Poopoo," he sobs to me.

"Do you have to go to the potty, buddy?" I ask him. He nods at me. "Okay, go ahead. You'll do great. Remember, everybody poops." I feel oddly like a cheerleader on the sidelines of some kind of a sick, twisted fetish sport.

"Noooo!" he yells. He toddles over to me and grabs my hand and starts pulling on it. "Poopoo, mohn."

I look at Stacey. "Did he just say poopoo, man? Is his mother a Rastafarian?"

"No," she says, impatiently. "He said 'poopoo, come on.' He wants you to go with him."

"Seriously?"

"Seriously."

Oh, I don't know about this. No pun intended, but this is really beyond the call of duty. I mean, the puke was one thing, but pooping? I have *issues,* for God's sake. I have *baggage.* I look at my watch.

"I don't think I can, Stace. I have stuff to do today, and I'm already running late. I think I should just call it a day and you can take it from here."

Aiden is still crying, and now he's pulling me with one hand and holding the other hand over his stomach. "Tummy huts. Poopoo potty. *Mohn.*"

Stacey looks at me. "Lara, *go. Now.*"

"*Fine,*" I say. I stand up and follow Aiden as he runs into the bathroom, and when he gets there he stops in front of a wooden thing that looks like nothing more than a glorified chamber pot that's been embellished with a few Elmo stickers. This, I take it, is the potty. Interesting. I notice that it contains neither water nor a flushing device, and I am wondering how exactly that is supposed to work. Aiden, for his part, is still standing in front of it, staring at me.

"Okay," I say to him, placing my palms in the air front of me. "Go for it." He looks down at his legs.

"Pants. Diaper. Off."

Oh, you've got to be kidding me. I kneel down and tug on his pants, and then I un-Velcro the sides of his diaper. I wonder if I'm supposed to throw it away, or if I should save it for when he's finished? I decide to save it, just in case. Not that I know how to get it back on him, mind you, but I can figure that out later. Or, to be more exact, I can give it to Stacey to figure out later. I pull the diaper through his legs, and I suddenly find myself eye-to-eye with his penis.

Whoa. He has balls. And they're big. Like, I've had boyfriends with smaller testicles than his. Oh, that is so gross. Forget everything I said about wanting to have a boy. I can't imagine having to clean balls every day. Ew.

The now pantless Aiden sits down on his chamber pot, and he immediately starts making loud grunting noises.

"Mmmmrrrrrr. Mmmmmmmmrrrrrrrr," he says, but it doesn't sound quite right. I think he's faking it. I get the sense that he thinks that that's what he's supposed to be doing when he poops, so he's going through the motions just to impress me.

"Are you really pooping?" I ask him.

He shakes his head no. "Can't," he says.

"Yes, you can, Aiden. Everybody poops, remember? The whale, the mouse, the snake, the bird. They all pooped, and you can poop, too." Suddenly I feel my stomach rumbling again, and out of nowhere I am overcome with an urgent feeling to go. A thought flashes through my head, and I realize that this is a seminal moment for me. A life-changing moment, really. Yes. I'm going to do it. I am.

"You know what?" I say. "I'm going to poop with you. Right now. We'll do it together." I lock the bathroom door and then I pull down my pants and sit down on the toilet that is next to his potty. "Okay," I say. "Let's do it. Come on, when I count to three, we'll both start pushing, for real this time. Ready? One, two, *three*."

I want to, but I can't do it. I just can't do it in front of him. My grunts are totally fake, just like his were. I realize that I'm no better than a two-year-old. I'm pathetic. And Aiden, who is watching me with a keen eye, totally knows it. But then, suddenly, all of the antics that I've gone through to avoid pooping in public, all of the excuses that I've had to come up with for why I need to leave wherever I am—and leave fast—all of the stomach pain that I've endured over the years—all of it is flashing before my eyes, as if I'm in the middle of a terrifying, fecal, near-death experience. Honestly, it's been a horrible way to live. Horrible.

I realize that I have to do this. I have to do this for Aiden. I cannot be even partly responsible for making this kid a poopaphobe like me. How could I ever live with myself, knowing that I contributed to the hangups of a poor, innocent child?

I close my eyes and take a deep breath, and then I push. For real.

"Hnnhhh." I open one eye and look at Aiden. "Okay, buddy, your turn."

He smiles at me. Suddenly his smile disappears and his face squinches up. He lets out a loud grunt. "Hunnnhhhh." As he does this, he passes some gas, loudly. When he hears it, he is startled. He abruptly stops pushing and looks at me for a response.

"It's okay," I tell him. "Totally normal. Come on, let's keep going." We both grunt and push for what must be close to fifteen minutes, and as we get more comfortable, each of us is getting louder and louder until we're practically screaming. I have to say, it's quite liberating. I don't think I've ever been this relaxed about anything in my entire life.

When all is said and done, it turns out that we've both been successful. I don't know about Aiden, but I feel like my stomach has shrunk about three feet.

"Good job, Aiden," I say. Still sitting on the toilet, I hold up my hand and we give each other a high five.

"I ditt!" he says.

"Yes, you did. You did it. We both did it." He beams at me.

"Ehybody poops!" he declares.

I think that that is just about the cutest thing that I have ever heard anyone say. Ever.

"That's right. Everybody poops. You know what, Aiden? I'm going to let you keep my book. I hope you'll think of me whenever you read it. But take care of it, okay? It's very special." I'm not sure that he gets this, but he doesn't have to. I get it, and that's good enough.

From the hallway I hear Stacey calling out to us. I can't even imagine what she's thinking right now. But I don't care. For once, I really don't care.

"Is everything okay in there?" she asks.

"Yeah," I yell. "Everything is perfect."

On the way home, I stop off at the toy store where I bought that gift for Julie's niece so long ago. Inspired by my success with Aiden, I decide that it's time to start training somebody else.

When I get home, Zoey is waiting for me, as usual, by the front door. Perfect. Just the person I wanted to see.

"Hi, Zo," I say, scratching her back and giving her kisses while she licks my face and sniffs me, trying to determine where I've been. "Mommy has a surprise for you today," I tell her. Her ears perk up, and I know she thinks that I have food.

"No, it's not steak from the Mexican place, sorry. It's better. Much more exciting." I walk into the den with the bag that I've brought in from the car, and she trots after me, curious to see what could possibly be better than steak from the Mexican place. Her tail is wagging a mile a minute. Oh, I hope I didn't talk it up too much.

I open the bag and pull out a life-size, bottle-sucking, diaper-wetting, goo-goo-gaa-gaa-saying baby doll, and I cradle it in my arms. Training is about to commence.

Zoey stands up on her hind legs and leans her front paws against my thighs, trying to get a look at this thing that is allegedly better than Mexican beef. I rock the baby in my arms and begin talking to it in the high-pitched voice that, prior to this moment, I have reserved for Zoey, and Zoey alone.

"Hi, Parker," I say to the doll. "You're so cute. What a good girl my baby is." I begin to walk up and down the hallway, cuddling the doll and talking to it. Every time I say something in the voice, Zoey wags her tail but then stops when she realizes that I'm not talking to her. Then she jumps up again to get my attention, but I ignore her. She stays right next to me as I pace, trying to figure out what I'm doing and what, exactly, this has to do with her. Finally, she stops in her tracks.

"Okay," says the scruffy voice. "What the hell is going on here?"

I crouch down to her level and put the baby in front of her face.

"I'm trying to prepare you for when the baby comes. I want you to see what it's going to be like. You're going to be a big sister, and that means that you won't always be the center of attention anymore."

Zoey shakes her head at me. "You're making a big mistake," she says. "I've heard about these baby things. They're no good. They turn everything upside down. They ruin the routine, and you know how I like my routine."

"I'm not making a mistake. Yes, things are going to change, and that's why I'm doing this. Now look at it."

She sniffs it for a few seconds, and then she looks back up at me disdainfully. "It's a piece of plastic." She shakes her head. "You are *so* weird." She walks off, and I can hear her muttering to herself, "Better than Mexican beef. What*ever*."

I close my eyes and sigh. So much for training. I guess she'll have to figure it out the hard way, just like the rest of us.

21.

The Butcher, the Baker, the Burned-cookie Maker

've been working the phones with colleges all week, and it looks like it's shaping up to be a pretty good year. The kids don't know yet (and I'm not allowed to tell them), but I've been assured that we will have at least one admit to each of Stanford, Yale, Harvard, Dartmouth, and Princeton, and I've got six in at Penn, three at Cornell, two at Columbia, and two at MIT. Wisconsin is taking almost half the class, BU is admitting about nine kids, and we're looking at twelve or thirteen admits to George Washington University.

All in all, it looks like everyone is going to get into college, which makes me breathe a whole lot easier, considering there were a few that I wasn't so sure about. Especially Tick. I've been on the verge of cardiac arrest all week because both Trinity and U. Conn are wait-listing her, and I haven't been able to get a hold of Ed or the rep at USC. But I finally spoke to USC this morning, and they're going to take her. They were a little concerned about her grades, but her dad has done some work with the film school, and there was simply no way that they could deny the only child of the brilliant Stefan Gardner. That's a quote, by the way. Only in LA, I know.

So now I just need to talk to Ed. We've been playing phone tag all week, and my anxiety level at this point is through the roof. I just don't know what's going to happen. Through a last-minute effort, she ended up with a B-minus in math and a twelve-eighty on her January SATs. Better, but not quite what I was hoping for. If it was a thirteen hundred and a B, I think that I could have made a compelling case, but with this . . . I don't know. I'm going to have to get creative on this one.

I pick up the phone and hold my breath as it rings.

"New York University, this is Ed Jellette."

"Hi, Ed, it's Lara."

"Oh, *finally*. You're harder to get on the phone than the pope. By the way, I hate the last week of February. There is nothing worse than talking to high school counselors all day long. As a general population, they're entirely too uptight. Between you and me, these people need to get laid more often. Present company excluded, of course."

Oh, don't be so sure, my friend. Except for a bout of makeup sex after the credit card debacle, anything resembling intimacy between Andrew and me has come to a grinding halt. I just can't do it comfortably anymore. There's no position that doesn't make me feel like either a beached whale or a potbellied pig, and blow jobs are out of the question. It's bad enough that I can't even take a deep breath anymore without a big old penis to suffocate on.

"Um, Ed?" I say. "Have you seen a high school counselor lately? They're generally not the kind of people who have sex. Except for me, of course, which is why I am here, on the phone, ready to whore myself out for any information that I can squeeze from you. And, of course, to persuade you that my kids are better and more deserving than all of the other self-entitled kids from Los Angeles."

Ed laughs at this. "Well, it's definitely the most honest description of your job that I've heard in a while. So, who are we going to be chatting about today?"

"None other than Ms. Tick Gardner, of course, and also Mark Cooper, one of my all-time favorites."

"Okay. Let me pull up those files. . . . Tick Gardner. Wouldn't I love to be her for a day. Let's see, deferred from early, new SAT scores are twelve-eighty, so-so midyear grades. I don't know, Lar, she's not looking all that enticing." I'm prepared for this. I have a whole spiel ready for him.

"Here's the deal, Ed. Tick's had a hard time here. She's an outcast, she doesn't have a lot of friends, it's been a rough few years. And it's not because she's a snob. She's just more mature than the other kids. She doesn't get caught up in the teenage angst and the petty high school bullshit that goes on around here. She's beyond that. She doesn't relate to it. She could care less about who is going to be homecoming princess and whether student government has a car wash or a raffle to raise money for prom. But it affects her academically. It's hard for her to focus on school because of the environment—the other kids don't get her and the teachers write her off because of who her dad is—but she's really a smart girl. You've seen her writing; it's fantastic. She's just not working to potential. And her home life is a mess. This is off the record, but her mother is a total bitch, couldn't care less about her as long as she stays out of the tabloids. And the dad is never around. Trust me, you would not want to be her. Not even for a day. You should hear the way people talk about her behind her back, and all because she was born into a family that happens to be famous. I think she'll do great at NYU. It's a perfect place for her. She can blend in, get out of the LA scene, nobody will care who she is, and she can just concentrate on school and her music. She's a talented singer and musician, and I think she'll have a lot to add to the campus. She'll thrive when she's in the right environment. I'm positive." There. That's my pitch. I cross my fingers, and Ed sighs.

"Lara, sweetie, I hear you. I do. But the poor-little-rich-girl thing doesn't usually play well in committee. Come on, bottom line, are the parents going to donate? Because I think that that could really help."

Damn.

"I talked to them about it, and they're just overcommitted this year. But she's definitely a prospect. They have a history of donating to places that they have a relationship with—they're huge donors at our school. I think that if she's happy there, and she's doing well, they'll definitely be players in the future." Ed sighs again. "Please, Ed. I have never asked you to look at a kid who isn't up to par, but she's different. She's a good kid; she's just misunderstood."

"Okay. Okay. I'll take her to committee, and I'll push for her. But I'm only doing this because I trust you, and I trust your judgment. I can't make any promises, but I'll see what I can do."

Yesssss. "Thank you. Thank you so much. I promise, she's a good risk."

"We'll see," he says. "Okay, what about Mark? I liked his application. Grades are good, SATs are about average for us, love his extracurriculars. Not the strongest curriculum, though. Regular-level English and History is kind of weak, but the APs in math and science might make up for it. He's not a sure thing, but I think it's looking good. Anything you want to add?"

"I love Mark. He's fun, he's got a great sense of humor, he works so hard—really, I've never seen a kid work so hard. He has managed to pull off As by sheer determination. He's a mover and a shaker, very into politics. You can't go wrong with Mark. He's terrific."

"Yeah. I like him. I think the committee will, too. I don't think it'll be a problem, but I'll have to see how he does compared to the rest of the applicant pool. By the way, applications are up almost fourteen percent, and the kids are stronger than ever. Average SAT score of *applicants* is a thirteen-sixty. I don't know what they're putting in the water, but these teenagers get smarter and smarter ever year. Anyway, is that it? Only two kids from Bel Air Prep this year? Last year we had around ten."

"Yeah, kind of weird, I know. I think that this is just an off class. Don't take it as a sign. Listen, can I call you again before decisions go out, to get a heads-up?"

"Yeah, yeah. Use me and abuse me. Of course you can call. We'll be in committee until March fifteenth, so anytime after that. By the way, how are you feeling, Miss Mommy-to-be?"

"Fat. I'm feeling fat. But thanks for asking. Okay, babe, I'll talk to you in a few weeks. Be good to me."

"I'll do my best."

Oh, thank God it's Friday. Only five more weeks until I start my maternity leave. I'm not that excited about the maternity part of it, but I'm very much looking forward to the leave.

The next morning I am up at the butt crack of dawn, going through the piles of paper that have been littering the kitchen counter for months (and that are comprised of scraps on which I have written notes to myself that I no longer can interpret, coupons that I didn't remember to use before they expired, a lab bill from my doctor that I have forgotten to pay, and various other things that at one time seemed important enough to keep but that I am now able to toss away without the slightest hint of remorse), putting away the many pairs of shoes that I have left in random places throughout the house (*oh, that's where my black Pradas have been*), and essentially trying to make the place look as if it is completely unlived-in and not at all as if it is inhabited by a slob (me) and a semi-neat person who has given up on trying to reform said slob (Andrew).

In case you were wondering, my cleaning frenzy draws its inspiration not from any maternal instinct to nest (an instinct that I either lack or just have yet to experience, but which the pregnancy books have warned about in the third trimester, telling tales of women hauling wheelbarrows around in the backyard and perching precipitously upon top-ladder rungs in an effort to Windex each individual crystal of their foyer chandeliers, all just minutes before their due dates), but rather from the fact that today, Andrew and I will be spending the day interviewing people for the job of live-in nanny/housekeeper.

And before you go attacking me for being a princess, you should know that the whole thing was Andrew's idea. Andrew grew up in LA, and his mother always had live-in help when he was a kid. When I was growing up, I knew of only one family who had a live-in—they were former New Yorkers whose company had transferred them to our town—and everyone in the neighborhood used to talk shit about them. But apparently everyone here does it, and Andrew swears that it's the way to go. I suppose I like the idea—I mean, realistically, I was planning on having *some* kind of a nanny, so why not have one there all the time?—but I'm definitely concerned about my privacy. Plus, I have no idea how this kind of an arrangement works. Do I have to eat dinner with this person every night? Will I be expected to make conversation when we're alone together in the house? The very thought of such things makes me shudder. Not to mention the whole "lady of the house" aspect of it, which completely freaks me out. I mean, I can barely manage to tell my twenty-three-year-old assistant what to do, let alone a woman who will most likely be twice my age and has undoubtedly raised seven or eight kids of her own. But Andrew is convinced that I will get over these things, insisting that the benefits (total flexibility and freedom to go out whenever we want, never having to worry about cars breaking down or finding a babysitter at the last minute) far outweigh the costs.

Which brings me back to my point, which is that I have been cleaning since six o'clock this morning, simply because I wouldn't want any of these potential hirees to think that I am anything less than immaculate.

254 · Risa Green

Of course, it has crossed my mind that one of these women may actually end up living with me, at which point, I suppose, the jig will be up, but at least the other four candidates can go back out into the world believing that I am as perfect and domesticated as I am pretending to be. Hence, by nine A.M., my house looks as if Martha Stewart herself has come to call (preconviction, of course), complete with fresh flowers sitting on the coffee table in the den, which I have arranged in a crystal vase that I received for my wedding and have never before used, and the smell of chocolate-chip cookies wafting from the oven. I had no idea that baking cookies was so easy, by the way—the batter actually comes in little perforated squares, and all you have to do is literally stick them in the oven. Very good to know for the PTA events that this perfect version of me is going to not only attend but chair in a few years.

"Wow," Andrew says, when he finally emerges from the bedroom at nine forty-five, shirtless and still in his boxers. "If I had known that you would be so motivated by a bunch of Latin American strangers, I would have been hosting La Raza meetings here."

"Very funny," I say. "Go get dressed, would you? The first one is supposed to be here in fifteen minutes." After scarfing down an English muffin with peanut butter and jelly and leaving his knife and plate sitting in the sink, he retreats to the bedroom. *Ugh*, thinks perfect-me, as I put them in the dishwasher. *A woman's work is never done.*

The doorbell rings at exactly ten A.M., on the dot. I consider for a second whether I should throw on the mint-green gingham apron that my former colleagues from my law firm gave me as a bridal shower gag gift, but then reject the idea as being a bit too much. I quickly check my list— ten A.M. is . . . Esperanza—and I run to get the door.

Esperanza, by the way, is the only person we are meeting who is not from the agency that Andrew called. (Or, I should say, the "agency" that Andrew called. I have no idea how he found out about it, but it's basically run by an illegal woman named Myrna who is tapped into the underground nanny community. She still charges an agency fee, but it's way cheaper than what the legitimate places charge.) Esperanza is actually a referral from the nanny who works for my next-door neighbor. When she heard that we were looking for someone, the nanny called me up and told me that a friend of hers from church needed a job, and asked if she could set up an interview for her. The only thing I know about this woman is that her name is Esperanza and that, according to the nanny next door, she "doesn't speak real good English." I was inclined to say no, thanks, but Andrew insisted that we meet her, assuring me that real good English is not actually a necessity. In fact, he considers it to be a liability, because the more fluent she is, the more money we'll have to pay her. Apparently, in the world of Los Angeles nannies, how much money one makes is directly correlated to how much one has assimilated into American culture. For example, a fluent, legal resident with a driver's license and a car can command top dollar, while a fresh-off-the-boat, in-hiding-from-the-INS, bus-taking resident might be better off working in a sweatshop. Andrew, obviously, would prefer the latter. As long as she can communicate with us, he said, we don't need much else. Plus, if we ended up hiring this Esperanza person, we wouldn't have to pay any agency fee at all. Needless to say, Esperanza is the front-runner at this point, at least in Andrew's mind.

I open the door and on the porch are two women. One of them is hanging back, and the other starts talking immediately.

"Hi, are you Lara?" Her English is perfect. She barely even has an accent. If this doesn't qualify as real good, I don't know what does. I nod and she sticks out her hand. "I'm Maria." She points to the woman behind her, who flashes me a smile. Her right front tooth is gold. "This is Esperanza. I came to help her with the interview, since she doesn't speak English so well. She can speak a little, but she gets nervous, so she asked me to come."

Okay, I think. *So let me get this straight. The woman came with an interpreter?* Somehow I get the feeling that this does not bode well.

I invite them inside and we start walking up the stairs to the den, just as Andrew is coming out of the bedroom. I raise my eyebrows at him.

"Andrew, this is Esperanza, and this is her friend, Maria. Maria came along to help Esperanza in case she doesn't understand us." I turn to Maria and Esperanza. "This is my husband, Andrew."

"Hola," Andrew says, and they both giggle like schoolgirls.

When we get to the den, Maria sits down on the couch next to me and Andrew, and Esperanza sits on the club chair across from all of us. Maria turns to us.

"So, what do you want to ask her?"

"Well," I say. "Does she speak any English at all?" I feel bad talking about her as if she isn't in the room, but I don't really have a choice. I mean, I haven't practiced my Spanish since high school. When I ask this, Maria gets a concerned look on her face.

"She speaks a little, but she can learn. She wants to learn." She glances at Esperanza and says something to her in Spanish. Esperanza answers, and Maria looks back at me. "She says she wants to learn. She's only been in this country for seven months."

"It's okay," says Andrew, grinning at them both. "No problem. We can work with this. *No problema,* okay?" Esperanza smiles at him. Maria smiles at him. I shoot him a look of death.

"He speaks Spanish?" asks Maria. "*¿Usted habla Español, sí?*"

"*Sí,*" he says. "*Muy bueno.*" Oh, here we go. Andrew thinks that he's fluent in Spanish because *his* nanny taught it to him a million years ago and he used to practice on some guys from his high school baseball team. It's so annoying. Whenever we go to Mexico, he insists on having entire conversations in Spanish, even though he never knows the words that he wants to use and it takes him forever to figure out an alternative way of saying what he's trying to say. It drives me crazy. But it's beside the point. Andrew is not the one who is going to have to be home with this woman all day for three months (and, if Ed cooperates, for two days a week all of next year). I am. And while I do have a limited vocabulary of Spanish words, I have absolutely no recollection of how to form sentences, how to conjugate verbs, or how to speak in the past or future tense. And, despite Maria's insistence that Esperanza knows English but is just nervous, I have yet to see any signs of understanding in her eyes. As much as I would love to not have to pay an agency fee, I can tell already that there is absolutely no way that this is going to work out.

But Andrew seems to have other ideas.

"*¿Dónde está trabaja antes de ahora?*"

Oh, please. Even I know that that's not the right way to ask where she worked before. But Esperanza doesn't flinch.

"*En un centro para bebés.*" Andrew looks to Maria for help with this one.

"She worked in a day-care center."

He beams at me, as if this fact should make up for her inability to utter even one word of English.

The three of them continue to have an exchange like this—Andrew mangles a question in Spanish, Esperanza answers in real Spanish, Andrew doesn't understand her, and Maria interprets—and from this, I learn that Esperanza will cook, clean, do laundry, and whatever else we want her to do, that she raised three babies that she left behind in Guatemala with her husband, and that all of the money she makes gets sent back to them.

When Andrew hears this last part, he begins shaking his head. "I'm so sorry. *Lo siento*," he says. *Es muy terrible.*

Oh, God. I'm going to have to put an end to this before he offers to let her move in tonight.

"*I'm* sorry," I say, "but she doesn't speak any English, and I don't speak any Spanish. How are we going to communicate with each other?"

Andrew and Maria look at me like I am the biggest party pooper that has ever walked the planet. Sensing that I am not as enthusiastic as my compadre, Maria turns to Esperanza and starts speaking to her very fast in Spanish, and Esperanza starts speaking very fast back to her. Maria must have told her that she'd better start speaking some English soon or she's going to lose whatever chance she has for this job, because all of a sudden Esperanza slams her hand on the coffee table.

"Table," she says. I'm not sure if I'm supposed to act impressed or not, so I look at Maria, who smiles and gives me a see-I-told-you-so glance. Esperanza flashes me her gold tooth. Then, in yet another non sequitur, she speaks again.

"Grandmother," she declares.

I gather that these are the only two words that she knows in the entire English language, and neither of them would be able to help my baby in an emergency. I look at Maria quizzically.

"She says she knows some words, and you can teach her. She says if you want her to clean the table, you can put your hand on the table and say *table* and make a cleaning motion. If you want her to change the baby's diaper, you can point to the diaper and she'll understand what you mean." I have no idea how *grandmother* fits into the picture, but Andrew chimes in before I can ask.

"We can send her to an ESL class," he says. "They have one at the high school down the street, and we can buy an English tutorial program for the computer that she can practice on. She can learn it really fast, maybe a few months." I look at him like he's crazy. He asks Esperanza in Spanish if she knows how to use a computer.

"*Sí, sí,*" she answers, totally unconvincingly. I have to cut him off before the poor woman gets her hopes up any higher.

"Okay, well, I guess that's all we need to know," I say.

Maria smiles at me. "So does she have the job?"

Whoa, there, lady, I think. I didn't realize she was expecting an answer on the spot.

"We still have to interview some more people, so we'll let you know," I say. Maria frowns and translates this for Esperanza, who looks extremely disappointed.

"Okay," Maria says. "Here's my card. You can call me when you make a decision. But she's good. She loves babies."

"I'm sure she does," I say, ushering them down the stairs. When we've closed the door behind them, Andrew turns to look at me.

"So, what do you think?" he asks, sounding excited.

"What do I think? I think you're insane. This woman needs to take care of our baby. She needs to know how to speak English, Andrew. What if there's an emergency?"

"They have nine-one-one operators who speak Spanish. This is LA; everyone speaks Spanish."

"Well, I don't, and since she's going to be living with me, it's not going to work. What is wrong with you? 'We can send her to an ESL class. She can do a tutorial on the computer.' I'm sure that back in her village in Guatemala she spent her days surfing the internet on their DSL line. Have you lost your mind? From now on, I'm in charge of the interviews. Don't say a word." He pouts. "In English *or* Spanish."

When the doorbell rings again, Andrew and I open the door and are met with Marguerita, a tiny little woman with a short haircut who is wearing white pumps and what appears to be an Escada suit in bright yellow, and carrying what is definitely a white, quilted Chanel purse circa 1987. She speaks perfect English and she shows us her driver's license without my even having to ask. I gather that she's the equivalent to a four-star general in terms of ranking in the nanny community. Andrew frowns.

I show her into the den, fully prepared to pepper her with questions, but I can't even get a word in edgewise. She does not even pause once to take a breath as she tells us, for twenty minutes, about Joyce, the previous woman for whom she worked. Joyce's family is also Jewish, they keep kosher, they live in one of the most expensive neighborhoods in the city, and, despite her protests, Joyce used to take her shopping at Neiman's on a regular basis. The kids are in college now, and they just don't need her anymore, but Joyce is heartbroken over having to let her go. She informs us that she makes a perfect brisket, she can do potato latkes for Hanukkah, and she has Joyce's grandmother's recipe for sweet kugel that is out of this world. She asks if we keep separate dishwashers for milk and meat, and she seems almost insulted when we tell her that we are a one-dishwasher family. When she finally stops talking and I am able to ask her some of my questions, she waves all of them away and says, "Of course, of course."

I didn't know that they made yentas in Honduras. All I can picture is having this woman in my house, constantly criticizing me. I decide that I already have a Jewish mother, and I don't need a second one. Next.

The next three interviews consist of: (1) another woman who barely speaks any English and shows up with her uncle to help her along in the interview. From the little that she says, she strikes me as a potential serial killer, and it doesn't help that her uncle repeatedly praises her ability to clean but keeps curiously silent about her way with babies. She makes me very nervous and I get rid of her immediately; (2) a chatty woman in her sixties named Paulina who has wild white hair that she wears in a long, teased ponytail and a voice like Betty Boop and who reminds me of my crazy aunt Dora who used to talk to pigeons. She was a nurse in her country and spent the last six years working with a family whose child had Down syndrome, and while she's very nice and obviously qualified, I just can't shake the image of Fran Drescher in *The Nanny,* but dubbed in Spanish for the Telemundo channel. Pass; and (3) a Mexican woman in her forties named Lupe whose only question for me is whether it is okay with me if she puts the baby in front of the television while she cleans and eats her lunch. Uh, no.

When they've all left, I kick off my shoes by the front door, and Andrew and I stare at each other blankly.

"Maybe we should just wait until after the baby is born to find someone," I say.

"And you for sure don't want to go with Esperanza?"

"Andrew," I say sternly.

"She's definitely the best one. She seems very nurturing."

"Forget about her. It's not up for discussion When we get home from the hospital I'll call a real agency, and I'm sure we'll find someone good. It's worth the extra money."

"Okay, okay," he says. "Where do you want me to put their phone numbers?"

"Just put them on the kitchen counter," I say. "I'll call them all to tell them no later."

Just then Andrew wrinkles his nose and starts sniffing the air. "Do you smell something?" he asks.

I inhale through my nose. "Oh, shit," I say, running into the kitchen. "The fucking cookies are burning."

22.

Hi, Ho, the Dairy-o, the Counselor Is in Hell

On the morning of March sixteenth, I arrive at work almost an hour early. I was so anxious that I barely slept last night at all. At two thirty, when I had four hours before the alarm went off, I tried counting sheep, but every sheep had a letter from NYU in its mouth and I couldn't read what it said, so I gave up on the sheep. At four thirty, I decided to count backward from one thousand, but I kept seeing every number in flashing Broadway lights, which reminded me of New York, which then got me thinking about NYU again, so I stopped at six hundred and seventy-three. By the time five forty-five rolled around and I was still staring at the clock, I was so stressed about the fact that I hadn't slept and worried about how I would ever be able to function at work today and do all of the things that I have to get done, et cetera, et cetera, et cetera, that I just decided to get up and take a shower. By the time the alarm actually went off, I was packing up my lunch and getting ready to leave.

Of course, I've called Ed three times already this morning and he hasn't picked up the phone. But I haven't left him a message because I don't want to wait for him to call me back. I'd much rather just keep calling every ten minutes on the chance that he'll pick up.

I still have six more minutes to wait before I can call him again, so I decide to check my e-mail. There's only one new one since the last time I checked five minutes ago, and it's from Your Baby. I click to open it.

YOUR BABY NOW: Thirty-seven Weeks

Hello, Lara!
You're in the home stretch, and your baby may be ready to make an appearance at any time now! If you haven't already made all of your final preparations, now is the time to do it! Pack a bag for the hospital, and stock up on diapers, wipes, formula (if you're bottle feeding), and anything else you may need for your nursery. See the Your Baby newborn page for a checklist of what you'll need!

Today's Hot Topic: Are you having trouble sleeping? Lots of women in their third trimester can't get comfortable. Join our live chat to see how other moms-to-be are finding ways to get some rest.

For curiosity's sake, I enter the chat room, but I quickly leave it when I see the advice, and, more important, how it's spelled. One woman, for example, advises "taking a lookewarm bath before bed, and then mehditaihting for twenty minutes about what you're baby will look like! I have six kids (and am pregnant with my seventh!) and this rehmedie always works! The baby always looks just like I imajined it!" Apparently exclamation points are contagious among pregnant women.

I smugly hit the delete button. Smugly because I don't need to look at their checklist, as I am already prepared for the baby. Well, stuff-wise, at least. Emotionally, psychologically, and informationally are a very different story. But all of the baby's furniture has been delivered. Of course, it's still sitting in the baby's room, unassembled, because the painter has canceled on me three times and I don't want to set it up until after the room's been painted (don't ask—the painter actually did already come and paint the room, but the shade of pink that I picked came out a horrible bubblegum color, and I cried for three days until Andrew finally said that he would call the painter back and have him come out and repaint the room in a paler shade, but the painter is annoyed with me because he told me that it wasn't a good color and I didn't listen, so now he's just trying to make my life as difficult as possible), but he swears that he's coming this week, and once he does Andrew can put everything together.

And last week I went shopping with Julie to buy all of the little stuff that we need. Mind you, it was totally overwhelming, and I nearly had a nervous breakdown in the middle of Babies "R" Us, but the point is, I got the stuff. The whole thing just caught me off guard, though. I mean, I knew there was a lot of stuff, but I was totally unprepared for how many choices there are among the stuff things. To give you an idea, there was an entire wall of mobiles, including teddy bear mobiles, puppy dog mobiles, clinically proven brain-enhancing mobiles that play classical music, and mobiles that are non–brain enhancing but also play classical music and are controlled by a wireless remote. Julie asked me which one I wanted, but when my eyes glazed over and I started to convulse, she just threw the brain-enhancing one into my cart.

She then took me through aisles and aisles of bottle warmers, wipes warmers, car seat mirrors, car seat covers, nursing pillows, bottle liners, nipples for newborns, nipples for infants, nipples for toddlers, angled bottles, small bottles, big bottles, disposable bottles, bath slings, convertible bathtubs, inflatable bathtubs, large yellow rubber duck–shaped bathtubs, newborn carriers that sit on your hip, newborn carriers that sit on your chest, carriers for children up to twenty-five pounds that can be carried like a backpack, a Diaper Genie, a Diaper Champ, a Diaper Dekor, a Diaper Dekor Plus, white diaper rash creams, clear diaper rash creams, gel-based diaper rash creams, baby monitors with two frequencies, baby monitors with three frequencies, baby monitors that produce light shows, baby monitors that double as portable television sets, and, my personal favorite, baby monitors that come equipped with United States Army–developed night-vision technology.

I deteriorated further and further with each aisle, until I finally lay down somewhere near the eighteen different kinds of bouncy seats (three-point harness or five-point? with music or without? four vibrating options or two?) and curled up in the fetal position, humming the theme song from *Mahogany*. But, thanks to Julie, who just ignored me and kept tossing things into my cart, all of the necessities have at least been purchased, and they are now sitting in giant plastic Babies "R" Us shopping bags in the closet of the bubblegum-colored nursery, just waiting for me to misuse one or more of them and consequently kill my soon-to-be-born baby. But, like I said, I'm prepared.

The phone rings, and I grab it. Maybe it's Ed. Maybe he knew that it was me leaving hangups on his voice mail all morning, and now he's calling to tell me the good news.

"College Counseling, this is Lara," I say anxiously.

"Hi, it's me." I recognize the voice, but I can't place it.

"Hi," I say with fake recognition, trying to be polite in case this is someone whose voice I should, in fact, be able to identify.

"It's Stacey." Busted. But in my defense, it is *so* out of context. Stacey never calls me at work. Ever. I didn't even know she had my work number.

"Oh, hi," I say. "Why are you calling me at work?"

"Can you go hiking tomorrow?" she asks. "I really want to go."

"You called me at work to ask me if I could hike tomorrow?" I ask her. "Is something wrong?"

"No. Can you?"

"Stace, I'm due in three weeks and its a hundred degrees outside. I don't know if I can make it the whole way. I do not want to go into labor on the trail and have my baby delivered by one of the Persian men."

"Oh," she says, sounding disappointed. "Are you sure?"

"Is something wrong?" I ask again. "You sound weird." She sighs.

"Todd proposed to me."

I scream. "He did? You're getting married? Oh, my God, I never thought this day would come. Please tell me that you're not going to make me wear a lavender taffeta bridesmaid's dress."

"I'm not," she says. "I said no. Actually, I broke up with him."

I gasp. "He asked you to marry him and you broke up with him? Why? I thought you liked him so much."

"I did," she says. "I do."

"So then why are you not planning a wedding right now?" I ask.

She sighs. "I just couldn't take the kid. And don't tell me that you told me so, okay?"

Oh, fine. But I did tell her so. "But Aiden is so sweet," I say. "Shit, I gave him my book, too. If I had known you were breaking up with him, I never would have done that."

"Okay," she says. "Not about you, here, remember?"

"Sorry. He just seemed like a good kid."

"He is a good kid. But he's a kid." All of a sudden her voice chokes up, and she's crying. I'm totally shocked. I honestly did not know that Stacey possessed tear ducts. She was the only person in my first-year Property Law class—male or female—who didn't break down in tears the day that she got called on by the horribly mean Professor Williams. Every day he would pick a different victim, and he would make the person stand up for the entire class, firing questions at them and humiliating them if they didn't know the answers. For a frame of reference, the wussiest girl in our section started crying as soon as her name was called, and I was a puddle after five questions.

"I just don't want kids," she cries. "I don't like them, and it's not something that I can compromise on. It sucks, though, because I think I really could have married him."

This is horrible. I've got to make her change her mind. "But he's only there part-time. And he's not *your* kid."

"Come on, Lara. I don't want to be the wicked stepmother, and you know that's exactly what I would be. And even though he's only there part-time, my life would still revolve around him full-time. It already does, and we're just dating." She catches herself. "*Were* just dating. I'm just being realistic, that's all."

I want to tell her that she's being stupid, and that she's throwing away the best thing that ever happened to her, but I can't. She's right. I know that she's right. And plus, I'm incredibly impressed by her resolve. If not a little bit jealous, even.

"Well, then you did the right thing," I say.

She sniffles. "Do you really think I did?"

"Yes. Definitely. I really admire you for this. You're a total bitch, but at least you're true to yourself. It's more than a lot of people can say." Including myself.

She takes a deep breath and composes herself. "Okay, I've gotta go. I have so much work to do. Sorry to bother you."

Have you ever seen a sci-fi movie where the main characters find a vortex into a parallel universe? It appears only once every twenty-five million years, and they have only a small window of time to jump in, do some exploring, and get back out before it closes up and traps them there forever? That's how I feel right now. I just had a ten-minute glimpse into Stacey's vulnerability, and now the vortex has been sealed for the rest of eternity.

I start to hang up the phone, but then I hear my name, muffled in the airspace between the receiver and the phone cradle.

"Lar?"

"Yeah," I say, putting it back up to my ear. "I'm still here."

She pauses. "Forget it. I'll talk to you later," she says, and quickly hangs up.

Yeah. That was something that I'll never experience again.

Two hours later, I've got him.

"New York University, this is Ed Jellette."

Finally. This is the sixteenth time I've called. But I'll act casual, like I just happened to get him on the first try.

"Hi, Ed. It's Lara."

He huffs. "Are you the one who's been calling me all day and hanging up?"

"What?" I say, pretending that I have no idea what he's talking about.

"I only told three counselors that we would have decisions ready today, and someone has hung up on my voice mail sixteen times this morning. Like, just leave a message and I will call you back, moron."

Oops. "It wasn't me," I lie. "But if whoever it is has all that spare time, I've got plenty of work that he could help out with over here."

"I know, right?" he says. "Some people just have no concept. Anyway, how *are* you? Aren't you, like, ready to pop any second now?"

"You have no idea. I'm so glad that you don't live here, because if you even saw how huge I am, your image of me would be ruined forever."

"Well, then I'm glad, too," he says. "Because your image is all you've got, doll."

I laugh. "Well said, my friend. Anyway, listen. You know why I'm calling. This has been the longest two weeks of my life. *Please* tell me that you have good news."

Ed goes into business mode. "Well, like I told you last time, our applications were up fourteen percent, and this is the strongest applicant pool we've ever had. And because we overenrolled our freshman class last year, we were told to underenroll this year because we don't have enough space. So we're wait-listing a lot of kids who normally would have gotten in. It was a very tough year for us."

Oh, that kind of talk is never a good sign. That kind of talk is a hedge against what's coming next. I cross my fingers.

"So, given that, we're admitting Mark Cooper—which is a gift, by the way; he was very close to being wait-listed—and we're unfortunately going to have to deny Victoria Gardner."

I close my eyes in defeat. *No. No, no, no, no, no.*

"Ed, listen, I am begging you. Is there anything that you can do?"

"There's nothing I can do, Lara. We don't have room for one more kid. Honestly."

I hesitate, and then I say what I have never said before. What I told myself I would never say. "Ed, I'm asking this as a personal favor." There is silence for almost a full minute.

"Okay," he says, sounding uncomfortable. "Here's the deal. Our class is completely full. Literally. We were told that we could admit seven thousand, three hundred and seven kids, and not one more, and that's how many we admitted. One of those admits is from Bel Air Prep. If it is that important to you"—he hesitates for a moment—"then I could switch the decisions. I could deny Mark and admit Victoria. It's your call."

Butterflies are slam dancing in my stomach. I feel like I'm in a bad remake of *Sophie's Choice.* How can I possibly choose between Mark and Tick? They're my two favorites. I want them both to get in. But they can't. Ed just told me that they can't. It's one or the other. I start weighing the options in my head.

If I choose Tick, I get to work part-time next year. I get to spend time with the baby, which means that I won't have to feel guilty about never being around. I can do that Mommy and Me class with her, I can take her to the park, and we could go on play dates with all of the new mommy friends that I am bound to meet. And let's not forget about me. I'll get to work out at least two days a week, which will save me from becoming just another fat-assed, X-percent-of-women-are-not-back-to-their-prepregnancy-weight-at-one-year-postpartum statistic when I throw Parker's first birthday party. And, of course, Tick gets to go to NYU, which is her dream. She gets to leave LA, leave her parents, and concentrate on her music. It would be so good for her. And I already know that Mark is getting into BU, and that's one of his top choices. He could go there and be really happy. . . .

But if I choose Mark, I work full-time. Which means full-time guilt. Which means leaving the baby with a nanny five days a week. Which means nanny cams, and a baby whose first word is *agua* or *leche,* and that I'll have doubts for the rest of my life about whether I screwed up my child forever by not being around during that crucial first year. It also means that Tick goes to USC, so she won't leave LA, she won't get away from her parents, and she'll probably end up dating Marcus again, or someone just like him. And, of course, even if I do pick Mark, he might not even decide to go to NYU. He may choose to go to BU anyway. I mean, he never told me which one was his first choice; I just know that he likes them both. . . .

Well, then, that settles it. I have to choose Tick. How can I not choose Tick? It makes the most sense. If I choose Tick, everyone wins.

"Okay," I say to Ed. "I really appreciate this. I'm going to . . ."

But then I start thinking again. How can I choose Tick? Tick doesn't deserve this. She has bad grades, and she just doesn't care about school. And it's so unfair to Mark. Plus, if I do this, I'll be just like everyone else. I'll be one more person who gives her the easy way out, who doesn't think about who she is, but only about who her father is, and what he can do for me. I'll be selfish, and she'll go on thinking that she can get whatever she wants without having to make an effort. If I pick her, I really will be using her. And that's not what she wants from me. I know that's not what she wants from me. She needs someone in her life to teach her the hard lessons. She's practically crying out for it.

I sigh.

". . . leave it the way it is. Go ahead and admit Mark."

"Are you sure?" he asks, sounding surprised.

"I'm sure," I say. "But thanks for the offer. It means a lot to me."

"No problem," he says. "I don't know what you just gave up, but I'm proud of you. You did the right thing."

"Yeah," I say. "Tell that to my head of school."

When I get off the phone, my assistant is waving at me urgently.

"Lara, there's an emergency faculty meeting in the theater. Everybody has to go down there right now."

Oh, God, I am so not in the mood for a Bel Air Prep "emergency" right now. These meetings are always the biggest waste of time. They make everyone rush down to the theater in a panic, only to tell us that a kid was found smoking pot in the parking lot and that we should all be on the lookout for telltale signs of drug use, or that somebody was caught getting a blow job in the bathroom and that they're bringing in a team of specialists from a teenage sexuality clinic. I don't know why they insist on gathering us all together for these things. It's never anything new and it's never anything that can't be said in a quick e-mail.

I grab my purse and head down to the theater, and when I reach the door I try to open it as quietly as possible so as not to call attention to myself when I walk in. But when I peek my head in, there's nobody there. Where is everyone? Is she sure it's in the theater? Just then about sixty people jump out from behind the stage curtains.

"*Surprise!*"

The entire senior class and a handful of teachers whom I actually like are standing in front of me, and when they pull back the curtains I see that the stage has been decorated with pink balloons and *It's a Girl* banners. I am stunned. Speechless. I really had no idea that any of them even noticed that I was about to give birth.

"You guys," I say. "You are so adorable. You are definitely my new favorite class." They all laugh, and the class president, a very pretty girl named Janie who has clearly seen the movie *Election* one too many times, comes forward with a bouquet of flowers.

"We just wanted to thank you for all of the help that you gave us this year. None of us could have gotten through the hell that is college applications without you, and even though you made most of us redo our essays thirty times, we still love you anyway." At this, all of the kids start clapping, and Janie steps forward and hands me the flowers. I give her a big hug.

"Thank you," I say. "You guys are lucky. Usually I make people redo their essays forty times." They all laugh again, and from behind me I hear another voice. It's Tick, and she's holding two boxes.

"And we all chipped in and got you some things. These are for the baby. . . ." She opens the first box and pulls out a tiny pair of red pants and a tiny red and blue T-shirt that says University of Pennsylvania, which is my alma mater (and Andrew's). Oh, I love that. That is perfect. Andrew is going to die when he sees this. "And these are for you. . . ." She opens up the second box and inside is a gorgeous full-length hot-pink satin robe, a gift certificate to a spa, and a two-hundred-and-fifty-dollar gift certificate to Barneys. Oh, you gotta love rich kids with good taste.

"Oh, my God," I say. "This is so unnecessary. Thank you so much."

Janie steps forward again. "You should know, Mrs. Stone, that this whole thing was Tick's idea. Like, we all thought it was great, but she co-ordinated everything."

I look over at Tick and she is blushing. *Oh, man*. I feel so guilty right now.

"Well, thank you to all of you, and thank you to Tick. This was incredibly thoughtful and generous of you." I go over to Tick and give her a big hug.

"Thanks," I say, so only she can hear me.

"I owed you one," she says. "Or two."

"No," I say. "You don't owe me anything." *Believe me,* I think. "This is one of the nicest things that anyone has ever done for me. I really appreciate it."

"You deserve it," she says. "You help a lot of people."

Oh, God. That knife just keeps digging in. I nod at her, trying not to cry.

"Listen," I say. "If you get a chance this afternoon, can you come by my office? I need to talk to you."

"Yeah," she says. "No problem. I'm free sixth period; I'll come by then."

"Great." I flash her a fake smile. "Thanks again for all of this."

* * *

At two thirty, Tick appears in my doorway.

"Come in," I say, waving her into my office. She drops her huge bag and falls into a chair.

"God, this has been the longest day. Oh, guess what? I got an A-minus on the math quiz I took yesterday. I've never gotten an A on a math test in my life. Can you believe that?" Oh, she's going to make this as hard as she possibly can, isn't she?

"That's amazing," I say. "Good for you." I clear my throat. "Tick, I have to talk to you about something, and I want you to know that the party today and the A-minus on your math quiz are so great, and they only make this that much harder for me to say."

She looks at me with alarm. "What's wrong?" she says. "Am I in trouble for something?"

"No, no. Not at all." I pause, and then I blurt it out. "Tick, I wanted to be the one to tell you that you're not going to get into NYU."

Her face goes pale. "You know that already?"

I nod. "I talked to Ed Jellette this morning."

"So why are you telling me? Why not just let me get the letter like everyone else?"

"Because," I say, trying to fight back my tears. "I'm the one who made the final decision not to admit you, so I thought you should hear it from me."

She squints at me, like she can't believe that this is real. "What are you talking about?"

I bite my lip in an effort to keep it from quivering so much. "I can't go into all of the details without compromising the privacy of other students, but basically, I was given an opportunity to make a decision that would have resulted in your being admitted, and I turned it down." Her eyes are watery, and I can tell that she is furious with me.

"Why?" she says. "Why would you do that?" I can feel my throat starting to choke up, and I don't think that I can get through this without crying. Oh, fuck it. Who cares if she sees me cry? I don't know who I'm kidding with this tough-guy act, anyway. The kids totally know that I'm a sucker.

"I'm really sorry," I say, my voice breaking. "But I didn't think that it was the right thing to do." I am in full-fledged crying mode now, and making no attempt to stop it. Tick, by the way, is totally unfazed by my tears, and she is staring at me coldly, awaiting a better explanation. I take a deep breath, but it is shaky and does nothing for my composure. "Look," I say, "I just don't think that you deserve it, and it's not fair to the kids who do."

She rolls her eyes at me in disgust. "Oh, so now you're the one who decides who's worthy and who isn't? It must be fun to play God, huh?"

I shouldn't expect her to understand. Perhaps telling her myself was not one of the brighter ideas I've ever had. But at least I'm not crying anymore. Although I'm not angry, either, which is surprising to me, because the "playing God" comment should have me completely riled up right now. But I'm not. I just feel sad for her.

"Tick," I say in a soft, slow voice that I have never heard myself use before. "You haven't worked as hard as the kids who got in and you haven't tried as hard. And if I had told them to admit you, they would only be doing it because they want to help me, and not because they want to have you there. And while I'm very sorry, that is just not a good enough reason for me."

Now she's the one sobbing. "So what am I supposed to do? Stay here and go to community college, or to USC, if I even get in? You were my only chance to get out of here next year, and you know it. You talked me out of going to New York with Marcus. Because of you Marcus broke up with me, and I lost my band, and I've had the worst year of my life. The only thing that got me through this year was the thought of getting out of here. You knew that. You knew that and you still screwed me."

I shake my head. "I didn't screw you, Tick," I say. Still the same voice. Where is it coming from? It's like I just started speaking in a foreign language that I can't ever recall having learned. Like I'm a sleeper agent for the CIA, and I was trained to do things I didn't know I could do—you know, fire a gun, kill people with my bare hands, be calm and sympathetic in the face of an angry, accusatory teenager. I keep talking, trying to conceal the fact that I have just discovered that I've been walking around for all of these years with a secret identity. "Believe it or not, I did this to help you. You might not understand it now, but someday I think you will. I'm sorry that you'll have to stay here next year, I really am. But I think that it's the best thing for you."

"Whatever," she says, and stands up to go. "I can't believe I went to all that trouble for you and this is how you repay me. Thanks a lot." She grabs her bag and slams the door behind her.

I wipe my eyes and take a deep breath. Believe it or not, that was the easy part. Now I have to tell Linda.

Or maybe I'll just wait until Monday.

23.

One, Two,
I Can't Buckle My Shoe

Here's how bad things have gotten: I am so big that I no longer fit in my car. Remember my little two-seater Mercedes convertible? Gone. I've been inching the seat back farther and farther every month, but when I tried to get into it on Saturday morning, the seat wouldn't go back any farther and I couldn't squeeze my stomach behind the wheel. Look, I knew I'd have to get rid of it eventually—it's not like I can put an infant car seat that, by law, must be placed in the backseat of a car into a car that has no backseat—but I never thought that I would literally outgrow the thing. Anyway, Andrew took it to the dealership this morning and traded it in (I couldn't bear to go with him—I said my good-byes and then stayed home and cried, mourning the loss of my salad days), and now I'm driving—big swallow—a station wagon. It's a Mercedes station wagon, but still. In the course of twenty-four hours, I've gone from being Christie Brinkley in *National Lampoon's Vacation* to Ellen Griswold. Talk about depressing.

What's more, in the middle of my crying stint, when I passed by the bathroom mirror to grab another handful of tissues, I realized that I have become officially revolting. I have. I'm pushing forty pounds of total weight gain—well over the twenty-five that was absolutely, positively *the limit*—and I've swollen up so badly that I look like a float version of myself. Honestly, if you tied me to a string and stuck me in the Macy's Thanksgiving Day Parade, nobody would know the difference. And the worst part of it is, I have failed miserably in my pregnancy rebellion. Everything that I swore

I would not become, I have become. The pregnant woman who was at Julie's niece's birthday party? I'm her. A taller, not-quite-as-fat version of her, but her just the same. My stomach arrives in a room a good twenty minutes before the rest of me does, and since none of my maternity shirts even come close to covering it, I have taken to wearing size XXXL wife beaters that I bought in packs of three for $9.99 at Marshall's (paid for in cash so as not to incite any further credit card maternity-wear wars). Not a hideous, kitchen-looking dress, no, but still, I'm no fashionista. My boobs? Totally gross. They're so weighted down that it looks like I have two goiters growing out of the top of my stomach instead of the two perky things that used to stick straight out from my chest, and my nipples are not only twice the size they used to be and at least four shades darker, but they've also sprouted four-inch black hairs that seem to grow back almost the instant that I tweeze them. High heels? Forget it. Although I valiantly teetered around in stilettos despite my waning sense of balance and shifted center of gravity, I have finally been forced to take them out of the rotation and resort to nothing but flip-flops, as the puffiness of my feet makes trying to squeeze into any pair of shoes like being subjected to an ancient Chinese foot-binding session, let alone a pair of three-inch heeled, strappy ones made by a misogynistic Italian man that for some reason always, *always* rub against the same spot on the side of each foot just like a cheese grater. And don't even get me started on my fingers. Let's just say that Andrew has taken to calling them his little sausages and then snorting like a pig whenever he so much as glimpses them, and I can't even get mad at him about it because the analogy is dead-on.

Yes, dear reader, as much as I hate to admit it, it's all true. I, Lara Stone, who swore like Corey Hart that I would Never Surrender, who fought the good fight against pregnancy and all of the evils that it brings upon good little calorie-counting, gym-obsessed, tragically hip girls who just want to look the way that God and fashion magazines intended, have finally given over to the other side.

Touché, Mother Nature. You win.

When Monday morning rolls around, I decide to take the day off from work. Besides the fact that I'm petrified of telling Linda about how I deliberately sabotaged the admission of her biggest benefactor's child into the college of her choice, I have things to do. Really. I've made a to-do list and everything:

1. Go to doctor.
2. Suck up pain and get bikini wax.

See? This definitely warrants a sick day.

After I get dressed (white XXXL wife beater, black maternity cargo pants that barely close, and black terry-cloth flip-flops) and blow-dry my hair (I've stopped throwing it up into ponytails because the lack of hair around my face only accentuates the fact that I am bloated to the point of being a dead ringer for Mrs. Potato Head), I cruise over in my new mommy mobile to Dr. Lowenstein's office. I'm T minus two weeks to my due date, and the good doctor and I have an old score to settle.

"Hi," Dr. Lowenstein says when he finally breezes into the exam room, where I am lying in wait in a green paper gown. He gives me a kiss on the cheek. "You're looking ripe and ready." Is this a compliment?

He listens to the baby's heartbeat, measures my stomach, and then flips on the ultrasound machine.

"Let's see what this kid is up to," he says.

Silently I begin to recite the prayer that I have been saying for the last six months. *Please be breach. Please be breach. Please be breach.*

The by-now-familiar-looking baby blob appears on the screen, and I hold my breath.

"How does she look?" I ask.

"Perfect," he says. "She's already turned, and her head is in just the right position for takeoff." He does some measuring on the screen. "Looks like she's around . . . maybe six pounds, so in two more weeks she'll be close to seven. Shouldn't be too bad of a delivery."

I bite my lip, trying not to cry.

He tells me to put my feet in the stirrups, and while he's poking around in my crotch, he looks up at me.

"Nothing's going on down here yet. No dilation, no effacement." He sticks what feels like his entire upper torso inside of me, and I flinch. "Sorry. Just feeling for the head." He takes his hand out. "So, have you thought about a birth plan?"

Why, as a matter of fact, yes. Yes, I have. So glad you asked.

"Uh-huh," I say.

He looks up from between my legs. "Oh, good," he says with a smile. "What do you have in mind?"

"Surgery."

His smile disappears. "Did you read any books like I asked you to?"

"Uh-huh." I did. I read the whole section on labor and delivery in *What to Expect When You're Expecting,* and it made me sick to my stomach. Did you know that some women can have discomfort and burning for months after an episiotomy, and some even have permanent scarring?

"And did you take a class?"

"Uh-huh." Okay, okay. Maybe I didn't *physically* take a class, but I did *vicariously* take one. I did. I made Julie tell me all about her Lamaze class, which sounded horrible and like nothing more than an opportunity for granolas to preach their natural-childbirth propaganda to a captive audience. It's probably a good thing that I didn't actually attend. There is no way that I would not have gotten into a fistfight with the instructor. Plus, it's totally pointless. I mean, I saw Julie's birth experience firsthand, and a lot of good the stupid class did her, right? Oh, and get this—Julie and I had dinner a few weeks ago, and Julie had had a few too many glasses of wine, and she let it slip that ever since her delivery, her vagina has been all hangy and stretched-out, and sex doesn't feel nearly as good as it used to. Now, come on, how much does that suck? And, as if I really need another reason, I have four little words for you: pooping on the table. Potty training with Aiden or not, this is one area where I simply refuse to give in. Mother Nature can kiss my fat, pregnant ass on that one.

"So you read about it, and you took a class, and you still want a C-section?" Dr. Lowenstein asks incredulously.

"Desperately," I say.

He sighs and shrugs his shoulders. "Look, it's your body. I'm not going to make you do anything that you don't want to do."

"Really?" I ask. I thought it would be a much harder sell than that. I was prepared to give him all kinds of arguments. I had memorized statistics about infant mortality rates in natural versus surgical births, and I was all ready with a speech about the horrors of episiotomies, stretched-out vaginas, and incontinence as a result of prolonged pushing.

"Yeah," he says. "We can schedule it for a week from tomorrow."

"Really?" I say, practically squealing with excitement. I get to have a C-section *and* my sentence ends a week early? There really is a God.

"Really. I'll schedule it for seven A.M."

"Yay," I say, clapping my hands while I am still lying, half-naked, on the examining table.

Dr. Lowenstein consults my vagina-that-will-now-remain-tight-and-intact one more time, and then he looks up at me. "Are you planning on getting waxed between now and then?" he asks.

I stop clapping.

I feel like I'm at a party that just got broken up, and the deejay ripped the needle off the record player, making the *zzzzzzppppp* sound of scratching vinyl. Is it my imagination, or did my gynecologist just insinuate that I am in need of some personal grooming? Well, I guess this clears up the question as to whether doctors notice such things.

"Um, actually, I've got an appointment for a wax right after I leave here."

"Oh, good," he says.

Okay, now I'm really starting to feel insulted. If he's relieved that he won't have to traverse the jungle again in a week, that's fine, but he should keep it himself, don't you think? I mean, really. It's downright rude.

"Here," he says, lifting up my gown. "Let me show you how low to have her wax you. We're going to have to put surgical tape on the incision, and I would hate for you to have your pubic hair ripped out twice in the same week."

Oh, so *that's* why he's asking. Okay, I feel much better now. Actually, it's quite thoughtful of him, when you think about it.

With his pen, he draws a two-inch line just above my pubic bone.

"There," he declares. "Have her go all the way down to this line." I look down. The line is really low. Even the lowest of low-rider bikinis will cover that sucker. I beam at him.

"Only in Los Angeles is your obstetrician going to be concerned with your wax job," I say. He smiles at me.

"Hey, I'm just looking out for you."

"Well, I appreciate that, thanks."

"No problem," he says. He takes my hand to help me heave myself back up into a sitting position, and then he smoothes out his hair. "All right. I guess I'll see you next week!" He gives me a kiss good-bye—I am tempted to use tongue, I am so grateful for the C-section—and then I head off to the salon.

I arrive for my appointment right on time, and my Russian waxer, whom I have not seen since I was eight weeks pregnant, acts like I am a long-lost cousin from the old country. She hugs me and kisses me on both cheeks, and pats my belly several hundred times. Normally I wouldn't tolerate such behavior for more than a nanosecond, but I say nothing, because (a) she is scary to begin with, and (b) she is about to rip out my pubic hair with hot wax while I lie, belly-up, on a table beneath her.

"I thought you ahlreahdy had bebe, no? Vhere have you been, dahling?"

"I'm having her next week," I say. "I thought it might be a good idea to get cleaned up first." While I am taking off my pants, I share my good news. "I'm having a C-section," I announce joyously.

"Good for you, dahling. It vill be much easier this vay. No puhshing, no big deahl." See? I am not alone in my craziness. She glances at my stomach again. "But it's a boy, no?"

"No, it's a girl."

"Ahre you sure? Because I am never wrong about dese tings."

"I'm sure; we saw her on the ultrasound."

"You see de peepee?" she asks with a note of distrust in her voice.

Naked from the waist down, I climb onto the table. "I saw the peepee. Front and center." She makes a *harrumph* sort of noise, and I quickly change the subject before she has a chance to get angry about it. "This will probably hurt more than the surgery," I say.

"I know, dahling, but you must have a pehrfect peepee for de baby." She clucks her tongue as she takes in the unruliness of things, and then spots the ink line. "Vat is dis?" she asks, pointing to it.

"I just came from the doctor. He drew it for you so that you could see where the incision is going to be."

She looks up at the sky and says something in Russian. "Only in Los Ahngeles, dahling."

I nod at her. "I know. That's exactly what I said."

* * *

After my wax, I decide to meet Julie and Lily for lunch. If I'm going to play hooky and have a girlie day, I figure that I might as well go all-out. I have to say, the only good thing about being hugely pregnant and looking as if you are about to blow at any second is the fun that I am able to have at the expense of random strangers. It's like payback for the months and months that I had to endure their endless, annoying questions. For example, I arrived at the restaurant first, where, although there was a line of at least ten people ahead of me, I was immediately seated by the maître'd. I'm sure that my quiet moaning and clutching of my stomach might have had something to do with it, and after he seated me he pulled the waiter aside and began urgently whispering to him. While they talked, the two of them kept throwing me nervous glances, in response to which I hammed it up, wiping my brow and wincing as if I were in excruciating pain. It's highly entertaining. You definitely should try it sometime.

By the time Julie shows up, pushing Lily, who is clad in a pink rhinestoned tank top and a pair of cropped jeans with matching rhinestones lining the hem, I have the entire restaurant staff in a tizzy.

"What is going on?" Julie asks as she wheels Lily up to the table. "I told them that I was with you and they asked me to find out if you needed them to call an ambulance. Are you okay?"

I give her a wicked smile. "I'm fine. I'm just having a little fun with them."

She takes Lily out of her stroller and sits her in the high chair. "You are evil," she says to me.

"Not evil," I tell her. "Just spiteful. So, how are you?"

She affixes a plastic place mat with a sticky backing to the table in front of Lily, whips some plastic containers out of her bag, and starts preparing a bowl of mush.

"We're doing great," she says, in a high-pitched baby voice. I hope she's not planning to use that voice during the entirety of our lunch. "But the real question is, how are you? You look good."

I make a face at her. "Please. I look like I ate a pair of six-month-olds whole for breakfast this morning. I need for this to be over."

"I know," she says. "The end is the worst part. But it's so worth it." She begins spooning the mush concoction into Lily's mouth, which Lily eats as daintily and neatly as if she's just completed a round of finishing school. When she sees that I'm staring at her, she gives me a big, toothless smile.

"Does she ever cry?" I ask.

"Not really. Only if something is wrong with her. She's an angel baby." Of course she is. Julie reaches over to pinch Lily's cheek, and then she drops the baby voice and leans in toward me.

"So, do you know what you're getting for your push present?"

"My what?"

"Your push present. You know, the present you get for having to go through labor?" *Now* she tells me that you get a present for going through labor, ten minutes after I schedule a C-section?

"I didn't even know about that," I say, starting to panic at the idea of having unknowingly passed up a gift opportunity. "What did you get?"

"My diamond studs," she says matter-of-factly, lifting up the hair in front of her ears to reveal two gigantic sparkly solitaires. "You never noticed them?"

"No," I say. "I've only seen you with your hair down. Congratulations to you." I hesitate. "Do you still get a push present if you have a C-section?" I ask her.

"Of course," she says. "Then it's called a gash gift." She eyes me suspiciously. "So you decided to go ahead with the C-section, huh?"

"Yeah," I say, a little surprised. I had forgotten that I'd told her about it.

"You know, my sister had a C-section with her first one. I used to think it was so awful—like she had somehow missed out on real womanhood—but now I'm not so sure. Maybe it's not such a bad idea after all."

Wow. I don't think I've ever heard Julie sound so enlightened. Her vagina must be *really* stretched out.

"But my God," Julie exclaims. "Next week! That is so soon!"

"I know," I say. "Only eight more days of being a cow. I swear, if I lived in India, people would be praying to me." Julie laughs. "Listen," I say to her. "I don't think that Andrew knows about this push-present thing. You need to talk to him. Or get Jon to do it. But it has to be discreet. He can't think that I'm behind it."

"Done," Julie says. "I will make absolutely sure that you don't leave that hospital empty-handed." Julie raises her water glass to make a toast. "To babies, and the many gifts that they bring," she says.

"To girlfriends," I say. "And the many ways that they find to make themselves useful."

We both laugh, and clink our glasses.

24.

Sunny Day,
It's My Last Day Today

When I knock on Linda's office door on Tuesday morning, my stomach is in knots. Yes, I've accepted the fact that I'm going to be working full-time next year. I've accepted the fact that Spanish will be Parker's first language, that she will call the nanny Mommy, that she will mistake me for a ship passing in the night, and that I will spend all of my retirement savings putting her through multiple bouts of rehab. I have made my peace with these things, and at this point, I'm just hoping that I don't get fired.

"Come in, come in," Linda says, waving her hand at me while she finishes typing something. I take a seat in one of the chairs across from her, where I nervously kick my right leg until she looks up. When she does look up, she gives me the once-over and makes no attempt to hide her mortification.

"Jesus, Lara, when are you having this baby? I didn't know people could get that big without exploding."

"Thanks," I say. "I'm having her next week. This Friday is going to be my last day."

"Oh, good," she says. "Excellent timing. Is everything taken care of in your office? You have someone to cover for you until June?"

"Everything is fine. I did all of the mailings for April and May ahead of time, and Rachel just needs to send them out on the dates that are on the letters. And she's going to mail out final transcripts to colleges as soon as they're ready. She can handle it. She runs that office better than I do."

"Okay, well, I'll check in on her now and then, and make sure you leave your home number and your cell phone in case there's an emergency." Oh, I am so getting called every week.

"No problem," I say. My hands are trembling. "Actually, I wanted to talk to you about Tick Gardner. I have some news about her college decisions."

"Oh, I've already heard all about her college decisions. Cheryl called me first thing yesterday morning." She gives me a knowing look. "It was very auspicious of you to be out sick. What the hell happened?" Oh, this is bad. This is very, very bad.

"I know," I say. "NYU just wouldn't take her. I tried everything. I played every angle, I used every connection, but her scores and her grades were just too low. It was extremely competitive this year. But, you know, the good news is, she did get into USC, so she has somewhere to go at least."

"At least?" Linda is staring at me as if she is totally confused. "It's her first choice. She got her acceptance letter on Saturday, and Cheryl said Tick was jumping up and down and screaming, she was so excited. Cheryl thought she still wanted to go to NYU, but Tick said that she changed her mind weeks ago. She said that you convinced her that USC had a better music program, and that she would like it better there." She shakes her head. "I have to tell you, the Gardners are thrilled. They didn't think she was ready to be running around on her own in New York *at all,* and Cheryl thinks that USC is very prestigious. Stefan even got on the phone to tell me what a great job you did. He said he met you at some party, and that you made such an impression on him. He even congratulated *me* for having had the foresight to hire an ex-lawyer to be the college counselor. Honey, at this point, you could work from home five days a week next year and the board wouldn't even blink. So congratulations. You've got a deal."

What? What? What is going on here? No—don't be stupid. Just go with it, and figure out the details later.

"Wow," I say. "That's great. I had no idea that they would be so excited. Honestly, I was just as surprised as anyone that Tick changed her mind."

Linda is grinning at me from ear to ear. "It just goes to show you that kids have no idea what they want. They get their hearts set on something for no reason, and then just like that"—she snaps her fingers—"the wind blows and they want something else. It's a wonder that half the class doesn't transfer every year."

"I know," I say, nodding my head. "They can be so fickle." I take a deep breath. "Okay, so, do we need to work out any details for next year, then?"

"I don't think so. You'll work two days from home, available by phone and e-mail, and the other three days in the office. If it's okay with you, I'm going to pay you the same thing you make now for next year. You would have gotten the standard three percent increase, but since your hours will be reduced, I think it's fair to forgo that."

"Fine," I say. Is she kidding? She's not even cutting back my salary? "I think that's totally fair."

"Okay. Great. New contracts won't be out until May, so we'll mail it home to you when it's ready, and you can just sign it and send it back in." I feel like I should get out of here before she changes her mind, or before I wake up and realize that this is a dream. I stand up to leave.

"Great. Thanks. Okay. I'll see you later." Linda turns back to what she was working on, and I open the door to her office and start to walk out.

"Lara!" she yells after me.

Shit. She definitely realized that she just got scammed. I hold my breath, expecting the worst.

"Yes," I say, sticking my head back in.

"If I don't see you before you leave, good luck with the baby."

I exhale. "Thanks. I'll see you in September." She nods at me, already engrossed in what she's working on. I walk out of her office, and as soon as the door is shut behind me, I do a nine-and-a-half-months-pregnant version of a touchdown dance.

My last day in the office is chaos. It seems that every college in the country mailed decision letters on the same day, and I have had a line of kids outside of my office all morning long. The kids usually try to keep poker faces until they actually get inside—the ones who are upset don't want anyone to know that they're upset, and the ones who are excited don't want to seem like they're gloating (except for the one asshole every year who comes to school wearing a Yale sweatshirt the day after he gets his acceptance letter), but I've been doing this long enough now that I can still tell what the news is just by looking at them. Before I open the door, I sneak a glance out the window to see the face of the next kid in line, and I immediately know whether I should be ready with a solemn hug and a tissue in my hand, or whether I should approach with claps and wide-open arms. So far, I've never been wrong.

Mark was one of the first ones I saw this morning. Of course, I already knew that he had good news for me, but I still got goose bumps when I saw how excited he was. Really, nothing makes me happier in early April than meeting with ecstatic seniors. Well, to be exact, nothing makes me happier in early April than the annual shoe sale at Neiman Marcus, but ecstatic seniors are a very close second.

"You knew, didn't you?" he asked me.

"I swear, I had no idea." There's an unwritten rule in college counseling that you never admit to having insider information. If the parents ever knew that I found out decisions early, I'd be bombarded with phone calls, and, with this crowd, probably bribes. Which might not be so bad, come to think of it, but still. It's best if they don't know. I don't want to ever have to be the one who delivers bad news again. We've already seen how well that went.

"So where are you going to go?" I asked him. "Have you decided yet?"

"I'm not sure. I liked NYU, but my mom really liked Boston. She thought it was more of a college town."

"It *is* more of a college town," I told him. "It's much more student-friendly than New York." I know, I know. After everything I went through, it's hard to believe that I was actually talking him *out* of NYU. But you know, if I made a decision to do the right thing, then I might as well go all the way with it. And plus, now I have no reason to be bitter if he doesn't go.

We left things with him still undecided. He doesn't have to make a decision until May first, so I told him to shoot me an e-mail at home when he knows for sure. I assured him that he wouldn't be bothering me—I definitely will want to know.

I get up from my desk to see who is next, but the line has dwindled down to nothing. There's just one person out there, a redheaded girl, sitting with her back to me while she reads a book at the table outside of my office. I don't recognize her—it must be a sophomore who wants help with scheduling classes or something—so I clear my throat.

"Can I help you?" I ask. She turns around, just as I realize that it's Tick. "Sorry," I say. "I didn't know it was you. Your hair is red."

"Yeah," she says. "It's my new look for USC. You know, red and gold. Go, Trojans."

I give her a concerned look. "Do I need to worry about you running out and joining the cheerleading squad?"

She nods her head with mock sincerity. "You know, I hear they get all the cute football players."

"Ha," I say, as I lead her into my office. "Seriously, Tick, what really happened?" She takes a seat in one of my chairs, which by now is an old, familiar scenario. But she looks different, somehow, and it's not just the hair. She looks . . . smaller. Lighter. Not thinner. Just lighter somehow.

"I was really mad at you," she explains. "*Really* mad. I was ready to tell my mom the whole story, just to see her go ballistic on you and try to get you fired, or shot, I don't know. But she wasn't home, and when I woke up on Saturday the letter from USC was there. . . ."

She pauses to think for a minute, and I realize that it's the bag. That's why she looks different. She doesn't have that enormous bag that she always schleps around with her everywhere. I don't think I've ever seen her without it before—well, she didn't have it at the Christmas party, but that doesn't count. I've definitely never seen her without it when she hasn't been dressed in couture.

". . . and I don't know; it just hit me all at once. I'm always complaining about how I don't want special treatment, and how I just want to be looked at like everybody else, and then the first time in my life that I didn't get special treatment, I freaked out. And I realized, that, like, you were totally right, you know? I didn't deserve it, so why should I get in? It wasn't your fault. It was my fault for goofing off for four years." She shrugs. "So I pretended that I wanted to go to USC. You shouldn't have to suffer because I screwed up." She pauses again, and looks down at the floor. When she resumes talking, her voice is so low that I can barely hear her.

"And I want you to be with your baby. Your baby is lucky that you want to be with her. I wish my mom wanted to be with me when I was little." I think that she realizes that things have just gotten a tad too heavy, so she looks up at me and laughs. "I mean, I wish she would leave me the fuck alone now, but it would have been nice when I was a kid."

I smile at her. "I don't even know what to say, Tick. You've really grown up since last summer. Look at you. In August you were dropping out of school to run off to New York with some guy, and now here you are, so mature, and with a sense of perspective. Who would have thought it?"

"Yeah," she says. "And who would have thought that you would have been the one to stick by me? In August you would have sold me down the river for ten bucks."

Good point. She's smart, this one. I've always said it. "I'm sorry that I made that deal with Linda."

"I'm sorry that you had to."

"So are we okay?" I ask her.

"Yeah," she says. "We are. Anyway, I've got to go, but I wanted to say good-bye. I heard that today is your last day."

"Yeah," I say, nodding. "I'm having the baby on Tuesday." I stand up to walk her out. "Listen, don't forget about me when you're off in college. Drop me a line once in a while, okay?"

"Promise," she says. "And good luck with the baby." We are both standing in the threshold of my office, unsure of what to say next. Without warning, she throws her arms around me.

"'Bye, Mrs. Stone," she says.

"Good-bye, Tick. You're going to do great."

She nods at me, and I watch her as she walks out my door for the last time, her combat boots squeaking on the linoleum.

It doesn't feel like a last day of school today. I don't have any of my normal giddiness, or the sense of anticipation. I feel sad, like I'm closing a chapter of my life that I'll someday look back on with wistful smiles, much like the way I look back on pictures of myself from high school and wonder how my arms were ever possibly so skinny.

As I shut the door and lock up behind me, I realize that the next time I open it again, I'll be somebody's mom. *Whoa.*

25.

If That Mockingbird Don't Sing, Daddy's Gonna Buy You Some Nice Bling Bling

t's Monday night, eleven thirty-seven. I'm supposed to be at the hospital in five hours and twenty-three minutes. It's my last night of uninterrupted sleep for God knows how long—possibly even forever—and I'm wide-awake.

"Andrew," I whisper. "Andrew."

He rolls over and opens one eye. "Huh," he says.

"I can't sleep." He closes the eye and rolls back over. I tap him on the shoulder. "Honey, please. I need to talk."

He sighs loudly and rolls toward me again. "What's wrong?"

"I'm really scared."

"Of the surgery?"

"No. Of the baby. I don't think I'm ready. I don't think I can do this."

"It's a little late for that, don't you think?" he says, chuckling.

"No, I'm serious." I can feel my heart pounding faster and faster. "I really don't think that I can handle it."

Andrew gives me his I'm-going-to-humor-you-for-the-sake-of-my-own-sanity look and sits up. "Okay. Tell me why. What are you thinking about?"

"First of all, it just occurred to me that this baby is serious baggage. What if something happens to you? What if you die? Or what if you meet a normal woman and decide that you like that better and we end up getting divorced? What will I do? How will I ever remarry? Nobody wants to be with someone who has a kid. I'll be damaged goods. I'll be a 'she's

great, but.' You know, 'She's great, but she has a six-year-old.' You see? Serious baggage."

Andrew shakes his head in disbelief. "Nothing is going to happen to
me, and we're not going to get divorced. I could never be with a normal
woman. I wouldn't even know how. Okay? Is that all?"

"No," I say. "That's not all. I am not going to be a good mother. I've
been saying it all along, and you didn't listen to me, and now we're having a baby and it's too late and I'm going to be terrible. Terrible. I should
have held my ground. I should have been like Stacey and stood up for
myself." I'm really worked up now. My breathing is getting shallow, my
voice sounds unnaturally high, and I'm starting to sob.

"Dolly," Andrew says. "I don't know what you're talking about. You're
going to be great. Look at how far you've come. You potty trained a two-
year-old. You cleaned someone else's throw-up. You made one of the
most unselfish decisions that you've ever made in your life. You're totally
ready."

"No," I cry, trying to breathe. "I'm not. It's different. Those were other
people's kids. It's easier with other people's kids. You deal with them, and
if you screw up you just send them back to their own parents to clean up
the mess. But now I'm going to be the parent. It's my mess. And this whole
blank-slate thing—it's so intimidating. What if I make a mistake? What
if I really fuck her up? I'll have to deal with the fallout for the rest of my
life." I am completely hyperventilating now, and I feel like I'm going to
faint. I'm trying to inhale, but no air is coming in.

"Are you okay?" Andrew asks.

I shake my head. "I." Inhale. "Can't." Inhale. "Breathe." Inhale.

"Seriously? You can't breathe, for real?" I nod my head at him, gasping
for air in between sobs. He jumps out of bed and races to the door. "Hold
on," he yells. "I'll be right back. I'm going to get a paper bag."

I nod again and try to calm down, but I just can't catch my breath.
The last time I was this upset was when I was seven and our family dog
died in my bed while I was sleeping. She was a Cockapoo named Shana
Lula Love, and it turned out that the people we got her from knew that
she had kidney failure and didn't tell us. When I woke up and found her
lying next to me, already cold and rigor mortised, I freaked. I had night-
mares about dead, worm-ridden zombie dogs for years afterward.

About a minute later Andrew comes running back into the bedroom. He's carrying a brown paper shopping bag. The big kind. With handles.

"Here," he says, thrusting the open side into my face. "Breathe into this." Miraculously, I have completely recovered and am now not only able to breathe, but also able to summon my full range of sarcasm and derision.

"Andrew," I say. "It's a shopping bag. My whole head fits inside of it."

He looks at me and sheepishly shrugs his shoulders. "It's the only paper bag I could find. We didn't have anything smaller."

I start to laugh. "Honey, are you kidding me? This won't work. You're supposed to use the lunch bag–size ones."

He shrugs again, defensively. "Sorry, I didn't know. You said you couldn't breathe, so I got you a paper bag."

It occurs to me that perhaps I should not be so worried about me messing up our kid. There are much higher odds that Andrew will be the one to do it. "Anyway, you seem fine now."

"Yeah," I say. "I guess I am. At least I can breathe again."

Andrew gets up and walks over to his side of the bed, where he opens up the drawer in his nightstand. "Here," he says. "I was going to give you this tomorrow, but now seems like a better time." He hands me a tiny box wrapped in silver paper and tied with a pink bow. Could it be? I carefully unwrap it. It's a jewelry box.

"Did you talk to Julie?" I ask him, cocking my left eyebrow.

"What? No. But it's funny you asked that, because she's been leaving me messages at work all week and I haven't been able to get in touch with her. Do you know what she wants?"

"No," I lie. "No idea." *Huh.* So Julie didn't coach him. I really can't believe he knew to get me a push present all by himself. I briefly wonder what else he knows that I don't give him credit for. I lift the lid to the box, and inside are two tiny platinum hoop earrings, each one lined with pavé diamonds. They're perfect.

"They're for making our baby from scratch," he says earnestly.

My eyes well up with tears. He is so damn cute sometimes. "I love them," I say, putting them on. "You're incredible."

"I know. Don't forget it." I get them both on and hold my hair back for him to see. "They look pretty," he says. He gets back in bed and leans over to give me a kiss. "You can't be a perfect mom, Lar. It's not possible. You're going to make mistakes just like everyone else. But you'll be great because you'll be you. That's what I love about you, and that's what Parker will love about you, too."

"Can you hand me a tissue?" I ask him. He pulls one out of the box on his nightstand and hands it to me. "Thanks," I say. I blow my nose and snot gets everywhere. "Romantic, huh?"

"Always," he replies. "Do you feel better now?" he asks me.

"I guess so." I lean over and give him a kiss on the cheek. "I love you."

"I love you, too." He moves closer to me and puts his hand on top of my stomach. "So," he says, "do you think you're ready to do this now?"

I fold over the tissue and blow my nose again, then pause for a moment to think over my answer. I nod my head.

"Yeah," I say. "You know, I think I am."

About the Author

Risa Green grew up in a suburb of Philadephia, PA, and graduated from both the University of Pennsylvania and The Georgetown University Law Center. She has worked as a corporate finance attorney and, more recently, as a college counselor at a private day school. She currently resides with her husband, their daughter and son, and their dog in Los Angeles. This is her first novel.

Notes from
the Underbelly

Risa Green

A CONVERSATION WITH
RISA GREEN

❈

Q. *How much of this novel came from your own experience?*

A. The events that take place in the novel are completely fictional, but many of Lara's thoughts and feelings about being pregnant derive from my own experience with pregnancy. Writing this book was very therapeutic for me—I definitely used Lara to vent some of my hostility over the silly things people say to pregnant women, as well as to express some of my fears and anxieties about the changes that were happening to my body. By creating Lara, I was able to say things that I never would have had the guts to say out loud to anyone, and I think that her honesty makes it easy for readers to relate to her character. I also drew very much on my background as a high school college counselor to write the storyline involving Tick and her mother. The college application process as described in the book is absolutely the way that it works in real life.

Q. *Why did you decide to write this book?*

A. It wasn't really a conscious decision. About a month after my daughter was born, I was on maternity leave and I was bored to tears, so I thought that it might be a nice idea to keep a journal, if only to have something "adult" to do every day. But when I sat down at the computer the words just started flying out of me, and it was incredibly cathartic. Every morning after that I woke up itching to write, and before I knew it I had written an entire book.

Q. *Were there any themes or ideas that you wanted to get across to readers while you were writing the novel?*

A. Yes, definitely. I think that books and television and movies do a great job of romanticizing pregnancy and motherhood, and as a result women are set up to believe that those nine months should be a perfect, joyous time. And maybe it is that way for some women, but I had the opposite experience. And so it was very important to me to tell the story of a woman who didn't find pregnancy to be so wonderful, because I remember feeling very alone in and betrayed by the world. I was furious that no one had warned me that I might feel the way that I did, and I felt a responsibility to let other women like me know that it's okay to feel anxious and insecure and ugly while they're pregnant, and to give them someone like Lara who could help them laugh about it.

I also wanted to put a real, human face on a college counselor, because I think that high school counselors often get a bad rap. People are always telling me stories about how their counselor was so discouraging and told them they would never get into any college, and then they ended up getting into Harvard, and so this book was my chance to defend the profession, and to show it from the other side. Plus, college admissions is such an emotional thing for people, and there are so many books written about it, I thought it would be interesting to show the process from a fictional point of view.

Q. *What role does the city of Los Angeles play in this novel?*

A. Los Angeles is such a wonderful and strange place to live, but I'm not sure that you can truly appreciate either of those qualities unless you grew up somewhere else, like I did. In Los Angeles, the entire city revolves around the entertainment industry—people actually refer to it as *The* Industry, as if there is no other—and I think that it can give kids who grow up here a warped view of the world. A lot of them have no concept of how the rest of the country lives, and they don't understand that you can still be successful even if you're not in entertainment, and then they grow up to be adults who think that way. I tried to convey this through the teenagers who attend Bel Air Prep, as well as through their parents. Also, on the west side of Los Angeles, where the story takes place, it often seems as if everyone has an obscene amount of money, and they spend it like it's going out of style. The Julie character is very much representative of that side of LA—she's the sweetest person in the world, but she is absolutely ridiculous in her spending habits. As an outsider, Lara is more grounded than the other characters, but she has to keep herself from getting caught up in that world. I think that that is a real choice that many people consciously make when they move to Los Angeles.

Q. *What books have you loved? What authors have influenced or inspired you?*

A. I've always been a bookworm—my husband would say that I'm more of a hermit, really—but to me, there is nothing better than spending the afternoon with a great book. Much better than spending it with people, I think. I definitely prefer American authors, and I'm drawn towards stories that are narrated with a strong, humorous voice. Coming of age in the eighties, Judy Blume was a huge influence on me, but as an adult I have loved

John Irving, Philip Roth, Tom Ford, John Updike and David Sedaris. I read *A Heartbreaking Work of Staggering Genius* by Dave Eggers just before I started writing this book, and his style was very liberating for me as a writer, because it made me feel that it was okay to write self-consciously, and to break up the narrative with long, only somewhat-related tangents. It's funny that these are all male writers who tend to write books with male lead characters, but for some reason, I just relate to them more.

Q. *What are you working on now?*

A. I'm working on another Lara Stone novel that will pick up where *Notes From the Underbelly* left off, with Lara having the baby and adjusting to her new life as a mother. I originally was going to include all of that in this novel, but it would have been entirely too long, so I decided to split it up into two separate books. I want to continue to explore the idea that not every woman is a natural at motherhood, and in the next book Lara certainly will struggle with figuring it all out.

QUESTIONS FOR DISCUSSION

1. Over the last several years, critics have bemoaned the rise of elective Cesarean sections in the United States. Do you think that women should have the right to choose the type of childbirth experience that they have?

2. Throughout the novel, Lara struggles to tap into her maternal instincts, and at times she wonders if she is just simply missing the "maternal gene". Do you believe that all women are born with maternal instincts?

3. At Bel Air Prep, Lara interacts with kids who are spoiled beyond belief. But even in less affluent areas, many people complain that kids today are overindulged. Do you think that parents are to blame, or do you believe that it is an inevitable by-product of living in a consumption-obsessed society?

4. Before Lara becomes pregnant, she and Andrew fight about when she will be ready for motherhood. Do you think that anyone can ever be ready to have a child?